FOR THE LOVE OF BARBRY . . .

"You must have loved her very much."

"Yes. Very much," he said. "I miss her." More than anything else in the world, he wanted her back. "I love you very much, Barbry." And he looked Sadie straight in the eye when he said that.

Fear danced in her eyes, and then something else. "I lo—" Sadie's left cheek twitched and she stood and trembled like a fawn. "Don't feel good," she said.

Henry caught her as she collapsed, and carried her back to the bedroom. Her cheek was twitching constantly now. Henry could swear he saw the cheekbone beneath it *flow*. He pulled up a chair next to the bed and sat there.

Sadie's hands clenched into fists that twisted and wrung the sheets. A scream trickled through her tightened throat. Henry could not move. *The nanny will try to restructure as well as repair.* But, dear Lord, he had never imagined that it would *hurt*. Henry saw the tension build in her muscles. She began moaning, and the moaning would have ended in a scream except her jaw was so tightly clamped that nothing but a whine escaped. *I can't take this,* Henry thought, and he pushed himself from the chair to go.

But her eyes snapped open and pinned him there. She spoke; and the timbre of the voice was more than Sadie, but not quite Barbara, and there was pain and hurt in it. "What are doing to me?" she cried. "*Why* are you doing this to me?"

The scream,

Henry's.

when it finally came, was

THE NANOTECH CHRONICLES

MICHAEL FLYNN

THE NANOTECH CHRONICLES

This is a work of fiction. All the characters and events portrayed in this book are fictional, and any resemblance to real people or incidents is purely coincidental.

A Baen Books Original

Baen Publishing Enterprises
P.O. Box 1403
Riverdale, N.Y. 10471

ISBN: 0-671-72080-5

Cover art by Gary Ruddell

First printing, September 1991

Distributed by
SIMON & SCHUSTER
1230 Avenue of the Americas
New York, N.Y. 10020

Printed in the United States of America

Portions of this book have appeared in slightly different form elsewhere. The following parts of this book first appeared in Analog magazine:

"Soul of the City" in February 1989

"The Washer at the Ford" in June and July 1989

"Remember'd Kisses" in December 1988

"The Laughing Clone" in October 1988

"Blood Upon the Rose" in February 1991

"Werehouse" first appeared in *New Destinies*, edited by Jim Baen, September 1990

Portions of this book have appeared in slightly different form elsewhere. The following pieces of this book first appeared in Weird Tales magazine:

"Soul of the City" in February 1989

"The Master of the Crows" in [illegible] and July 1990

"Remembered Tears" in December 1987

"The Laughing Clone" in October 1988

"Blood upon the Rose" in February 1991

"Whorehouse" first appeared in New Destinies, edited by Jim Baen, September 1990

Dedication

To Margie, Sara, and Dennis
For their understanding and tolerance.

Contents

Prelude

Pavel Denisovitch d'Abreu studied the eager faces arrayed before him and sighed. How young they all were! And each year they grew younger. Or was that only his own age speaking? Perhaps, though Pavel Denisovitch did not believe it. He sucked in his breath and inclined his head slightly in superior-to-inferior mode. "Gakusei!" he greeted them.

"Sensei!" the students chorused in unison, bowing deeply from the waist. Alas! Some had forgotten to anchor themselves properly, and conservation of angular momentum set them tumbling around their centers of gravity. A few squawked in embarrassment, neglecting their dignidad. Pavel Denisovitch caught his lower lip between his teeth, lest he laugh and they lose face. For the same reason he did not suggest putting the module under spin gravity. Such would be wretched insult. He himself was not too proud to use an anchor in zero gee.

When his students had sorted themselves out, Denisovitch grew himself a lectern. He unclipped the kit from his belt and tore open the pouch. Then, bending carefully, so as not to loosen the grip of his Velcro slippers, he troweled the agar to the deck with a putty knife. He immersed himself in the Tao of the moment, letting the immediate task become his reality. He felt the cool plastic handle of the putty knife; he felt the way the agar packed and spread. The pungent smell assaulted his nostrils.

When he was done troweling, he placed the container pouch atop the carefully shaped mound, pressing it firmly into the gelatinous mass. The skin of the pouch contained the activators, so that the entire lectern kit was self-contained.

Some of the younger students hissed their excitement as they watched the lectern grow. Even the older students were self-conscious in their studied indifference. Denisovitch himelf kept a stoic face, yet allowed himself an inward thrill. He knew the chemistry of it. He knew how the assemblers pieced together the molecules of the agar as they reproduced; how the lectern was in some sense the nest, the offspring and the excrement of an artfully-made pseudo-life. But, still . . . *Any sufficiently advanced technology,* he reminded himself, *is indistinguishable from magic.*

Sometimes even to the magicians themselves.

"Modern orbital society," he began his lecture, "is both a revolutionary and an evolutionary outgrowth of groundside society. Revolutionary, because we have made a break, politically and socially, with 'those we left below us.' But evolutionary, because our way of life grew out of theirs as surely as this lectern grew from its agar. Though much of what we now take for granted would seem strange or even impossible to our great grandparents, the seeds of modern life were being sown even then.

"We need look no further than nanotechnology itself, without which our society would be impossible. We are accustomed to using molecular machines to grow what we need when we need it from little more than raw moonstuff. Our groundside ancestors would have been astounded.

"And yet . . . And yet, they routinely used molecular

machines—to construct beer or penicillin, for example. Ah. Senhor Williamson-san, you have a question."

Takeshita Williamson managed to bow without tumbling. He sucked in his breath. "Sensei! Beer-building was known to the ancient Egyptians. Your statement implies that nanotechnology is thousands of years old."

Denisovitch bowed his acknowledgement. Williamson had artfully framed his question, managing to express his doubts without contradicting his teacher. "Hai!" he agreed. "Perhaps it is merely a question of perspective. What were brewing yeast or vaccines but primitive nanomachines? I grant you that they were bred from nature and that they were applied in bulk. The enzyme that increased the milk production of cows, for example, was simply the cow's own natural enzyme bred in quantity. But the first consciously designed nannies were already being built at the turn of the twenty-first century. An enzyme that dissolved dental caries without attacking enamel. A bacterium that ate crude oil in salt water. An antigen that bound to the surface of the HI virus and prevented its functioning. The manufacture of synthetic human insulin. Ah. Senhorita da Silva-san."

Gabriella da Silva spoke. "Sensei! We were taught that the groundsiders rejected these wonders."

"*Sim*. Ultimately, they did; but at first, they welcomed them. At least some did. But, any new technology causes dislocations. Old opportunities are cut off, resentment grows. Though, of course, new opportunities spring up, too, if one has the wits to grasp them. Sometimes these new opportunities are most zen-like, surprising and at the same time gratifying. Senhor Takeda-san?"

"Sensei! Would you give us an example?"

Pavel Denisovitch nodded thoughtfully. A good example was worth more than a thousand bald assertions. All the great roshi had known that. So easy to forget in the course of numberless, repeated lectures. Too easy simply to spoon-feed facts. The eager, open faces around him deserved more. And it was important that they know their roots.

Closing his eyes, he selected a koan and used it to empty his mind of conscious thoughts. Then he tongued his datalink and accessed the main storage drives in Old First Module. Pseudo-memories cascaded into his mind. A thousand crises. A thousand comedies. A thousand dramas, large and small. Quietly, he let them sort themselves out. He scanned first one, then another. Finally, he paused. "Ah."

He opened his eyes to see the class waiting eagerly. Someday soon enough, the older of them would have implants of their own. Until then, though, there was still magic in the Teller of Tales. "There is one instructive episode," he said. "Though only one of many. It begins of a dark evening in the deserted streets of a once-great city. Smell the damp decay. Listen to the far-off, underground rattle of the subway. Watch as a stealthy figure scampers swiftly down a darkened alleyway. . . ."

1. Soul of the City

The blank, grey stone wall was a canvas crying out for art, and Diego Salazar was the artist to rise to the occasion. He set his bag softly against the hard cement sidewalk, the cans within rattling, and studied the building in the harsh glare of the sodium vapor streetlights. He tried to feel how the building felt; the colors that would warm it, the shapes that would soften it. His brother, Jaime, and his friend, Pablo, stood watch at the two corners at the ends of the block, ready to whistle a warning should any cars approach. They fidgeted impatiently, knowing that speed was vital.

But Diego was not to be hurried. Sometime in the dim past he had been told of a famous architect—an Anglo, he could not remember the name—who had been hired to build a house on a certain hill. After several weeks had gone by, the owner had visited the site and found the architect sitting in the shade of a great tree, chewing upon a stem of grass, and admiring the view. Have you not begun upon my house, the builder cried? Have you not even sketched its floor plan? No, the architect had replied, for how can I design a house for this hillside until I know how it feels to be a house on this hillside?

Diego smiled as he remembered the story. That Anglo

had understood. Diego liked to think that he and that man were soul brothers. That they would have recognized and understood each other immediately; knowing one another for artists. That, despite the gulf between a wealthy Anglo professional and a poor Dominican street artist, there would have been a bond of *simpatico.*

And yet, there was an urgency about Diego's work. Speed and timing were integral to his art; indeed, a part of it. The City Fathers, for whatever reason, did not approve of color and shape. They walled in the streets with hard, flat towers of granite and steel and glass; and in doing so, they walled in the souls of those who swarmed and toiled within. A breath of free thought, a soaring of the spirit, disturbed them. Why, place a mural before the swarming workers and, who knows? They might pause and admire it and be late for work. And so, artists like Diego worked by stealth, in the small hours of the morning. A half-remembered story nibbled at the corner of his mind.

Suddenly, decision came upon him. He reached into his bag and pulled forth a spray can of bright crimson paint. Quickly, he set to work.

He worked swiftly but carefully; placing his colors and shapes just so; using an old piece of cardboard to mask his edges so the colors would not run together; using an old broom handle to steady his arm for the finer work.

The centerpiece of his creation was a two-word quote from that long-ago story. It cried out: "Repent, Harlequin!" in bold, explosive lettering, block shaped, but coming unraveled at the corners. Words unwilling to be confined by straight lines and angles. Behind the lettering and embracing it with outstretched arms he sketched a jester's face thrown back in laughter, his cap o' bells cocked at a defiant, jaunty angle. The costume was straight pantomime; the motley that had graced a million English country Christmases. A cry from the long-suppressed, carefree heart of Anglo culture; one that belied the joyless facade behind which they had imprisoned themselves. But the face he painted as the faces he knew: Brown skin. Narrow, oriental eyes. Straight, black Indian braids. Somehow, it all harmonized. Somehow it was exactly right.

When he was done, Diego stepped back and considered his work. It was flawed, as all such art is flawed. The dictates of speed meant that touch-up was not possible; that minor details went uncorrected. Still, he admitted even to his own critical and seldom-satisfied eye, it was one of his best works. Better than the west support on the Williamsburg Bridge, now sadly sandblasted out of existence. Better even than last year's E-train (which had told a complete story, each car in line continuing the narrative thread). He dubbed his new painting *The Unrepentant Harlequin.* Simple and understated as it was in the garish and colorful vocabulary of his medium, the painting had captured the soul of the City. The clown, in his irrepressible, multi-ethnic gaiety seemed to burst forth from the flat, grey wall of the building, as the spirit of the people would burst from their grey, pin-striped suits, were they only given the chance.

Hastily now, he stuffed his tools into his canvas bag and sprinted to the corner where Jaime waited. The paint cans clattered as he ran.

"Good, no?" he said to Jaime when he had arrived.

"It is wonderful," his little brother breathed. "Never have I seen so fine a painting."

Jaime was ten and easily impressed. Still, Diego's chest swelled with pride at the compliment.

Pablo joined them. "Twenty three minutes," he said, breathless. "A new record." Pablo was obsessed with numbers. He knew all the odds; he knew all the statistics. He worked in numbers the way Diego worked in spray paint. He paused and surveyed Diego's work. "You didn't finish it," he said. "Why?"

"What do you mean?"

Pablo pointed. "The lettering. You left it grey."

Diego looked and saw that, indeed, the lettering was

grey, and not the bright, insistent red that he had used. "I don't understand," he said. And then he understood even less, because, as he watched, the other colors faded slowly and the drab walls of the building emerged, like a mildew growing on a basement wall. Diego's heart faded with the colors.

Last to go were the jester's eyes and grin; and, as they vanished, they struck Diego not as a laughing affirmation of life, but as that rictus of uncomprehending terror that the joyful have always worn when the life was sucked from them.

They sprinted to the wall and stared at it. It was as barren as the hearts of the City Fathers.

"Mother of God," said Pablo, crossing himself. "What magic is this?"

Diego knelt and fingered a trace of sooty powder at the foot of the wall. He rubbed it between thumb and fingers. It was gritty and slightly greasy and left a drab stain on his fingertips. The breeze down the canyon-like street caught the powder and it flashed away on the wind.

Diego gritted his teeth. "Not magic," he said. "Only another blow in the fight between the City and the street artists. They think they have found a way to proof their walls against our colors." He glanced down at Jaime, who was sniffling and rubbing his eye with a fist, crying for the now-vanished beauty.

"They think they have," he repeated.

He discovered the reason that very night. Diego was in the kitchenette, cooking supper for Jaime and his mother when he heard the word "graffiti" from the television set in the other room. He quickly turned the gas off on the stove and hurried over to where the tube flickered on Jaime's face.

Mama, who worked nights, had woken and had turned on the evening news as a backdrop to her primping. Diego sat on the floor next to Jaime and watched the screen carefully.

There were two men, both Anglos, standing before a clutch of microphones. The fat, jowly one was talking, while the other, a spare man with a brush cut and laughing eyes, stood a little behind and aside.

". . . an end to this vandalism," the jowly man was saying.

"Could you explain for the folks at home how this chemical works?" asked one of the reporters. Since he worked for the station that Diego was watching, the camera cut quickly to show the reporter's face, looking wise and curious. Diego laughed, because he had once painted such a face on the wall of Black Rock, the NBC building. Only, he had painted the face as a masque, held before yearning cameras and phallic microphones. Behind the masque had been the same face, but with a bored and vapid expression. That work had lasted long enough to be photographed, and had appeared in full color in *City Magazine.* Diego kept a clipping of that picture, the only permanent record of a sadly evanescent art form.

"I believe I'll let Dr. Singer answer that one," the fat man said.

The second man stepped to the microphones. "Which means that Mr. Cardrick doesn't know the answer." The reporters laughed at the sally, and even Cardrick chuckled unconvincingly. Diego took an immediate liking to the second man.

"As you all know," Singer said to the reporters, "nanomachines are built on a molecular scale. Proteins, viruses, and the like are natural, biological nannies. This new machine which my Team and I have developed is called EverKleen™. It is a clear, solar-powered coating that will protect buildings and windows—any reasonably flat surface—from picking up dirt and grime, thus eliminating the need for and the cost of periodic cleanings; not to mention the dangerous work of window-washers on the skyscrapers. When the nanny is sprayed onto a surface its built-in nanocomputer, Tiny NIM™, memorizes the molecular structure of the substrate. Afterwards, anything applied overtop of it is recognized as foreign matter and the nanny's restrictor enzymes dismantle the molecules. Thus, the dirt or the bird droppings are converted into pure atoms of carbon, oxygen, and what-have-you."

"You say it destroys dirt," said a reporter who, being from a competing station, remained invisible and anonymous. (Instead, the director inserted a quick cut of his own man so the viewer would have the impression that was he who had asked the question.) "Does it also recognize graffiti paint and destroy it, as Mr. Cardrick has claimed?"

Singer paused, pursed his lips, and nodded. "Yes."

"What about people leaning up against the building? Won't your nanny try to take them apart, too? Or at least their clothes?"

"Well, that would discourage loitering, wouldn't it?" said Singer. The reporters laughed again. "Seriously, though, we did give that considerable thought. Tiny NIM™ has some built-in safeguards. For one thing, the coating doesn't act immediately. Depending on the thickness with which the coating is applied, the foreign material must remain in place anywhere from fifteen minutes to many hours. In fact we can specify the thickness in minutes. Each layer of molecules is fifteen minutes 'thick.' Secondly, the foreign material must not move during that time. No person or animal can remain so perfectly still even for a short time. So, birds are safe; birdshit is not."

The scene cut away from the press conference to the studio, where the anchor proceeded to tell the viewers what they had just heard. Diego didn't need the summary. He understood perfectly well what had happened. The City had a spray coating that ate art.

His hands clenched into fists. They couldn't do it! They couldn't take the color out of life! He wouldn't let them.

But how could he stop them? They would go through the City, painting over the graffiti or removing it, and spraying the drab, monotone surfaces with their graffiti eater. Already, one building at least had been treated. Diego realized that now. The building he had tried to paint last night had probably been a test.

"Hah!" his mother said to his back. "You finished now with your spray cans, Diego. You finda job now, eh? You go t'work, like respectable people."

It was a long-standing argument. He didn't answer back, as he usually did, that he was an artist and artists lead different lives. He had a greater obstacle now than his mother's attempts to shoe-horn him into some clock-punching, shuffling, ass-kissing office. His enemy was Cardrick, the man who owned more buildings than anyone in the City. Cardrick was the enemy, not his mother. Not even, Diego realized suddenly, not even that scientist, Singer. No man with laughter in his eyes could be his enemy.

It came to him then what he had to do. He leapt to his feet and hurried to the telephone. He called Pablo. Pablo had a cousin who ran a Dominican restaurant on the Lower West Side. Its facade was grimy and scrawled with graffiti of no artistic merit at all. Only names and boasts and obscenities. Pablo's cousin would help.

They made it a public event, as Diego knew they would. There was no way Cardrick could allow such an open challenge to pass unanswered.

The building was new, unfinished and, hence, Diego had reasoned, unsprayed with the new material. Now it sported a giant mural, sprung into life in the small hours of the morning: *The Unrepentant Harlequin* laughed again. This time, the laugh was unabashedly triumphant. Diego had also added a little bit of Singer to the eyes. Not enough to be recognizable, but enough that Singer himself, when he made his appearance, gave a double-take and barely suppressed a grin.

Below the Harlequin, Diego had painted Cardrick. A pasty, joyless face the color of fishbellies, at once greedy and sorrowful, defeated by the laughter of the Harlequin. A comic book balloon emerged from the jester's lips: "Hey, nanny, nanny-o!"

Twice as large as its predecessor, the mural had required the help of seven other street artists to complete quickly enough to avoid being caught in the act. Yet, despite the committee approach, Diego was unable to detect where each of the artists had worked. They had followed his instructions and sketches perfectly; and he had paid them in what he knew would be the new coin of the demi-world of art.

Diego worked his way to the front of the crowd, where he could see better. He kept his ear open for the comments and scattered remarks that he treasured. His morning-after reviews. "Seems a shame ta paint it over, don't it?" "That Cardrick, he ain't got no sensa humor." "Oh, I think it's rather funny, don't you, dear?" "Damn vandals gotta spray paint everything."

Well, no one loves a critic.

He reached the front of the crowd just as Cardrick began the press conference. Diego glanced at his watch and did some quick mental arithmetic. It would be close. He hoped Cardrick would hurry.

"This act of blatant vandalism," Cardrick humphed into the microphones that had been set up on a temporary platform, "is so obviously a challenge to our program, announced last week, of creating a graffiti-free City, that we felt a public response was called for." He waved a hand awkwardly at a small group of men and women dressed in green coveralls labeled "SingerLabs" across the back. They wore goggles and air filters and pressure tanks strapped across their shoulders. "We will paint over this monstrosity," Cardrick continued, "this affront to the sensibilities of the people of our fair City, and prevent forever any future acts of vandalism."

Diego heard his name called. He looked over his shoulder and saw Pablo pushing his way through the crowd. Pablo had Jaime and his cousin, Esteban, in tow.

"I thought I would find you here," he said. "Best seat in the house, eh?"

Diego was growing more nervous as the time grew shorter. He cupped his hands about his mouth. "You gonna stan' up there an' talk, gringo? Or you gonna start painting?"

Cardrick stopped, surprised, in mid-sentence. He searched for the source of the interruption and glared at him. Singer, standing to one side, raised his eyebrows and looked at Diego speculatively. Cardrick waved an arm at the painters. "Go ahead. Paint the damn thing over."

Jaime looked crestfallen. "Diego, why did you do that? It only made them mad, so they ruin your picture."

Singer's crew began spraying over the mural with a white basecoat. When they obliterated the Harlequin's head, a sigh ran through the crowd. "They were going to paint over it anyhow," Diego told Jaime. Pablo, he saw, was biting his lip to keep from laughing.

Singer's people left Cardrick's visage to last. Little by little, they buried the mural under a layer of white until finally only the pasty, hangdog face remained. Singer, Diego realized as he watched Cardrick's scowl deepen, was something of an artist himself.

Finally, the cover-up was complete and Diego checked his watch. He breathed a sigh of relief. It was just in time. Oh, the exquisite agonies of the artist!

Cardrick launched into another speech, the gist of which was that, when the basecoat had dried, the regular coat would be applied; then, after that, the EverKleen™. The crowd began to turn away. Watching paint dry was not a New Yorker's idea of excitement. Diego sighed, watching the white spot where his mural had been.

Esteban was an older man, about forty. He took Diego's hand and pumped it vigorously. "I cannot thank you enough," he said, "for the fine job you and your friends did on my restaurant. Never has it looked so bright and clean. And your mural across the facade, your painting of *La Trinitaria* and their struggles against the black invaders—it is the talk of the neighborhood. Already the Haitian gang from across the street has tried to deface it; but their pitiful scrawls have faded, even as you said they would."

"It was the coating that man invented," Diego told him, pointing at Singer. "The one I had you buy."

"It was very expensive," Esteban said. "This Singer hombre charges dearly for his product. And to have it delivered by courier was even more so." Esteban shook his head.

"But it was worth it," Diego reminded him. "You will save in cleaning expenses far more than what you have paid out."

"Yes, as you said. It is not the price, but the cost that matters. Did you obtain the rebate?"

"Rebate?" Diego was paying Esteban only half a mind.

"Yes. I realize how easy it is to overestimate the amounts needed for a job, but I would hate to see you lose that money."

He spoke to the restauranteur without turning. "Oh, no. I did not want a rebate for the extra material. I wanted the material itself. This 'nanny' of Singer's."

"The material?" Esteban was puzzled. "Whatever for?"

"For my art. To pay my friends for their help. Because one layer of it is fifteen minutes thick," he replied.

Esteban turned in desperation to his cousin. "Pablo, he makes no sense."

Pablo was grinning. "He will."

A shout went up from the dispersing crowd. "The graffiti! It's back!" Heads turned. People stopped.

And indeed, while they stared at the wall, the white basecoat gradually faded and the laughing jester face returned. Repent, Harlequin, shouted the wall. Hey, nanny, nanny-o, the Harlequin replied.

Cardrick turned and saw what was happening and his face turned mottled with surprise and anger. Singer had seen it, too, and, after a moment of pure astonishment, was doing his best not to laugh. Instead, he approached the wall and touched it with an instrument he pulled from his pocket. He touched a few buttons on the face of the instrument, read the results. Then he did laugh, long and hard.

"What is it, Singer?" demanded Cardrick.

"I'm afraid someone has beaten you to it, Mr. Cardrick."

"Beaten me . . . What do you mean?"

"I mean someone painted this graffito, then covered it over with EverKleen™. The nanny now recognizes the paint film as the 'correct' surface and rejects anything applied overtop of it. Including your paint."

"What?!" Cardrick swelled up. "Do you mean to tell me that that piece of trash is—"

"Permanent? I think so. It will reject paint remover, certainly. Maybe sandblasting would work. The nanny layer would be dog's breath to bust through. We made it tough on purpose."

The crowd was laughing now. Some of them were slapping each other on the back. Some were pointing at Cardrick and Singer. Diego saw others run off and come running back with friends. Then they began to applaud. Slowly at first; only a few of them, an arrhythmic patter, like the first drops of a rainstorm. Then others joined in, and others, until it was a thunder in Diego's ears. Diego grinned widely enough to split his face in two.

Repent, Harlequin!

Never!

Jaime was jumping up and down and clapping his hands. "Diego! Aah, Diego," he said. Esteban was staring slack-jawed at the wall, the corners of his mouth twitching up. Pablo looked at Diego over his cousin's head. Diego stretched up his arm and tapped the crystal of his watch. How long?

Pablo looked at his own watch and held up a handful of fingers. Five more minutes. They waited the time out patiently.

When the Harlequin's left arm began to fade out, the

watching crowd let out a groan. It rippled through their ranks like windblown paper down an alleyway. The disappointment was palpable. A patch of something that twinkled like cellophane fell away from the wall. The crowd sighed as the arm faded out.

Ah, but they loosed a cheer when it faded back in.

The new arm, painted beneath a second layer of EverKleen™ thirteen hours thick, had its thumb planted firmly against against the jester's nose. It's fingers, caught in mid-waggle, danced contempt at the Cardrick-face. A tongue slowly appeared, lolling out from the jester's mouth. The crowd whooped and pointed at the property magnate, who grew steadily more angry.

Esteban leaned over to shout into Diego's ear. "I don't understand," he said. "What did you do?"

"We painted many paintings last night," Diego told him. "And covered each painting with a thick layer of the chemical. Then we painted overtop of it. The 'nanny' waits before it dissolves the material atop it. Depending on how thick it is laid on, it may wait many hours; even days. As each layer dissolves from the actions of the 'nanny' beneath it, it reveals the next level of painting. That was the tricky part, deciding how many coats of EverKleen™ to use for each layer. I was afraid the mural would start to change before Cardrick tried to cover it up; but the timing worked out very well, I think."

"I helped him calculate the timing," said Pablo. "The bottommost layers are many days thick, while the one on top was only fifteen minutes thick. You see, each layer had to be thinner than the one underneath it, otherwise, several layers of the painting might vanish at once."

"And that would be bad art," finished Diego.

Esteban grinned. "I like it," he said. "But what happens to the paint caught between the layers of the coating? It breaks down, you said; but where does it go?"

Diego shook his head. "Each layer of paint except the very first has a layer of EverKleen™ below it and above it. The outer layer of EverKleen™ bonds to the paint beneath it. When that paint dissolves from the inner layer of Everkleen™ it becomes a powder, and the upper layer, having no surface to bond to, simply falls away. What is left of the paint drops to the ground and becomes a pile of soot at the base of the wall."

Esteban smiled. "Have you become a chemist, now?"

"An artist learns how his medium performs. It takes no genius to realize that a coating does not outlast the surface it coats."

Esteban looked back at the mural. "How many layers of the painting are there?"

Diego shook his head. "That would be telling."

"People will come from all over the City to see this painting," Pablo announced, "hoping to be here when it changes again. Perhaps, even the City Fathers will grow to like it; or at least, to like the tourist money it will bring."

"Ah," Esteban sighed. "But you will gain nothing from it, Diego. That is not right."

"I am an artist," Diego told him. "And for me the art itself is sufficient."

The crowd was jostling around them, trying to get a better view, but Diego managed to maintain his place at the front. He leaned on the police barricade and admired his painting. A glance at his watch told him the next change was not due for several hours. He thought perhaps he would wait for it. Cardrick and Singer were arguing by the platform and Diego could make out some of the words. He heard "warranty" and "antidote." Finally, Cardrick turned in disgust and stalked off, tossing "lawyers" back over his shoulder at the scientist.

Singer watched him go, a twisted smile on his face. Then he turned and stared at the painting. Diego watched him pull a stick of gum from his shirt pocket and shove it into his mouth. After a while he turned away from the painting, and Diego saw the thoughtful look on his face.

Singer called one of his people over, someone named

Eamonn, and began talking with him in low, excited tones. Diego heard him say something about "Belusov's Reaction." The skinny, freckled man he was talking to looked at the mural, thought for a moment, and nodded vigorously. He grinned and Singer slapped him on the back and they parted. Singer glanced at his watch and again at the painting.

Somehow, Diego knew without asking what Singer was thinking. Timed paint. Colors that would evaporate and change with subtlety and precision. Diego's heart beat faster. He had painted in space for many years. Now he could paint in time, as well. Painting in time. There was a new art, for you. How he longed to express himself in it!

As Singer turned to go, he caught sight of Diego. Their eyes met and locked for a moment. Singer looked from Diego to the painting, then at the way Diego looked at the painting. Then he grunted and shook his head slowly and Diego smiled bashfully back at him.

Slowly a grin spread over Singer's face. He gave Diego a cocky salute and, after a moment, Diego gave him an equally cocky bow. They recognized and understood each other perfectly. Artists always did.

Interlude

Pavel Denisovitch allowed himself a small smile to match those upon the faces of his class. There was a certain satisfaction in in the tale of Diego Salazar. From such small beginnings . . . For many years, his "active murals" had been much in demand. Cities had vied for his talents, and few indeed were the public places that did not boast at least one Salazar original. Why Old First Module itself sported a holographic reproduction of Salazar's *Inquisition,* in which the artist commemorated his hearing before the NEA Racial Purity Board. The Board had ruled that, because his grandmother had been half-French, he was tainted with "Eurocentric bias" and was thus ineligible for a Minority Artist grant.

In his later years, when age had bent his fingers so that he could no longer hold a spray can, Salazar's studio had turned out younger artists who painted in his style and whom he had taught to master the intricacies of Singer's "Tempo" line of paints. Although it was said that only Salazar himself had ever truly mastered "Con Brio."

Gabriella da Silva spoke. "Sensei! Singer, the man who invented EverKleen™. Was it not he who . . ."

Denisovitch laughed. "Yes."

The class laughed with him. Denisovitch hunkered over his lectern and said, "Yes. Mention the birth of nanotechnology, and Singer's name is spoken as if the two were synonymous. His many undeniable accomplishments; his struggles against economic decline and America's failure of will; his dramatic death. They are the stuff of legend. Soon enough we will hear that it was Singer who invented the Saturn rocket and the Aswan Dam; and that he built the Great Wall and the Moskva Metro. This is certainly unfair to Matsumoto, to Rita Bedford-Contreras and the others. The Age of Nanotechnology would have come about had Singer never been born. And yet—!" He leaned toward them and paused for dramatic emphasis. "And yet," he continued more quietly with a crooked smile, "we can be sure that it would not have come about in quite the same way."

2. The Washer at the Ford

I

Charles Randolph Singer looked at the door with its bright magenta-and-yellow trefoil warning and licked his lips. The door was gunmetal grey; the handle, one of those bank-vault kinds that spun like a wheel. Through the thick lead-quartz window beside the door he could see the rows of waldos used for handling the fuel rods. The guide had just demonstrated how they operated, showing a dexterity in manipulating the gloves that most people did not show with their own hands. *And I'm putting this off,* he thought.

"Dr. Singer? We're going to see the waste storage pool now."

He glanced at the tour group where they waited on the mezzanine, at the doorway back to the control room. Half of them were already through it. Biologists and medical/health practitioners in suits and ties. The yellow visitors' hard hats sat awkwardly atop their heads. The nuclear engineer in the long, white lab coat seemed an alien being.

He waved a hand at them. "You go ahead. I just want to see something here." To demonstrate his intention, he leaned against the quartz window and cupped his hands around his eyes to block out reflections.

The engineer herded the other biologists out. "You can't stay here without an escort," he said.

"Oh, very well." Singer turned to follow the others out of the room; the engineer stepped through the doorlock ahead of him, and he was alone for just a fraction of a second.

And that was all he needed.

A quick turn of the handle and the heavy door unlatched. Immediately klaxons sounded and an insistent red light began flashing above the hatchway. A pleasant, female contralto spoke through the loudspeakers: "The pile door is unlatched. The pile door is unlatched."

The engineer-guide stuck an astonished face through the doorlock, saw what Singer was doing, and sprinted down the stairs from the mezzanine. "Hey!" he shouted. "The plenum's been cracked for fuel replacement! You can't go in there without a suit!"

The heavy, dull-white radiation suits hung on rows of hooks. Their shapeless hoods, with the single, rectangular visor set like Cyclop's eye in the center, gave them a weird, unearthly appearance. Singer ignored them and stepped through the open door.

He pulled it shut just as the engineer reached it. It slammed with a satisfying chunk, and he spun the inside wheel. That wouldn't keep them out for long, but he only needed a moment.

With movements long rehearsed in his mind, he turned to the inner door of the airlock and punched in the five-digit number that was supposed to unlock it. There was a pause, and Singer wondered if the number he had been given was correct. Then the door clicked and hissed.

Once the inner door was unlatched, the outer door could not be opened. Singer leaned his right arm against the doorframe, and rested his forehead on it. He let out a slow breath. He had made it.

He straightened up and stepped into the containment structure. A maze of plumbing filled most of the interior. Steam pipes. Condensate pipes. Coolant pipes. All of them were color coded and marked with arrows showing the direction of the flow. The codes and symbols were runes, without meaning, save to the engineers that interpreted them. Singer was able to identify the coolant pump only because it was making pump noises. He knew that the other large structures were the steam generators and the pressurizer, but he didn't know enough about engineering to tell them apart. It was all very mysterious; like an immense abstract sculpture. A mix of symmetry and chaos. *"Touch nothing, no matter how bored you get." Good advice,* thought Singer. Though, considering where he was, caution seemed a little silly. Like wearing galoshes during a hurricane.

He walked to the reactor and inspected it curiously. The pile itself was contained inside a larger plenum assembly, now open, which also contained the control rods, guide tubes and other auxilliary equipment. Singer gazed for a moment at the exposed "guts." Murchadha had told him it was a CANDU, whatever that meant.

He stood by the edge of the pile. He could feel the heat from it; feel the neutrons piercing his skin. Or was that his imagination? Who knew? Who had ever lived to describe it? He closed his eyes and imagined himself on the beach, sunbathing; the solar radiation turning him a nice golden tan. He stretched and turned slowly. It was like sunbathing. A smaller sun perhaps, but much closer.

When he looked over his shoulder, he saw his erstwhile companions pressing their faces against the quartz glass window, like children at a candy store. Or at a zoo. That was a more apt comparison, he decided. A zoo. Peering at a very strange critter indeed. The faces he saw there were a mixed lot: distraught, curious, and even—in one instance—eager! *Ghoul,* thought Singer. The engineer was talking animatedly on a red telephone.

Singer waved at his audience. He found an exposed Ibeam in full view of the window and monitoring cameras and sat down on it. It was important that they realize he was not a terrorist; that he was no threat to the reactor. So, after his first curious inspection, he paid no further attention to the pile or other generating equipment. Instead, he pulled a paperback book from his jacket pocket and opened it. Classic Heinlein. *The Man Who Sold the Moon.* He began to read. *I should have brought* The Green Hills of Earth, he thought. Rhysling's story was more *apropos* his current situation. Especially that last part, in the ship's reactor room.

As the word spread through the power plant, more and more people crowded up against the viewing window. Singer ignored them and concentrated on his book. Once or twice, he glanced at the window for a casual headcount. Then he would lick his thumb and turn a page in the book. He tried to ignore the voices in his head. *"You don't take failure very well, do you, Charlie?"* said one voice. *"The problem with edges,"* said another, *"is that it's too easy to topple off them."*

And a third: *"Then, you do not believe it is possible?"*

And *"Please, don't talk yourself into doing something I can't live with."*

Resolutely, he stared at the pages gripping the ancient, tattered paperback. *"There are no final solutions, Charlie."*

"Maybe not," he muttered aloud. Then he realized that the people crowded at the viewport could probably hear him over the intercom. Talking to himself. He flushed. *They must think I'm nuts.* Then he remembered where he was and laughed.

"Maybe not," he said again, as much to himself as to the voices. "But at least there are temporary ones."

He remembered the emptiness of the Lab when he last visited it, just before coming here. Everyone gone, scattered. His footsteps had echoed in silent rooms. The terminal screens were dark; the equipment, shut down, mute and accusing. And who knew when, or even whether, they would be powered up again? *How did it come to this?* he asked himself. But it was a rhetorical question, because he knew very well how it had. He could remember every step along the road. Every stumble. He could remember the insistent ringing at his door that had started the whole thing.

II

When Singer answered the doorbell on the first floor of the laboratory building and saw Masao Koyanagi standing outside, he did not know who it was.

His door opened only an inch, held in place by a diamond-fibre chain that he had knitted himself. It was built up from intricately bonded layers of carbon atoms grown in a vat. No in-mugger's bolt cutter could break it. He peered through the crack and saw a short, thin Japanese man, wearing a bluish-grey suit with the faintly irridescent, diagonal pinstripes that were the fashion rage among businessmen that year. The man's hair was impeccably groomed; his nails, buffed to a sheen.

"Yes?" said Singer suspiciously. It might be a *zaibatsu* sales rep. The Niprazilians were constantly after him for permission to produce or market his inventions. Singer preferred his own privately held company and subcontracted whatever manufacturing work was necessary to local concerns. He was small and, God willing, he would remain small. Giant corporations had been the death of American business, and were already strangling Japanese and Brazilian enterprise with their bureaucratic inertia.

"Dr. Singer?" the stranger asked. "Have I the honor of addressing Dr. Charles Randolph Singer?"

"You're doing it," Singer allowed. "Whether it's an honor or not is up to you."

The stranger chuckled nervously and glanced behind him. "May I come in for a moment?" he asked.

Singer closed the door, unlatched the diamond chain,

and opened the door again. The stranger scurried through, and Singer banged the door and shot the bolt.

"You're taking a big chance, going out alone," he said. "Not only out-muggers. There's plenty of folks around the Northeast who like to play 'Trap the Jap,' Mister—?" He let the word drawl out.

"Ah. I am Koyanagi-sensei Masao; ah, that is Dr. Masao Koyanagi." He bowed partway, equal-to-equal, and a business card appeared, as if by magic, in his cupped, outstretched hands.

Singer sighed inwardly. *Meishi.* He took the card, using only his right hand, though, strictly speaking, he should have used both hands. The Japanese made a big deal out of presenting their business cards, and a powerful lot of Americans, he knew, were taking up Japanese customs and behaviors; all the *giri* and *gimu* nonsense. But, Singer didn't hold with that and delighted in displaying "American crudeness." After all, Koyanagi was wearing Western clothing, not a kimono. And a lot of the Japanese in Brazil were picking up Brazilian manners; or at least, so he had heard. Crudeness was all a matter of culture and taste.

However, he was not so crude as to take the card with his left hand.

"All right, Dr. Koyanagi. What do you want?"

"I would like to do business with you," his visitor replied bluntly.

Singer sighed. "I thought so. Another sales rep. Which *zaibatsu* are you from? No, never mind; I don't want to know." He walked to the door. "Don't let the doorknob ream your ass on the way out."

Koyanagi grimaced. "Please, Dr. Singer-sama. It is not that at all. I am a scientist; I represent only myse—"

"A scientist. Wait a minute!" He pointed a finger at him. "You're not the M. Koyanagi of São Paulo Biophysics Laboratory, are you? The '*Further Study of* M. radiodurans *under Robust Levels of Gamma Radiation*'? That Koyanagi?"

The visitor bowed again, much lower this time, showing gratitude. "I am honored that you know of my unworthy efforts."

Singer reached out and tapped the man on the chest with his forefinger. "You owe me a half-million novocruzeiros! The nanomachines you used to enhance that bacterium were proteins that I patented."

Koyanagi winced. "Please, Dr. Singer. That is an issue you must address to São Paulo. If it were only myself, I would pay you the NCr 500,000 and more, and welcome to it. Without your nanomachines my work would have been impossible."

Singer paused. "Then what . . . ?"

"I bring you an opportunity to become rich and famous."

"I'm already rich and famous," Singer grunted, "but now you've got my attention. Come on upstairs and set a spell."

Singer had converted the second floor of the building into a comfortable apartment. It was equipped with a kitchen, living room, two bedrooms, a library, and some rooms that varied in their functions. The living room ran the full width of the building and had a picture window at each end. In square footage the apartment was as big as most houses. Singer also had a home in the country, but normally spent only his weekends there. He liked to stay close to the action.

He let Koyanagi into the apartment and looked around. "My wife's out right now," he said. "Go on. Have a seat, son, and keep talking about making me rich." He gestured to the couch in the apartment's living room. "Can I offer you anything? Tea?"

Koyanagi smiled. "No, but a shot of *cachaça* would be fine."

Singer jerked his head around. He grinned. "Acculturating, are you? Let me see what I have." After a few moments he returned with a glass of dark liquid. "Couldn't find any *cachaça*, will Barbados rum do?"

"Very nicely, thank you." Koyanagi took it and tossed it off in one swallow. "At the train station," he said, "I felt as if all eyes were on me. Not friendly eyes, either."

Singer shrugged. "What do you expect? They have to blame somebody for the economic mess they're in, so it might as well be you. Brazilians have the same problem, except most of them pretend to be Puerto Ricans to make themselves socially acceptable. Did you walk here from Metropark Station?"

"No cab would take me."

"Hmm, no. Not without a Nisei badge; and maybe not even then." He took a seat facing his visitor. "So, tell me, Dr. Koyanagi, why are you here? This is no casual visit, obviously. How do you plan to make me rich?"

Koyanagi drew himself up and launched himself into what seemed a prepared speech. "Dr. Singer, you are the world's foremost authority on nanotechnology. You hold more biogenetic patents than any living individual. People have compared you to—"

"Thomas Edison. Yes, yes; I know. That's why I built my laboratory here in Menlo Park. You see that tower outside the north window? That was where Edison built his original 'invention factory.' But, son, you did not come eight thousand miles just to tell me I'm a great man. I already knew that."

"So. I am buttering you up. Is that the phrase? Most peculiar. The Persians say 'I am putting melons under your arms.' No. I have a request to make of you." He hung his head and rotated the empty highball glass between his two hands. "I have made a most intensive study of *Micrococcus radiodurans,*" he said, after a moment of silence. "You know of it?"

Singer nodded. "Microorganism with a high resistance to radiation. It can survive radiation levels that are, what? A thousand times the lethal dose for humans, right? A million years' worth of normal background radiation delivered in one punch."

Koyanagi nodded vigorously. "Yes. Yes. Kitayama and

Matsuyama studied it extensively in 1979. I have expanded on their original work. I believe the organism's resistance is due to internal protein structures, rather than to its simplicity, as everyone has assumed—"

Singer nodded. "All right," he interrupted. "You're a certified genius and a pioneer. Go on. How does *M. radiodurans* make me any richer than I am now?" Singer leaned forward eagerly. There was a cash flow problem developing in the Lab and new ideas for income were always welcome.

"Hmm. Does the *senhor* recall the *Mir* disaster?"

Singer blinked at the change of subject and sat up straight. "The Soviet space station? Yes, of course. The solar flare caught them unprepared. There were three cosmonauts up there and two of them died almost immediately. It set their space program back by half a decade."

"The third man also died, from delayed cancer, a few years later."

"Yes, I remember. What of it?"

"I was wondering." Koyanagi looked up, then out the window where the Edison tower stood. "What if those cosmonauts had been . . . well . . . 'inoculated' with *M. radiodurans?*"

"Inoculated?" Singer felt a tingle move through his body and leaned forward again. "What are you trying to say?"

Koyanagi looked at him. "Proteins are strings of lumpy beads. If they fold up the right way, the lumps can fit together like the pieces of a Chinese puzzle and form enzymes and hormones. There are . . . 'sticky?' Yes, 'sticky' places on molecules. Could the proteins that *M. radiodurans* uses be folded in such a way that they could stick to, say, the white blood cells, so that—"

Singer straightened. "So that humans would become radiation resistant, too?" he finished. "So the proteins could repair human cells, instead? Son, that is the craziest, most off-the-wall notion I've ever heard!"

Koyanagi's face crumpled. "Then you do not believe it is possible."

Singer laughed. "Hell, I said it was crazy. I didn't say it wouldn't work! Crazy ideas are the only ones worth trying." Singer stuck out his paw and engulfed Koyanagi's manicured hand. He shook it vigorously. "Welcome to Singer and Associates, Dr. Koyanagi!"

SingerLab's conference room was centered on a round wooden table, inlaid with touchpads and sunken terminal screens. A portable lectern with a Mystica pad stood in the front of the room, and the entire front wall was taken up by a flatscreen electronically connected to the pad. Singer and the other associates sat in padded swivel chairs, listening while Koyanagi outlined his concept. Singer wanted everyone to have the same, clear vision; and where better to get it than from the original visionary?

"If only small areas of the body are affected," Koyanagi was saying, "human beings can tolerate remarkable levels of radiation. Even though the affected tissues die, the organism survives. That is the basis for radiation therapy for cancer. However, even small doses can be fatal if delivered as whole-body irradiation. Tolerance varies from person to person, but generally speaking, dosages in the 600–800 rad range are one hundred percent fatal; while doses running 400–600 rads are fifty percent fatal. To put these numbers in perspective, recall that the levels reported twenty kilometers downwind of Chernobyl fell in the range of 450 rads."

Singer listened carefully, taking notes on his terminal. Masao wasn't telling them anything new, of course. That wasn't the purpose of the initial briefing. The idea was to tune everyone's thoughts to the same channel.

"Our task," Koyanagi continued, "is to raise the radiation level that human beings can tolerate. The old term for this was 'hardening.' We have long known of ways in which people can be hardened to some extent. For example, a diet rich in green vegetables coupled with large doses of Vitamins A and E can effect a thirty percent reduction in the damage done by radiation. What I envision, however, is a prophylactic, taken in the form of a pill, perhaps, or an injection, that will 'install' in the human metabolism the same sort of molecular machinery that some lower life forms possess."

"A vaccine against radiation," mused Jessica Burton-Peeler. She was a mature woman with a Rubenesque figure; the kind that men once found attractive, in the days before anorexia became fashionable. She wore owlish glasses and a dark blue suit with a ruffled blouse. She was the second-best geneticist in North America.

"Correct, Dr. Peeler," replied Koyanagi. "A vaccine. But how is it to work? Radiation consists of fragments of shattered atoms: broken shards of nuclei, individual particles, high energy photons. Alpha, beta, gamma. These act like subatomic 'bullets.' When they strike atoms within the tissues of the body, they knock electrons loose, ionizing the cell material, and causing abnormal chemical reactions. Since living tissues depend upon precise and elaborate sequences of chemical reactions to perform their functions, these abnormalities can easily prove fatal. The cells reproduce themselves too slowly—they are destroyed faster than they can be replaced—or else the replacement cells themselves are abnormal. The problem, therefore, is one of broken molecules. What I envision is quite simple. A nanomachine that will paste these broken molecules back together as fast as ionizing events can fracture them."

There was a moment of silence before Kalpit Patel blurted, "Then I am glad that what you envision is not complex!" The microbiologist was a second generation Indian-American. His skin was coffee-colored and he sported a caterpillar moustache and thinning, grey hair. At fifty-two, he was the oldest of the group.

Koyanagi smiled. "Yes. The goal—to harden humans; and the objective—a cell repair nanomachine—are easy to state. Perhaps not so easy to do. However, I am sure that if anyone can do so, it is this illustrious group."

Singer thanked Koyanagi for his briefing. Koyanagi bowed and took his seat, and Singer strode to the front of the room, where he activated the Mystica pad. He looked over the group and grinned, tossing the electronic stylus in the air and catching it.

"I can see by your faces that you think Masao has dreamed up a pretty hare-brained scheme. I agree. Let's go for it." There was a round of laughter and Singer added in his mountain drawl, "Aw shucks, folks, if'n it were easy someone would a-done it already. Besides," he added more sternly, "easy jobs bring small rewards. The profit potential in this project is enormous. The market includes not only cosmonauts and nuclear plant workers, but people living *near* nuclear plants, afraid of a melt-down. And radiologists. X-ray technicians. Miners. Any-one who works around radioactives. I estimate near total market penetration within five years of product launch; and the market itself will expand as *Bandierantes Inter-planetarias* adds to its L4 manufacturing complex."

He paused and let his eyes sweep the group, pausing on and challenging Jessie's thoughtful gaze. "Make no mistake. The investment will be substantial; our operating margin, paper thin. So, we need to put a hold on all non-commercial projects"—he saw the looks the others exchanged among themselves—"and push to com-pletion those projects with high profit potential, espe-cially the monomolecular telecomm cable and the aerosol room freshener. On the other hand . . ." He leaned across the podium toward them. "On the other hand, the return on Masao's project can be equally substantial, *if we can make it work.* I think we can.

"The good news is: I don't expect competition. Only Dr. Koyanagi here has any evidence that *M. rad's* resis-tance to radiation is due to special proteins, and not to structural simplicity. Now, that may or may not be true, but the data he showed me looks very good. So, we get a head start on everybody else. If we can humanize those proteins, we can pretty much write our own ticket. People will line up outside the door there with cash in their hot little hands. The question is: Can we make it work at a reasonable ROI? What are the issues that want to be solved?"

"Configuration, for one," said Patel. "What is the design envelope to be relative to cell size? How fast should it act? What are the limits of radiation flux against which we should design?"

Singer nodded without speaking and began writing on the Mystica pad. He wrote "Rad Repair Nanny" on the right-hand side and drew an arrow pointing to it. A larger than life version sprang into existence on the flatscreen set in the back wall. The other associates swiveled in their chairs to face it. Singer drew a forty-five degree branch off the main arrow, which he labeled "Configuration," and added three stems corresponding to the three points Patel had raised. He did not address any of the points, nor did he allow anyone else to discuss them.

"What else?" he asked.

"We must identify the protein," offered Koyanagi.

"And tailor it to fit human molecules," added Patel. He looked at Koyanagi, who nodded.

"Concept," said Eamonn Murchadha. He was the youngest of the group. A redhead with freckles, he seemed hardly older than a college student. Yet, he had already made a name for himself as a nanomachinist. "There are at least a half dozen ways of designing the little darling. We need to decide on the best approach before we can talk about specifications. We could flood the bloodstream with millions of nannies, so they would circulate throughout the body looking for damaged cells—"

"Yes," interjected Koyanagi. "They could be designed as a variety of leukocyte."

Patel gazed thoughtfully at the ceiling. "Or we could," he said, "hard-wire it into the chromosomes."

"And access," said Murchadha. "The nanny must be able to get inside the cells."

"Only for free-swimming designs; access isn't an issue if it's permanently installed in the cell."

"No, regardless. You still have to get the 'construction company' inside the membrane."

Koyanagi agreed. "I used a modified T4 phage in my work."

Patel rubbed his moustache. "T4, eh? Nature's own hypodermic. Inject the instructions into the cell and let the nanny build itself on-site?"

"What about incision-and-sew? That's faster," Murchadha commented.

"Jessie," said Singer. "You're being unusually quiet today. "Do you have any thoughts on this?" He knew she did. She had opinions on everything. Sometimes several. She had been staring pensively at the idea tree, her lips working like they always did when she was deep in thought.

"Very well," she said slowly. "This is a more difficult task than I think you appreciate. If the cash flow is going to be as tight as you say, perhaps we should not get into this at all."

Koyanagi looked shocked, but Singer wrote the comment down anyway. Jessie had a point. A negative point, but still a point. If the nanny couldn't be built for a profit, there was no purpose to it. Only he wished that she wouldn't go out of her way to phrase things negatively.

"Furthermore," she continued, "it won't do any good to repair the enzymes and hormones if the RNA has been damaged."

"That's right," added Patel. "And fixing the RNA won't help if the DNA has been hit."

"Then write these down, dear," said Burton-Peeler—a bit smugly he thought. "We must address three levels of repair: first, corrective action on the proteins; second, repair of the RNA; third, re-editing of the DNA."

"Product, tooling and blueprints," said Murchadha. "What about the raw material? Defective amino acids?"

"It's not necessary to repair those," she told him. "If the RNA tooling is right, it will reject any defective components."

"No critique yet," Singer reminded them as he recorded Muchadha's comment. Cells were nano-scale factories. They took in amino acids and converted them into proteins in mitochondrian "workshops." The RNA were the "stamping dies" delivered from the nuclear "design department" where the DNA "blueprints" were kept. Glandular chemical plants. Neural telecommunications. Food and transport. The body was a complete economic system in miniature.

He realized he was letting his mind wander. "I'm sorry, Kalpit. What did you say?"

"If the nanny is to work on the DNA, it must cross the nuclear membrane, as well," said Patel. "I think we will use your $T4_2$," he told Koyanagi.

"No decisions yet," warned Singer.

"Recognition," said Eamonn Murchadha. "It would be a shame if the nanny didn't know a damaged cell from a healthy one. What if it starts to 'repair' a healthy cell?"

"Then it needs to be able to detect ionization."

"Ionization that doesn't belong. Remember, there's ionized calcium in the intercellular space."

Koyanagi pointed to the diagram growing on the wall. "Please. Would you place a DNA library on the recognition branch, Dr. Singer?"

"And don't forget standards. The nanny will have to create its own standards for the DNA library," Patel pointed out. "That goes on the recognition branch, too."

"Then the nanny must enter the cell nucleus and inspect the DNA tapes," said Burton-Peeler. "And be able to tell if those tapes are damaged or not. There are millions of codons on a single strand, you know. That's an awfully large information load."

"We'll need a processor to control the whole thing. How about Tiny NIM?"

"Does NIM have the capacity for this job?"

"What does the, ah, nanny do once it identifies a damaged cell?" asked Koyanagi. "It must be able to tear down the old structures and replace them."

"That's right. Create another major branch would you?" said Murchadha. "For assembly and disassembly. The nanny needs restriction enzymes to cut and paste the strands. I think we can use commercial grade mutS and mutH and maybe build on a DNA polymerase."

"Prioritization," said Patel. "The nanny must know to concentrate on the most critical tissues. Nervous system first."

"Why nervous system?" asked Burton-Peeler. "Aren't the lymph tissues more sensitive?"

"Yes," said Koyanagi, "but the body doesn't replace nerve cells. Death from radiation sickness is almost always a nervous system disorder." He faced forward again. "We should also address the bone marrow. Since blood cells turn over more rapidly than other cells, symptoms generally appear there first."

The brainstorming continued for another two hours, until everyone was exhausted and wrung dry of ideas. Singer was a Socrates, controlling the discussion without appearing to. If the talk turned to critique, he squelched it immediately. The important thing was to keep the ideas flowing freely. If a participant became reticent, he drew him or her out. If the discussion wandered off the topic, he tapped the arrowhead of the diagram with his wand and brought them back.

Afterward, they cleaned up the diagram; moving ideas from one branch to another, adding details, clarifying comments. Then they prioritized the list in order of importance. First priority was to identify the relevant protein structures of *M. radiodurans*. That job went to Koyanagi and Burton-Peeler. Meanwhile, Patel and Murchadha were to simulate alternate design scenarios. Once the relevant design decisions were made, Burton-Peeler would tackle the access and recognition systems; Murchadha would prepare the restrictor enzymes and other features of the nanny itself; and Patel and Koyanagi would collaborate on designing a protein that would simulate the benefits of *M. radiodurans*, but which would fold in such a way that it would stick to human bloodstream molecules.

Singer promised to document all the tasks on a PERT chart and awarded himself the job of specification and configuration control. All the parts of the project had to fit together properly, just as the parts of a machine did. Design decisions must harmonize. Otherwise, the solution to one problem could end up blocking the solutions to others.

After the meeting broke up, Koyanagi lingered, studying the idea tree that they had generated. Singer sat at the table watching him. There was something on Masao's mind. He could tell from the man's self-conscious absorption with the diagram projection on the wall. Singer pressed a button to get the hard copy. "So. What do you think of my little crew?" he asked.

Koyanagi turned. "What? Oh. They are very able. If any team can solve this problem, it is yours. But I do not think they would solve it if not for you."

"Oh?" Singer pulled out a stick of sugarless gum and popped it in his mouth. "Are you putting them down? We've been together for a coon's age, you know. Longer'n that for Jessie 'n me."

"Putting them down?" Koyanagi frowned over the idiom. "Oh, you mean am I disparaging them? No, by no means, *Senhor* Singer-sama! It is just that you are the. . . ." He waved a hand in the air, searching for a word. "The motivator. The driving force. You define what problems are to be solved."

"Hunh." Singer was not impressed by praise. A fact

was a fact. Patel or Murchadha would be brilliant researchers in any setting, but under his tutelage they were brilliant creators, as well. Picking the right problem was at least as important as solving it. Edison had had that talent, mostly, and Singer knew he had it, too. That rare ability to separate the vital few ideas from the trivial many. No brag, like Walter Brennan used to say on that old TV show. What was its title? Singer had forgotten. No brag; just fact. Even Jessie admitted it.

And Jessie never admitted much. She didn't like being the "second best" geneticist.

"What is Tiny NIM?" asked Koyanagi. His finger traced the twig on the idea tree. "I wanted to ask during the discussion, but I did not want to interrupt the flow of ideas."

"Tiny NIM is our nanocomputer. It stands for Nanoscale Integrating Machine. It's only a prototype right now, limited functions; but someday we hope to expand it into a general purpose computer. It's mechanical, actually. All gears and wheels and cogs. But it's faster than electronics because its parts are the size of molecules."

Koyanagi frowned. "Is that possible? That a mechanical computer can be faster? After all, electronic signals propagate at the speed of light."

"Flap your arms."

Koyanagi stared at him. "I beg your pardon?"

"Flap your arms. Like a bird. Like this." He did a Red Skelton seagull imitation to show him. "Do it as fast as you can."

Koyanagi looked doubtful, but complied. Singer could see he felt foolish. "That's enough," he told him. "Now, compare how fast you could do that to how fast a bird can flap its wings, or a hummingbird, or a bumblebee. You see? The smaller the scale, the faster the motion. Take my word for it, Masao. Nanocomputers are very fast because they're very small."

Koyanagi nodded. "I see."

Singer swiveled in his chair and faced the Japanese.

"All right, old son, spit it out. You didn't stick around for small talk. What's eating you?"

"Eating me?" Koyanagi looked confused for a moment. Then he tilted his head back and sucked in his breath. "Ah, so." He hesitated.

"Don't hand me that oriental bullshit," Singer snapped. "Out with it."

Koyanagi pursed his lips and considered Singer. "Very well," he decided. "There are some aspects of the design envelope that disturb me."

"Such as?"

Koyanagi pointed to the idea tree. "You have specified that the nanomachine be copy-proof and non-replicating."

Singer nodded. "What of it?" he asked. "If it weren't copy-proof, then any Jimmy or Jane could pirate it and undersell us. They wouldn't have any development costs to amortize, so—bingo!—there go our profits. As a former employee of São Paulo Biophysics," he added drily, "you should appreciate the risk of piracy."

Under patent law, such theft was illegal, regardless of whether the product were copy-proofed or not; but Singer didn't trust pieces of paper. He was more interested in preventing the loss in the first place than in calling it illegal afterwards. Besides, a New York Court of Appeals, citing the attractive nuisance doctrine, had ruled that the lack of copy-proofing constituted contributory negligence. Like leaving your car keys in the ignition; or like a rape victim wearing provocative clothing. Once again, the victim was at fault. Trust a New York court to discover that.

"Are profits so important," asked Koyanagi, "compared to the benefits this machine could bestow on humanity?"

Singer laughed. "Son, profits are always important. A business needs 'em the way any critter needs food. If it doesn't get enough, it dies. And second—" His grin broadened. "I like money."

Koyanagi looked at him sadly. "So I have heard. Is

that all that this project means to you? Recovering your investment? What of serving mankind?"

"Serving mankind is how I recover my investment." Singer didn't like Koynagi's implication. Another head-in-the-clouds do-gooder. He felt his face flush, but controlled his voice. "Me, I'm in business to make money; not out of altruism or scientific curiosity. You don't stay in business unless you offer people goods or services with the qualities they need. A lot of American businesses forgot that. They sold stock instead of products. That's why your folks undercut them. This nanny will satisfy a real need for space-based companies and the nuclear industry. There's always money in serving mankind. That's why I gave it the go-ahead."

"But . . ."

"I'm listening."

Koyanagi looked at him and took a deep breath. "*Senhor.* I regret if I cause you discomfort. But, I worry that your, ah, 'concern' for profit will put this product out of the financial reach of many who need it. Will we create two classes of people, the Immune and the Vulnerable, widening the gap between rich and poor?"

Singer shrugged. "Of course we will, but what of it? How many solar panels can you find in Harlem? How many backyard windmills? Does that make solar energy elitist? Sure it does! But that's no reason not to do it. The rich always get first cut on any new technology. That's just a fact of life. What do you want me to do, give it away for free?"

"I am not suggesting that—"

"Because you're getting mighty generous with my money. Look, those who need the nanny will get it," Singer went on. "The greedy power companies and space stations will include it as part of their workers' benefit package. The unions will see to that, even if management is too dumb to realize the potential for reduced insurance costs."

Koyanagi flushed and Singer marveled how the man

could look both angry and embarrassed. "Dr. Singer, I . . . dislike argument. But what would you say to a mother living downwind from a mismanaged nuclear powerplant, whose child has died of radiation sickness because she could not afford your shots?"

"I would say that her community should have supplied it, just as they do flouridated water." He jotted a quick note on his desk pad: *Water-borne vector?*

Koyanagi was silent and Singer looked at him. "What's the matter? Do you wish my motives were purer?"

"Frankly, *senhor* Singer-san, yes."

Singer grunted. "Have you ever been poor? I mean, really hard-scrabble, ricket-ridden, dirt-poor. Have you ever gone to bed hungry?"

"No," admitted Koyanagi.

"Then shut up about my motives! You don't know what you're talking about. Why should I care about the respect of future historians? That and 75new¢ will buy me a cup of coffee. And not even Brazilian coffee, at that."

Koyanagi bowed slightly. "I see. Then the reason for the non-replication requirement is to assure repeat sales. Otherwise, a single injection would be sufficient for life."

Singer wagged a finger at Koyanagi. "Now, hold on there, Koyanagi-sama! Money isn't the only issue. I don't like to release self-replicators into the general public because they're too hard to control."

"*Sim.* We would not want an epidemic of radiation resistance to break out. If people could catch it from one another, they wouldn't need to buy your product."

Singer drummed his fingers on the table and said nothing. Masao was beginning to annoy him. Who did he think he was, coming in here with an idea—a very good idea, granted—and then trying to tell Singer how to run his zoo? Sure, it would be nice if everyone could have the nanny; and maybe someday the price would drop to where anyone could afford it. Until then, the books had to balance somewhere. Altruists like Masao were generous folks, but they were mostly generous with other people's money.

Koyanagi fidgeted, looked uncomfortable, then bowed reflexively. "I meant no offense, Dr. Singer-san. It is just that the sound of the cash register is perhaps a little too jarring to me."

"Hunh. What sounds constitute music depend on whose ear it is. Maybe for you, it's the applause of your peers at some technical conference. But, son, *someone's* got to pay the rent on this shack."

"Yes. I see."

"And, Masao. Tell me one more thing."

"What?"

"Did you plan to refuse your share of the profits from this?"

Koyanagi stared at him for a moment. Then his eyes fell.

"No."

"Uh-hunh. I didn't think so. So, don't give me any of that holier-than-thou crap."

III

Singer took his seat at the conference table and watched while Kalpit Patel set up the computer interface. Murchadha passed copies of their report around the table. Koyanagi immediately opened his copy and began reading. Singer glanced at the first-page summary, then tossed it back on the tabletop. "So what is it, good news or bad?"

Murchadha handed the last copy to Dr. Peeler. "Yes," he said.

Singer cupped his chin in his hands. It was going to be one of those briefings. "Would you care to elaborate on that, son?"

Patel faced the group and cleared his throat. He looked down at his notes and hunched his shoulders. Patel hated talking in front of other people, which was why Singer insisted on it. It was good training to do something you hated. He remembered Patel's first briefing, years ago. His hands had shaken so badly he could hardly read his notes.

Patel looked at Murchadha, who nodded and dimmed the lights slightly. Patel was more at ease when he couldn't see his audience. "As you know," Patel began, "Eamonn and I were given the assignment of simulating alternative design scenarios."

Singer wished people would not begin sentences with *As you know* . . . "Get to the point," he told them. "Can we do it or can't we?" Koyanagi looked up from his private perusal and blinked around at the group. He laid his copy of the report down, and listened with a troubled frown on his face.

"Well, Dr. Singer," said Murchadha. "We can and we can't."

Sometimes Eamonn annoyed him. Eamonn could carry that Irish act of his a little too far. He was a damn good nanomachinist, and he knew it; but he tended to act like an eccentric. A prima donna. Hell, they were all prima donnas—including himself, Singer admitted. But he wondered if any of the others appreciated just how much money was already involved in the project. Sunk costs, regardless of whether the project flew or not.

"Okay. Just skim the details. We don't need a blow-by-blow account. I assume all that's in your report. Just give us the straight skinny."

Patel dropped his eyes to his notes and discarded the first three cards. "We, ah, looked at several promising scenarios; but we will only present two of them." He activated a program and a graphic animation began playing on the large wall screen. Duplicate displays appeared on the smaller screens set into the table at each seat.

Singer watched a large, irregular blob fill the screen. A cell, magnified many times. It had hairy tendrils, and darker splotches within it, like some creature from a bad sci-fi movie. A nanomachine, represented by a miniature black box, swam up to it. It passed through the cell's membrane, closing it up behind it.

"The nanny," said Patel, "has recognized the cell as being abnormally ionized."

The scene shifted to the cell's interior, where the nanny was seen disappearing into the nucleus. Shortly, a cloud of nannies emerged and spread throughout the cytoplasm.

"The nanny checks the DNA library to determine the cell's proper configuration. Then it spins off slaves and inspects the cell top to bottom until it finds the damaged structures."

Singer watched as the view magnified to molecular scale, showing a protein strand with a carbon group hanging loose where the linking electron had been knocked off. The black box crawled down the strand until it reached the defective part. There, its restrictor enzymes snipped it off and replaced it.

"Very nice," said Koyanagi. "That is exactly what I had in mind."

"I thought the nanny was not supposed to be a self-replicator," said Burton-Peeler.

"It is not, truly," Patel told her. "The slaves self-destruct once the repairs are completed."

Peeler studied the now blank screen. She shook her head. "It won't work," she decided.

"How do you know?" Singer asked sharply. Jessie was always too ready to criticize.

"Too many bits to bite," she said. "Isn't that right, Eamonn?"

" 'Tis beyond the state of the art," Murchadha admitted. "Tiny NIM can't handle the information load yet. Maybe in another couple years—"

"Maybe in another couple years we'll be bankrupt," snapped Singer. "Don't tell me what we can't do, damn it. Tell me what we can do." He scowled and glanced quickly around the table. He hated losing his temper. But why did they have to treat it like it was some kind of game? Research. As if success or failure did not matter. He could feel Jessie's eyes on the back of his head.

Murchadha licked his lips. He gestured to Patel, who activated the next simulation.

"This nanny is much cruder," explained Patel. "It kills the abnormal cells and lets natural reproduction replace them. We based the model on the cytotoxic *T* lymphocytes, or 'killer *T* cells,' because its recognition system is more discriminating than that of other killer cells. It inspects the MHC—the major histocompatibility complex—on the target's surface. This will assure that the nanny does not attack healthy cells. It binds to a target cell only when the MHC presents abnormal antigens."

Singer watched the killer cell bind itself to the target cell and secrete nanomachines from its granules. "This nanny is based on the protein, perforin," Patel commented. "It masses an average of 70 kilodaltons; and, in its monomer form, it will penetrate the target cell wall like a nail. Then, in the presence of ionized calcium, it polymerizes, barrel-stave fashion, creating a pore in the target membrane."

The protein molecule *was* shaped somewhat like a railroad spike, thought Singer, but its penetration reminded him more of a worm burrowing into the earth. Once in place, it popcorned duplicates of itself, forming a circle of "spikes." Water and salt from the intercellular space poured through the resultant pore into the body of the cell, which swelled like a balloon until it burst.

Murchadha, of course, had added sound effects to the simulation. The bang of the explosion caused the others to chuckle and even brought a smile to Singer's face.

"Hmm. What stops the nanny from polymerizing in the intercellular space?" asked Burton-Peeler. "Ionized calcium is plentiful there. I can imagine it filling up with these killer pores."

"Ah, and isn't that the beauty of it?" Murchadha answered her. "Only the monomer can penetrate cell walls.

Once the little bugger polymerizes, it's harmless. Check Young and Cohn." He turned the lights back up.

Koyanagi looked troubled. "But, this method will simply accelerate the destruction of the radiation-damaged cells."

"Aye, Masao, that it will. That means they won't be hanging around, putting out the wrong chemicals or popping abnormal daughters."

"But . . ."

"But you wanted more," Singer told him. He looked at Patel. "So did I."

"And so did we," answered the microbiologist. "So what we did is—"

"—we combined the two concepts," finished Murchadha. "Poor Tiny NIM can't repair *all* the damaged cells. But, if we restrict it to certain tissues—"

"The nerve cells," guessed Burton-Peeler. "Am I right?"

Patel nodded. "Yes. Those cells *must* be repaired, but the others can simply be removed."

"Have you spec'ed any of this out?" Singer asked.

"No," answered Patel. "We think we can find the recognition system in *M. radiodurans.*" He looked at Koyanagi, who nodded. "The granule system, we'll steal from the *T* lymphocytes."

"You'll need the protectin protein, also," said Koyanagi, who had resumed his private reading of the report. He was flipping from page to page. Singer wondered if he was a speed-reader. "Otherwise, the perforin could attack the nanny itself."

Murchadha looked hurt. "We already thought of that. 'Tis in the appendix."

Singer made a decision. "All right," he told the group. "We'll go with the dual nanny concept. But I'll spec out the costs before we proceed. I've already done some preliminary market checks, on the QT. I want to know if we can make this thing for a price people are willing to pay. If not, we'll have to terminate it now."

"Don't worry, Dr. Singer," said Koyanagi. There was an edge in his voice and Singer turned his head and looked at him. "Don't worry, Dr. Singer. Demand at the margin will be very elastic."

He woke up gasping for breath and sat upright in the bed. His heart thudded like a hammer in his ears. He looked around the darkened room, recognizing nothing. Shadows and shapes, ominous in the night. Panic and confusion. Where am I?

He took several deep breaths, calming himself. He wiped his palms on the sheets. What a dream.

"Pillow talk, Charlie?"

Singer looked over at his wife's side of the bed. Jessie was a shadow within shadows. "Sorry. Did I wake you?"

"No," she replied. "But I talk in my sleep. What's wrong?"

"Nightmare."

The sheets rustled as she rolled over. "What about?"

"The nanny, I think."

"Don't you remember?"

"It's not the sort of thing you'd want to remember." Confused images of the nanny's failure; of Jessie saying "I told you so"; of his mother boiling roots for dinner. Waves crashing on a midnight beach. "I guess I got spooked today when I ran the design envelope simulation."

"It didn't work?"

"No. The limits of the design envelope projected a nanny too weak to be marketable." He shook his head, knowing she couldn't see him and hugged his knees to his chest. "We're running on a knife edge, you know. All we need is one big flop and we're finished."

"Do you think we should bail out now, while there's still time?"

"No. I'm going to rerun the simulation tomorrow."

"Oh?" He thought he heard surprise in her voice. "Why?"

"Because the journal data I used today must have been

garbled. I looked at the raws and they didn't look right. I think some of the digits were scrambled during transmission. I'll get another copy from the data bank in the morning."

"Are you sure?"

"What do you mean?"

"I mean when you start questioning the data because you don't like the results. . . ."

"I can smell spoiled preserves when I open the jar. Don't worry. I know it will work. We'll *make* it work. This is just a minor little glitch, is all. No more'n a wart on a bullfrog."

"You don't really think so. Not deep down."

He looked toward her, surprised. "Why do you say that?"

"Because it's one in the morning and you're lying awake in bed."

Singer couldn't think of an answer to that. Forgotten wisps of his dream fogged the corners of his mind with images he could not quite make out. He lay back down and put his arms behind his head and waited for sleep to return.

Singer watched the curve trace its way across the CRT screen. The rate of cell destruction increased as a direct function of the radiation level. That made sense. Careful gleaning of the biophysics data banks had yielded the data for the curve. And this time he had made sure the numbers were right, cross-checking and sampling at random against hard copy. The curve climbed toward infinity as it reached the right-hand edge of the screen. Singer grunted and entered a series of commands that would activate a simulation program. Murchadha's design for the nanny was still at the black box stage, but he had given Singer the working parameters to use for simulations.

A second curve, representing waste heat, replaced the first. In order to stay ahead of cell destruction, the nanny would have to work hard and fast, and that meant heat.

Higher rad levels meant faster cell destruction; which meant more work for the nannies, which meant more waste heat. Which meant running a fever.

Which meant there must be a limiting level to the amount of radiation the nanny could guard against without cooking the patient.

Singer pursed his lips and rested his chin on his hands, staring at the screen. Then he sat back and pulled a stick of sugarless gum from his pocket. He queried the data base again and the heat curve grew a probability band around it. A given rad level produced a probability distribution of heat levels, due to random variations in the cell repair rates. The band shaded off from black—the fitted curve was the maximum probability—to successively lighter shades of grey. *Now, how much fever can a body take?* He added a second probability distribution, a bell curve sitting along the temperature axis. Given the variation in human metabolisms, people suffered severe impairment, or even irreversible brain damage, at different temperatures. He studied the lower end of the bell curve. The probability that temperatures below the 3σ limit would harm anyone were less than one quarter of one percent. He propogated a horizontal line corresponding to that maximum tolerable heat level across to the upper edge of the regression band and read the ordinate value on the radiation axis. That was the maximum rad level that the nanomachine could safely handle.

For a moment he toyed with the idea of trading off the probabilities. After all, by making the vaccine "cool" enough to be safe for everyone, he was in effect condemning those robust individuals who could tolerate a "hotter" vaccine. Make the rad nanny cool enough for "Emily Dickinson," and "Arnold Schwartzenegger" could die if the rad dosage exceeded the design limits of the nanny. But make the nanny "hot" enough to protect Arnie against extreme doses and you could wind up cooking Emily.

He could calculate the joint probabilities. It should be

possible to solve the probability equations for minimum deaths. For any given design limit, there were Arnies and Emilies. Those for whom the design limit was too "cool" and those for whom it was too "hot." That had to be weighed against the probability of actually encountering a radiation level exceeding the design limit. Somewhere along the scale, the sum of those two components had to equal a minimum. That was first semester calculus. He could trade off a small increase in the first category for a big decrease in the second, giving him a lower overall death rate.

But he aborted the program without running it.

There was no point in cutting it too close. Let one person die because the rad nanny cooked his brains and the market would go west. Not all deaths are created equal. Any medicine could kill if it were too strong, and any medicine could kill if it were too weak to do the job. Sins of commision and sins of omission. But better ten deaths because of low potency than one death because of high. There was something especially terrifying about medicines that killed; and sins of commision were harder to forgive. Even *one* death due to an adverse reaction to the nanny could have severe financial repercussions. People would become afraid; refuse to buy the nanny. That had happened with the swine flu vaccine.

The public did not understand risk assessment. Not the difference between the α-risk and the β-risk; nor the relationship between them. People who refused to enter airplanes thought nothing of driving their cars. His equations would tell him the design limit that would minimize total deaths, but there was no term in the equation for human cussedness.

He decided on a 4σ safety margin for the design envelope. That gave him a maximum tolerable heat level, that would be safe for the *entire* human population, the delicate individuals as well as the robust.

He studied the design limit. *Not too bad, after all.* Perhaps he was worrying over nothing. The safe limit was well above the level of the Chernobyl release or the usual solar flares. Good. At least the nanny would actually be able accomplish its goals. After yesterday's simulation, he had been afraid that the safe limit would be too low. There was no market for a rad vaccine that only protected against sunburn.

Or was there? A sun tan was a mild form of radiation poisoning. He made himself a note to check into the possibility of a nano-sunscreen, perhaps injested in the form of a tasty soft drink. If they could produce a "cold" version cheaply enough, they might be able to penetrate that market, as well. He chuckled to himself. *We may have tapped into a real gold mine here.*

The noise woke Singer up. He fussed for a moment, twisting and turning under the covers. Closing his eyes, he willed sleep to return. No good. Grumbling, he pushed himself out of bed. He struggled into his housecoat and wandered out to the kitchen, where he found his wife with her head in the refrigerator.

"Jessie?"

"Hi, Charlie," she said to the lettuce. "How does a midnight snack sound?"

"Not bad." He yawned. "You woke me up."

She looked at him. "Sorry. I was working on the identification problem and got so caught up with it, I forgot to punch out. I just now closed up downstairs."

Singer shook his head. "You're the only person I know who apologizes for solving a problem."

"Do you want a sandwich or don't you?"

"Hmm. Yes, but—" He pulled her away from the refrigerator and pointed her toward the table. "—you sit down and talk. I'll do the fixin's."

Burton-Peeler pulled a chair out and sat, smoothing her skirt. Singer began pulling odds and ends from the refrigerator.

"How does an error rate of one in a million million sound?" she asked.

"On identification? Not bad. How?" He gathered the tuna salad, bread, and other materials and carried them to the sideboard.

"Well, I approached radiation sickness as a kind of proofreading problem."

"Proofreading?"

"Yes. Ionizing radiation causes typos."

He did a double-take and gave her a quirky grin. "That's one way of putting it."

"Yes. It's difficult to rebuild damaged cells if the DNA blueprints are themselves bad. Thank you." Singer set a plate in front of her with a tuna salad sandwich on it. The tuna was garnished with slices of onion and tomato and sprinkled with paprika, just the way she liked it. He had cut her sandwich diagonally. His own sandwich was much cruder, uncut and without embellishments. He could never figure out why she insisted on cutting sandwiches diagonally. It made no sense. He sat down across the table from her.

"Go on," he said.

"We have two issues, right? Cell replacement rate and faulty cells. Quantity and quality. Murchadha's nannies are the answer to the first. They'll be considerably faster than the body's natural mechanisms. Repairing when they can; removing when they must." She took a small bite from her sandwich. "He hasn't worked out all the details yet," she said when she had swallowed, "but the idea is that his repair enzyme will crawl down the DNA chain by touch. Selective stickiness, he calls it. It reads each nucleotide in sequence and checks it against the blueprints via Tiny NIM. If they fail to match, the nanny uses its restrictor enzymes to tear the molecule down and rebuild it to specs."

"Unfortunately," Singer commented, "the blueprints themselves may also have been damaged."

"Are you telling me my job, Charlie? What do you think I've just solved for you? That's where the proofreading comes in. Broken links in the DNA chains produce typographical errors in the genetic code. Hence, faulty cell reproduction, our second problem."

"So, how does the nanny know when the prints are correct?"

"Simple. We instruct the machine to work in triplicate. Imagine three DNA strands that have been randomly mutated by ionizing events. My program compares the nucleotides at the same addresses on all three strands. If they match, all well and good; but if they don't, majority rules."

"What if it's the odd one that's correct? Or if all three are different?"

She gave him a sour look. "Didn't you ever study statistics, Charlie? Of course you did, so stop asking silly questions. That would be like two or three independently recorded cassette tapes being garbled at exactly the same spot. It could happen, but it's not probable."

"One in a million million, you said."

"That's right. If you want better odds, you'd have to use quadruplicate or quintuplicate comparisons. That would slow the nanny, though probably not enough to matter. The real limit is Tiny NIM's capacity. Triplicate's the best I can do for now without a larger nanocore. So if you don't like the odds, tough."

Singer nodded slowly. It was a nice solution to the problem, though he did wonder why it had taken her so long to develop it. The concept was simple enough. Possibly the execution was more complex. Technical details. All solutions seem simple in hindsight.

"There's one other problem, Charlie. I've checked over our idea tree and it isn't there. Nobody thought of it. Not even me." She took another bite of her sandwich. Singer wondered how anyone could manage to project smugness in the way she chewed. He knew she was doing it on purpose, to make him ask what it was she had noticed. And when she had said, "Not even me," she had meant, "Not even you, Charlie."

"All right," he said. "What is it?"

She looked at him innocently. "What makes the *nanny* immune to radiation?"

Singer opened his mouth and closed it again. "It's a small target," he said finally. "A lot smaller than a cell. The probability of a hit is pretty low."

"But not zero. Given a high enough particle density and a long enough exposure time and, sooner or later . . . whammo. And the killer cell 'aircraft carriers' are nano-giants."

"Well, so what?" he told her. "There'll be hundreds of thousands of nannies in the bloodstream! So what if a few of them are knocked out?"

"The more nannies there are, the more likely it is that some will be hit. It's a Poisson process. You're missing the point, Charlie. What happens if a nanny is damaged?"

"Nothing."

"Are you sure?"

"What?"

"Are you sure that it fails safe? What if it starts 'repairing' proteins incorrectly? Or what if damaged killer cells attack healthy targets? Like a wounded tigress. That will only make things worse. Remember AIDS? That was a natural nanomachine with bad instructions. The HIV injected itself into the T-helper leucocytes and reprogramed them so that instead of fighting infections they would produce more HIV's."

Singer looked at her and pursed his lips. "You're right," he admitted at length. "I think we've all assumed fail-safe modes without actually designing them in. Have you spoken to Eamonn or Kal?"

"Not yet. I'll catch them first thing in the morning." She hesitated.

"What is it?"

She studied her sandwich. "I don't know. Is it worth it?"

Singer looked at her blankly. "Is what worth it?"

"The nanny. So much of our capital is tied up in it

and we don't even know yet if it will work. Maybe it's time to cut our losses."

"Of course it will work," he told her.

"How do you know? How many more problems like the one I just raised are lurking under rocks we haven't even thought of rolling over?"

"Every project has unanticipated problems."

"Maybe. But this project has such vital implications that—"

"All the more reason to push on. The profit potential was the reason we decided to go with it. How often do we get a chance to make a bundle on a product with such clear benefits and with no drawbacks?"

"How—" She locked glances with him briefly, then looked away. "How do you know there are no drawbacks?"

Singer laughed. "If we find a flaw, we design it out. Besides . . ." And now it was he who avoided her gaze. "We're in too deep financially to back out now. It's got to work."

"But—" She seemed about to say something.

"What?

She touched her lips with her tongue. "But what if we come across problems we can't solve? What if we roll over a rock and find Godzilla?"

"Then we'll deal with it. Where's your optimism? We're a can-do bunch, aren't we?" He stuck his jaw out.

Jessie looked at him and shook her head.

"What is it?" He was growing irritated with her hesitancy. But it was late, after all. She had put in a long day, and was tired and irritable; so he had to make allowances.

"I just have a hunch. That's all. There's something so big that you haven't seen it. Some blind spot."

When Jessie had a hunch, it usually meant something. Singer picked up his own sandwich and stared at it. He wasn't hungry anymore, but he ate it anyway. It was a sin to waste food.

IV

Singer rubbed his face in his hands, leaned back in his office chair, and glanced at the clock on the opposite wall. Quarter to six. How long had he been concentrating on the screen? Did he suppose that sheer will power could change the debits and credits around?

With a sigh of disgust he leaned forward and deactivated the bookkeeping program. There was no way around it. Cash flow was drying up. Aire Fresh was doing well. It more than covered their operating expenses—maintenance, power, utilities—but it was not enough to offset the research costs on the radiation nanny.

Aire Fresh was an aerosol nanomachine that rearranged odor molecules into more pleasant-smelling configurations. With it, a person could fall into a pile of manure and come up—literally—smelling like a rose. It was selling especially well in areas beset by air pollution; and Murchadha had already suggested an industrial strength version to be installed in emission stacks and auto exhausts. Since the nanny actually uncoupled the harmful molecules, there were profound environmental implications. Someday it would be a major cash cow in their product line.

None of which helped pay the bills today.

Dammit, he would have to go to the banks. He hated that. He hated borrowing money. Being in debt to another person twisted his gut into knots.

He rose from the desk and stretched his arms. He looked again at the clock. Time to close up shop.

It struck him that that could be taken literally, as well. If they did not get a cash infusion sometime in the next few months, he might have to close up the Lab.

The thought filled him with dread. The Lab was his life. Everything he owned was tied up in it. Without it . . . *without it, I'll be where I was the first time.*

And the first time had taken him out to the shore below Tom's River on a cloudless midnight in October.

Is there any place as dreary and deserted as an October beach? He remembered how the sea breeze had felt on his face as he stood there staring out to sea. Black sky and black ocean. Black future. Restless breakers luminescent under the stars. The muted rush of the water as it stroked the land, patiently rubbing rock into gravel and gravel into sand. His business was in ruins, being ground away by creditors as ruthlessly as the beach was being ground away by the waves. It would take so little effort to dive into that surf and swim out so far he could never swim back.

It was the touch of the sea breeze that had stopped him, one bare foot in the tide. That and the sheering of the gulls. Or perhaps the distant lights of a tramp freighter working its way down the coast. Something in him rebelled against surrender, and he had made up his mind to succeed in spite of everything. And he had. He had turned his back on the beckoning ocean and had made his name a household word.

Yet, even today, it could bring out a sweat on him to remember how close he had come to taking that long swim.

He roused himself. *Tomorrow,* he thought. *I'll hit the banks tomorrow.*

He wandered to his office window and looked out at the shop. He grunted in sour amusement. Everyone was working late. There was Kal quietly building simulations at his terminal. And Masao running microdisc after microdisc through his own terminal. Jessie and Eamonn were sitting at Eamonn's workstation, surrounded by his pumps and pipes, deep in discussion. Jessie was talking animatedly, gesturing with her hands, while Eamonn listened, smoking his briar and nodding occasionally. *What is wrong with this picture?* Singer thought wryly.

Answer: Why, with all this overtime, are we falling farther and farther behind the PERT schedule? We should be much further ahead by now. The project was moving as slowly as a legislature on tax reform. It was like swimming in molasses. Every time things started to look good, Jessie uncovered a new problem. Or Eamonn's pumps quit on him. Or two molecular subassemblies would not fit together. They had had to redesign one particularly promising enzyme completely from scratch. *My fault,* he told himself. *Configuration control was my job. But I've been spending my time going over Peter's books, taking out a loan for Paul.*

Patel called Koyanagi to join him. Masao looked up and saw Singer watching from the office window and gave a little start. Then he shoved his microdiscs into his drawer and rolled his chair across to Patel's side, where they huddled over the simulation. Singer grunted again. He must look like the wrath of God, lowering over His creation.

Patel looked at Koyanagi, then at the screen. A CAD drawing of an elaborate molecular chain was displayed there. Patel crossed his fingers and pressed a button on the computer console. They watched the diagram fold up into a ball.

Koyanagi sighed. "Are you sure the angles on those molecular bonds are correct?" he asked.

"Trouble, boys?" Singer had come up behind them. He laid a hand on both their shoulders and stared at the tangled mess on the screen. "It doesn't look very pretty."

"Three months of work," said Patel, shaking his head. "It would do the job. It is the structure that gives *M. radiodurans* its resistance. It recognizes radiation damage. Mister Murchadha has a machine that it can insert into nerve cells."

"But . . ." prompted Singer.

"But it folds improperly," said Koyanagi. "It will not nestle with other bloodstream molecules."

"And it should," declared Patel. He stared at the screen, daring it to contradict him.

Singer tapped the screen with his fingernail. "So, why not roll your own?"

"I beg your pardon?" Koyanagi looked puzzled. Patel cocked his head and looked interested.

"Kal knows what I'm talking about. Tackle the problem like an engineer, not like a scientist. Build the molecule you want, *de novo*. If what you find in nature doesn't fold up right, then design something that does. Start with the final configuration and work backwards until you have the design."

"Yes," said Patel thoughtfully. "That could work. It has been done before on simple molecules. In fact, the first nanny designed from scratch was built in 1983—a bee toxin. You must have heard of it, Masao," he added, turning to his partner. "And Gutte and the others were building short chains that nestled onto the surfaces of other molecules exactly as planned even as early as 1979. This is only more elaborate." He paused and looked again at the screen. He rubbed his forefinger back and forth across his moustache. "Much more elaborate," he said.

Koyanagi smiled broadly. "If we must fold our own molecules, Dr. Singer, then I have every confidence in our success."

Singer blinked. "Oh? Why is that?"

"Because my hobby is *origami*."

"Dr. Charles Singer?"

Singer looked up from his newspaper. The mid-afternoon train from New York was nearly empty and Singer had been enjoying a quiet ride home following a round of visits to the banks. He had been trying to arrange for a line of credit to finance his "unspecified, but potentially profitable research program." Singer hated borrowing money. Fortunately—in a way—the banks hated lending it, at least on mystery collateral; so Singer was leaving New York with his principles, but with no principal.

He saw a man standing in the aisle, balancing himself against the rhythmic swaying of the coach. The wheels of the car chattered underneath, and the telephone poles ticked past the windows. He was a thin man with a plain face, the anonymous kind that came off bargain basement racks. "Dr. Singer?" the man repeated.

"Yes, but if you're a salesman, I'm not interested. I don't do business on the train." To emphasize the point he raised the newspaper back to reading positon.

"No, Dr. Singer. I'm not selling. I'm buying."

"I ain't selling, either," he told him through the paper.

"We understand you are working on a method of hardening human beings against radiation."

Singer put the paper down and stared. The thin man had taken the seat facing him. "Is that so?"

The man nodded. "Yes. That is what we want to talk to you about."

"I never discuss rumors," he told him and shook the paper open again.

"Don't play games, Dr. Singer. We *know* what you're working on."

Singer looked at him. "Are you threatening me?"

"Please calm down, Doctor," he said placatingly. "Perhaps, you don't understand. My name is Royce. John Royce. I represent the government."

"Whose?"

The thin man blinked, startled. "Why, ours, of course." He opened his wallet and showed Singer an identity card. A bad photograph of Royce peered earnestly from beneath the plastic. Governmental acronyms and numerology bordered the photograph. Office of Technology Assessment.

Singer handed the card back. "Hunh. The government. Then you *were* threatening me."

"Not at all, Doctor. What I was trying to say is that we are very interested in your invention."

"Alleged invention."

The thin man looked pained. "Please, Doctor. Give us credit. There is no other possible explanation for the kinds of journal articles you have been accessing from the data banks. In combination, they add up to what we like to call a 'capability.' If you are not working on such a program, Dr. Singer, you should be."

"Information on my research plans is proprietary!"

Royce nodded and looked apologetic. "I'm truly sorry, Doctor, but sometimes the vital interests of our country force us to cut corners on legal technicalities. National security, you know. Community interests must occasionally take precedence over purely private interests. The inconvenience is minor compared to the outrages other governments commit routinely." He leaned forward. "And you must realize, of course, that this new drug of yours—"

"Medical device," said Singer automatically.

"Eh?"

"The courts have ruled that nanomachines of this sort are medical devices rather than drugs."

Royce waved his hand in irritation. "Never mind that," he said. "The point is that this new, er, device is of tremendous importance to the people of this country. So much so that the government is prepared to underwrite your costs of development and to take responsibility for its manufacture and distribution."

Singer had had a retort ready on his lips, but it died unspoken. "Underwrite my costs," he said.

"Yes." Royce was emphatic. "We are prepared to designate you as prime contractor to develop a radiation immunity device for the government, on a cost plus basis."

"Cost plus." Singer realized he was repeating Royce's words back to him. He shook himself. "I've never dealt with the government," he said gruffly. "I've always preferred the private market."

"As well you should, Doctor. Free markets are what made America great. But, the private marketplace is so uncertain. Profits are not guaranteed. A product might not even get to market. There are regulations to be met. Papers to be filed. The public must be protected—"

"I've dealt with the EPA and FDA for many—"

"All sorts of bottlenecks could develop, bottlenecks that can delay your entry into the market." Royce shook his head in contemplation of bottlenecks. "Not only bureaucratic foul-ups—you know how mid-level drones love to demonstrate their importance—but Luddite lawsuits and protests, as well. And all the while your costs would continue to accrue, with no incoming profits to offset them. If things drag out long enough, the entire venture could become unprofitable. You and I both know of companies bankrupted, or of project costs tripled due to such circumstances.

"On the other hand"—and here Royce brightened—"when the government is your customer, EPA and FDA filings have a habit of fast approval. There would be no hang-ups over petty technicalities. No long waiting periods to evaporate your profits."

Singer ran a hand over his mouth. "Cost plus," he repeated. "Cost plus how much?"

Royce waved a negligent hand. "That can be negotiated. Say twice your usual net profit?"

"And SingerLabs retains all creative control. No second-guessers from Fantasyland-on-the-Potomac. I would insist on that."

"Surely. Not everyone in the government is a mindless paper-shuffler. My office is interested in results, not rituals. You produce for us and we'll restrain the i-dotters and t-crossers."

Singer thought it over. The government was a bad customer and a worse boss. But, this looked like a way out of the financial corner they were in. Not only that, but the government could carry out the kind of widespread distribution Koyanagi wanted without cutting into the Lab's profit margin. "I tell you what, Mr. Royce. You come and see me in my office. Not on the street or on the train or anywhere else. Bring the papers and I'll look them over. I can't promise anything till I've seen the fine print."

Royce smiled. "Of course not. How about next week?"

"After I've reviewed your proposal," he said, "I'll bring it up with my Associates."

Royce frowned. "You consult your employees on such matters?"

"Why not? It's called democracy. Jefferson and Paine thought well of it. Besides, they're not exactly employees. They're Associates. Partners. They own shares in SingerLabs. I don't muzzle the oxen that tread the corn."

Royce seemed oddly reassured by that. "Deuternomy 25, verse 4," he said. "But you do retain controlling interest, do you not?"

Why was it, Singer wondered, that representatives of the Greatest Democracy on Earth were so shy about dealing with democratic organizations? Why did they always look for an autocrat? A sheik, a shah, a caudillo. Someone who could make the decisions. Was it a love for neatness and order? Democracy was inherently messy. "My wife and I do," he told Royce.

"Ah, your wife. Good." Royce smiled pleasantly. "There's no problem, then. I'll bring the papers by next week. Naturally, we would prefer to work with SingerLabs, rather than with some other nanotech firm. You have already done the preliminary research. But you know how competitive the nanotech industry is. So don't take too long on the formalities." He held a hand out, still smiling, and, after a moment, Singer took it.

Singer stood by his apartment window staring out at the Edison Tower and twisted his neck back and forth to get the kinks out. The tower was surmounted by an enormous light bulb and, beyond it, Singer had a glimpse of the first street in the world to be lit by electric lights. Edison's lab. Now long gone. Dismantled board and nail by Henry Ford and taken to Dearborn for his odd collection of buildings. Singer thought about how much had been done in that lab; done for the first time anywhere. There was a thrill in that, in doing something for the first time, that was unlike any other thrill imaginable.

What hath God wrought? Come here, Watson, I want you. My God, the damn thing works! Say, Ridley: there's somethin' wrong with this ol' machmeter. The Eagle has landed. No, there was nothing like it, because there could only ever be one first time. He wondered what kind of tower they might someday build to him.

Suddenly, hands encircled his neck and began rubbing the tired muscles. He reached up and patted the hands.

"Jessie. I didn't know you were up here. I thought you were chewing the midnight bytes downstairs in the shop." He tried to turn, but her insistent fingers held him tight. Her thumbs worked the shoulders and the base of his neck. Singer relaxed and enjoyed his wife's ministrations.

He had met Jessie in graduate school, where they had become both lovers and rivals. Lord A'mighty, that was an eternity ago. It was an affair of the mind that bound them to each other, a passion and a genius for genetics; because—Lord knew—there was little enough else to draw them together. He, the rough-edged boy from the ghost towns of the Kentucky coal fields; she, the polished, upper-class emigré from Devon. For three years they had traded top honors back and forth; and they had graduated first and second, respectively. Sometimes over the years, he had wondered whether there wasn't an undercurrent of that rivalry in their marriage. Whether Jessie had said "I do" in part so that she could continue competing with him. Maybe so. Singer told himself he didn't mind that. What was the old saying? A man wants a woman to walk beside him, not behind him.

He told Jessie about the meeting on the train. About Royce's offer.

She let go of his neck, and after a moment, he turned and faced her. She was frowning. "Since when do you deal with the government, Charlie?"

"I know, I know. But the offer is tempting. You know how thin our margin is on this one. And Royce did promise hands-off."

Jessie snorted. "Tell the Red Indians about government promises. They even got them in writing."

Singer took a deep breath. Jessie was running true to form. "The banks turned us down, you know."

"We'll get by somehow, without taking the King's shilling."

"Cost plus."

"Cost plus hassle. It's just throwing good money after bad."

"It's government money."

"Then it isn't even good money. I'm still not used to red-and-blue banknotes."

It wasn't any use to argue. After twenty years, you'd think he would have learned that. Jessie was as stubborn as a badger in a burrow. He turned and stared out the window once more. Without operating capital from somewhere, the Lab could go down the toilet. Didn't she understand that? No. When it came to money, she understood nothing. "You won't approve this contract, will you?"

"Approve? Goodness, no! That's inviting the camel's nose into the tent. Pretty soon the rest of him is in there with you. That mightn't be so bad, if you like camels; but they stink, they're foul-tempered, and they spit a lot."

"Dammit, Jessie, I've never seen you so negative as you've been on this project. You're not pulling your weight, you know. Not like Masao or Kalpit. They're putting a lot of skull sweat into this. You're just coasting. You hardly participate at all in our brainstorming sessions. And it seems as if every point you bring up is an objection, or a roadblock, or it exaggerates the difficulty or complexity of the project."

"Have any of my points been invalid?" she shot back. "Dammit, the project *is* difficult and complex, and wishful thinking isn't going to simplify it one whit. Pointing out the pitfalls doesn't make me an enemy. What about that fail-safe issue I raised?"

"We've got a consulting topologist working on it. But that's not the point—"

"Bloody hell it isn't! Charlie, you were never a nixon. Questioning doesn't have to mean opposition. The fail-safe business had to be raised. You know that. You'd have raised it yourself, if you had thought of it. But you didn't. And that makes me wonder if you can see clearly on this one."

"What do you mean by that?"

"I mean you are so obsessed with our financial predicament that you can't see the real issues. You want this project to succeed—"

"Don't you?"

"You want this project to succeed so much that you think that means it *will* succeed. That there *can't* be any problems. And that makes everyone who points one out into some sort of traitor. Well, wishful thinking is no substitute for hardheaded engineering."

"You've got to think positive," he told her.

"No. You've got to think negative. If you always have your eyes on the stars, you don't see the pitfalls under your feet."

"What pitfalls? Name them!"

"I have, dammit. Read my reports. But you've got to think of some of them for yourself. Don't expect me to do everything on this project."

Since Singer had been thinking precisely the opposite, her protest sounded incongruous. He snorted and flashed her a wan smile over his shoulder. "Royce seemed to think that I controlled your vote." Royce, he reflected, was probably not married.

"He what?"

Singer turned. "When I told him that you and I together held controlling interest, he seemed to take it that *I* held controlling interest."

She snorted contempt. "Where does he come from, then, Iran? Should I veil myself?" She glared at him, arms crossed.

He shrugged. "It wasn't me that said it. Come to think of it, though; when I quoted Scripture at him, he did come back with the chapter and verse."

"A Sawyerite, then." She waved an arm in dismissal.

"And," Singer said patiently, "a bona-fide government flunky. And . . . Look. He was very polite and apologetic. Never came right out and said so, but I got the very distinct impression that it was his deal or no deal."

She scowled. "What do you mean by that?"

He left the window and walked to the sofa. He sat and ran his hands over his face. "I don't like the government any better than you do. You know that. There's something about power that tempts people to push its limits a little further out each time they exercise it. Look at the way presidents have expanded their war powers, or how bureaucrats have defined 'wetlands' to include outright deserts. Royce dropped little hints: about using the reg agencies to keep us off the market; about leaking our project idea to NanoTech or General Molecule. It was the old carrot-and-stick approach. Do what we want, and we'll shower you with gold and silver. *Don't* do what we want, and you get diddly squat."

"So that's why you want the deal."

"Dammit," he said, pointing a finger at her. "The offer would have been tempting, regardless. We need the money."

"Then why the *angst?*"

Singer paused with his arm outstretched. He hesitated, and the arm dropped slowly. "I didn't like his approach. It was a blatant appeal to my greed." He stuck his hands in his pockets and slouched in the sofa. "Are my motives so transparently simple?"

"Since when do you let your emotions interfere with making a buck?"

"Since when have you complained about making bucks?" he retorted.

She was silent, her eyes cast down. The silence grew

in the room. "Charlie?" she said after a while. "Do you recommend that we accept this contract?"

Singer grunted. "Cost plus if we do; nothing if we don't. What do you think?"

"Beware of Greeks bearing gifts. Especially government Greeks." She turned and walked to the window where Singer had been earlier. He could see the tower over her shoulder. She crossed her arms. The silence lengthened. "Well, you haven't convinced me," she said finally.

He sighed. "I didn't think I would." He wouldn't look at her. "Jessie, without this money, the project is dead. Maybe the Lab is dead, too. If that doesn't mean anything to you, it does to me. I don't need your shares to approve this, you know. Masao wants this nanny so bad he aches. 'To benefit humanity,' " he mimicked the Niprazilian's voice. "And to benefit his own career, of course. The government will assure the kind of wide distribution he wants, and we'll still get to make a profit. So, the do-gooder will vote my way. And between us, we can convince Eamonn and Kalpit. They'd like to keep their jobs as much as anyone. The four of us together out-vote you."

"Go ahead, then. Why bother arguing with me."

He did look at her then. "I said I didn't *need* your votes, Jessie. I never said I didn't *want* them."

"Hunh. Getting romantic in your old age?" She looked away, working her lips like a fish in an aquarium. "All right," she announced. "If everyone else agrees, *maybe* I'll go along. But, Charlie? Ask yourself one thing."

"What's that?"

"Why did they bother? As far as they knew, you were going to build these nannies whether they offered you a contract or not. They could have bought all the nannies they wanted at fair market prices. By giving you this contract, they get to buy the exact same thing, but at inflated, cost-plus prices. You've been telling me what

SingerLabs gets by doing things Royce's way, *but what in bloody hell does the government get?*"

V

Singer celebrated the signing of the contract by letting Royce treat him to lunch; and, even though it was government money, Singer picked a moderately priced restaurant in Perth Amboy. Habit. Never spend more than you had to to get what you needed. There was an upper limit on what he was willing to pay for food, even when someone else was picking up the tab; and he refused to pay extra for what he considered non-essentials, like "ambience" or fancy dinnerware.

The restaurant was set on a converted sailing ship permanently moored to the dock in Raritan Bay, just off Front Street. *The Amboy Clipper.* It specialized, naturally enough, in seafood. The maître d', who was dressed like Captain Bligh, greeted them warmly and led them to Singer's usual table, one with a good view of Raritan Bay. They settled themselves into leather-padded captain's chairs. The waitress was also dressed nautically, though her uniform would hardly have passed muster on a genuine sailing ship. Royce ordered shrimp scampi; Singer asked for the broiled seafood platter.

"I'm surprised," Royce said, when the waitress had brough them their drinks.

"Oh?" Singer sipped his manhattan. "At what?"

"Well," the government man gestured vaguely, "for a man of your fame and notoriety, you don't seem to attract much of a crowd. I would have thought that here in your own back yard, so to speak, more people would recognize you."

Singer shrugged. He stared out the window at the bay. Staten Island was absurdly close; the Arthur Kill was little more than river-wide. To the south was a marvelous view of Sandy Hook. A scrubber ship was criss-crossing the bay, cleaning up a garbage spill from the Kill by seeding it with plastic-eating nanomachines. Plastiphage had been one of his first inventions, and the one that had made him famous. The view of the scrubber ships was one of the reasons why he like to eat here so often. To remind himself what fame was worth.

Which was: not much, because General Molecule had pirated the Plastiphage design and marketed it themselves. He had sued, of course, but the courts had caved in because G/M had the resources for immediate mass production of the nanny and the Public Welfare had demanded a Clean Environment Now. So, while Singer had the inventor's fame; G/M had the retailer's profit.

"I try to keep my face out of the news," he said. "As long as I know who I am, it doesn't matter who else does. I'll leave the groupies to the athletes, musicians, and politicians."

Royce chuckled. "It's refreshing to talk to someone who's not all caught up with himself. You wouldn't believe some of the egomaniacs I've had to put up with in the Public Service."

Singer looked at him and grinned crookedly. "Oh, I'm an egomaniac, too. I just don't advertise it."

They ate their lunch in a half-silence. That is, Royce talked and Singer didn't. Royce's monologue generally covered his life and career, a topic in which Singer had less than consuming interest, so he listened with only half a mind. The rest of his attention was focused on how he would accelerate the research program now that federal money would be coming in. He wondered if he could buy sufficient stocks of research quality mutS and mutH without any of the big companies getting interested.

He speared a scallop with his fork and chewed on it thoughtfully. Scallops had the shape, taste, and consistency of rubber bottle stoppers, but he almost always ordered them when they were on the menu.

"I envy you, Dr. Singer," Royce was saying. "You don't

know what it's like to be surrounded by drones. Too many of my colleagues in Public Service want nothing but more pay for less work. But, then," he sighed, "Gideon's Band has always been small."

"Gideon's Band?"

"Many are called," said Royce enigmatically, "but few are chosen."

"You take it seriously, don't you?" said Singer, a little surprised. "Public Service, I mean. Usually, someone uses those words to me, I think he's a damn hypocrite. A passenger on the Federal Gravy Train."

Royce looked embarrassed. "I've always tried to give an honest day's work."

Singer laughed. "Then you're working for the wrong company, son."

"Maybe. Maybe not. Someone has to look out for the interests of this country. The whole country, I mean; not just good old Number One. Look at those people." He waved at the other diners in the restaurant. "Do you suppose any of them are genuinely concerned about anything beyond their own personal lives? Our waitress. Does she even feel a loyalty to the restaurant? I doubt it. She's worried about her paycheck and her tips; or maybe what her husband is up to; or whether the kids need braces. Maybe the maître d' feels a loyalty; he probably has a piece of the action. The owner certainly does. But do his loyalties extend beyond his restaurant? Does he concern himself with the county or the state or the nation, except to the extent to which they impact his business? I doubt it."

"Not everyone is so self-centered," Singer demurred. But he realized uncomfortably that he did not even know the names of his own representatives and what—if anything—they stood for.

"It's not the self-centeredness," said Royce. "We're all self-centered, fixed in the absolute middle of our personal universes. We all look out first for Number One. The Book says we must love our neighbors as ourselves, which implies that we must love ourselves first. No, it's the scope of that love. How far *beyond* Number One do our loyalties extend? To our family? Friends? Employer? Profession? Hometown? Country?"

Singer waited for Royce to add "humanity" or "The World" to his list, but was not surprised when he did not. "I think you'll find that most people are loyal to their country," he said.

"That's not what I meant. I don't mean that painless, motherhood-and-apple pie loyalty. The kind that waves flags, but makes no sacrifices. No, I meant, how many people really work at it? How many have the vision or the 'self-less-ness' to see where some private interest must be sacrificed for the common good?"

"And you do?"

Royce stiffened. "I like to think I have tried."

"A'right, a'right. Don't git up on yer high horse." Singer used the down-home accent he always used when he wanted to set someone at ease. "I wasn't accusing you of hypocrisy. What I meant to say was, how could anyone—however well-intentioned—know what was really for the common good?" He twisted in his seat and pointed out the window toward the bay. "You can't see Long Island from here; but out there is where the Shoreham nuclear plant used to be. The politicians never let it start up; instead they delayed it until it had become such a financial albatross that the utility caved in. Then the state stepped in and dismantled it, brick by brick. All in the name of the common good."

"As I recall," said Royce, "the plant was in too densely populated an area. There was no provision made for emergencies—"

"You mean the local governments refused to make such provisions."

Royce shrugged. "Have it your way. But the area was still too densely populated. People would have been subject to radiation leaking from the plant."

Singer laughed. "So instead they built coal-fired plants, and got irradiated anyway."

Royce frowned. "What do you mean?"

"That was my point, about knowing what is for the common good. Even when one's intentions are the best, it isn't always obvious; and sometimes the 'obviously right' solution does more harm than the problem itself. You see, burning coal releases carbon-14 and radioactive thorium. It goes straight up the stacks and into the air. No scrubbers. No containment." He made a mental note to market the nanny to coal plants as well. "Coal plants put out more radiation every day than nuclear plants do in a year. Yet, there are stringent limits placed on the one, and none at all on the other. Do you know what that means?"

Royce looked puzzled. "What?"

"It means that the target of the regulation was not dangerous radioactivity. The target was the nuclear industry."

Royce pursed his lips and looked uncertain. "Not necessarily," he said. "It might mean that the lawmakers were ill-informed. They were trying to do the right thing. Trying to protect the people. If they had known that about coal, I'm sure they would have extended the law. After all, radiation kills. Everyone knows that."

Singer smiled his crooked smile. It was remarkable what "everyone knew." "Well, yes and no," he said. "We live in an ocean of radioactivity. We're surrounded by it and don't even notice it. Normal background radiation runs 100 rads a year; even higher in places like Denver. Take solar energy—"

"Solar energy?"

"Certainly. That's a nuclear pile up there in the sky, or didn't you know?" Maybe he didn't, Singer reflected. Science education in the schools had been deteriorating for a long time; and a lot of pressure groups had succeeded in bowlderizing the textbooks so that unpleasant topics, like evolution or nuclear power plants were mentioned only with politically correct disapproval. "It's ninety-three megamiles away," he continued, "but it can still strike people dead."

"Mad dogs and Englishmen, anyway."

Singer chuckled. "Yes," he agreed. "But think about it. Solar radiation gives us skin cancer as well as sunstroke. Up in LEO or GEO"—he pointed toward the ceiling— "on the *Novy Mir* or the L4 complex, solar radiation is an even greater hazard than it is down here. Then there are bricks—"

"Bricks?"

"Yes. They're naturally radioactive, more or less, depending on where the clay was mined. And granite. Dental porcelain. Television sets. Even our own bodies: the potassium-40 in our blood. You get a lot of radiation standing in a crowd. Radiation is everywhere. Burning tobacco releases polonium-210. A heavy smoker can accumulate 8000 millirems a year—"

"You've convinced me, Doctor. I'm quitting!"

Singer laughed along with him. "Yes, you should. And the Earth itself is naturally radioactive. It exhales radon gas, which can be trapped and accumulated inside houses, especially those 'environmentally sound' ecofast houses." He smiled ruefully. "It's ironic when you stop and think about it, but environmentalism has put more people at risk of radiation-induced cancer than has the nuclear industry. The natural radiation inside some homes has exceeded the amounts released at Three Mile Island."

"Hmm. I see what you mean. We really can't escape radiation, can we? That makes your nanomachine all the more important." Royce stared past Singer's shoulder with a thoughtful look in his eyes and scratched his cheek. "All the more important."

Leaving the restaurant, they passed a group of protesters near the pierhead where the Bay Maintenance scrubber ships docked. They were carrying signs with the big e symbol of the Green Party. "MOTHER EARTH, RIGHT OR WRONG." One of the signs read: "OUR EARTH! LOVE IT OR LEAVE IT!" Singer got a chuckle out of that one.

"Damn radicals," muttered Royce.

"Oh, I don't know," Singer allowed. "Their hearts are in the right place, even if their brains aren't."

"It's brains that solve problems."

"Agreed, but it's the heart that tells you the problem must be solved."

Royce gave him a suspicious look. "Are you a Green sympathizer?"

"Hell, no. Like I said, their brains aren't in the right place. And this new Gaea religion of theirs rubs me the wrong way. Mother Earth. They forget what a cruel goddess she was."

"Paganism," said Royce.

Singer looked at him and considered saying what he thought of Sawyerism, too, but he thought better of it. It wouldn't do to bite the hand that fed him. "Still, whether the ecosphere is 'alive and conscious' or not, you can't deny that it has a way of striking back when you don't treat it right."

"Mother Nature," said Royce. "Gaea worship. Paganism and feminism."

Yes, thought Singer. And environmentalism, too. But also anti-science. And anti-evolution, because that contradicted their beloved Dogma of Entropy. How long, he wondered, before those commonalities led the two wings of fundamentalism to merge? Sawyerites and Greens despised each other, but Singer could see how their shared emnity toward "materialist science" could bring them together someday. "Behold, I have given you stewardship over the earth and all that is in it." Genesis 1, 28-30. Amen, brother. Amen.

They came to Royce's car, a black Olds. Royce unlocked the doors but paused before getting in. He looked back at the protesters. "One thing I don't get," he said.

"What's that?"

He pointed. "If they're in favor of cleaning up the environment, why are they demonstrating in front of the scrubber ship dock?"

Singer looked at where Royce was pointing. "I guess the idea is not to make a mess in the first place. I was reading where the number of spills has been increasing lately. They should be over at the Staten Island landfill to make that point; but I guess not as many people would see them there, or hear their message. Besides," he grinned. "It stinks over that side of the Kill."

VI

It was late and Singer was closing up the laboratory when he noticed Eamonn Murchadha sitting at his nanolathe, a pipe clenched tightly between his teeth. He was staring at nothing in particular and the pipe was not lit. Singer wondered, as he sometimes did, how such an ungainly assemblage of pumps, vats, and reactors could machine components so ungodly small. Things had come a long way since IBM first spelled out its initials by lining up xenon atoms.

"Problem, Eamonn?"

The Irishman jerked in his seat and turned around. "Dr. Singer," he said. "Sure, you'll be giving me a heart attack, sneaking up that way."

"You had your input/output system buffered," Singer replied. "I could have marched through here with the entire British Army and you wouldn't have noticed. Which planet were you on?"

Murchadha's face fell. "This one, I'm afraid."

Singer scowled. Something was obviously troubling the young nanomachinist. He pulled a stool from under the lab table and perched himself on it. "I see. Anything in particular, or just general Celtic melancholy?"

Murchadha took the pipe from between his teeth and inspected the bowl. He rapped it sharply against his left palm; then he took a tool from his pocket and began to worry the plug. Fragments of tobacco fell onto the table. "Tell me, Doctor. Have ye ivver thought about the implications of what we're doin' here? With the radiation nanny, I mean."

Singer frowned and cocked his head. "I take it you don't mean the obvious."

"That we won't fry any cosmonauts or depopulate the Ukraine? No, I didn't mean that."

"Then what?"

"The spin-offs," he replied enigmatically. He inspected his pipe bowl again, and sucked on the stem experimentally. "You can't change human nature, you know."

Singer was puzzled. "Human nature? I'm not sure what you're getting at."

Murchadha sighed. "Neither am I. But . . ." He shrugged and looked off into the distance. "Supposin' you're the operator of a nuclear plant. You've got strict safeguards and procedures to follow. There are guards around guards around guards. Fail safes and 'Tell Me Thrice's.' And all because the danger is after being so great." He shook his head. "But what if the danger were *not* so great? What then? What if all those folks livin' outside th' perimeter were immune to accidental releases?"

"Hardened, not immune. They're supposed to be. That's the whole idea."

"Aye, and a noble idea it is." Murchadha smiled and looked at the ceiling. "Did you know there's many a policeman refuses to wear a bullet-proof vest? 'Tis a fact, it is. Flat refuses. They say the wearing of it gives a false sense of security. It makes a lad take chances."

Singer stirred uneasily. "And you think that if we give people a 'vest' for subatomic bullets, that they'll grow careless? I don't believe it!"

Murchadha shook his head sadly. "Ah, 'tis a touching

faith in human nature that you have. It doesn't matter whether ye believe it or not. People are people. You can't change human nature. We might wish that folks were reasonable and logical and compassionate; but the sad fact of it is that they're not, and they never will be, God bless 'em."

Singer pursed his lips. A similar thought had crossed his own mind, when he had decided on designing the nanny to a "cooler" tolerance. Individuals might be reasonable; large groups were not. "But the vaccine isn't really a bullet-proof vest!" Singer protested. "It doesn't confer immunity. It raises the level we can tolerate above what we would expect from nuclear accidents. That's all. I've pushed the edges of the design envelope in simulations. There are limits. To the rad level. To the exposure time—"

"Ah, you know that, and I know that. But what will the folks out there be knowin'? Only that 'tis no longer so important to be careful. And managers—business-trained managers, anyway—have taken short-cuts before, even without bullet-proof vests." He shook his head. "They don't understand, at all. They think maintenance and weld inspection and the like are overhead. They think they are *financial* issues." He pulled a pouch of tobacco from his shirt pocket and hefted it in his palm. "But that isn't the worst of it, not at all." He sighed and filled his pipe. " 'Tis an evening for gloomy thoughts, it is."

Singer sighed with him. When Eamonn put on his stage-Irishman act it could mean anything. "Then what is? Worse, I mean."

Murchadha was silent for a long moment. "Have ye ivver heard," he asked finally, "of the Washer at the Ford?"

"Who?" Singer shook his head. "No."

Murchadha nodded. "I wouldn't think so. Who has, these days? We've no time for myths anymore. Leastwise, not for the old myths. We've got new ones, we do." He tamped the tobacco into his pipe bowl with his thumb. Then he looked off, past Singer's shoulder. "It happened a long time ago, they say; back in the time there was before there was time. The Daghdha, the Good God, was out walking on the eve of the great battle of *Magh Tuiredh*, with the Fomorians. Taking the evening air, he was. *Feis Samhain* had begun at sunset." He paused and looked at Singer. "Samhain was the old pagan New Year. It began at sunset on the last day of October."

"You mean Halloween?"

Murchadha snorted. "All Hallow's Eve. Aye. And All Hallow's Day that follows. Sunset to sunset. That's all that's left of the Old Feast. It's still a Holy Day for Catholics, you know. At any rate, while the Daghdha is out walking he meets a woman doing her wash in the river. A good-looking woman, she was, with a fine shape wearing the bones of her. She makes the offer and he accepts, being a fine Irish lad as well as a god, and not wishing to seem ungracious. Afterwards, the woman promises her aid in the coming battle. So naturally the Daghdha laughs. 'Your aid, is it?' he says. 'And what might that be?' Then he sees that the woman is not a woman, at all; but the Morríghan, the Triune Goddess, in her manifestation as *Nemhain*, the Spirit of Battle. He sees in her eyes death and skulls and rotted bodies. Decayed flesh dripping from the white bone beneath. She is the War Fury, that dreadful female who is seen just before a battle, washing the severed heads and limbs of those about to die."

Singer shivered. "The Morríghan," he repeated.

"Aye. The Phantom Queen, the War Fury, and *Badhbh*, the Raven of Battle. Three in One. We never needed Padraig to teach us about Trinities. The Three Morríghans she was called by those who feared her. And what Hallow E'en skeleton or witch's costume has ever captured the horror of Herself?"

"None," Singer agreed. "But why was she washing the heads and arms?"

Murchadha turned and stared at his work. "It was *Nemhain*'s cleansing itself that brought death. The Washer at the Ford was also the Chooser of the Slain."

"A chilling story, son," Singer told him. "But what has it to do with our nanny?"

Murchadha looked up. With his thumb, he again tamped the tobacco firmly into the bowl. "Tell me, Doc. What is the worst radiation problem of all? The very worst."

Singer felt a spark of anger. He leaned forward. "Quit playing around with me, Eamonn! Get to the point!"

Murchadha lit his pipe. It was a butane lighter and the sudden flare was so large and so bright that Singer instinctively pulled back and almost fell off the stool. Murchadha sucked the flame into the bowl and the tobacco ignited. He glanced sidewise at Singer.

"Nuclear war," he said.

"Nuc . . ." Singer felt fear. He looked at Murchadha and added two and two. "Are you trying to tell me that by making people more resistant to radiation, we'll make nuclear war more likely? That's absurd! Impossible! You can't really believe that!"

"I can believe anything. I'm Irish, remember? We're all fey. The Queen of Hearts could believe six impossible things before breakfast. Sure, she had no imagination at all. We'll be handing the politicians a bullet-proof vest for fallout. And they are no brighter than the utility managers, are they? Won't they wonder? Won't they wonder if this might not be the very edge they need? Oh, maybe not our own president, fine lady that she is, or the old first secretary over on the other side of the world. They won't throw the Big One, because they'd both be losing more than they could ever hope to gain. But what of folks like that al-Qaysar? Or the new Homeland Party in Japan. Or the Indians and Pakistanis? Or . . . Need I go on? How do you think their minds would run if they believed *Nemhain* had washed their soldiers?"

"But . . . But . . ." Singer felt anger and frustration

building in him. "Dammitall! It's absurd. It doesn't matter if people are hardened to fallout if the rest of the ecosystem isn't. We can't tailor nannies to every species on the planet. And, besides, there's more to nuclear war than radiation. There's the blast itself, and nuclear autumn, and the collapse of the health and food delivery infrastructures. An increased resistance to radiation won't help a man who's starving to death, or dying of infection. So, what you're saying doesn't make any sense."

"It doesn't have to. People make decisions based on the facts as they see them, not as you see them. And if they don't like the facts, well, they just explain them away." He glanced at Singer and his eyes flicked away. "Tell me, Doctor. Have ye ivver read Thucydides?"

"Thucydides? No. He was an ancient Greek, wasn't he?"

"So he's not 'relevant' to modern times?" Murchadha sighed. "Why did our monks bother saving all that stuff?" He shrugged. "Well, this Thucydides lad, he wrote once. . . . Let me see if I can remember how it goes." He tilted his head back and closed his eyes. "He wrote: 'Their judgement was based more on wishful thinking than on sound calculation of probabilities; for the usual thing among men is that when they want something they will without reflection leave that to hope, while they will employ the full force of reason in rejecting what they find unpalatable.' " He opened his eyes and looked at Singer.

"Remember," he continued, "these are politicians we are speaking of, not technicians. They are not used to reason. They live in a world where the words on a piece of paper are reality and everything else—matter and energy and physical laws—are only abstractions. They judge things by political 'agendas' or 'bottom lines.' They don't ask whether something be true, but only whether 'tis consistent with their political philosophy, or their investment strategy. They don't understand any of this. Nary a corporal's guard is technically trained. Nuclear bombs are only large firecrackers. They play children's games, chattering about throw weights and windows of opportunity and numbers of deliverable warheads. Deliverable? As if they were speaking of postal packages. EMS pulse? Nuclear Autumn? The collapse of the health care system? It cannot be true, because they do not want it to be true. Only theories, they say. The theories of weak sister scientists with politically suspect beliefs. As if a neutron cared what ideology a man professed."

Singer was silent, taken somewhat aback by the vehemence of Murchadha's speech. He waited for the man to continue. When he did not, Singer spoke into the silence. "You could be wrong," he said carefully. "You're probably wrong."

"Aye." Murchadha blew a cloud of bluish smoke toward the ventilator. "I could be, at that. But I could be wrong believing the other way, too; now couldn't I? On the whole, I'd rather worry and be wrong. It's me duty, you might be sayin'. Me duty." He smiled thinly, as if at a joke.

"Your duty?"

"Sure, and is Murchadha not the Gaelic form of Murphy?"

Singer's sleep, when it finally came that night, was troubled, disturbed by dreams whose meaning he could not quite discern. A part of him knew he was dreaming, that he was inside himself and watching himself from afar at the same time. Sounds had a peculiar, muffled quality to them.

He found himself in the laboratory, but the laboratory looked somehow like the old cabin he grew up in. The floor was hard-packed dirt, and he was barefoot. Everything was backlit by a strange sourceless lighting. Jessie and the others were sitting at their workstations, intent on their work, and when they moved, it was in slow motion. They ignored him as he walked through. "How is it going?" he asked, and heard his voice echo as if he were in a vast cavern.

Patel shook his head slowly. Left. Right. Left. Right. He held an intricate Tinkertoy molecule in his hand and he showed it to Singer. "It should fit, but it doesn't." He tried to jam it together with another Tinkertoy structure and they both fell apart into sticks and balls. Patel stared at the wreckage and wept.

Koyanagi was running discs through his terminal. His screen flashed in manic images that never lasted quite long enough to register on Singer's mind. "We must benefit humanity," Koyanagi told him, "even if it costs every penny you have."

Murchadha was sewing fancy, brocaded vests. He took out a tape measure and measured Singer. "Take a number. Line up." Royce was taking the vests from Murchadha and stacking them in piles by size. "Radiation is everywhere," he announced. "Everywhere. Everywhere."

A file of Green protesters goose-stepped through the lab. DON'T GO AGAINST NATURE, read their signs. RAD NANNIES KILL! WHAT IF THEY FAIL? Mysteriously, there was another door at the far end of the lab and, as the Greens filed out, Thucydides tied blindfolds around their eyes.

Thucydides was dressed in the waitress's nautical outfit. When the Greens were gone, he came over and tied blindfolds on Muchadha and Koyanagi and the others. They all laughed and began playing blind man's bluff. Though Singer was not blindfolded, he could not connect when he swung his paddle at them. Yet, they never seemed to miss when they swung at him. They began knocking equipment over in their play and Singer tried to call out a warning, but no sounds issued from his throat.

Thucydides stood before him with a blindfold and said something. It was Greek to Singer. The blindfold came up and over his eyes and everything went impossibly black. Singer stumbled forward, laughing. "Where is everyone?" He felt faerie fingers groping in his pockets. He clapped his hand over his wallet, but the ghostly hand snaked in anyway and his pocket was suddenly empty.

Then his hand touched flesh. It was soft and yielding and covered with a gentle fuzz. He ran his hands up and down, feeling the smooth, familiar shape; the hills and valleys of baby-like skin. "Jessie?" He pulled her to him and for a wonder she came. Their lips met, suddenly passionate; and Singer realized that they were both nude.

He pulled off his blindfold and looked at her, and it wasn't Jessie at all but the Morríghan. He watched the soft, round flesh melt off her, into a red, sticky horror. The skull spoke to him through lipless jaws. "We've washed everyone," said a hoarse whisper. "We've cleansed the world." And a white flash scoured everything of color. Singer tried to scream, but all that came from his throat was a low moan.

The shout that woke him was his own. He jerked upright in bed, his heart thudding, drenched in sweat. A feeling of *deja vu*. He flicked his reading lamp to low. Beside him, Jessie stirred and said something unintelligible, but did not awaken. He took a long, slow breath to calm himself. *Another nightmare.* He looked at his wife's still form.

She was sleeping with her back to him. The curves of her body rose and fell with her breathing. He remembered how her flesh had felt in the dream. She began to roll toward him and Singer was struck by the sudden fear that the dream was not over, after all, and that the face he would see would be the face of dripping horror.

He didn't want to know. He squeezed his eyes shut and lay down, facing away from her. As he waited another dread stole over him: that a skeletal hand would reach from behind and place itself upon his shoulder. *This is crazy.* Knowing was better. He raised himself upon his elbow and glanced at Jessie.

And it was only Jessie, after all. Her face quiet and peaceful. *So, what did you expect?* he chastized himself.

This project is getting to me. But with the government funding coming, our worries will soon be over. He wondered if sleep would return and, if it did, whether he would dream again.

VII

The phone warbled the code that meant an outside call. Singer grimaced and, with a flourish, let the report drop to the desk. He glanced at Koyanagi. "Give me a minute, would you, Masao?" Koyanagi nodded and crossed his legs.

"Dr. Singer here," he told the mouthpiece.

"Hello, Charles." It was Royce. "I was wondering if I could borrow a few moments of your time."

"Only if you promise to give them back."

"What?"

"Nothing. What did you want?" he asked with a touch of asperity. "Everything is going fine. Just as it was two days ago. And last week."

"I'm not trying to ride herd on you, Charles." Royce sounded aggrieved. "I don't know your job well enough to give you instructions."

"That wouldn't stop some people."

Royce laughed. "I know. I know. I work with some of them. No, the government just likes to keep an eye on its investments. I'm only checking in to see if you have any roadblocks you need cleared. That's my job: to make straight the path before you. You're the quarterback in this game. Just think of me as your offensive line."

Singer sighed. He had no problem thinking of Royce as offensive. "No, we don't have any problems of that sort. Only technical hurdles that you can't help us with."

"Do you need more personnel? We can always round up a bunch of experts for you."

"No, John. You cannot solve research problems by committee. More than five or six people cannot decide when to eat lunch, let alone how to tackle a problem."

Royce laughed and Singer decided that the man's most irritating quality was his complete sincerity. He really did want to help, but he didn't know any way of doing that except to throw people and money at the problem. Well, Singer reflected, it could have been worse.

"Is that all you wanted? You'll be getting my regular progress report at the end of the week. If I do run into any bureaucratic snafus, I'll call you."

"Well . . . there is one other thing."

Royce sounded oddly hesitant. "What is it?" Singer asked.

"That Jap you have working for you? I'm afraid he'll have to go."

Singer frowned. He pulled the phone away and looked at it, as if he could see some defect with its mechanism. He glanced at Koyanagi, who was sitting calmly next to the desk.

Koyanagi was doing nothing. He wasn't fidgeting, or twiddling his thumbs, or looking around, or reading a magazine. He was simply . . . waiting. Singer had seen him do that before and it always bothered him, as if a person had to be constantly occupied at something. He wondered if it were some sort of Zen thing.

He cupped the mouthpiece of the phone and motioned to Koyanagi to leave the office. "Give me a few minutes here, would you?" Koyanagi raised an eyebrow, then nodded. He rose and shook out his pants. "I will come back later regarding my report," he said. He closed the door behind him as he left.

"All right, Royce," Singer said into the phone. "What are you talking about?"

"That Koyanagi-san of yours. He's one of the roadblocks I was telling you about. It's either him or the appropriation. You can't keep both."

"What? That's absurd. The nanny was his idea in the first place. He came to me. He's our protein expert. I couldn't finish the job without him."

"Look, Charles, I just found out myself this morning."

Royce sounded genuinely apologetic. "If it were up to me, I'd say what the heck. You can't always get real Americans, so you get by with what you have. But, you must see our point as well. With the economy the way it is, the government is extremely reluctant to let a contract on such a vital matter if it involves a foreign national. Especially a Brass Jap. There are powerful individuals on both the Senate and House science subcommittees who are disturbed. They had a hard enough time with your other employees."

"My other . . . What the devil does that crack mean?"

"Well, one senator wanted to know why you didn't hire Americans instead of a mick, a limey, and a dothead. His words," Royce added hastily before Singer could speak, "not mine. I told him that Dr. Burton-Peeler was your wife and a citizen by marriage, that Mr. Murchadha was a naturalized citizen; and that Dr. Patel was a citizen by birth. That calmed him down somewhat; but it did create an issue over Koyanagi, who is most definitely an alien. We have enough problems with the Japanese-Brazilian co-dominium without having one of their nationals on a vital project of ours."

"But—"

"And didn't he steal one of your designs when he worked for São Paulo Biophysics? SPB never paid royalties on that, as I recall. Another drop in the foreign exchange bucket. So it makes some of the committee members wonder what he's up to. It makes me wonder; and, frankly, Charles, shouldn't it make you wonder, too?"

Singer took a deep breath, unsure how to answer the man. Royce hadn't worked with Koyanagi like Singer had. Creating this nanny was Masao's life's goal. It was the nanny he cared about, not São Paulo.

Nor, come to that, SingerLabs.

He looked up at the office door and saw Koyanagi through the glass. He was waiting just outside for Singer to call him back in. Masao wouldn't care if SingerLabs developed the nanny or someone else, as long as it was developed. And as long as Masao had a hand in it. So why had he come to Singer? Why not stay at São Paulo and do it? *Because we're frigging geniuses here, that's why*. Because breakthrough comes before development. But if another lab could market the nanny at a lower price, making it more widely available to "humanity" . . . No, with the government handling that end, Masao had no concerns. They would probably make the nanny a civil right; find something in the Constitution that said everyone should have it. That was fine with Singer, as long as he got paid.

He thought there was something he should ask Royce, but he couldn't think of what it was. Something about distribution? Never mind. That wasn't his concern. The problem right now was what to do about Masao.

Singer turned back to the phone and swiveled his chair just a bit away from the door. "It comes down to this, John," he said. "My choice isn't between Masao and the nanny. Without Masao, there is no nanny. He is key to this project. Can you get your congresscritters to see that?"

"Maybe," Royce admitted. "I don't think they recognize the importance of individual excellence. To them, people are pretty much interchangeable. The senator will want to know why we can't use just any old biophysicist."

"Okay, if they can't understand why 'people' isn't the same as 'headcount,' try this on them. If I dump Masao, he'll go straight back to São Paulo with everything he knows." *Could he do that?* Did his Brazilian patriotism outweigh his loyalty to SingerLabs? Singer remembered what Royce had said that day on *The Amboy Clipper*. Loyalties spread outward from Number One in concentric circles. How far out did Masao's loyalties extend? Some Englishman—who?—once said that, given the choice between betraying his friend and betraying his country, he'd hope he'd have the decency to betray his country. By coming to Singer for the breakthroughs, was

Masao betraying the Nippo-Brazilian co-dominium? Brasilia would certainly see it that way; but did Masao? *What is Masao's plan?*

"We'd have to start over," he told Royce, "and the Niprazilians would have a leg up. Our government couldn't stop Masao from leaving the country because the co-dominium would raise a stink about it and, if it stank bad enough, Tokyo might not reschedule our debt payments. Maybe your senator can understand that."

"I see your point. But, perhaps a compromise is possible. Surely, even if you need this man's services during the research and development phase, you could dispense with them afterward. The work then would be routine, wouldn't it?"

"Well . . ."

"And, of course, the government would be aware of the extra costs you would incur in the event of hiring and training another man to take this Koyanagi's place."

"And you would 'defray' those extra costs?"

Singer could almost hear Royce's smile over the phone. "Cost plus," he heard him say. "Cost plus."

Singer cradled the phone and stared at it. Absently, he pulled out a stick of gum and popped it into his mouth. Cost plus. How much for stringing Masao along, then dumping him? Thirty pieces of silver? What was the alternative? Losing the contract and the Lab. Throwing Eamonn and Kalpit on the street. He and Jessie losing everything they had worked to build. It is expedient that one man die for the whole nation. Was it also expedient that one man be fired for the whole Lab? He thought about it long and hard, but found no easy answers.

VIII

The report from the consulting topologist was four inches thick. Singer looked at the report, then looked at Patel. "Good news or bad?" he asked.

Patel smiled. "It is very good news," he said, but he didn't sound very enthusiastic.

Singer pulled out a stick of gum and unwrapped it. "I could use some good news," he said. He stared at the report lying on his desk. How many pages thick was it? "Did she have to take so long saying it?"

He flipped to the back of the report and winced. As with most technical reports, it suffered from appendicitis. Twelve appendices in this one. He grunted humorlessly. It was probably better to put the gory details in an appendix than to have them strewn about the body of the report like the aftermath of the Texas Chainsaw Massacre.

He tried to read through one of the appendices. The derivation of some theorem or other. But he gave it up after a few lines. He was used to mathematics that used Greek letters, but general topology as often as not used Hebrew and Logic as well. This one-line equation here . . . it wasn't really an equation, like in calculus. It was more like a statement in logic. The one line would probably require an entire page of English. If it could be expressed in English at all.

And even the parts that appeared to make sense seemed to elude his grasp. "A topology that is both conjoining and splitting must be maximal splitting and minimal conjoining." "A space is compact iff it is both H-closed and set-bounded." "Flynn's Theorem states that every function space in a class C^Y has a conjoining and splitting topology if the universal space of the class, U^Y, has such a topology." Hot stuff. He could picture topologists staying up late at night, flashlights on under the bedsheets, unable to stop turning the pages. Anxious to see how it all turned out.

"It is not entirely mathematical," Patel pointed out. "The conclusions are rather simple and straightforward. Only two of the structures we have designed so far do not fail safe. Furthermore, the report defines an envelope of structures within which we must design in order to assure safe failures."

With a sense of relief, Singer retreated to the main body of the report and read through it quickly to make sure he understood it. When Jessie had raised the fail-safe issue with the group, Kalpit had suggested tackling the problem through topology; so Singer had retained a general topologist from the university—something the professor had found sufficiently intriguing in itself. Topologists were not in high demand for consulting jobs. But he remembered how the woman's eyes had lit up as he and Kal had outlined the situation. Singer thought she would have an orgasm right then and there. The topologist had spent a week in the Lab with Kal and Masao, learning about molecules, and had then disappeared to wherever it was that such people disappeared to, muttering about H-closed, B-bounded δ-structures and Harris proximity spaces. A month later, she had returned smiling with the report they had commissioned and enough research ideas to burn out two dozen graduate students.

"The basic idea," said Patel, "is that molecular structures are points in a topological space; and 'mutation' is a topological operator that defines a proximity on the space. Two molecular structures are 'close' if one can be transformed into the other by a mutation. The 'distance' between two structures, Π_0 and Π_K, is the inverse of the product of the probabilities of the chain of mutations that link them. For example, if Π_0 could be changed into Π_K by means of a chain of three intermediate mutations, $\Pi_0 \rightarrow \Pi_1 \rightarrow \Pi_2 \rightarrow \Pi_3 \rightarrow \Pi_K$, each having a probability p, then the distance between them is p^{-4} This metric creates regions in the space of all molecular structures."

It was the most pleasant sounding gibberish that Singer had ever heard. "Do you understand any of what you just said," Singer asked with a grin.

Patel did not return the grin, which surprised Singer. "I understand it well enough to apply it," he said. "The set of structures that we developed for the rad nanny is a closed and bounded region that does not intersect any actively harmful structures. Except for the two instances I mentioned, no possible chain of mutations can change the nanny into anything but a broken nanny."

Ever since Jessie had raised the issue, Singer had been contemplating a host of Luddite "what-if" lawsuits, based on the chance that the nanny "might" malfunction. The sort of thing you would expect from people whose ideas of mutants came from Marvel comics. No probability greater than zero impressed that crowd. If it was possible, it had to be guarded against; even if the probability was one in a billion. *Do you mean to tell the Court, Doctor Singer, that you are willing to take* chances, *no matter how slim, with human lives? Why not,* he imagined himself responding. *We do that every time we drive a car.* Polite circumspection was not Singer's long suit. He knew he made a hell of a witness, and was the despair of his lawyers.

"You're right. This is good news," he told Patel, tapping the report with his forefinger. "We can actually prove that harmful mutations are impossible, not just improbable."

"Except for the two I've pointed out," Patel said.

Singer looked at him. "That's the third time you've mentioned that. Is something bothering you?" He realized he still held the unwrapped stick of gum in his hand, and he popped it into his mouth.

"Bother me," Patel repeated. "I don't know. Perhaps it is only my imagination."

"Son, if you don't tell me pretty damn quick what's on your mind . . ."

Patel shook himself. He nodded at the report. "After I had read that thing and I went back over the structures we had designed, I became interested in the two that did not fail safe—"

"Can we redesign those two so they are safe, but they still do the job?"

"Charles, this is serious."

It was indeed if it meant that Kalpit was calling him Charles. "I'm sorry, Kal. You talk; I'll listen."

"Thank you. In answer to your question: Yes, we can redesign them, provided we modify a few other structures to compensate. Masao and I went through the entire system, component by component. But . . . one of those structures I designed myself and . . . and I could swear it had been altered."

Singer sat upright in his desk chair. Its spring threw him forward, catapault-like. "What? Altered how?"

"Charles, there is no other way. It had been altered deliberately."

"Wait a minute. Wait a minute. Do you know what you're saying?"

Patel looked at him, then dropped his eyes to the floor. He found something in the carpeting intensely interesting. "Yes, I know what I am saying. Some of the groups on the chains, they are not the proteins I put there."

Singer shook his head angrily. "Impossible. There are too many codons, too many bonds, even in the simplest structure. I know. I've reviewed them myself. You couldn't possibly remember what you put in each and every address."

"I do not," Patel admitted, still staring at the carpet. "It is not that. It is the . . . the aesthetics. An artist has a style, a certain way of doing things. And an artist recognizes his own style. A painter knows his paintings. An engineer knows his drawings. And I know my molecules." Patel looked up at him, his brow furrowed, his jaw firm. "I know my molecules," he repeated. "And one of them has been altered so that its failure would endanger the organism using the nanny."

Singer stared at him expressionlessly. "What about the other?"

"That would also endanger the organism. But it was

Masao's design, not mine, so I do not know if it has been altered."

"Does Masao know? Did you ask him?"

Patel shook his head. "No. I did ask him if the structure was as he remembered it, but he laughed and said who can remember such things." Patel looked troubled and again would not meet Singer's eyes.

"All right. All right," said Singer, thinking aloud. "You say that one, maybe two, structures have been altered—"

"Possibly more."

Singer felt offended. "You said two."

"No. Two would fail in a dangerous fashion. But, there have been other problems. Configuration problems. Interference fits on tolerances. Incompatibility between components. Little things, the kind of problems that we have always had on past projects. But more of them. Perhaps, too many more."

"And you think . . ."

"That someone is tampering with the design. To slow it down. Or to sabotage it completely."

There. It was out in the open now. A cold, horrible fact. No, not a fact; a speculation, Singer reminded himself. Kalpit had no proof. Nothing with which to confront anyone.

Configuration problems. Singer knew he had not been paying enough attention to the technical side. Money worries had been on his mind. Configuration control had been his job, and he had muffed it.

"These alterations that you suspect," he said. "They weren't out and out sabotage." Sabotage. From the French *sabot,* the wooden peasant shoe, which they had kicked into the gears and wheels of the strange, unfamiliar machines of the industrial age. "I mean, no one reached in with a hammer and smashed the molecule. They were altered subtly, weren't they? They still performed their design function?"

"Yes. Only not as well. And they caused problems elsewhere. We were slowly painting ourselves into a design corner. Had the situation gone unchecked for much longer, we would have found ourselves with a nanny that was ninety-five percent complete; but with the remaining five percent impossible to realize."

Like a jigsaw puzzle whose last piece didn't fit. "All right. The million yen question: Who has the brains to do something like that?"

Even as he asked it, he knew the answer. All of them. Except maybe Eamonn. But, he saw the way Patel had dropped his eyes at the question, and it suddenly occurred to him why Kalpit was so wrought up; why he was so hesitant to mention his suspicions. Configuration control had been Singer's job. So maybe the problems were of Singer's making?

"It wasn't me," said Singer.

Kalpit looked at him and his skin flushed darker. "Nor I," he said. He clasped his hands together, as if he were praying, and laid his forehead on his knuckles. After a while, he looked up and his eyes were pleading. "Masao was my friend," he said.

Then you're thinking the same thing I am. Singer ran a hand across his chin. "Look, Kal. Don't say anything about this to any of the others. Not even Masao." He wondered. *Especially* not Masao? *Didn't they steal one of your designs?* Royce had asked. *Shouldn't you wonder what he's up to?* "Give me time to check into it," he said. "Maybe it's a misunderstanding, not deliberate." But it *was* deliberate. He knew it. He knew the work had been going too slowly. He remembered how the data for his design simulation had been garbled. How structures hadn't fit together properly. How they had had to redesign one enzyme from scratch. Sure, it could have been coincidence. Accident. And he and Patel could pretend to believe as much of that as they liked.

Patel nodded and left, without saying anything further. Singer watched him go. Patel? Configuration control was Singer's job, and sooner or later, he would have discovered the sabotage. Patel knew that. Had he come forward simply to divert suspicion from himself? Perhaps. But what motive could Patel possibly have?

What about Masao? He had been standing just outside the office when Royce had called to demand his firing. Could he have overheard? Was he taking revenge? But Masao wanted the nanny more than anyone. More than Singer, even, since to Singer it was the profits that the nanny would bring that mattered. Still, he disagreed with Singer's marketing strategy. He wanted Free Nannies for All. And he *had* been a party to São Paulo's piracy, hadn't he?

Then there was Eamonn and his *angst* about the side effects the nanny might have. Could his concern be deep enough that he would try to ruin the project? But Eamonn didn't have the expertise to do so subtle a job. Or did he? Just because the man wasn't a geneticist or microbiologist, it didn't mean he was ignorant. Nanomachining required extensive knowledge of molecular structures, and no one was more intimate with the *details* of their proteins than the machinist.

Or Jessie? His own wife? They had been rivals for years. Friendly rivals—hell, they were married! But . . . she had been dragging her feet on the project, had not shown her usual flash and brilliance. Why, Singer didn't know. But lack of enthusiasm was not a motive for sabotage. Try as he might, he couldn't make the connection.

He couldn't make the connection with any of them. Except for Masao, they had been with him for years. He knew them. They wouldn't do such a thing to him. It just wasn't in them.

And that left Masao. The man from São Paulo.

Which would make it much easier to comply with Royce's demand.

Singer turned and spat his gum into the wastebasket. It had gone sour and tasteless.

IX

Royce got off on the wrong foot with Jessie from the moment he complimented her on her dress.

Singer and Burton-Peeler stood in the doorway of the restaurant's cocktail lounge, searching for their host, while their eyes adjusted to the dimness. Royce saw them and waved them over, and they made their way through the chattering lunchtime crowd to his table. He had a half-finished, bright yellow drink in front of him. Singer wondered if it contained any alcohol.

Royce stood and held a chair out for Jessie to sit. "I see you brought the little woman along," he said to Singer. Then he turned to her and said, "That's a very charming dress you're wearing, my dear."

Whoops, thought Singer. He waited for Jessie to say something, but she only smiled and held her peace, and Singer breathed a prayer of thanks. The three of them chatted for a while, exchanging meaningless pleasantries about the weather. Royce twisted in his chair and signaled to the waitress.

"So. How are things going on the project, Charles?" he asked, turning back.

"Not as quickly as I would like," Singer admitted. "But I think I've got a handle on the biggest roadblock, now." Roadblock. That was one way of putting it. He had said nothing of Koyanagi's sabotage to Royce. Considering his earlier warnings about the Niprazilian, Royce would probably take the news as evidence of Singer's bad judgement in defending him. He might drop the funding and move the project elsewhere.

"It's a rather difficult project," Burton-Peeler interjected. "I think Charlie underestimated the difficulties from the very beginning. He's been very moody the last few days, but he won't say why."

"Hmm. Is there any way to make up for the lost time, Charles?" The waitress arrived at their table, and Royce picked up his drink and tossed the rest of it off. He handed her the empty glass. "The same for me, missy. And my friends will want . . ." He glanced inquiringly at Singer and Burton-Peeler. "Feel free. It's on Uncle."

"Gin and bitters," said Jessie.

"Beer," said Singer. "Whatever's on tap and domesticated."

"I've tried to explain, John," he continued after the waitress had left. "Research isn't like production. You can't make it go faster by putting more people on it. You can't expedite it."

"Sometimes," added Jessie, "it depends on a flash of insight. And the flash never comes."

"I suppose." Royce scratched the side of his nose. "I'm not a creative man myself. I admit it. So, I'm not telling you how to do your job, Charles. You know that. I've seen too many projects ruined by colleagues who were too zealous in their oversight. Constantly nit-picking. Changing specifications on a whim. Generally getting in everyone's hair. And as often as not, the end product would not perform anyway, because some key factor was overlooked."

"There may be a connection," Jessie commented, "between overseeing things and overlooking things. Thank you," she added to the waitress, who set their drinks down in front of them. Royce seized his and took a long swallow. *Orange juice*, thought Singer. *It's got to be pure orange juice*.

"Excellent." Royce handed the woman a bright red-and-blue ten note. "Keep the change." He looked at Singer. "Oversee and overlook. That's pretty clever. You've got yourself a bright little lady here, Charles."

"I've always thought so," he replied, hoping to forestall Murder One. "So did the university. We both graduated *summa*, you know."

"College sweethearts. I know. I've read your files."

"I've always tried," Dr. Burton-Peeler said sweetly, "to be a credit to my sex."

Singer almost burst out laughing and lifted his mug to

hide his face. *Please, Jessie. Keep that hold on your temper. You promised.* It was obvious that she didn't care for Royce. Singer could see that as plain as a tick on a hound dog's ear. It came across in her body language and in the tone of her voice—to which the government man seemed oblivious. Singer knew Jessie was angry; and he knew that the anger would be unleashed later, at him. But at least he knew how to roll with her punches. He wasn't sure how Royce would react, and Royce held the purse.

"I suppose," Royce continued to Burton-Peeler, "that you are working on the woman's angle of the project."

"Woman's angle? There is no—" Jessie began, then stopped and pouted her lips. She cocked her head. "Yes, of course, I am. Someone has to consider the unexpected problems. 'Damn the torpedos' is a workable strategy only if there are no torpedos ahead."

"Hmm, yes." Royce nodded slowly. He looked at Singer. "What is the woman's issue here?" he asked.

"I think I'll let Jessie answer that one. It's her assignment." *Just what the hell has Jess thought of? Royce didn't have anything particular in mind when he made that remark, I'm sure. But it sure made Jessie think of something.*

"Well, it's nothing earth-shattering," she said, twirling the stem of her cocktail glass slowly between her thumb and forefinger. "It's just that not everything in a mother's bloodstream makes it through the placenta into the f . . . into the baby. We need to assure ourselves that the nanny will protect the unborn as well as the mother."

Damn, thought Singer.

"And, of course, there's Weismann's Barrier, which normally separates germ plasm cells from somatic cells. A general principle of genetics is that somatic changes are not hereditary. That would be Lamarckism."

"Lamarckism?"

Jessie smiled at him. "The inheritance of acquired characteristics, a theory that Stalin pushed because Darwinism was contrary to communist principles. We must assure ourselves that the design permits the nanny to cross the barrier and repair the reproductive material. Otherwise—"

"Otherwise," Royce finished for her, "mothers exposed to radiation could still give birth to deformed babies, even many years later. Could that be a real problem, Charles?"

"Yes," said Burton-Peeler.

"No," said Singer. He looked at his wife and she returned the look calmly. "No problems that genius and creativity can't handle," he continued, holding Jessie's gaze.

"Glad to hear it," Royce said, picking up the menu. "Glad to hear it."

Dinner was uncomfortable, at least to Singer. Jessie continued to emphasize the difficulties they had had in developing the nanny. Singer just as consistently pointed out how those difficulties had been overcome or, in some cases, would be overcome. Once, when Royce excused himself and left the table, Jessie turned to Singer and vented some of her frustrations.

"Your government buddy is a 24-karat chauvanist," she said.

"He's not exactly my buddy."

"Who invited his nose into our tent? I'm sure he's a Sawyerite now. He hardly heard a word I said. Did you see it?" Singer nodded, but said nothing, knowing that it hadn't been a real question. "I'm only a woman," she continued, "so I cannot have a worthwhile opinion." She twisted her voice into a squeaky imitation of Royce. "What a nice dress, my dear. Oh, are you handling the woman's angle? I could have told him his zipper was on fire and would have smiled and told me my hair looked nice."

"That's life on the pedestal," Singer said. "Some

women like it. Don't take him so seriously. We have to deal with him, so let it roll off your back."

"Easy for you to say. He wasn't being condescending to hillbillies."

"Jess—"

"Besides, I've got to dump on someone, so it might as well be you. I've been a good little girl, haven't I? I didn't kick him where I should have."

She had done that one time, he remembered. The SOB had deserved it, but Singer still winced at the memory. When Jessie had a few gins in her she became more than a little unpredictable.

"Look. Try to go easy on the problems we've been having, would you?" he told her. "You keep emphasizing our problems—"

"We have had problems!"

"I know. I know. This project has had more bugs than the embassy in Rio." He thought again of the sabotage and his voice tightened. "That's not what I meant. If he keeps hearing you bitch about the difficulties, he may think we're hinting around for more money."

Her eyes bored into his. "So let him think that. Maybe he'll up the ante. Why should that bother you? You'll do anything for a NewDollar, won't you?"

Singer looked over Jessie's shoulder and saw Royce returning. "Not anything," he said. "I've never crawled."

"I'm sorry to have to tell you this," Royce said as he wiped his lips with his napkin. He pushed the empty plate from him. "But I haven't been able to convince the committee members on that nationality issue."

Singer grunted. "I didn't think you would." Xenophobia was running rampant in the country since the Embargo and the congresscritters knew enough arithmetic to add votes.

The waitress brought the check and Royce handed her a debit card without checking the figures. He picked up the salt shaker and toyed with it. "Will that cause you any difficulties?"

"Not as many as I had thought before. In fact, it might solve some."

"Oh? Then you've decided you don't really need him?"

"What are you two talking about?" Jessie asked. "Need who?"

Singer grimaced. "The timing has to be right. Like I told you before, we do need his expertise for a while longer. And . . . there are still some things I need to check out. I'll get back to you."

"I'm glad you saw the light on this one, Charles," Royce said with a smile. "We couldn't buck the Joint Committee over just one man, and not even an American, at that. Don't worry, you'll get by without him."

Jessie said nothing until they were seated in their car in the parking lot. She watched Royce's Olds disappear onto Stelton. Singer started to put the keys in the ignition, but Jessie reached out and stopped him.

"All right, Charlie . . ." He glanced up and saw the grim look on her face. "You know what part of the camel's anatomy is in the tent now?"

"No, what?"

"The prick."

"What?"

"Yes, he's trying to screw us."

He started to give a flip answer, then thought better of it. Her face told him this was not a joking matter. "What do you mean?" He knew what she meant and had been dreading this moment.

"What was that business back there? Who were you two talking about firing?"

"Firing? Oh."

"Don't 'oh' me, Charlie. Open up. You know you can't fire anyone. It takes a majority of the shares to force someone out."

His hand reached for his shirt pocket, but Jessie seized

him by the wrist. "And don't go for the chewing gum, either," she told him. "You do that every time something's bothering you."

Singer twisted his arm in her grip and she let go. "Royce tells me that we won't get the government financing unless we fire Koyanagi."

Her eyes widened. "Koyanagi? Why?"

Singer didn't answer her. "And without the financing, there's no project. And that's the end of the Lab."

"Then what's the problem, Charlie?" she said. There was acid in her voice. "Dump the gook, and you'll get wealth beyond the dreams of avarice."

"Don't go slinging clichés at me! Dammit, Jessie. I've been rich and I've been poor. And all things considered, I'd rather be rich."

"Now, that's original."

He turned his head and stared out the windshield. "I'm not joking. I was there once. You don't know what it was like."

"You're right, Charlie. I don't. I only know that no amount of money is worth selling out a friend. Not even in Appalachia."

"Don't patronize me! I'm not some sort of Judas. I wouldn't sell a friend for thirty pieces of silver. It's just that . . ."

"Just that what?"

He ran his hands around the steering wheel, then batted it with his hand. "Who says Koyanagi's a friend of ours?"

A frown creased her forehead. "What are you talking about? This whole project was Masao's idea in the first place! He wants this nanny more than anything in the world."

"Sure. *He* wants it."

She gave him an odd look. "What is that supposed to mean? I thought you wanted it, too."

Singer shook his head. "I do, but not the way he does. Look, he doesn't want the nanny built. He wants to build the nanny. Get the difference? He wants to do it himself, and the way things stand now, there's only one way he can."

"I'm not sure what you're getting at."

"Look, if we keep him on, we'll lose the contract. Royce will leak everything to NanoTech or one of the others. They wouldn't hire Koyanagi, either. So whether he stays or goes, he's out of it. Unless . . ."

"Unless what? I don't like where this is going, Charlie."

He gave her a sharp look. "I don't like where it's been! I thought he was our friend."

"He is."

"Friends don't sabotage."

"Sabotage?" Jessie dropped her hand from Singer's arm. She leaned away from him. "What sabotage?"

Singer waved his hand at her. "I have evidence. Molecules have been altered, very subtly, to slow the project down and prevent its completion. Kal says it has to have been deliberate, and I believe him. Someone is to blame."

"The new kid on the block."

"Well?" he demanded angrilly. "Who else? Eamonn doesn't have the smarts for it. And Kal is the one who found out and told me about it."

Singer balled his right hand into a fist and hammered once on the dashboard. "Dammit!" The dash was padded, but it hurt his hand nonetheless. The pain felt good. "Masao's been the guiding light. If he goes, the project might drag out for another couple years."

"We might never finish it at all," said Jessie with an odd twist to her voice.

"I thought I knew him," he said. *But who ever knows another person? Masao doesn't like my attitude. He's made no secret of that. He's a bleeding-heart idealist and I'm a money-sucking mercenary. But I wouldn't have thought he would go this far.* But the trouble with idealists was that they were fond of grand, futile gestures.

Sure, Koyanagi wanted to "benefit humanity." But he wanted the applause, too. The peer recognition; the gratitude of humanity. Sometimes Singer thought his own monetary motivation was not only simpler, but cleaner. At least, he made no bones about why he scratched where it itched. Everyone wants payment for their work; but those who demanded their payment in intangibles could be far more arrogant and hypocritical than those who just wanted the cash, thank you.

"Why?" said Jessie. "Why would Masao deliberately sabotage his own project?"

"Why? I don't know! Maybe he planned it this way all along. Maybe he was playing us for suckers, so we would help him solve some of his research problems. Maybe he overheard my phone call with Royce and resented being dumped."

"Just a moment! You mean the sabotage is not the reason Royce wants him out?"

"No, he doesn't even know about it. If I told him, he might decide SingerLabs is a bad security risk and cancel the contract anyway."

"Well, we wouldn't want that."

"Don't be sarcastic. No, all the government cares about is that Koyanagi's a 'Brass Jap,' a citizen of the co-dominium."

"So, you were going to try squeezing him out even before you discovered the sabotage. Is that right?"

"I . . ." He wouldn't look at her. "No. I was playing for time." He wouldn't look too closely at himself, either. What would he have done? He wanted to believe he would have done the right thing, but it was impossible to remember clearly the feelings of the past, given the feelings of the present. "I thought if I strung it out long enough, something might have come up."

"Maybe the horse will learn to sing."

"What?"

"Never mind," she said bitterly. "Play it your own way, Charlie. You always do. Just one thing."

"What's that?"

"I know you, Charlie. I know you like a book. I know every damn misprint and torn page between your covers. So, please, don't talk yourself into doing something that I can't live with."

X

Singer lay awake in the middle of the night with a knot in his stomach. *I have to* know. He lay on his back in the bed, gazing up at the blackness of the ceiling. Beside him, Jessie snored gently on her side. It had taken her forever to fall asleep.

He had *trusted* Koyanagi, and the little Jap had betrayed him. If he was going to believe in betrayal—believe such a thing of anyone—he needed hard evidence, not deduction. *Maybe I'm wrong*. Maybe Kalpit was wrong. Maybe there was a harmless explanation for everything. An outsider. A hacker. Not a harmless explanation, exactly, but at least one he could live with. He wondered if that was what Jessie had been trying to get at in the car, earlier in the day. *Don't do anything I can't live with*.

Of course, she expected him to guess what she meant. She always did. Was he a mind reader? Was he supposed to read her every mood?

And Kalpit. Kalpit suspected Koyanagi, too, but he would want hard evidence before he would believe it. He and Koyanagi had become friends.

Christ! Did it matter who it was who was doing it? It was someone's friend. Everyone's friend. No wonder there was a knot in his stomach and the clock read one in the morning.

Gently, he eased the blanket back and slipped out of bed. He picked up his robe and houseshoes and, grabbing his keyring from the dresser, crept out of the bedroom, shutting the door silently behind him.

He didn't bother turning on the lights in the Lab.

The windows were made of diamond glass, assembled molecule by molecule in Eamonn's tanks, and they admitted enough light from the streetlamps to throw everything in the room into a ghostly relief. He knew the floorplan well enough to walk it in pitch black.

From his office, he retrieved the copies of the altered structures that Kalpit had given him. Then he sat at Koyanagi's workstation and activated the terminal. The glow from the screen created an island of light in the center of the room. *All right,* he thought. *Let's see what we can find.*

He downloaded Koyanagi's disc and went through each document, one by one, using FileComp. FileComp was an applications program that compared two versions of a file and displayed the differences. He wasn't sure what he was looking for. Evidence. Evidence of something, anything to prove that he was right. Or wrong. Unconsciously, his hand searched out a non-existent shirt pocket, fumbling for a stick of gum. When he realized what he was doing, Singer grunted in sour amusement. Jessie was right about his habits.

It was four-thirty before he finished reading. And there was nothing that he could find to prove Koyanagi's piracy. The altered structures (if they had been altered and were not simply errors) were on Koyanagi's disc as well as Patel's. Surely a saboteur would keep the original, correct copy. *Could I be wrong?* But, no. Kal had been sure of himself. And deliberate sabotage would explain so much. All that overtime, and so little progress. Singer remembered thinking that not too long ago, when the money situation had just begun to reach critical. He glanced over his shoulder at his office window. He had stood by that window looking out at a beehive of activity: Kal contemplating his screen, Koyanagi copying discs, Jessie and Eamonn deep in conversation. And he had wondered then why they had been falling further and further behind their schedule.

Well, now he knew. Someone had been holding them back. Koyanagi, if only he could prove it.

Copying discs?

Singer sat rigidly in the chair. Koyanagi had been running discs through his terminal. Then he had glanced up and had seen Singer watching and had started as if caught in the act.

In the act of what?

In the act of making unauthorized duplicates.

Of course! It had to be. Singer pulled on the drawers of the desk. Locked. They would not open. He yanked on them several times, hard enough to rattle the desk. Dammit, did he have a spare key? Every desk came from the furniture company with two sets of keys. Where was the second set?

He pushed himself away from Koyanagi's terminal and strode to his office. He flicked on the light. *I usually toss the spares in the bottom drawer.*

He opened the drawer and rummaged through it until he found a tangle of small keys that had migrated toward the back of the drawer through Brownian motion. He seized them and hurried back to Koyanagi's desk. He noticed he was breathing hard. *Anxiety attack*, he thought. *I'm afraid of what I'll find. Or what I won't find.*

The third key he tried fit. The drawers unlocked and he pulled them out one at a time and groped feverishly through them. His hand closed on a small case in the back of the bottom drawer and he paused. He pulled the case out. A minidisc holder. The discs inside were unlabeled. He picked one and inserted it in the terminal.

‹THIS DISC IS UNREADABLE. DO YOU WISH TO INITIALIZE IT?›

Singer ejected that disc and tried another. It, too, was blank. So was the third. The fourth booted up. . . .

The remaining discs contained duplicates of the files. Not the regular backups that sat in their racks over the filing cabinets. These were secret duplicates, squirreled away. He scanned for the folder he wanted and opened it.

Carefully, he studied the two structures that Kal had believed altered. He compared them to the versions that Kal had given him. FileComp went down the chains, codon by codon, and . . . *there!* A thymine group at that address instead of an atropine. A double bond there instead of a single bond. Subtle differences. Easily unnoticed.

He sat in front of the terminal, staring at the evidence, an aching in his body, in his chest. Of all the sins, betrayal was the worst. Dante had found the deepest circle of Hell reserved for those who betrayed their benefactors.

How long he sat there, Singer did not know; but suddenly the overhead lights came on. He spun around in his chair and faced the entrance.

Jessie stood in the doorway, an astonished look on her face. She was wrapped in her housecoat. Her hair was rumpled and her face had the naked look of an habitual glasses-wearer without her spectacles. "What are you doing down here at this time of night?" she demanded. She took a step closer. "You're going through Masao's desk!"

"Yes."

"That's pretty shabby," she said distastefully. "Spying on your own people."

"Yes. But so is betrayal." He turned suddenly and shoved the open desk drawer closed with a violent motion. It bounced and opened again halfway. "Damn him."

A worried look crossed Jessie's face. "That business of sabotage? You can't really know for certain. Kal may have been mistaken. Those might have been honest errors he found, not deliberate."

"No," Singer said wearily. "Kal was not mistaken. I found the original, correct versions. Your Jap friend had them hidden on a secret set of duplicate discs." He waved his hand at the case he had found, at the screen with the betraying diagrams, at Koyanagi's workstation, at the heartless world in general.

Burton-Peeler stepped closer and squinted at the screen. "Oh." She studied the diagrams near-sightedly. "These are different from the ones in the regular files?"

"I just said that, didn't I?" Singer said irritably.

She pouted her lips. "Yes. Yes, you did." She was silent for a while. "This doesn't prove that Masao sabotaged the proteins. It only proves that they were sabotaged after he made these copies."

"Well? Why did he make the copies?"

"Backups?"

Singer said nothing, but pointed silently at the rows of backup discs atop the cabinets.

"He must have had a reason."

"Of course, he had a reason!" Singer exploded. "Everyone has reasons! He was stealing the design and wanted to make sure that our copy wouldn't work. So he and São-fucking-Paulo would get a head start on us."

Burton-Peeler took a deep breath and let it out. She walked past him to Patel's terminal and ran her hand over the cabinet. "What will you do now?" she asked, her back to him.

Singer rubbed his hand across his brow and squeezed the bridge of his nose. "What else can I do? I'll have to fire the sonuvabitch."

"You can't do that, Charlie. I told you before. You need a majority of the shares to do that."

He looked at her, not believing what he had heard. "You and I have a majority," he said.

She stopped toying with Kalpit's terminal and wrapped her arms around herself. "Yes." She turned and faced him. "Is that what you want?"

"What I want?" He held empty hands out. "No, it's not what I want. I wanted Koyanagi's friendship."

"Intangibles? From you, Charlie?"

"Screw you." He had thought that finding proof of Koyanagi's piracy would make him feel better, would end the ache of uncertainty. But it hadn't. He felt angry and bitter.

She cocked her head and chewed on her lower lip. "You two were arguing all the time. About profits and altruism."

"So what? I don't require my friends to agree with everything I say. If Eamonn or Kal had been the saboteur, I would feel just as badly."

"What if it had been me, Charlie?"

He waved an arm. "You know, that's what hurts the most. The betrayal. You expect things like this from your enemies, but not from your friends. You don't know how much I was hoping to find a break-in by a hackercorp." His right hand was a fist. He sighed and rubbed it with the left. "Well, it's a dirty job . . ."

"Charlie, I can't let you do it."

"Eh? Do what?"

"Fire Masao. Force him out."

"What are you talking about? You want to keep him with us? In spite of Royce and the government? In spite of *this?*" Again, he waved at the screen. "No. Eamonn and Kal will vote him out, even if you don't help." He looked at her, trying to understand why she was opposing him again.

"No, Charlie. It was me."

"Who? What?" She wasn't making sense.

"I did it. I sabotaged those designs."

"You?" He blinked slowly. Then, more alertly: *"You?!"*

She pulled out Patel's chair and slowly sank into it. Singer watched dumbly, stricken speechless. Jessie studied her hands in her laps. The silence lengthened. "You," he finally managed to repeat.

She looked up, a defiant look on her face. "Yes, me! I did it. Every chance I had, I introduced tiny changes into the designs. Little incompatibilities. I deliberately suboptimized each of my assignments, so that none of the parts would quite fit together."

"And you always pointed out problems," Singer said. "Every time you opened your mouth, out came another stumbling block."

"Real problems," she told him, with just a touch of beligerency. "That needed real solutions."

"Solutions that could have been planned for if you had brought the problems up earlier. You held back. You held out."

"Some of it." She turned her gaze on her hands again. "Even I can't think of everything, Charlie. I brought up the fail-safe issue as soon as I realized that some of my alterations had made the nanny potentially dangerous. I didn't want to hurt anybody."

"You didn't want to hurt anybody. Oh, great. Then this isn't blood on my shirt." He slapped his chest with his fist. "Why, Jessie? What on Earth was worth doing this to me? To the Lab?"

"Why?" She looked at him. "You still can't see it, can you. Even after Eamonn explained it to you."

"Eamonn? You mean—"

"Yes. If you give this nanny to people, they will become more careless about radiation. It's as simple as that. Government leaders, especially, will find the nuclear option to be more thinkable. Do you want that on your conscience?"

"Do I want . . . ? You're being ridiculous!"

"Dammit, Charlie!" She stood up and glared at him. Patel's chair rolled across the carpeting, spun and fell. "Don't you ever call me ridiculous! You're so blinded by dollar signs that you can't see anything, any other ideal—"

"Oh, you're an idealist, are you? Well, idealists make me sick. You're so caught up with your lofty goals that you forget about people."

"What do you mean by that crack?"

"I mean you were perfectly willing to let Masao take the blame for the sabotage, weren't you?"

"I . . ." Her eyes shifted away. "No, I told you it was me. I told you I couldn't let you fire him."

"Sure. Tonight. When it came down to the wire, you couldn't go through with it. But why didn't you say anything earlier, in the car? *Why did you let me go on thinking it was Masao?*"

"It . . ." She wrung her hands together. "It didn't seem as important as stopping a war."

"Stopping a war? Be realistic. Even if what you say is true, you're not talking about stopping a war. All you're talking about is an increase in a probability. From one chance in a trillion to two chances in a trillion."

"When the payoff is minus infinity, does it matter how long the odds are?"

"Any excess, if the cause is good? Where have we heard that before?" He stood abruptly and stalked to the door.

"You've heard nothing. Nothing at all."

"Don't talk to me." He held his hands out, as if to shield himself from her.

"Where are you going?"

"Out."

"In your pajamas?"

He said nothing for a moment; then he stamped up the stairs to the apartment, where he found a pair of jeans in the clothes hamper and pulled them on. He couldn't think. His mind was racing in circles, thinking the same thoughts over and over. He was tying his sneakers when Jessie finally appeared in the bedroom doorway. He concentrated on his laces.

"Are you coming back?"

He stopped tying, but wouldn't look at her. "Maybe." He resumed tying.

He finished, rose, and pushed his way past her. At the front door he heard her call him from the top of the stairs.

"Charlie?"

He froze with his hand on the knob. "Yeah?"

"Promise me one thing."

"What?"

"Promise me that you'll think about what I said. About how people will react. I mean, that you'll *really* think about it."

He yanked the door open and slammed it behind him.

XI

Singer returned to the Lab later that morning, his sweatshirt stained under the arms and his hair matted down with perspiration. His breath was ragged with exhaustion. He had spent the last three hours alternately walking and jogging the back streets of the township, being barked at by dogs, being paced for a short while by a police car. Running had become an end in itself. While he ran, there was nothing except the physical reality of feet slapping the paving; of the shocks running up his legs; of the air bellowing in and out of his lungs. He had rested for only a short while, on a stone bench in Roosevelt Park, staring sightlessly at the pond, unable to pull his thoughts together. He would be there still except that he had seen storm clouds gathering in the northeast.

Physical exhaustion had calmed him, at least to the extent that he could conjure up no feelings from the early morning argument. He paused in the doorway of the Lab and saw the others staring at him curiously. *I must reek,* he thought. He noticed Masao brush at his sharply creased trousers and finger the knot on his tie. Eamonn, whose work required him to get dirty from time to time, always dressed more casually than the others; but even he was staring at Singer with surprise.

Jessie walked by with a hard copy in her hand. She paused when she saw Singer standing there. Her lips parted slightly, as if she were about to speak. Then her eyes hardened and she turned her back on him abruptly and walked away.

Singer stepped into the Lab and slammed the door hard behind him. Kalpit, engrossed in the display on his screen, jumped at the sound and turned around. Masao blinked with owl-wide eyes. No one spoke.

Singer strode past them with barely a glance. He ignored Jessie when he passed her workstation, and she ignored him. Part of him knew that this was not the way an argument should be handled. Let it all hang out. Wasn't that the advice everyone gave? Don't hold anything in. But he was afraid of what might happen if they did let loose. He was afraid that one of them would say something that could never be unsaid. And so it was safer to barricade himself behind his desk and dare the world to come to him.

He sat there, his two hands clasped together into a ball on the desktop. *How could she do this to me?* Didn't she realize that, with their financial situation as precarious as it was, sabotaging the project would ruin them? Didn't she care?

After a while he looked up and out the office window. The others were going about their tasks with the care of a squad of soldiers crossing a minefield. They could feel the tension, and no one wanted to be the spark that accidently ignited it. They spoke to each other; but lowly and briefly, and in whispers. And none of them looked at him or at Jessie, where she sat staring fixedly at her screen, her face set in the granite of righteousness.

No way out. He shook his head slowly. No way out. Jessie. Masao. Eamonn. Bitterly, he wondered what Kalpit was up to that he didn't know about. Jessie had been right. You don't sell out a friend. But Masao was pirating. And Jessie was sabotaging. So, who was selling out whom?

He put his face in his hands. *Oh, Jessie. What are we to do?*

* * *

A time went by, while Singer remained seated at his desk, thinking and feeling nothing. In every direction he looked, he saw nothing but wreckage. His thoughts, his feelings were numb.

Gradually, however, his strength returned and, with it, his anger. The anger built slowly, from a dull, red glow of hurt and resentment to a bright flame licking at the edges of his mind. One by one, he laid the sticks of memory on the fire. His hands slowly balled into fists on his desktop.

He glanced out the window again and saw Jessie talking with Eamonn. He remembered the Irishman's musings about— What had he called that spook? The Washer at the Ford. Memories of a nightmare tickled him. *Jessie must have put him up to it.* With her talk of nuclear war and atomic carelessness. She hadn't had the guts to come to him herself, so she had used Eamonn as her cat's paw. Dammit, he hated cowardice.

Jessie said something to Eamonn and it must have been funny, because he laughed. Somehow, that enraged him even further. He shoved himself from his desk, rose, and threw the office door open. Everyone looked and froze; but he ignored them and stalked across the floor toward his wife and the machinist.

He stood before them silently, suddenly at a loss for words. He didn't know where to begin. He knew he must look angry, for Eamonn was staring at him with frightened eyes. Jessie looked him up and down.

"Don't you think you should shower and change, Charlie?"

He gave a spasmodic half turn toward her and his hand came up a fraction of an inch. "You can't brush everything off so glibly," he told her.

Eamonn began to ease away from them and Singer turned on him. "And you don't get off, either, Murchadha." He let his gaze slide from one to the other. "So, you put him up to it," he said to Jessie. "I should have known. Dammit. Why didn't you come to me first?

Why did you have to hide your doubts; drag your heels; pump poor Eamonn here to bring them up to me?"

"Just a moment, Charlie—"

"And you," he turned to the nanomachinist. "Did you have to parrot everything Jessie told you? Can't you think for yourself? You and your Morríghan. Bullet-proof vests."

Murchadha's face grew red. "Dr. Singer, I am not such a lackwit that I cannot see a plain possibility. Had you taken the time to reflect on it, you would have come to the same conclusion yourself."

"No, he wouldn't have, Eamonn," said Burton-Peeler with a sigh. "He can't see it even now. You've told him, and I've told him, and he still thinks we're worried over nothing. And he can think of no more plausible explanation for why the two of us reached the same conclusion than to suppose that one of us coached the other."

"Aye," said Murchadha. "That *you* coached *me*." He looked at Singer with smoldering eyes. "I have not the wits for independent thought."

"That's why I didn't say anything to you," she said, turning to Singer. "Every word out of your mouth told me you weren't prepared to listen. The *only* thing about this project that meant anything to you was the money. You can't see past the dollars."

"And you can't see them at all. Or doesn't being poor worry you?"

"Charlie, we're a long way from being poor."

"Perhaps," said Murchadha, "if I am so poorly endowed with the powers of reason, I should seek employment elsewhere."

Singer looked at Murchadha. "Perhaps you should. Take your worries somewhere else."

"They are more than worries, Charlie," said Jessica. "They are moral issues."

"*Moral* issues? Then maybe you shouldn't dirty your hands on the project, either. Leave that to us sinners."

"Maybe I should."

"And making a profit is what business is all about, or haven't you heard? A company makes a profit or it dies."

"So. People need to eat, or they die. Does that make eating the purpose of life? I never said that profits didn't matter. I said that you saw *only* the profit. But what about the nuclear issue Eamonn and I raised? What about the social issue Masao raised? What about everything else in the world *besides* profit?"

"Please! What is going on here?"

Singer turned and saw Koyanagi and Patel. They were standing side by side, Patel with a bewildered look on his face; Koyanagi wringing first one hand, then the other. "Why are you arguing?" Singer had not realized how loud their voices had grown.

"Do you want to tell them?" Singer crossed his arms and stepped aside.

Burton-Peeler stuck her chin out. "Eamonn and I believe the nanny could be dangerous if it were released to the world."

"What?" Masao seemed confused. He looked from Peeler to Singer to Murchadha.

"Because it may encourage folk to carelessness around nuclear matters," said Murchadha. "Meltdowns and heavy releases will become more probable, and thus in the long term, more frequent."

"But," said Patel, "the nanny will protect people. That is its purpose."

"Aye, it will protect people; but what of the birds and the squirrels and the cattle and the trees?"

"Perhaps that lack of protection," said Singer drily, "will encourage people to be *more* careful."

"It's not symmetric, Charlie," Jessie told him. "The worst of it," she continued to Patel and Koyanagi, "is that people will consider nuclear weapons less dangerous than before, and if less dangerous, then more likely to be used."

"Surely, not!" Koyanagi protested.

"It's a question of probabilities," Burton-Peeler insisted.

"What if just one ayatollah, or one caudillo believes it? How many is too many? Just tune into the UN debates later this year, when all of the world's so-called leaders will be here, and you'll see what I mean."

Patel looked thoughtful. "There may be something in what you say."

"No!" That was Koyanagi. He seeemd agitated, almost ready to burst into tears. "It cannot be true! No one would behave so irresponsibly."

"You tell 'em," said Singer. Koyanagi had a lot of nerve coming to *his* defense.

Jessie's mouth opened. "Masao. Charlie's blind to anything but the bucks; but I would have thought that you would see the truth of it."

Koyanagi said nothing, but shook his head slowly and firmly. "I am a Buddhist. I have greater faith in human nature than you." Singer almost choked to hear Koyanagi say that. Singer had placed some of his own faith in Koyanagi's nature.

"Of all the world's religions," said Murchadha, "those that place their faith in human nature have the shakiest foundation."

"Eamonn and Jessie told me they're quitting the project," said Singer. It was an overstatement. A provocation. He had deliberately phrased it so. He saw Jessie stiffen. "That way," he finished, looking her straight in the eye, "they won't share in the moral blame."

"Charlie, it goes beyond that. Believing what I do, how can I let *you* work on the project?"

"Oh? How do you plan to stop me? More sabotage?"

Dead silence fell on the group. They looked at each other; at Burton-Peeler. Koyanagi was openly shocked. "Dr. Peeler sabotaged the project?" He stared at her as if he had never seen her before. Patel looked as if he were about to burst into tears. "It was she?" he asked.

"Yes, our illustrious vice president has been sabotaging the project. What do you think of that?" He crossed his arms once more over his chest.

"I was trying to delay the project; drag things out," she explained. "I hoped that you and the others would see sense. But only Eamonn did."

"But sabotage?" asked Patel. "Why did you not raise the issue openly?"

"Why, so Charlie could dismiss it out of hand?"

"It was not right," Murchadha said—and Peeler flashed him an injured look. " 'Tis one thing to argue against a course of action," he told her. " 'Tis another to let down those depending on you. It wasn't honorable."

"Honor? We're talking about upsetting the nuclear stalemate, and you talk about honor?"

"So, Jessie," said Singer smugly. "How do you propose to stop us?"

"We'll vote the project down. You and Masao want to keep it going? Fine. Eamonn and I want it stopped. Between us, we control as many shares as you two."

Singer reflected that there was a fine irony in that the survival of the project now came down to an alliance between himself and the man he intended to force out. He turned to Patel. "Well, Kal? It's up to you."

Patel looked at the four of them and shook his head. He walked off a little distance and sagged against Murchadha's worktable. His hands pressed against the surface and he leaned on them, his back to the group. "Up to me?" he said. "Why should it be up to me? Who am I? All I ever wanted to do was design better molecules. I do not wish to be the center of attention. I do not wish to be the decision-maker."

"You can't help it, Kal," said Singer. "You're in center stage, whether you want it or not. You put yourself there when you came to me about the sabotage."

The microbiologist lifted his head and turned to them. He bit his lip. "I don't know. I see that Jessica and Eamonn may have a point; but I do not think closing our eyes will make it go away." He looked at Koyanagi. "Masao?"

The Niprazilian pulled himself up straight. "It is a task that must be done. I will stay on." Patel nodded.

"Then if Masao stays, I will stay."

Singer snorted. "Then good-bye. Because Koyanagi's not staying either."

"What?" Everyone but Jessie was startled.

"The government man," she said, "told Charlie that, unless he fired Masao, the government would not honor the contract."

Patel looked saddened. "But it was *not* Masao, after all, who was sabotaging the work."

"It had nothing to do with any sabotage," Peeler said. "The government just didn't like the slant of Masao's eyes."

"Ah, but you were willing to let me go on believing that Masao was the saboteur, weren't you? You didn't say anything at first, even though you knew better."

"You suspected *me* of the sabotage?" Koyanagi asked Patel. Patel looked miserable but said nothing.

"Sabotage was not Masao's intention," said Singer. "He was going to pirate the design. He was keeping secret duplicates of all of our work." Singer saw how Koyanagi jerked his head to look at his desk drawer.

"You searched through my desk." Koyanagi made it a statement, not a question.

"Piracy?" Patel shook his head. "No, I do not believe it."

Singer jerked his thumb. "Go ahead, ask him."

Koyanagi drew himself up. "That was improper, to search my desk like that."

"It was improper to steal our work."

"I . . . I was copying. But not for myself. For humanity—" Singer's laugh interrupted him, but Koyanagi raised his voice. "For humanity, I say! So that the poor are as protected as the rich. So that the love of profits does not condemn the helpless."

"But theft?" asked Patel. "Masao, I had thought better of you."

Koyanagi looked at him in disdain. "You had thought me the saboteur."

Patel hung his head.

"Saboteur, thief; what difference?" said Murchadha. "Is the one more honorable than the other?"

"I had good reasons for what I did."

Murchadha nodded at Burton-Peeler. "Aye, and so did she. And neither reason was good. What is life without honor? When the Green Knight comes, will you bare your neck?"

"But—"

Murchadha drew himself erect. In his eyes Singer thought he saw the righteous stubborness of countless Irish heroes. "Our opponents' motives seldom seem as right and pure as our own. Sure, is not every pettiness built on good intentions?"

"Look," said Singer. "I was wrong about you, Eamonn. You're welcome to stay on. So are you, Kal. Neither of you did any harm. But you, Koyanagi-san, and you, Jessie . . ." He couldn't look either in the eye, so he chose to look at the nanolathe. "I'll have to ask you to . . . distance yourselves from the project."

"Just how far do you want me to distance myself, Charlie?"

Singer still would not look at her. "You be the judge."

"Dr. Singer," said Murchadha. "I don't know if I can stay. I never knew you had so low an opinion of me, and . . . and I still believe that the Washer is waiting for us at the river. And maybe *Magh Tuiredh* on the other side. I don't know that I can work on the project in good conscience anymore." He scowled and stuffed his hands into his pockets. "I need to be thinking about it." He turned slowly and walked off. The others watched silently. When the Lab door closed softly behind him, Singer sighed.

"It's just you and me, then," he told Patel.

Patel shook his head. "It is a good project. I do not agree with young Eamonn, or with you, Jessica, but—"

Again he shook his head. "There may be too much bad karma here. Friends have turned upon friends." He looked at Koyanagi, then at Burton-Peeler. "I know you each had your reasons, but you have hurt people."

"Idealists don't care who they hurt," Singer told him.

Patel looked at him. "Nor do mercenaries. You were prepared to find an excuse to fire Masao, weren't you? If not his piracy, you would have found another, less legitimate reason. And why? Simply to please the government and obtain their money." He held his hand up. "I know. I know. You had good reasons, too. Without the money, the Lab might not survive." He shook his head. "But I do not think this would be a pleasant place to work after this. What if Indians were next on the government's list?"

"You're an American," Singer told him.

Patel smiled wearily. "Tell that to the dot-buster gangs." He looked at his workstation sadly. "Still, I will miss this place. I will miss the years we had together, before we discovered our true *atman.*" He looked at Koyanagi. "And I will miss the years we might have had together." He held his hand out for a moment, then dropped it. "No," he said. "It would be hypocritical, would it not? Well, perhaps in another life."

And he, too, left.

Koyanagi shifted uncomfortably from foot to foot.

"What will you do now?" he asked.

"Do? What can I do? You'll have to go. I can't keep you around anymore, can I?"

"I see."

Singer glanced at him. Masao's face was rigid and expressionless. The inscrutable oriental. That was bullshit. There was pain written all over him.

"Don't let the doorknob," Singer said, "ream your ass on the way out."

Koyanagi flushed and bowed his head. "You do not understand my motives," he said and turned and walked away.

When Koyanagi was gone, a silence settled over the Lab. Singer stood unmoving. Then he glanced over his shoulder where his wife sat on Eamonn's stool. "Well, you've got what you wanted," he said. "We're ruined."

"You did it to yourself, Charlie," she said wearily. "This was never what I wanted."

"Oh? What did you want, then?"

"I wanted you to see reason."

Singer grunted. "Your reasons."

She laughed sadly. "Now you know how he felt; don't you, Charlie?" She slid off the stool and shuffled toward the door. Singer felt fear in his stomach. He remembered their first day as lab partners in school; the dark times when he had failed and she stood with him. He remembered how they had created Plastiphage together, and EverKleen™ and all the others. The delight of discovery. Hugging each other; jumping up and down like giddy schoolkids. He wanted to shout, *don't go!* But he didn't want to give in to her, either.

"How who felt?" he asked her.

She looked around the empty Laboratory. "Samson," she told him. "When he stood in the ruins of the temple."

Singer closed his eyes briefly. "If I'm Samson, then you must be Delilah. The woman he loved and who betrayed him."

Jessie looked at him and worked her lips. She seemed about to say something, but then changed her mind. She shook her head and opened the door. "Good-bye, Charlie," she said.

Then he was alone.

He looked about him, at the terminals and the equipment. The empty chairs. The hiss of the air conditioner sounded like the breakers on a midnight beach. And that reminded him that there was always one way out.

XII

His indecision lasted only until he heard the front door slam. Then he bolted from the Lab after her. "Jessie!" He threw back the front door and raced across the broad, grass lawn that fronted the building. When he came to the street, he stopped and looked both ways. The black clouds he had seen earlier were boiling in from the northeast, and the trees and buildings had that aetherial appearance that marked the pause before a thunder-storm. He felt the hairs on his neck rise and, somewhere far off, lightning flashed.

He saw her at the end of the block, a specter turning left on Christie Street. He sprinted after her, his heart thudding. "Wait!" The upper branches of the trees thrashed as the front moved through; and he heard the distant rumble of thunder. "Jessie, wait!"

When he reached the corner, he saw that she had stopped by the fence ringing the Edison Tower. The darkness of the storm had tripped the automatic switches and the giant lightbulb atop the Tower cast a brightness around her. She was leaning against the fence, with her fingers curled through the steel mesh. Singer caught up with her and took her by the arm.

"Jessie!"

She pulled her arm away from him. "Don't touch me."

"Jessie, I'm sorry."

She turned her face away. "Does this mean I'm not fired?"

"I can't fire you. You own twenty-five percent of my business."

She shook the fence, hard. Waves of steel rippled and rattled down the line of posts. "*Our* business, dammit! Ours, not yours. You can't make one of your stupid jokes out of this."

"All right. Ours."

"And Kalpit's and Eamonn's and Masao's. We were partners, not underlings."

"I know that, Jess. I told Royce that myself."

"But you didn't act it. Not on this project, anyway. It changed you."

"I . . . was worried. It was a very expensive project. We were on the knife edge. It was twisting me up inside." Oddly, he realized that that knot was missing now. Now that his ruin was a fact, he could deal with it.

"Is that an excuse? I'm not stupid, Charlie. I know that the Lab needed money, but that gave you no right to do the things you did. You never closed your eyes and ears before. You were always willing to listen."

"And is that your excuse?" It was an automatic riposte. He had not intended to say it; or to say it quite so bluntly. "Because you thought I wouldn't listen, you went behind my back."

"Would you have listened?"

"I—" He stopped. "I don't know." He shoved his hands in his pockets, turned, and leaned against the fence. The links pressed into his back. "I like to think I would have, in spite of everything. But that's not the point. I did what I thought I had to do. Maybe I was wrong. But you and Masao also did what you thought you had to do."

She turned her head slightly and the light from the Tower illuminated her face in profile. It shone through the curled edges of her hair, and made a diamond sparkle down the curve of her cheek. "All right," she said. "I was wrong, too. Is that what you want to hear? You were wrong and I was wrong and Masao was wrong and now everything is just pralines and cream and we can all go back to the way things were."

"Can't we?"

"Charlie, sometimes you are the stupidest man I have ever known! Do you know that you have called me by my name more times in the last five minutes than you have in the last five months?"

"What?" Singer was puzzled by the irrelevancy of the remark. There was another crack and rumble; still distant, but closer than before. A car rolled down the street and its driver looked at them curiously.

"Never mind," she said. "It doesn't matter anymore."

"Dammit, it does matter. Otherwise we wouldn't be standing here right now."

She must have heard something in his voice, because she turned at last and faced him full on. "Yes. You came after me. I . . . wondered if you would." She paused and walked a few steps away from the fence. "Charlie, I said that I could see your viewpoint. About the money. I can even empathize with it, somewhat. Why can't you make the same effort to see my viewpoint?"

He started to remind her that he had good reasons for everything he had done. But wasn't that just the problem? Everyone had good reasons for what they did. He knew he was facing the most important crisis in his life. More important, perhaps, than even that October midnight. And the issue was not money; not who owned the Lab; not even the Washer at the Ford. It was Jessie and he and their life together. She was hard to live with. She was opinionated, assertive, and just plain ornery. She had shown just recently that she did not trust him. Yet, he realized, the one thing he did not want was to lose her.

He squatted and leaned his back against the chain-link fence. "All right," he said. "Explain it to me. I'll listen. I promise."

She walked slowly to one of the big elm trees that lined the street and ran her hand over the rough bark. Charlie waited patiently. Then she looked back at him. "Do you know anything about psychology, Charlie?"

"Sure. You pay a shrink sixty NewDs an hour to do what priests once did for free. To find out that you have a fixation because of some childhood trauma."

She gave him an odd look. "Yes. To find out that very thing. But that's beside the point. I asked you about psychology, not psychiatry. Psychology deals with behavior. Observable phenomena, not mental attitudes or beliefs." She pulled a small piece of bark off the tree.

"Tell me. If we needed money as badly as you say, why didn't you rob a bank?"

"Say what?"

"Why didn't you rob a bank? That's where they keep the money."

"Don't be silly."

She slapped the trunk with her hand. "I thought you said you would listen to what I had to say."

Singer took a long, deep breath and let it out slowly. "Yeah. I did. Do I do that often?"

"Too often, for someone as liberated as you are. I'll never mistake you for a Sawyerite, but in some ways that only makes it hurt more." She paused and flipped the piece of bark into the gathering gloom. Lightning flickered and washed everything of color. Singer thought that they should get indoors.

"So, why don't you rob banks?" she insisted.

Let her make her point her own way, he decided. "Because it's wrong."

"Who says?"

"Who says? God. The Law."

"So what?"

"So they put you in jail. Or in Hell, depending on Who catches you. It's not worth taking the chance."

"Not worth taking the chance," she repeated. "That's exactly right. Every act has benefits, but it also has costs. The probability of engaging in an action is proportional to the margin of profit. Lord, Charlie. This is your favorite language! Costs, benefits, profits. You don't rob banks because the probable profit is too small."

"Dammit, Jessie. You make people sound like rational robots! They aren't. If people were rational, we wouldn't be worried—"

"Wouldn't we?"

"—and I haven't avoided a life of crime because the cost/benefit ratio is too low. I don't rob banks because it's *wrong!*"

"So. If it's wrong because God said so, then isn't the

absolute certainty of Divine Punishment part of your probable costs? Or if it's wrong because it harms the fabric of society, then isn't that part of it? The costs and benefits aren't money, but intangibles like time, energy, self-esteem, comradeship. Things that we balance in here." She thumped her breast.

"But what does all that have to do with the Washer at the Ford?" Lord, why was he using that nightmare image? Because Eamonn told a good story? Because the afternoon was dark and stormy, full of premonition? "You can't tell me there's a profit to be had in a nuclear war."

"No? How do you measure the profit to be had from the satisfaction of destroying your enemy, even if it brings the temple down around you? Blast it, Charlie, people vary. We're individuals, making individual assessments of probabilities. Who can say what looks like a reasonable chance to another person? People play slot machines, for God's sake. They buy lottery tickets. No matter where you draw the 'break-even' line there will always be some who fall on the other side of it."

Singer thought about that. "Arnie and Emily," he said.

"Who?"

"Nothing. It's just that I had the same kinds of thoughts a while back. But that was a technical issue: biophysics and system analysis."

"People are part of the system, too, Charlie. And operant conditioning is about as well founded in psychology as Mendel's laws are in genetics. There's nothing robotic about it. People generally make reasonable decisions—in the light of the data available to them. The difficulty comes in deciding what is 'reasonable.' "

"Isn't that always the difficulty?" Singer said. "Isn't that what just tore our team apart? Everybody being so damned reasonable." The whole behavioralist notion of motivation seemed simplistic to him. People were more complex than Jessie gave them credit for. Although . . . Economics was also complex, yet the cost/benefit principle was an elegant simplicity lying at its heart. That the principle was more general than economics—that, in fact, economics was a "special case"—seemed attractive. Perhaps deceptively so.

"Still," he insisted, "you're talking about probabilities, not realities. That's why I couldn't buy the argument before."

"So. How do probabilities for individuals translate into determinism for populations? If the 'profit margin' of a behaviour puts its probability at, oh . . . let's say 0.001 and there are three hundred million people in the country. Then we can predict that three hundred thousand people will choose the behaviour and fall on the other side of that line."

"Plus or minus eleven hundred or so," he said, "assuming p was the same for all strata of the statistical universe. If not, it would depend on the prior distribution of—"

"Forget the technical details, Charlie. They're not important. The point is that an unpredictable probability for an individual becomes a predictable distribution for a mass of individuals. Statistical mechanics doesn't care whether the individuals are molecules or people. Now what do you suppose happens to p if you reduce the costs of the behaviour?"

"Jessie, I'm not stupid either. More people will choose the behavior. Maybe twice as many. Maybe two in a trillion instead of one in a trillion."

"*But it must increase.* Don't you see? By reducing the perceived penalty for nuclear war, our nanny will make it just a tiny bit more likely."

The trouble was, Singer suddenly realized, was that he *did* see it. Perhaps he had always seen it. He remembered the Green picketers that he and Royce had watched at the docks. He had assumed at the time that they were protesting the garbage spill; but now he realized that they must have been protesting the nanny itself. Plastiphage reduced the penalty for dumping garbage, at least plastic garbage. It was, in that sense, a license to pollute, and the Greens were less interested in cleaning up the environment than they were in not trashing it in the first place. They wanted to change human behavior, not accomodate it.

And he had read somewhere that the spills from the Arthur Kill landfill were becoming more frequent, not less; and that efforts to control them had been reduced. He had shaken his head sadly at the time at the foolishness of New York politicians, but it had never occurred to him that the nanny itself might have encouraged a "why bother" attitude.

He looked at Jessie. Or did the argument seem so reasonable now only because he did not want to lose Jessie? When you *want* the answer, you don't question the argument. Good old Thucydides. Those Greeks were pretty smart boys. Only how could anyone know whether his own convictions arose from reason or from desire?

No, dammit. Her argument *did* make sense. What was it Eamonn had said? People were people. They reacted to the facts as they saw them, not as Singer saw them. If people were all the same, there would be no problem. But they weren't. They were a wild statistical distribution of individuals. Arnies and Emilies. Stubborn and pliable. Thoughtful and impulsive. Prometheans and Luddites.

He should have known. He should have seen it himself. How long had manufacturers been plagued with customer misuse of their products? Card tables used as stepladders. Screwdrivers used as chisels. As long as there have been manufacturers and customers. It did no good to argue that people *shouldn't* do such things. It was a foregone conclusion that some percentage of them *would*. And the courts had ruled that manufacturers were liable for any "foreseeable" misuse.

So the basis for Jessie's concerns was firmly entrenched in case law. And probably statute law as well. Section 402A of the Third Restatement of Torts, or something like that. He wondered, if the rad nanny were to lead to a nuclear war, who would be around to bring suit.

How do individuals know whether their own convictions arise from reason or desire? They couldn't. But when different people reach similar convictions, and those convictions are tested rigorously, in laboratories or courtrooms, they achieve a kind of objectivity, an inter-subjectivity. It didn't matter whether Jessie's argument was rational or not. It was real, and that was all that mattered. A scientist learns nothing if he doesn't learn to deal with reality.

"What's wrong, Charlie?"

He yanked a tuft of grass from the ground and pulled it apart. "I'm afraid you may be right."

"Afraid?"

"Certainly, afraid. The fact that you're right doesn't mean that I'm wrong. If we scuttle this project, it still means the end of the Lab. Creditors aren't impressed by noble motives." He sighed and used the fence to pull himself erect. "It's been a hell of a day, and I haven't had any sleep."

"What will you do? About the project, I mean."

He looked at her. "There's not much I can do, is there? The team is scattered. And, even if they weren't . . . I'd have to give the whole thing a serious second look." He turned and kicked at the chain-link fence. "Damn."

"You don't take failure very well, do you, Charlie?"

"Failure, is it? Was it a contest? Was one of us supposed to win?"

She shook her head. "I don't know. It doesn't feel like winning."

The storm broke then, and large raindrops pelted them with the force of small stones. Flowers of water blossomed on the concrete and asphalt. The rain came down like a waterfall and they were both drenched within seconds. There were more lightning flashes and Singer became suddenly aware of the tower and the trees around them. "Come on," he said, "we'd better run back to the Lab!"

Jessie pulled her sodden blouse away from her body.

"Why bother running?" The rain running down her hair and face made her shine, as if she were sheathed in glass.

He took her by the arm. "Because I'm not Gene Kelly," he told her; and thought that it had been quite some time since they had laughed together, even if it was only for a moment.

XIII

All right. What are you waiting for?

Singer eyed the telephone, picked it up, hesitated, then re-hooked it. *I don't know.* He rose and walked to his office door and looked out. Kalpit's terminal was dark; Eamonn's vats, empty. Overhead, he could hear Jessie's footsteps criss-crossing the apartment. The muffled thunder of the storm accentuated the emptiness. Quietly, he shut the office door.

Damnfool thing. Behavioral psychology? Why couldn't they argue over sex, like normal people? He pulled his robe together and listened to the rumble of thunder as it shook the walls. At least he was dry. Snug as a bug. He picked up his cup of steaming coffee and sipped from it.

Everybody has reasons for what they do. Everyone, in his own eyes, is reasonable. And what did that mean? When others behaved differently, then they must be unreasonable. Never mind that they might have reasons of their own.

Reasons of their own. Even when others behaved the same way, when they seemed to have the same goals, they still might have reasons of their own. He returned to his desk and, before he could change his mind again, grabbed the phone and punched in the eleven numbers and waited.

"Royce here."

"Yes, John," he pumped his voice full of hearty enthusiasm. "This is Charles Singer at the Lab. I'm glad I caught you still in."

"The work is never done."

"Isn't that the truth. Look, the reason I called. We've got a problem."

"What is it? Anything I can help with?"

"I don't know." He hesitated. As far as he knew, Royce had always played square with him. If the government man had been a son of a bitch, this would be a lot easier. Well, one more betrayal to add to his list. "Look, do you mind if I ask you a policy question?"

"That depends." Royce's voice was guarded. "I may not answer."

"Fair enough." Singer took a deep breath and put as much worldly-wise cynicism as he could into his voice. "I've been thinking. When you said the government would handle distribution of the nanomachine, you didn't mean you were going to give it to everyone in the country, did you? That wouldn't be very smart."

"Is that what you thought?" Royce sounded surprised. "Oh, no. Not at all. You can rest easy on that score. This is all *very* hush-hush. Why do you think we were so insistent on secrecy?"

Singer's knuckles stood out white where he held the phone. *What in bloody hell does the government get?* It gets to sit on the secret. "It wouldn't do to have everyone know about it," he allowed.

"Certainly not. Half the advantage of having an edge is when the other side doesn't know you have it."

"And this would be a considerable edge."

"I can see you think strategically, Charles. But, you're right. If, God forbid, nuclear weapons are ever used on the battlefield, our forces would be able to move directly through the interdicted zones. Catch the enemy flat-footed. Nuclear war isn't something any of us want to see; but as long as the possibility exists, it would be criminal—treasonous—not to seize every possible advantage. I know it's fashionable these days not to give any thought to Armageddon. To pretend as if there is no danger. But that's our job. Thinking the unthinkable, so people can go on pretending. The more of an edge we have, the safer those folks will be."

"You will stockpile them for civilian casualties, though. In all the big cities. The nannies, I mean. If there's ever an . . . an exchange—"

Royce interrupted him. "Yes, and near all the other target areas. Europe, too. Don't worry, the logistics have all been worked out. If the balloon ever does go up, we'll get your drug—" He chuckled. "I mean your device—to the people who need it. There won't be any point to secrecy after the first attack. You needn't worry about that end of it. Just get the bugs out of your bugs."

Singer looked out his office window at the empty workstations. He could see Patel and Koyanagi in his mind's eye: Masao pointing to something on the screen, Kalpit nodding vigorously. He remembered how Masao had argued with him about profits and altruism. *Are profits so important compared to the benefits this machine could bestow on humanity?* He thought of the cosmonauts and space station workers. Few of them were Americans. There'd be no nannies stockpiled for them. Royce's loyalties might extend well beyond Number One, but they did not extend farther than the nearest border.

Poor Masao. But the altruists always lost in the end. Nice guys finished last. Wasn't that the way the world worked? Words of wisdom from a baseball coach. When it came to insight, Durocher was right up there with Thucydides.

So, it looked like *Nemhain* was going to take in laundry, after all. Hell, she could set up a goddam laundromat. If a man as decent and well-intentioned as John Royce could be led astray, what hope was there for the others? For the crazed, or the ambitious? New technologies were ink blots. People saw in them what they wanted to see. Illusions. And, who could say? Maybe those who saw only an ink blot were the most deluded of all. *All right, Charlie,* he asked himself. *What can you do about it?* He would have to kill the project. No rad nanny, until humanity grows up and is ready for it. And too bad, John Royce, Masao Koyanagi, and Charles Singer. Disappointment and frustration for each. No secret weapon; no universal benefit, no profit. (Damn! He even sounded shallow to himself. No profit? At least Royce and Koyanagi had, in their own eyes, noble intentions.)

Disappointment was a bitter herb, but he could drink his hemlock and smile.

Jessie wins.

And he had only to form the thought to wonder about it. Win? Was it a game? Did everyone else have to lose? No, we all win. We banish the Washer from the Ford. *But how do I kill the project at this stage? Even if SingerLabs is dead in the water, Royce could move the project to another company.* The nanny would eventually be produced, even if they were out of the picture. *I'll have to set this up carefully.*

"Speaking of bugs, John," he said. "We've run into quite a few lately."

"Don't worry, you'll work them out. I have faith in you."

"I'm glad to hear that. But I think you should be prepared, just in case . . ."

"In case what?"

"In case the nanny may not be possible, after all."

"What do you mean, not possible? You mean in case you can't do it? We can always line up—"

"No, I mean, in case it can't be done at all. Period. Not just beyond the current state of the art, or beyond the abilities of my staff, but physically impossible. Our initial protocols didn't look too good."

"That doesn't sound right. Not after all those glowing weekly reports you've been handing in. And which I've been passing on to my bosses," he added pointedly. "Look, are you trying to send me a message? I told you, the money would become available as soon as you got rid of the Brass Jap."

And that was really going too far. "I don't send subtle messages, John. And there's no reason to be disrespectful of Dr. Koyanagi. He's a brilliant scientist. He's as responsible as anyone for bringing this project as far as it's gone. You can't hold him to blame for his government's unfortunate behavior."

For his own behavior, yes. Very much to blame. But Singer wondered to what extent he had forced Koyanagi into choosing piracy by his own rigid attitude. What if he had remained open? Would Masao and Jessie have come to him instead of working behind his back? Maybe. Maybe not. But they would have lost a rationalization for doing so.

Royce grunted. "You're right, Charles, and I apologize. It isn't fair. But we've all had to do things we've hated at one time or another."

Yes, thought Singer. *And once we have, there's no turning back.* It changes you, doing things you hate, no matter how you rationalize it or try to justify it to yourself. From his tone, Singer judged that Royce had made his own choice a long time ago. He wondered what it had been, and how the man had felt afterwards. *I guess I'll know soon enough.*

"Feelings are running pretty high against the codominium," Royce continued, "and Japanese Brazilians are getting the worst of it. What I told you earlier still goes. Twenty years from now, we and Brazil may be the closest of allies; but right now, having your friend on the staff can torpedo this whole thing. If it were just me, I wouldn't care; but the damned subcommittee is still sitting on final approval. You know what politicians are like. They follow the polls like they were rings in their noses. If only we had a leader with backbone and moral principles, like . . . Well, you didn't call to hear me gripe."

Oddly, Singer realized that Royce was asking for Singer's forgiveness. One of Royce's most disturbing traits was his wholehearted sincerity. *He's in the wrong line of work for that.* Still, it was important to realize that people who opposed you could believe sincerely in what they did. He had had his nose rubbed in that lesson. "*Absolvo te, filio meo,*" he said.

"What?"

"Nothing. I'll talk to Koyanagi tonight."

After he had hung up, Singer spent some time staring at the phone. Royce thought the nanny would give the country an edge. It probably would. But the problem with edges was that it was too easy to topple off them.

The trick was going to be to convince Royce that no radiation nanny was possible. To convince him so thoroughly that he would not try to keep the project going by shifting it to another company. Maybe he and Jessie could work out a convincing proof. Perhaps a dramatic failure. It would be for the greater good. *Greater love hath no man.* A dramatic failure? He felt a tingle move through his arms.

He sensed motion in the doorway and looked up. A rain-drenched figure stood there and his heart gave a sudden leap. A break-in? It took him a moment to recognize Masao Koyanagi. The man's clothing was sodden and wrinkled, his hair disarrayed. There was nothing left of the dandy he had known. *Drowned rat,* he thought, and immediately regretted the thought. Not a rat. Not really. Not by his own lights. Still, what he had done had hurt. A lesser betrayal than Jessie's, but a betrayal nonetheless.

Masao entered the office and slumped in Singer's visitor chair. He wouldn't meet Singer's eyes.

"Well?" said Singer. He kept his voice carefully neutral, neither hostile nor welcoming.

"I— came to return my keys." He stretched out his hand and dropped a key ring on the desk. Singer looked at the keys, but didn't touch them.

"Is that all?"

"It . . . Yes. That is all." Koyanagi started to rise and Singer grimaced.

"Oh, sit down. It's raining cats and hounds out there.

You didn't walk back through that kind of weather just to return my keys. Your keys."

"No."

"And I'm not going to let you sit there sopping wet. You're still covered by our group medical and if you catch pneumonia, I'll have to pay."

He meant it as a joke, to break the ice that had formed between them; but he saw immediately that it had gone flat. "Oh, dammit. I didn't mean that the way it sounded, Masao. Give me a second." He picked up the phone and touched the sensor that buzzed the apartment. He waited a few moments.

"Jessie? We have a guest down here who needs to dry off. Are you decent? No? Well, you don't look any worse than he does . . . Masao, that's who. Sure." He covered the mouthpiece and looked at Masao. "You know I bought several bottles of *cachaça* after you came here and you're the only one who drinks the damn stuff, so Jessie says you have to come upstairs and warm up."

Singer stood by the large front window, nursing his coffee. Across the street, the Edison Tower rose 131 feet into the sky. Singer paused and studied it. Not a very big monument, he thought, for the man who had single-handedly created the twentieth century. He wondered what Edison himself would have created if he had designed his own monument.

Probably nothing, he decided. Edison had been notoriously practical. He would have used the money to finance a new invention.

He turned and faced Masao and Jessie. They were sitting in separate chairs, trying not to look at each other. Masao was dressed in some of Singer's clothes, which did not fit him at all; and Singer wondered momentarily whether the man was as embarrassed by the baggy shirt and trousers as he was by everything else that had happened that day.

"Storm's over," Singer announced. The rain storm, at

least. He looked past them, to the far side of the room. The front room ran the full width of the apartment. At the other end, another window opened on the tops of the trees that surrounded the property. Between their waving branches he caught glimpses of the brightly burning windows of the office towers on the far side of the railroad tracks. There was an extensive office park there; a luxury hotel. *I'm still on the "wrong side of the tracks,"* he thought.

He drifted across the room to the other window and stood there, studying the lights and the silhouettes of the branches.

"Well?" said Jessie. "Isn't anyone going to say anything?" Singer turned and looked at her. "What is this, a wake?" she said.

"Yes," said Singer, and he saw her wince. *She doesn't like it any better than I do.* He twisted his hand, clenching and uncleching it, wishing for a stick of gum. "But, what the hell, it doesn't have to be a double funeral."

They both looked at him questioningly, and he scowled and added, "I'd rather bury a company than a friendship."

Koyanagi sucked in his breath. He shot from his chair and strode to Singer and embraced him. "Hey," said Singer. "I thought you people went in for polite bows."

Masao released him. "You forget, I am a Brazilian. My parents emigrated before I was born."

"Yes, I know," Singer told him, disengaging himself from the *abrço.* "I did some checking up on you a while back."

"Ah?"

"Yes. Your grandparents were killed at Nagasaki, weren't they?"

Koyanagi hesitated, then nodded. "*Sim, senhor.* They lived beyond the blast zone; but they died later, from radiation-induced cancer. I do not like to speak of it."

"That was your purpose all along, wasn't it? The radiation nanny. You didn't care about fame at all. You wanted to make it up to your grandparents by giving everyone fallout protection. The power plant and space potential was just to get me interested. You were going to pirate the design, once we'd helped you build it, and give it away for free." There was no one more ruthless, he reflected, than an altruist.

Koyanagi bowed and sucked in his breath. "I regret the miserable deception. But some needs go beyond price."

Singer swatted the air. "Don't apologize, dammit. Never apologize for doing what you think is right."

Koyanagi said, "That was why Dr. Pee— Why Jessie's arguments bothered me so. Perhaps even more so than her unfortunate actions. I wanted to protect people, and she was telling me that instead I was endangering them."

"And next to Charlie, you were my biggest obstacle."

They turned and looked at her. She was hunched over in the sofa, a thick mug of hot chocolate in her hands. She was staring into the chocolate. "You both wanted to build the nanny," she said to the room. "For different reasons, maybe, but you both wanted to build something that I saw mustn't be built." She looked at them. "I've been asking myself why I was so ready to let Masao take the blame for the sabotage."

"Oh, we're a fine crew, aren't we?" said Singer. "Let's invite John Royce over and we'll all party." He told them what Royce had planned to do.

Koyanagi sank slowly into a chair. "Classified? Top secret?"

"And what did you tell him, Charlie?" she asked.

"What do you think I told him?" he challenged her.

Koyanagi, who had been about to say something, looked back and forth and held his tongue.

Jessica parted her lips, paused, and studied him with narrowed eyes. "Yesterday, I would have said that you didn't care. That all that mattered to you was that you got paid for the job, and if the government wanted to stockpile the nanny in secret, that was their business."

Her words were like slaps, and he flinched from them. Was that really how she saw him? Did he really seem so shallow? Dammit, after all these years, she should know him better than that. Or maybe he did keep himself too close, never opening up to anyone else. *Perhaps, after all these years, I should know myself better.* He looked her in the eye. "And today?" he asked.

"Today?" She seemed unsure. "Today, I don't know."

"When I talked to Royce," Singer said, "I saw how neatly his intentions fit your argument. I mean the part about how the nanny would be used by society."

Masao sighed. "I do not want that to be so. It means the end of a dream that I have held for as long as I can remember." He clenched a fist. "Yet, my feelings on this matter are so intense and personal that I wonder if I can see the argument clearly."

"You and me both," grunted Singer. "But, if we make people radiation resistant, we reduce the penalties for wrong decisions. It's that simple. We make nuclear war just a little more thinkable."

"Just a little."

Singer grinned at Masao's irony. "Yes. It's all a matter of what one is used to, I suppose. Why twenty or thirty megadeaths should be any more thinkable than seventy or eighty, I don't know."

"Will you stop the project, then?"

There was a rumble behind them, heard faintly through the window. Singer turned and watched as a railroad train crossed his field of view. It shot from left to right, appearing in fragments between the waving branches. The rhythmic clatter of the wheels sounded far away and the brightly lit windows ran together in a blur. Sparks leapt from the overhead wires. It was an Amtrack train on its way to Philadelphia. The whistle blew and the sound floated back to them. Singer sighed.

"That's a lonely sound," he commented. "What is it about trains in the night time that sounds so damned lonely? You know, I used to lie awake nights when I was a kid, shivering and hungry in my bed, listening to them. The train whistles. It sounds melodramatic. Hell, it *was* melodramatic. I was a stereotype out of some damned Southern gothic novel. I would squeeze my eyes tight and wish for one of those trains to come and take me away from those Kentucky hills. One day, one did; and I left all that misery behind me. I left it behind," he repeated. "Maybe a part of me never realized that." He shook himself and walked slowly to the sofa. Sometimes, he thought, psychotherapy could be too damned expensive.

"It was a fool idea anyway," Singer told Koyanagi after he had sat down. "Giving it away. People just wouldn't believe you. Immunity from radiation, and a Jap is *giving* it away? Long before you'd convinced anyone you were on the level, you'd be in jail for fraud."

"But I could prove—"

"Do you think it matters what you could prove? The last headline anyone would see would be the one trumpeting your arrest. Jimmy and Jane Public saved from another quack. The truth never overtakes life."

"But, you will see the project through, Dr. Singer-sama? You will market it. You will not allow Mr. Murchadha and Dr. Peeler to dissuade you?"

Singer shook his head. "How can I finish it? Jessie and Eamonn won't help and you can't. We'd need the government money and your talents and we can't have both. And even with the government money . . . I don't know if we should."

"With their talk of increased risks?" Masao ran a hand though his hair. "I spent all day today thinking it through. Oh, not that Dr. Peeler was wrong. She wasn't, but one may be perfectly correct and still delude oneself. Wearing shoes makes people more careless where they step, but that is no reason for everyone to go barefoot."

Jessie raised her head and scowled at him. "This is a little more serious than ringworm," she said.

"She's right," said Singer.

Koyanagi made a sour face. "All this worry," he grumbled, "over such a slim chance."

Singer spread his hands. "Yes, all this trouble. But not everyone evaluates things the way we would, and wishing won't make it so. People are part of the system, and an engineer works with parts and materials as they really are, and not as he wishes they were. And, as Jessie said to me the other day, when the payoff is minus infinity, how slim of a chance will you take? Look. Suppose I make you an offer. I'll roll four dice. If the total is five or more, I'll pay you a million dollars. But if it's a four, I get to poke your eyes out with a stick."

Koyanagi blinked and his hands jerked toward his eyes. Jessie winced.

"The probability of rolling four ones is only one in 1300," said Koyanagi slowly.

"Actually, it's one in 1,296," Singer told him. "That's 1,295 chances of getting a million dollars versus only one chance of losing your eyesight. Does that mean you'll take the bet?"

The biophysicist shuddered. "No."

"That's right. Neither would I. For some things, probabilities don't matter. That's the issue I couldn't see earlier. We can't compute the rational choice. Or rather, the rational choice means foregoing the bet entirely. If you don't bet, you don't risk your eyes. You also don't get a chance at the million dollars; but you didn't have the million dollars to begin with, so you haven't really lost anything."

He sighed and pushed his hands into his pockets. "I don't like it, either, Masao. I'll probably . . . *we'll* probably lose the Lab over it. But, it's the only rational choice we have. It means foregoing the benefits, the radiation resistance; but we don't have those benefits now, so we aren't losing anything. The question is, can we scuttle the project in such a way that no one else will carry on? Remember, Royce and his committee already know what we're doing."

Koyanagi clasped his hands in from of him and looked at their faces. He seemed close to pleading. Singer hated to see people beg. "No," said Masao. "You cannot do it. I mean that literally. You *cannot* do it. We cannot 'forego the bet,' as you said. The dice will be rolled. You see, Mother Nature is a blabbermouth."

Singer felt the shock like a slap across the face. He closed his eyes tight.

"Nature keeps no secrets," Koyanagi amplified. "You may fool Mr. Royce, perhaps for quite some time; but eventually others will learn what we have learned. Royce will not need to tell anyone. I was not the only researcher studying *M. radiodurans.* Do you suppose I will be the only one to wonder at its powers?"

Thoughts tumbled chaotically in Singer's head. *The genie is dangerous,* he realized. *But he's already out of the bottle. We daren't go forward, and we cannot go back. The nanny will be built, but we mustn't build it. No way out. No solution.* There had to be a solution. His soul rebelled against the notion that there may not always be solutions.

He rose from the chair and stood by the front window again. Edison's tower. It had always inspired him before. Edison, his patron saint. Saint Thomas. Thomas the Doubter. *Unless I put my fingers in the nailholes. . . .* Singer had always thought of the apostle Thomas as the patron saint of science. The other apostles *believed,* but Thomas *knew.*

But Edison had never had to deal with this sort of problem. How could society misuse light bulbs or phonographs? He wondered if modern popular music constituted misuse of the phonograph. Motion pictures. Motion pictures had taken families out of their homes for entertainment. They had initiated the long, slow breakdown of the family, displacing the hearth as the center of people's lives.

Technological change. Social consequences. The industrial revolution had killed slavery. The home appliance had made women's lib possible. That photograph of the Earth taken from the moon . . . Would environmentalism have grown as dramatically without that galvanizing picture? He wondered if there had ever been a social change, good or bad, that was not the spin-off of technology.

Pieces began to fall into place. Fragments began to coalesce. He began to see it. Not a solution, but the way toward a solution. He turned from the window.

"We'll build it," he said.

"No!" said Jessie, and she half rose from her chair.

"Jess, if it can be done, someone will discover how to do it," he told her bluntly.

"And if someone's going to make money on it," she said bitterly, "it might as well be us?"

"Well, why not? But that's not what I meant. I meant that it will be done by people who haven't thought through the implications as thoroughly as we have. I think I see a way out. I'm not sure. I need time to reflect."

"What about Masao?" she asked. "You'll need the government's money and Masao's talents, you said. And you can't have both."

Masao pursed his lips. "Perhaps I can help secretly?"

"No," said Singer. "We can't risk having Royce find out."

Masao nodded. He walked slowly to the back window and stared at the trees. He gripped his hands behind his back, squeezing first one, then the other. Singer and Peeler watched him. After a while, he took in a long, slow breath and let it out. "I could defect," he said.

"Defect," said Singer. He looked at Jessie then at Masao's back.

Koyanagi turned. "Yes. Defect. I could make speeches, if your John Royce wishes me to. I could denounce the co-dominium. His senator may appreciate a defector even more so than a native-born American."

Singer frowned and nodded. "It may work," he said. "It just might work. We'll run it through Royce tomorrow."

Jessie looked at Masao. "You could never go back, then. After defecting and making such speeches. Can you bear that? Never to see your home again?"

Koyanagi shrugged. "I will miss São Paulo and the rain forest and Carnival. But this work comes first. Perhaps someday, when the word leaks out what we have done, I will be able to go back."

"And what about me, Charlie? And Eamonn? All you've said so far is that, if the dice will roll anyway, we might as well place our bets. But it's still an irrational bet! You were bloody well convinced yourself, Charlie. Then you flip-flopped back. What changed your mind?"

"We're going to load the dice," Singer said carefully.

A frown creased her brows and she cocked her head. "Are you going to let us in on it? Or is this more of Charlie Singer, the Lone Ranger?"

He shook his head. "Not yet, because it's not clear in my own mind yet. Besides, Eamonn and Kal should be here, too. I'm going to call a meeting tonight to discuss it. No, it's too late and there's some reading I need to do. Tomorrow. A lunch meeting." He rubbed his hands together, thinking furiously.

Koyanagi raised his eyebrows. "Load the dice?"

"Yes." Singer reviewed his plan mentally. It would scatter the team, he realized. But it was necessary. "Yes," he repeated. "We need to reformulate our aerosol."

He saw the most bewildered looks he had ever seen on a pair of human faces.

Singer cut his steak carefully into strips, listening to the strained conversation around him, but maintaining his own silence. Everyone was uneasy with everyone else. Jessie, the saboteur. Masao, the pirate. Charlie, who was ready to sell out his friend for government money. Kalpit and Eamonn, playing the roles of peacemakers. *Blessed are the peacemakers*, he thought sourly, *for they shall be mowed down in the cross-fire*. He wondered if there were any two people at the table who had not offended each other.

He speared a strip of steak on his fork and dipped it in the marinade. They didn't call it teriyaki anymore. It had a good American name now. He had forgotten what it was. *Liberty cabbage*, he thought.

They were eating in the banquet room of the Steak and Ale on Route One, the room the restaurant used for parties and meetings. He had had Patel make the reservations from a public phone booth using a phony name. He had made sure the room had no outside windows. There were microphones, he knew, that could read the vibrations of a window pane and translate them back into words. Unnecessary precautions, perhaps. There was no reason to suppose they were under surveillance. Still, it was the nature of the beast to be paranoid.

When the waitress brought deserts and coffee, Singer told her they were about to start their meeting and did not want to be interrupted. He paid the bill and added a generous tip. The waitress did some mental arithmetic and she grinned and nodded. "No interruptions," she agreed.

Burton-Peeler watched the waitress leave. "All right, Charlie," she said, turning back. "What's this all about?" She stared at him, daring him to say something she didn't like. The others waited, puzzled but uncomplaining.

"Yes," said Masao. "What is your plan?"

"Well, first off, we need an antidote—"

Koyanagi blinked. "An antidote?" The others' comments were lost in a babble. Singer shushed them.

"Next, we have to change some of the molecular structures—"

"The structures?"

"Which ones?"

"—and, of course, redesign Aire Fresh."

Now he had complete silence. They all looked at one another, then at Singer. Finally, Jessie spoke.

"All right, Charlie. It worked. You've got our attention.

Either you know something you haven't told us yet, or you've gone completely around the bend." Singer saw in her eyes that she wasn't entirely sure which it was.

He leaned forward, putting his arms on the table and clasping his hands. "Look, what is it about this project that's bothering us? Some reasonably foreseeable consequences. Especially the one that Eamonn and Jessie pointed out to us." He paused a moment before continuing. "The more I thought about it, the more I realized that every technological change is also a cultural change."

"Everyone knows that, Charlie," said his wife.

"So? Then why don't we act as if we did? It's become a cliché to talk about the social consequences of technology, yet do we really take them into consideration? I'm not talking about those circuses they hold in Washington, where some official panel takes 'testimony' from 'witnesses' so everyone can ride their favorite political hobby horses. Hell, everybody knows what the testimonies are going to be before anyone so much as opens a mouth. The so-called 'findings' are driven by ideology and the polls not toward serious extrapolation of consequences."

He paused and started to reach for his gum. Then he remembered that he had thrown it out. Bad habit, anyway. "Let me give you a small scale example," he said. "A company once decided to expand its chemical laboratory. They needed more room, and they could prove it: with layout studies and space planning and the testimony of the chemists. It was a safety issue, too. You certainly don't want chemists bumping into each other and dropping things. So what could they do?"

"Expand the laboratory," said Patel. He looked puzzled.

Singer smiled. "And that's exactly what they did. But there were social consequences. The larger lab building encroached on the parking lot, eliminating spaces. This threw more parking onto the already congested city streets. Workers had to leave for work earlier to find parking, disrupting routines at home. Who would drive the kids to school? Old car pools broke up and new ones formed; and with them, friendships. The ripples spread steadily outward. Who knows if they've damped out even today."

"How many people died, Charlie?" his wife asked sarcastically.

"Some," he answered. "Perturb the normal traffic pattern and you always get an increase in accidents." The others at the table stared at him thoughtfully. "It's all a question," he concluded, "of extending our fault tree into sociological areas; of not stopping when the technical issues have been dealt with."

"That's what I tried to do," Jessie protested. "Given human nature, it was possible to foresee how the nanny would be misused by managers and politicians."

"Yes," said Singer judiciously. "And Eamonn reached the same conclusion. You tried to broach the subject with me once or twice, didn't you?" he told her. "Looking back, I think I can see when. But you backed off when you saw that I wasn't even willing to consider the possibility. I'm sorry for that, and I apologize here and now to you and to the rest of you. This whole shindig was my fault. I didn't study my Thucydides." He saw how that remark puzzled everyone except Eamonn. "I thought that because I wanted *one* outcome of the nanny, that there weren't—that there *couldn't* be any other, less pleasant outcomes." He smiled at them to show how contrite he was.

"But!" And now he stabbed a finger at Jessie and at Eamonn. "You two were guilty of the same sin. You thought that because you could foresee a single, bad consequence, that none of the good consequences mattered." He repeated Masao's analogy with shoes and going barefoot.

Peeler shook her head. "No, Charlie. It's not the same thing, at all. As I said earlier, being more careless about where you step simply isn't in the same league with being more careless with nuclear piles or weapons."

"Yes it is," he answered, "because they both deal with

human psychology. Look, I've spent the day reading anthropology. It's pretty soft stuff. Anthropologists generally 'discover' exactly what they set out to discover—real science often takes its practitioners by surprise—but there is a core of basic principles that has been pretty well established. One is that every society has a pattern of culture—'rules of the road.' The major benefit of that pattern is its predictability. People know how they are expected to behave, whether they are bankers, burglars or revolutionaries. The underworld has its pattern of culture; so does Wall Street."

"Aye, the same one," said Murchadha.

"That's not the issue," Singer told him. "No matter what the pattern is, change—*any* change—is a threat. It breeds uncertainty. That's why people often resist changes that are clearly beneficial."

"I once told my superior at São Paulo," Koyanagi reflected, "that I had identified a simple process improvement that would save the company seven million novocruzeiros. He rejected it. He felt that having overlooked such an improvement for so many years would make him look foolish to his superiors."

"I once read of a tribe in South America," said Patel, "that was suffering from a diet deficiency. Their traditional diet was lacking in some amino acid. Or perhaps a vitamin? Well, no matter. The agronomists studied their situation and recommended they grow—I think it was soybeans. But the Indians refused and went on suffering."

"Exactly," said Singer. "I don't know the example, but I can guess why it happened. The tribe's resistance made no sense to the agronomists—the technological change was clearly beneficial. But the technological change was not the stumbling block. The cultural change was. Everyone in the tribe wanted to know, on some subconscious level, how the change would affect his place in society. Accepting the agronomists' advice would, for example, undermine the status of the elders as the local agricultural experts. And they were right, too. You can never change just one thing. Start growing soybeans, and who knows what will happen next? Revolution and anarchy." He spread his hands. "And before you go on thinking that that sort of thing only happens in primitive societies, let me give you another example that I know of, because an uncle of mine told me about it. The foundry he worked in was losing quite a few workhours to foot injuries. You lug a lot of heavy stuff around and some of it's going to get dropped on toes. So the company implemented a safety shoe program. They provided the workers with steel-reinforced boots." He paused and waited.

"Makes sense," said Murchadha cautiously.

Singer grinned. "You don't sound too sure, son."

"I'm waiting for the other shoe to drop."

Everyone moaned and Singer laughed. Some of the tension lifted and Singer made a note never to underestimate Eamonn's savvy again. "Yes," he said. "There was a catch. The boots were clearly beneficial, but the workers resisted. They wore them only under heavy supervisory pressure. Why? *Because their wives didn't like the shoes.* The shoes were heavy, unwieldy; and they marked their husbands as low-caste, blue-collar, factory workers. In my uncle's day, those were important considerations." He let his gaze circle the table. "As scientists and engineers, we have to do more than just shake our heads and say that the wives were being illogical—"

"Wait a minute," said Jessica, interrupting. "The answer is obvious. Redesign the shoe so it looks dressier."

"And that is what they did," Singer responded. "But the point is that that solution would never have occurred to anyone until the cultural root of the resistance was identified. Until then, the only response was coercion or persuasion: Wear the shoes, or else! Addressing the symptoms, not the problem. Well . . ." He shrugged. "I realized that these cultural issues are invisible to technical folks like us. We're used to dealing with systems, *but technology defines the boundaries of our systems.* All that cultural stuff is 'outside the system.' We make a proposal.

It's technically sound; it's economically viable. Yet, there's resistance, and the resistance makes no sense. A mysterious roadblock here. A pointless argument there. The old run-around everwhere. Since we don't realize that the resistance is cultural—the resisters themselves may not realize it!—we assume our opponents are simply being malicious and the whole thing turns into a urinary olympics."

Koyanagi frowned over the last phrase. Patel leaned over and whispered in his ear and the biophysicist made a face.

"So what are you trying to say, Charlie? Eamonn and I were resisting the nanny because it would affect our status in society? Don't be absurd."

"Hmm. The steel-reinforced work boot is on the other foot now, I guess."

"Don't make jokes! There's nothing funny about trying to avoid a nuclear war."

"No there isn't. But we were dealing with the symptoms, not the causes. *Why* should a nanomachine that enhances radiation resistance be destabilizing? Is refusing to build the nanny really the answer? Is it a *viable* answer? Does it really address the issue? Look, do you remember the Nuclear Winter fiasco? The net result of the TTAPS report was that it made nuclear war just a bit more likely."

Koyanagi was startled. "How so?" he asked. "I supported the position."

"So did I," said Singer. "But think. Suppose their scenario had been correct. It wasn't, but let that go for now. A potential aggressor might then be tempted to launch a pre-emptive strike *just below* the level that would trigger a Nuclear Winter. If the victim were to retaliate, it would drive the ecosphere over the edge. An aggressor might gamble that the world would accept the *fait accompli* rather than risk total destruction. Combined with a disarmament program, this scenario becomes even more destabilizing. Yes, Jessie, what is it?"

She pursed her lips and ran a finger around the rim of her water glass. "I was going to say that that scenario isn't too likely, but that was your counterargument to me, wasn't it?"

"But the TTAPS model was not correct," said Patel. "It overstated the effects. That's why we talk about Nuclear Autumn now."

"Yes. It's still a deadly scenario, worse than anything imagined before the TTAPS report. *But not worse than anything imagined* since *the TTAPS report!* The upshot of the whole contoversy was that many world leaders were left with the vague impression that a nuclear exchange was not as dangerous as some 'alarmist' scientists had thought."

"But—"

"But what, Jessie? Doesn't the same reasoning that applies to our nanny apply elsewhere? If our nanny makes nuclear war more likely, than so does the Nuclear Winter scenario."

"Oh!" That was Koyanagi. They all turned to look at him. "MAD is part of our pattern of culture." He looked at Singer, then at Burton-Peeler. "Don't you see? We resist anything that threatens the existence of Mutually Assured Destruction, *because it's what we're used to.* The cultural pattern provides predictability. We know what to expect from MAD: an uneasy peace. There has been no major power war since the invention of nuclear weapons, and both the United States and the Soviet Union have accepted defeat rather than use them in brushfire wars. We may not like what the pattern gives us, but at least we know what it is."

"Better the devil we know," said Murchadha, "than the devil we don't know."

"Yes, yes." Koyanagi was growing excited. "Change MAD and we don't know what to expect. It might be better, *but it might be worse.* That's what affects your status in society, Dr. Peeler. Status is not your personal prestige, but your relationships to everything else in your life."

"But that doesn't make my concerns less valid."

"No it doesn't," Singer agreed. "I've only suggested that we shouldn't use a double standard."

"Are you suggesting that TTAPS should have suppressed their original report?"

"No more so than that we should suppress the nanny. Certainly, there are risks involved in building this thing. Low level risks, but with catastrophic consequences. But there are also benefits. If we *don't* build the nanny, people will die."

"And as I said earlier," interjected Koyanagi, "Nature keeps no secrets. We *cannot* suppress the nanny because others will discover it independently. Think how often such duplication has happened in the history of science."

Patel spoke up. "Dr. Singer, we have two inevitable, but mutually incompatible consequences. One is that a radiation nanny *will* be built. By ourselves or by someone else. The other is that, along with its great benefits, it *will* bring some undesired consequences. In particular, a greater carelessness in nuclear matters."

Murchadha nodded. "Bullet-proof vests."

"And wishful thinking," Patel continued, "will not prevent either one from occurring."

"So what do we do?" Singer asked him.

"Cultural issues are part of the system," Koyanagi recalled. He was watching Singer carefully as he spoke. "What do we do when we identify a technological problem in the system?"

"We analyze the symptoms of the problem," Burton-Peeler told him, "diagnose the cause and effect relationships, and incorporate a preventative feature into the design. Oh, pest!" She looked at Singer. "That's what you're getting at, aren't you? How can we redesign the nanny to take the cultural effects into account?"

Singer grinned. "That's right. It's our great blind spot. Not many people in science and technology take courses in anthropology; so when we run up against a social consequence we find ourselves reduced to babbling about the symptoms. One side says the risk is so small that there's no point in worrying about it. The other side says you dassn't do anything at all, because no risk is too small. Yet, when we deal with technological issues, it's a different matter."

He reached out and took the wine list from the center of the table. It was printed on a laminated plastic card. He toyed with it as he spoke. "Al-Qaysar might be tempted to attack Iraq if his soldiers were radiation hardened. It's an edge, right? And he's got to do it quick, before Iraq gains the same edge. There's no point in attacking if you don't have, or think you have, some sort of edge. On the other hand, if Iraq learned that al-Qaysar was secretly hardening his troops—and what nation can keep secrets for long these days?—Iraq would be tempted to attack before the Iranians were ready. It's a dangerous time when one side has an edge over the other." He balanced the plastic card upright in front of him. He pulled his hands away and the card swayed and fell over. "Edges are always unstable."

"So what is the answer?" asked Patel.

Singer took the wine list again and folded it in half. "With two or more edges, you regain stability."

Koyanagi sucked in his breath and came out of his slump. Patel nodded slowly. "How do you plan to accomplish this?" he asked.

"You're going to market it everywhere, aren't you, Charlie? So everyone has it and no one has an edge. Will Royce let you get away with it?"

"No," said Koyanagi. "That will not work. Market forces result in diffusion patterns. Until penetration is complete, some groups will have it and some will not, resulting in the kind of instability Charles has mentioned." He looked at Singer. "It must reach everyone simultaneously; or, until it does, no one must know that it is diffusing."

Burton-Peeler laughed and clapped her hands together. "In the aerosol! Isn't that right, Charlie? You plan to put it in the Aire Fresh. My word, the way that is selling, the nanny will be all over the world within a year."

Singer smiled. "I thought that might work."

"No profit from it, though; unless you plan to double the price for the Aire Fresh."

Singer shook his head. "No profit," he said. "Or maybe just a little."

"What about the Lab?"

"It's like you said. We'll get by somehow. There's no such thing as defeat, you know. Not really. Except here." And he pointed to his head.

"Not everyone in the world uses Aire Fresh," Patel pointed out.

"No, but people use it everywhere in the world; and they can serve as focal points for infection."

"Infection?" Koyanagi blinked. "Then we must make it self-replicating."

"Yes. That's why I said we must redesign some of the structures."

"It will take time," cautioned Patel. "Successful self-replication is not so easy to accomplish. The nanny will be competing with millions of other proteins and viruses. Ones that have survived eons of ruthless natural selection. That is why so many genetically engineered organisms have failed to survive when released." He looked at Koyanagi, who nodded once.

"I already have some designs prepared." Masao paused, embarrassed at having reminded them of his attempted piracy.

"Nine months," Singer told them. "No more. I can't stall Royce forever."

"That will be sufficient," Masao responded, "provided there is no more sabotage." He looked at Burton-Peeler, who flushed.

"If we brainstorm this all the way through the cultural

implications," she said, "and come up with a design feature to address each pitfall, there'll be no need for sabotage. Anyway, everything will be out in the open." She turned to Singer. "That's what you meant by 'loading the dice,' isn't it?"

"But what of the possibility I spoke of?" asked Murchadha. "Not the calculated adventures of the leader with an edge, but the *carelessness* of the manager who thinks radiation no longer matters. If everyone is hardened to radiation, so that no one has an advantage, some leaders will still become more heedless of the dangers."

Singer nodded. "Like Nuclear Winter being overstated. Or like Plastiphage made polluters more heedless. Yes." He looked at the wall in irritation. "We should be in the conference room with the screen so I can write all this down."

"I have been doing so," Koyanagi said holding up a napkin filled with scribbled notes. Singer laughed.

"The engineer's proposal form," he said. He turned back to Murchadha. "That's why I want the antidote. One that causes the body to reject the radiation nanny. You see, when the UN session opens next fall, every major world leader will be there, for the keynote addresses. And if, as I suspect, there is a major odor problem with their air conditioning system, they will naturally want large quantities of Aire Fresh to fix it. And of course, we'll have some special batches stockpiled."

By now they were all laughing. "Sure," said Murchadha, " 'Tis one thing to have one's troops immune, but another thing to have no immunity yourself."

"Don't forget the various Parliaments and Congresses and General Staffs. And not every leader will be at the UN."

"And West Point and Sandhurst and other military academies. Can you see it? The grunts are immune, but their officers aren't!"

"What about the Kremlin? Even with this *glasnost* business, it won't be easy to give the KGB the antidote."

"We can make a start with their consulates."

Burton-Peeler leaned back in her chair and folded her hands across her middle. "You know we five aren't the only nano-geniuses around. Someone will figure out a way to counteract the antidote. And the antidote itself—"

"Right," said Murchadha. "You precede your attack with a bombardment of antidote bombs. That makes the enemy vulnerable to radiation again."

Koyanagi stabbed a finger at him. "But then you lose the element of surprise. An atomic attack can only work if it is a surprise attack."

"We can make the antidote slow-acting," said Patel. "Say it takes several weeks to establish itself and destroy the rad nannies already in the blood. No possibility of surprise then. The victims will know that they are being softened."

"But for now," added Murchadha, "we'll be keeping the antidote our little secret. No one will try to disable an antidote they don't realize exists. By then it should be well-established among the target population."

"I think we should be adding the owners and managers of nuclear power plants to the antidote group. To discourage them from cutting corners on maintenance and such."

"Let's not be forgetting," said Murchadha, "that there are people who don't want nuclear plants or space stations to be less dangerous. Just after that fiasco at Three Mile Island, an English professor at Dartmouth, I forget his name, wrote a newspaper column. Do ye know what his reaction was to the fact that, despite a totally unanticipated failure mode and unbelievable neglect on the part of the utility management, the engineering safeguards worked and prevented a disaster? He was actually upset that no one was killed! If only hundreds had died and Harrisburg had been evacuated, he wrote, people would realize how dangerous nuclear plants were."

Burton-Peeler snorted. "And they say technocrats are ruthless? He sounds like one of those early environmentalists who preached—what did they call it? Global Triage. Ehrlich and the two Paddocks. They claimed that countries like India and Mexico were doomed anyway, so we shouldn't waste *our* food by sending it to them. They began soft-peddling that line when they realized that even most environmentalists couldn't stomach the selfishness."

"I've got mine, buck-o," said Murchadha, "and you can't have any."

Patel only shook his head and Singer realized that Kalpit's parents were among those who would have been written off.

"And don't forget," he added, "that when Third World scientists in Mexico and the Philippines started the Green Revolution that eventually made those 'basket case' nations self-sufficient again, the same groups denounced it as 'elitist' because the bigger farmers got the most benefit. We can expect similar arguments against the nanny."

"It wasn't feeding the hungry that concerned them," said Kalpit with a touch of bitterness. "It was *how* they were fed. The Green Revolution was not Appropriate Technology."

"Aren't we getting off the topic?" asked Masao.

"No," said Jessica. "Because it's just this sort of thing we've got to deal with. We've identified some 'irrational' reactions, like the government's desire to stockpile the nanny as a military asset, which can destabilize the nuclear stand-off. But there are other non-technical spin-offs, like the Luddite callousness we've just been discussing. We need to consider how to deal with them, as well. Remember, in the context of their own belief system, the objectives of the Establishment and the Luddites are perfectly valid and sincerely held."

"Yes," said Singer, catching her eye. "That's what being 'realistic' is all about."

XIV

The airport was crowded and smelled of plastic and vinyl and jet fuel. People sat in hard rows of uncomfortable chairs and read books or talked or napped, waiting for their flight to be called. Singer paused on entering the gate area and looked around, searching for Jessie. Outside, through the huge, plate glass windows, a jetliner raced down the runway. Then it arched its back and bit the air with its wings and soared; as unlikely a bird as ever flew.

Singer watched its takeoff. Muchadha was already gone, on his way to Ireland; and Kalpit was hopscotching across the U.S. on a series of puddle jumpers. Masao would leave for Brazil, by way of Florida, Texas, and Mexico, later this morning.

He didn't see Jessie anywhere near the assigned gate and he wondered with a sudden stab of anxiety whether she had gotten the wrong gate number. He had dropped her off in front and parked the car. Now she was nowhere to be seen.

The gate area was circular, with a kiosk in the center. He began walking around the other gates. Most of them were filled as well with waiting passengers. *I hope she didn't go out the wrong concourse.* No, that was silly. Still, to check the other concourses, he would have to return to the terminal. A long walk in both directions. Why didn't airports have cross connecting tunnels between their concourses? Was it a deliberate ploy to discourage connections to other carriers? Or were airports designed by architects who never made connections themselves?

A hand tapped him on the shoulder and he jumped.

"Looking for me, Charlie?"

He turned and gazed at her, thinking how soon now she would be gone as well. She was dressed in a comfortable, loose-fitting blouse and skirt. She wore tennis shoes, which was probably why she seemed so much shorter than normal.

"I was looking for you in the seats," he said.

"No room. I stuck my carry-ons over there," she pointed vaguely across the gate area.

"Got your ticket?"

"Certainly, I have my ticket." Singer noticed her hand move toward her jacket pocket and he smiled to himself. *Of course, I have my ticket,* he thought. *I'm absolutely sure until someone asks me.*

"Don't worry," she told him. "We've been planning this for months, now."

Singer still felt uneasy. The team was dispersing. Breaking up. The Lab was dark and silent once more. "I know. It's just that . . ."

Just that what? That he would miss them all terribly? That he was scared to death that they wouldn't come back?

"Just what, Charlie?"

"Nothing. I'm just skittish, is all."

"Don't worry. Everything will be fine." She lowered her voice. "Think of how many people have already been infected just by our standing here."

"I know. Eamonn left from Kennedy and Kalpit and Masao are at LaGuardia."

Burton-Peeler smiled. "I wonder what the travel agent thought of Kal's itinerary."

"I think he's making connections at every hub airport in the country. Those that Masao doesn't hit on his way to Mexico."

"The passport people didn't give him any trouble, did they?"

"Masao? No. The reports we've been feeding Royce add up to failure. Who cares about a Brass Jap on a project that didn't pan out?" That had been the tough part, he thought. Developing a plausible scenario, consistent with the experimental evidence, that "proved" that a radiation nanny for the higher phyla was impossible. He was sure that Royce would check it with other experts, probably at General Molecule. Not because he suspected deception, but to assure himself that SingerLabs hadn't overlooked anything.

Masao had estimated one to two years before anyone figured it out. By then, the nanny and its anti-nanny would be endemic throughout most of the world. The people Royce would contact in the G/M hierarchy would be high enough that they would be unable to unravel the deception; while those with the competency to do so would be too far down in the trenches to be involved. He wondered if anyone had ever used the Peter Principle as a design parameter before. Unconsciously, perhaps. Every corporate worker he had ever known had taken the boss's stupidity into account when laying plans.

"Worried about your part, Charlie?"

"Hmm? No. I mean, yes. Who wouldn't be? Not the cocktail circuit, but the other part. The public announcement. But I wasn't thinking about that. It's almost a year away. Just things in general," he said, scuffing the floor with his shoe.

The idea of using the world's airports to spread the nanny had been Kalpit's idea. A bit of person-to-person infection. A supply of specially doped Aire Fresh, Eamonn's "industrial strength" version, installed in the air conditioning system. Airport authorities had tripped over each other for the chance to freshen the air inside their terminals, and what more natural reason for Singer's crew to hop around the globe from airport to airport than to oversee sales and installation?

They had worked out the epidemiology on the computer, developing a plan to achieve maximum spread of radiation resistance within a year and a half. The anti-nanny, they had given a six-month head start. It was already spreading through the upper classes.

Singer had been surprised to find that the two target populations barely overlapped. The world of private jets and exclusive resorts barely touched the world of workaday humans. So, while the nanny spread in the one group, the anti-nanny spread in the other. Each acted to immunize against the other. Inevitably, the two sets had fuzzy edges, but there was no help for that.

Spreading the anti-nanny had been Singer's task. It required going to country clubs and exclusive receptions. Meeting government leaders. Joining boards of directors. Hobnobbing with the rich. Singer's reputation and putative wealth—and his being the only Real American on the team—had given him entry.

Jessie brushed at her jacket. "You know, it's odd when you think about it. You were right. The firm needed profits. But I was right, too. And so was Masao when he said it didn't matter what we did because Mother Nature was a blabbermouth. And Eamonn was right. And so was Kalpit."

"Kal?"

"When he said that all we ever wanted to do was build better molecules."

"Oh." Oddly, he felt a tear in his eye. '*All we ever wanted to do* . . .' What was so sad about that phrase? The sense of lost innocence? The memories of the time before the storm? He paused, searching for the right words. "I'm just glad we found a way out of the woods on this one," he said. Those weren't really the right words, but they were easier to say.

She looked at him. "We haven't found a way out," she told him. "We never will. We live in the woods and there's always another bear. Remember, the automobile was once hailed as the solution to the air pollution problem. Do you know how many *tons* of horse manure New York used to produce in a single day?"

"Still does," Singer responded.

She laughed softly. "You've got a comeback for everything, don't you, Charlie? But the point is that the grandparents' solutions become the grandchildren's problems. There are no permanent solutions, Charlie."

"Maybe not," he said. "But at least there are temporary ones." Maybe that was all they could ever hope for.

To think things through all the way and take their best shot.

The PA system crackled something unintelligible. Singer could make out only the last part. London. Heathrow. He sighed.

"Well, Jessie. That's your flight."

"I know that."

He followed her to her carry-on bag and watched while she pulled the strap over her shoulder.

"Do you have the Aire Fresh kits?"

"Yes, Charlie. I have the Aire Fresh kits. They're going air freight. Half the airports in Europe want one, and the other half will, once the word gets around." She fiddled a little with her strap. The steward by the gate said something into the microphone and half the people in the waiting area stood. They shuffled into line, using their luggage the way a running back used an offensive tackle. Singer couldn't see what point there was in getting a few slots ahead in the line. They wouldn't slam the door shut in someone's face. "They're calling my row number," Jessie said.

"Yeah," he said. "Well. Good luck." He wanted to ask again if she had her ticket with her. They embraced briefly and she turned to walk on the plane.

Then he did find the right words. "Are you coming back?" he said, just loud enough for her to hear.

Jessie paused and looked over her shoulder. His pulse throbbed and his breathing was shallow and quick. He was afraid of her answer. Deep rifts had opened up between them; rifts that had been patched over by the work on the anti-nanny, but which remained just below the surface. They had done things to each other that neither could forget.

"I'm not sure," she said at last. "A lot has happened. I'm not sure anymore who you are. I'm not even sure who I am."

"Come back then, and I'll introduce us."

They stared at each other for a long, awkward

moment. Then Jessie sighed. "Oh, what the hell. I'm an old lady, too old to change my ways; and I'm used to having you around." She hefted the shoulder bag again and turned and walked down the jetway.

He watched her until she turned the corner and was out of sight. Used to having him around. Singer decided that that was the most tepid declaration of love he had ever heard. Maybe it wasn't much, but it was something. How did the old saying have it? You like "because"; you love "despite." With all his faults, with all her faults, neither of them were willing to give up on the other. Maybe it was pride, not love. Maybe neither of them liked to admit defeat. And maybe, he thought, not giving up was what love was all about.

"Please, Dr. Singer. You must come out. It's deadly in there."

Singer did not look up from his book. Slowly his mind returned to the present. The plant manager was a fool. Didn't he realize that Singer knew quite well how deadly it was? More to the point, didn't he realize how many rads Singer had already absorbed?

Probably not, he decided. Surely, like most in the upper echelons, the plant manager was financially trained, neither a biophysicist nor nuclear engineer. He no doubt knew everything there was to know about nuclear power plants except what was important.

"Entry to the containment building is for authorized personnel only!"

Singer didn't bother to answer that one either. If the lack of proper authorization had not stopped Singer from entering the containment, why on Earth should the man think it would persuade him to leave?

"You are trespassing! I'll have you in court, celebrity or no celebrity!"

That meant nothing either. Before this was over, he'd have a lot more than trespassing to answer for. *We must have violated every regulation in the books*. Sweat rolled down his brow and he mopped it with his handkerchief. Waste heat from the nanomachines in his blood. Either that or he was nervous as hell.

Probably both, he decided.

"Mr. Davis," he said, addressing the plant manager. "Have the media arrived yet?"

"They have. Someone tipped them off." Davis peered suspiciously, at Singer, at the engineer, at the tour group.

"Invite them in, then, if you please. I have an announcement to make." He saw two of the biologists in the tour group look at each other. One of them was making notations in a pocket notebook. The engineer was watching him with hard, appraising eyes. Estimating rads, thought Singer. He knows.

"I will not invite them in. This is a power plant, not a circus for ghouls. I will not have my operations disrupted."

"Mr. Davis, you are shut down for a PM. There are no operations to disrupt."

Singer gave him his best stubborn look and, after a few moments, Davis wilted. "Very well." He strode to the red wall phone and spoke into it.

Singer grinned at the two biologists and pulled a pair of sunglasses from his pocket and put them on. The biologists grinned back. The engineer shook his head, whether from pity or admiration Singer did not know.

All the while a little voice in the back of his head kept up a running commentary. There were limits to the nanny. Limits to the radiation level and exposure time. Kalpit and Masao had calculated how long he could stay in here. But what if they had made an error? Everyone had checked the calculations several times. He had checked them himself. Still, what if there had been an error?

Why then I'm already dead, he told the little voice, *and it doesn't matter at all*.

And that shut the voice up very nicely.

° ° °

The news people spent a considerable amount of time setting up and jockeying for position. Singer watched them, wondering what customs they used to settle issues of status. *I've got to explain everything to them.* The benefits. The limitations. The dangers. Especially that of increased carelessness. Everything but the antidote. Let them think that some people are immune to the nanny. Someone will figure it out sooner or later, but by then everyone should be used to the nanny. *It will be part of the cultural pattern and we'll have learned how to live with it.*

He was surprised to see John Royce file in with the reporters. Royce stood toward the back of the crowd, with his arms folded across his chest. His face gave no hint as to what he was thinking. He could be waiting to arrest Singer when he finally came out. Or he could have realized himself that this was the best way. Best for the country.

Finally, the reporters sorted themselves out. They stood with their tape decks and microcams aimed at him. One or two glanced nervously at their dosimeters.

Singer stood and put his Heinlein back in his jacket pocket. He brushed himself off and stood in front of the viewing window. He smiled at them.

"I've got some good news and some bad news."

Interlude

Pavel Denisovitch d'Abreu dismissed the class and they floated out, one by one, bowing to him as they passed by. Pavel detached another pouch from his belt and unzipped it. The applicator head was shaped like a paint brush, and he spread the disassemblers across the top of the lectern with a few broad strokes. It would take a few minutes for the podium to be reduced to its original agar paste. He hovered in space beside it, contemplating the process.

He always liked ending the first day's lecture with the story of SingerLabs and the Radiation Nanny. It was good story. Upbeat, as the Americans used to say. Without the rad nanny—Singer's Flu, they called it—life in the L4 and L5 complexes would be impossible. As it was, Pavel Denisovitch could remember fleeing to the storm cellar only once in his life, during the Great Flare of '93.

And yet, the tale held a cautionary note. Every silver cloud has a dark lining. And it was important to study both. Pollyanna and Gloomy Boris were both wrong in the end, because the real world was never quite so unambiguous. Singer had become quite good at what he liked to call "spin-off engineering." Too bad that he . . . well, there was no point dwelling on *that* tale. It was not one to be shared with first form students, anyway. No, they needed positive stories on which to focus. Perhaps Murchadha and the Molybdenum Settling Pond, or how Singer-Labs had revolutionized clay sculpture.

Ah, those were the great days, full of a sense of wonder, with new discoveries coming almost daily. Singer had saved his laboratory from the creditors' jaws—thank the gods for toxic waste dumps—and had gone on to other successes.

Perhaps on to too much success, because after Singer's death . . .

Pavel Denisovitch shook his head. Almost involuntarily he keyed his implant and downloaded the files on Henry Norris Carter. If Singer had still been around, things might have turned out differently. Certainly, the Lab would have remained a small research group. But that was not fair, either. Burton-Peeler had had her own vision, and who was to say that hers was less valid? And Murchadha had made an outstanding general manager. Still, in a larger organization things can sometimes fall into the cracks.

All you need is love, the poet once said.

Is that really *all* you need?

3. Remember'd Kisses

Click.

A mechanical sound. A relay, perhaps. A flip-flop switch or maybe a butterfly valve. Very soft. Almost muffled.

Sigh.

And that was hydraulics. Escape gas bleeding off. Pressure relief. Again, a muted sound, not particularly obtrusive.

Click.

It was a metronome. A syncopation. If you focused all your attention on it, it could become—

Sigh.

—quite relaxing. Hypnotic even. It would be easy to lose oneself in its rhythm.

Click.

The sudden hand on his shoulder made him start.

"Mr. Carter?"

Sigh.

He turned, unwilling; guided by the gentle but persistent pressure of the hand on his shoulder. His vision rotated, camera-like. Away from the equipment; along the tubing, hanging in catenary loops; past the blinking monitors; toward the sight that he had been avoiding ever since he had stepped into the room.

Click.

"Yes, Doctor?" His voice was listless, uninterested. He heard it as if he were a spectator at a very bad play.

"We did all we could, Mr. Carter. The medics stabilized her as soon as the police cut her out of the car. But I'm afraid there was little else they could do."

Sigh.

He looked at the doctor, turning his head quickly, so that the bed itself flicked across his vision without registering. But his subconscious saw the subliminal afterimage and began sending messages of pain and fear.

Click.

"I understand, Doctor . . ." He glanced at the name tag pinned to the white uniform, trying not to notice the little splashes of red on the sleeves and on the chest. "I understand, Dr. Lapointe. I'm sure you did everything possible."

"If we had gotten to her sooner, or if the trauma had been less severe, we might have been able to repair the damage. There have been incredible advances in tissue repair nanomachines in the last several years . . ." *Sigh.*

Henry Norris Carter wondered if the doctor thought he was being comforting. *Tell me more*, he thought. *Tell me all the different ways you might have saved her. If only. If only this advance had been made; if only that had been done sooner. If only. If only.*

Well, take it as he meant it. "Yes, Dr. Lapointe, but I'm sure you understand that such speculations cannot make me feel any better about what's happened." (And a part of his mind curled up and gibbered, *Nothing's happened! Nothing's happened!*) "I'm quite aware of the advances in nanotechnology. My wife and I both work—" He suddenly realized he had used the present tense and stopped, confused. "No, worked—" But that wasn't right, either. Not yet. "I mean we were both genetic engineers at SingerLabs over in New Jersey. We both donated DNA to the cell library there. As long as we're talking 'if only's,' if only I had had her cell samples with me—"

"No, Mr. Carter, you mustn't think that. As I said, the trauma was too severe. Even the most advanced nanomachines are still too slow to have saved your wife before irreversible brain damage set in."

So. Finally. He forced himself to look directly at the figure on the bed. The maze of tubing crawled snake-like around it. Encircling it; binding it; piercing it. Up nose. Down throat. Into vein and groin. Pushing the fluids and the gasses in and sucking them out, because the body itself had given up the task. The click/sigh of the respirator faded into the background.

The contours of the sheet were not quite right, as if parts of what was under it were missing. The doctors, he supposed, had cobbled the body back together as best they could, but their hearts hadn't been entirely in it. The whole left side of her face was an ugly purple bruise. And the symmetry of her nose and cheekbones and jaw was irretrievably lost. The right eye was closed, as if sleeping, and the left— The left eye was hidden under a mass of bandages. If it was there at all. Judging by the extent of the damage on that side, it was doubtful that the eye had remained in its socket.

He wanted to scream and his stomach gave a queer flip-flop and his knees felt suddenly weak. He trembled all over. Don't think about that. Think about anything else. Think about—

Quiet evenings at home. She, reading her favorite Tennyson in a circle of soft light cast by the goose-neck lamp; while he pretended to read, but watched her secretly over the lip of his book and she knew he was watching her and was waiting for just the right moment to—

Running through the rainstorm down 82nd Street from the Met, his trenchcoat an umbrella over both their heads. Laughing because it was so silly to get caught unprepared like that and they were soaked to the skin already and—

Hiking the Appalachian Trail where it lost itself in the granite mountains of New England and stopping to examine the wildflowers by the edge of the path and wondering why on Earth the stems would always branch in just exactly that way and—

Four-wheeling over Red Cone that summer in Colorado and how he had frozen at the wheel because all he could see out either side of the Bronco was sky because the road ran up a ridge only a little wider than the car itself and how could anyone expect to drive over a knob of rock that steep? And how the sign on the other side, by Montezuma, had said dangerous road travel at your own risk and wasn't that a hell of a place to put it and—

Her eyes had been a most lovely shade of hazel.

"Pardon me?"

Henry looked at the doctor and blinked away the memories that had blurred his vision. "I said her eyes were hazel."

"Oh."

He turned and looked again at his wife. The doctor seemed at a loss for what to say, and for a crazy instant Henry felt sorry for him. The doctor wanted to say something, anything to pierce Henry's shell of misery, but there was nothing that anyone could ever say or do that would make the slightest particle of difference in how he felt.

He felt . . . nothing. He was numb. He refused to accept what he saw.

"Barbara."

"She can't hear you. She's far too deep in coma for that."

He ignored the doctor's comment. It was patently absurd. Voices made sound waves; and soundwaves vibrated eardrums; and eardrums made nerve impulses; and somewhere, somewhere deep inside that dying body there had to be a tiny, glimmering spark, wondering why everything was growing so much dimmer and fainter, and he would be damned before he would let that spark flicker out all alone in silence.

He drifted toward the bed; and the doctor, sensing his intention, guided him toward her relatively uninjured right side. The doctor lifted the sheet, exposing her hand, and Carter took it in both of his. He noticed the mole on her right side, just above the curve of the hip, and touched it briefly with his forefinger.

"The other driver," the doctor said, "the one who ran

the red light, was killed instantly. An eighteen-year-old kid and dead drunk. Now he's just dead."

Henry shook his head. Did the doctor think that that thought would comfort him? He felt a brief regret that the drunk hadn't suffered, and a second regret that he would wish such a thing of anyone, and then he felt nothing once more.

"Barbry, I'm here. I came as soon as they called." He stroked her hand gently, fingertips on palm, and let his palm run under her limp fingertips; and was embarrassed to notice how his body, for a brief instant, responded to the remembered touch.

He began telling her about his day, because there wasn't much of anything else he could think of to talk about. (And why had she taken the day off to shop for his birthday? They should have been together in the Lab, safe. Instead—)

Instead, he told her how he and Bill Canazetti had finally made some progress on the Barnsleyformer; because the trick wasn't in the morphogenesis after all, but in the fractal geometry of the genes. They had gotten a brief, tantalizing glimpse of a simple and elegant recursion formula and would have continued to work on it well after quitting time except the phone call had come from the hospital and—

And the traffic at the tunnel ramp had been terrible. Backed up all the way around halfway to the turnpike gate. Wasn't it always that way when you were in a hurry?

At any rate, he told her, Dolph Kavin was doing a slow burn because he'd been passed over for project leader on the cloning team. Old Lady Peeler had picked Amanda Jacobs and Dolph had complained bitterly to anyone who would listen (and there weren't that many) how women always stuck together; but you know how it is with office politics. And he said it was probably a lot different in the old days before Singer had died and the Lab was run on a more personal level.

And—

"She's gone, Mr. Carter."

He jerked for the second time at the unexpected touch; and looked from the hand tentatively laid on his wrist, up the arm to the doctor's sympathetic face.

"What?"

"She's gone. All brain activity has ceased. I—" He broke off, looked uncomfortable, mustered his resolve. "If you would sign a few forms, please. Many of her organs can still be saved, if we act quickly." The doctor looked at him in mute appeal. *Your wife is dead*, his eyes seemed to say; *but we can still save others if you help*.

Others.

Strangers.

And why should he care about strangers?

Donate organs. A nice way of saying, let's cut up your wife's body into little chunks and sew them into other people. Intellectually, he and Barbara had always supported the organ donor movement, but it was different when the actual time came. And what the hell did it matter? Barbry didn't live there anymore.

"Yes," he said, and his voice came out in a sort of croak. "Yes," he repeated. "Go ahead. It's what she would have wanted."

"You're doing the right thing." the doctor assured him. "Your wife may be dead, but part of her will go on living through others."

Click.

The most awful thing about the whole business, Henry decided as he rose shakily from the chair, was the way the respirator continued to pump air and the way in which the sheets continued to rise and fall. As if the person beneath them had only fallen into a deep slumber and would awaken when the morning came.

Sigh.

Of course, they insisted that he stay and rest. They gave him a mild sedative and they made him lie down for an hour or so. He closed his eyes, but his mind wouldn't shut down. It kept spinning and spinning, trying to find a way out of accepting what had happened. When he arose only a short while later, he was unrested and unrefreshed.

It was the early morning pre-dawn hours when he left Roosevelt Hospital and made his way down Ninth Avenue toward the Lincoln Tunnel entrances. There was a mist off the Hudson that gave the West Side a ghostly and unreal appearance. Sounds echoed as if on a damp and abandoned stage set. His was the only car on Ninth Avenue, and in the distance a single pair of headlights drifted crosstown. If New York was the City That Never Slept, during these hours it at least dozed fitfully.

Some part of him had taken over from the gibbering, helpless personality crouching in the back of his head. It was a part of him that felt nothing and thought nothing. It was an automaton that made his body do all the right things, like some faithful robot dutifully carrying home its injured master.

The neighborhood north of the tunnel ramps had once been called Hell's Kitchen; but the new yuppy-fied City was a little ashamed of its rough-necked, blue-collar past, so they called it Chelsea North now. They could call it what they damn well pleased, but some things never change. It was still Hell's Kitchen, and if the police no longer walked the beat in squads of five as they once did, it was because they seldom left their patrol cars.

If Henry had been entirely himself, he would never have made the wrong turn. But automatons do make mistakes and the sign with the arrow pointing toward the tunnel was placed ambiguously. He meant to turn right at the *next* corner, but his eyes saw the sign and his hands spun the wheel, and there he was.

He realized his error almost immediately. He cursed for a moment or two and checked the street sign at the next intersection to get his bearings. He turned, and turned again, and then he saw her.

The streetlight was a stage spot highlighting a tableau. Brown, ratted hair hanging low around familiar eyes and nose, her body wrapped in a tattered pea jacket and huddled over a heating grate, hugging a tattered shopping bag to her. Three men—two black, one white—loomed over her, laughing, giving her little shoves, while her eyes darted like mice eyes back and forth, looking for escape.

"Barbry!"

Henry hit the brakes, twisted and grabbed the jack handle from the floor in the back. He burst from the car. "You! You, there! Leave that woman alone!"

The men laughed and turned on him, and the laughter died. If Henry had been entirely himself, they would have pounced without a thought, like any wolfpack. But he was not entirely himself, and he had a jack handle in his hand, and there was something in his eyes. A flame. They used to call it the berserker look. It was the look that said that, whatever came, life or death, he would accept it gladly.

The three liked long odds in their favor. Three strong young males against a lone woman, that was acceptable. But against a crazy man with the berserker look? No. You couldn't win against a man who didn't give a damn. They might walk out of it; but maybe not all three, and certainly not all whole. So they sought the better part and walked away, throwing obscene words and gestures after them to show they hadn't been afraid after all, not really.

Henry walked to the woman on the grate and took her by the hands and raised her to her feet. She looked at him with fear in her eyes.

"Barbry?"

And she didn't really look like Barbara at all; and that broke the spell. Henry blinked and his surroundings came crashing down around him. Hell's Kitchen? My God! How had he gotten here? He could remember nothing since lying down at the hospital. And who was this woman?

She looked like— But, no. Her hair was brown, like Barbara's, but it was a shade darker. The face had the same shape; but the cheekbones sat lower. And there was a scar that ran from under the right eye, across the cheek toward the ear. She stank: of sweat and booze and excrement. Whoever it was, it wasn't Barbara. And why on Earth would he ever have thought that?

"Who are you?" he asked.

She didn't answer and tried to pull her hands from his. Henry remembered leaping from the car, and looked around with sudden alarm. Those three punks might come back any moment. He began to shake as he realized what he had done.

He turned back to his car, remembered the woman, and hesitated. He couldn't just drive off and leave her here. If those punks came back, she'd be worse off than if he had never stopped.

"Come on," he said. "Get in the car."

She looked at him doubtfully and backed away a step, holding her shopping bag like Hector's shield. Henry pulled open the passenger's door. "Get in," he repeated. "They might come back."

That seemed to get through to her. She glanced down the street in the direction her tormentors had gone, then looked back at Henry's town car. Her tongue swept out and around her lips. She looked at him again. Then she made up her mind and darted into the safety of the automobile.

Henry slammed the door, ran around to the driver's side, and slid behind the wheel. He hit the door lock and all four doors snapped at once. The sound startled the woman who jerked around anxiously. She tried the door and it wouldn't open; so she slid across the seat from him as far as she could go, putting her bag between them and clutching it to her.

He took her with him back to Short Hills because he didn't know what else to do, and it was easier to make no decisions than to decide anything. Once home, he hustled her inside his house, glancing over his shoulder while he did so, to see if—despite the hour—any of the neighbors were watching.

In the kitchen, she pulled away from him and ran to the farthest corner and crouched there, making small sounds in her throat. Henry wondered how much human being was left imprisoned within her skull. There but for the grace of God . . . Barbry and this bag lady looked enough alike to be taken for sisters if not for twins; yet, Barbry had lived here, in comfort just short of luxury, while this woman had lived on a heating vent in Hell's Kitchen. How easily it might have happened the other way. What trauma might have been enough?

"Now that I've got you," Henry told the woman, "what do I do with you?"

She seemed to shrink within herself, and Henry held out what he meant to be placating hands. "Don't worry. I won't hurt you. If you want, you can have a shower and a meal. And a change of clothes." The thought of giving this woman one of Barbry's dresses was distressing. He wasn't ready to part with anything of hers, not yet. But there was a trunk in the attic, with some cast-offs that she had meant to donate to charity anyway.

He took the bag lady by the hand, noticing as he did so the track of needlemarks up the inside of her arm, and showed her the shower in the bathroom. He gave her a washrag and towels and one of Barbara's old housecoats and told her to leave her dirty clothing for disposal. The woman glared at him suspiciously, so he shrugged and walked away.

In the kitchen, he opened a can of beef broth into a pot and turned on the heat. Something not too taxing for her system. As the odor filled the room he realized he was hungry, too, and he added a second can to the pot. After it had come to a boil, he reduced the heat to simmer and walked to the kitchen window.

The kitchen faced on a woods protected by "greenbelt" legislation from development. No danger of ticky-tacky working class homes depressing the property values. The canopy of the trees looked like a silhouette cut from black construction paper, the false dawn providing an eerie backlighting.

He still didn't know her name. He had asked twice on the drive back, but she had remained silent, staring at him with ferret eyes, and he began to wonder if she even realized what was happening to her. Probably not much intelligence left. Etched away by years on the streets and a constant drip-drip-drip of heroin on the brain cells. Odd, how much—and how little—she looked like Bar— Like Barb—

He squeezed his eyes shut and willed himself not to think of her. The sound of her voice. A wisp of perfume. Remembered kisses.

After a while, he realized that he couldn't hear the shower running upstairs. What was that bag lady doing?

When he checked the bathroom she wasn't there, so he searched from room to room until he found her. She was hiding in the closet in the guest bedroom. She had taken the few odd garments hanging there and made a sort of nest of them. The wire hangers swung and tinkled like Japanese wind chimes. She looked at him with those ferret eyes; expecting anything, surprised at nothing.

Somewhere, she had found an old bag of salted peanuts. A relic of some airline flight Henry had long forgotten. She had poured the nuts into her palm and was gnawing at them. When she saw Henry at the closet door, she clutched the foil bag to her, as if she expected him to try to take it away.

Eventually, she did eat. Not the peanut bag, but the soup Henry had prepared. She wolfed it in great greedy gulps, her left arm encircling the bowl, and her right wielding the soup spoon like a shovel. She kept her eye fixed warily on him the whole time, except when she darted quick looks around her, like an animal guarding its prey.

When she was done he took the bowl, which she released only reluctantly; and this time when he led her to the shower she seemed to understand. She grabbed the towels from his hands and stared at them. Then she stared at him.

"Go on," he said gruffly. "You shower now. I'll go up to the attic and see if I can find some old clothes for you."

When he returned from the attic with an armful of clothing, Henry found the woman in the library, sitting in Barbry's favorite reading chair. Showered and scrubbed, she seemed like a different person. Certainly, she smelled different: fresh and clean. From the rear, in the soft light and wearing Barbry's bathrobe, she looked enough like Barbara to make Henry's heart freeze for a moment. The dresses fell from his arms and he braced himself against the back of his own reading chair.

And the illusion vanished. All he saw was a bag lady holding the portrait photograph that Barbara and he had had taken only eight months before.

"That was my wife," he said, and she jumped a little and turned and looked at him. Her eyes were childlike. Green, he saw, and not hazel. They didn't look at all like the suspicious ferret eyes he had seen earlier. "My wife, Barbara," he explained, pointing to the photo. "She was, she was killed today in an automobile accident."

There. He had said it out loud. Now it was true. All of a sudden, he couldn't look at the photograph. The bag lady looked from the portrait to him and back to the portrait. Then she stroked Barbara's face gently. She nodded her head up and down in a slow cadence and made a low keening sound. Henry dropped into his chair, crushing the dresses he had laid there. He covered his face with his hands and a time went by.

When he looked up again, he saw that the woman had gone to the mirror by the bookshelves and was staring at her own face. She was holding the photograph in her right hand so she could see both herself and Barbara side-by-side. With her left, she held the front of the housecoat gathered together.

"Yes, you do look a little like her," Henry said. "Not much, but that's what made me stop there on the street. I—" He suddenly realized he had as much as said he wouldn't have stopped otherwise.

But the bag lady seemed not to have noticed, or, if noticed, not to have cared. "I'm Sadie," she said, and Henry jerked his head in surprise at hearing her speak. "Sadie the Lady. That's me." She said it in a kind of sing-song voice. She returned her attention to the study of herself and the photograph.

Henry stood up and walked behind her so he could see the two faces from the same angle. "Yes. You know, if you did your hair up the same way, you would look even more like her." Barbry had always worn her hair piled up.

Sadie the Lady smiled, showing an incisor missing on the upper right. She put the photograph down and reached with both her hands to gather her hair into a rough approximation of Barbara's. She primped for the mirror, turning this way and that. Henry, watching her reflection, blushed. He should have known she would need new underwear, too.

The tableau in the cemetery seemed unreal. As if he were watching it from far away. Voices buzzed. Puppet figures stood about. He felt things only as if through layers of cotton. People he knew kept coming up to him and gripping his arm and telling him how sorry they were. He couldn't understand why they were so sorry, but he smiled and said everything was going to be all right.

Bill Canazetti, his lab partner, told him it was all right to cry. That he shouldn't hold it in. But Henry just shook his head. Later he would do that for Her. Just now, he couldn't.

There was a preacher. Barbara had been a churchgoer, High Church, and Henry had sometimes gone with Her. He wished now he had gone more often. It was a portion of Her life that he could no longer share.

The preacher— (Priest, he supposed. There was a difference.) The priest spoke of comforting impossibilities. Eternal life. The immortal soul. Barbara had gone to a better world. She had left behind this vale of tears. Henry listened. He wanted to believe it. He tried to believe it. It was better to believe such things than to believe that there was no Barbara at all, anywhere. Death was the Great Proselytizer.

"Most of all," the man in the funny collar said to the assembled group, "Barbara lives on in the hearts and minds of those of us who knew and loved her. We carry some piece of her with us always. . . ."

Now, that was certainly true. At least, since he had donated Her organs. There were no doubt several people already who carried a piece of Her with them. And there was the DNA sample at the lab. Under proper conditions it should last nearly forever. Immortality of a sort, though he doubted that that was what the priest had meant.

Henry decided that, if Barbry did live somehow in his memories, the first thing he should do when he got home was to record those memories on tape. Everything about Her. That way he could never forget.

He had kept Her clothes and other things. He couldn't bear to part with them just yet. They were memories, too, in a way; he wasn't quite ready to cast them out. In fact (and it would shame him if it ever got out), he slept at night with one of Her slips tucked beneath his pillow.

And then there was Sadie the Lady.

Henry had talked her into staying. He didn't know why. He had put her up in the guest bedroom and let her wear Barbara's old things. Suspicious at first, she had gradually loosened up. She spoke now, at least once or twice a day; and had wandered off to her closet nest only once. She was still hoarding food, Henry discovered, in several caches around the house, which Henry left undisturbed. It seemed . . . right that she should be in the house.

The worst part had been the heroin withdrawal. Henry hadn't believed that such agony was possible. Sadie had moaned and sweated and begged him to find her connection. But her connection was in Manhattan and Henry had not allowed her out of the house, despite her pleading, her tears, and her threats. At times, he had to restrain her, physically; and found that, for her condition, she was surprisingly strong. Together, they had finally weathered the crisis; and when it was over they were both drained.

Afterwards she had begun to show more interest in herself. She bathed more regularly, and brushed and combed her hair. She became a kind of housekeeper, doing odd chores around the house. Cleaning. Cooking his meals. Sometimes mumbling to herself. Once or twice saying a few words out loud. Perhaps it was gratitude. Her way of repaying him for what he had done for her that night on the streets. Or perhaps she was trying to help him through his bereavement. Henry didn't know.

Sometimes when he saw Sadie in the hall or in the kitchen, Henry squinted his eyes and pretended to himself that she was actually Barbara. The mental novocaine was wearing off and Henry was starting to feel the pain of Barbara's loss. His little game with Sadie helped numb the pain, at least for a little while. It was a harmless bit of self-deception.

And it was only a game, of course. He knew when he did it that he was only pretending.

It was two weeks before he returned to work.

No one else was in the Lab yet. Henry had come to work early on purpose. His cubicle was at the far end of the common room, farthest from the door, and he hadn't wanted to face the others, to run the gauntlet of their pity. Not right away. He had wanted some time alone, with Barbara, in the cell library.

She really was there, in a way. The culture dish contained all the information that was Barbara. Everything, that is, except the experiences and memories that had made Her a *person* rather than an organism. He told Her how much he missed Her, but mostly he was just silent, remembering things. Then he noticed the time and slipped hastily out of the cell library before anyone could see him there. People wouldn't understand and might think him a little odd.

He returned to his cubicle and looked around vaguely, as if he were in a strange country. He fiddled with the clutter on his desk and wondered how far Bill had gotten on their project. Bill hadn't been idle, he was sure. The guy was a certified workaholic. The two of them worked well together. The tortoise and the hare. Bill was a great one for leaping ahead in flashes of intuition, while Henry was the plodder who filled in the details and proved whether Bill's gut feeling was something more than what he had eaten for breakfast.

Well, he couldn't sit here all day looking like a zombie. Lord knows what the others would read into that. He activated the terminal screen and began studying the log book. Minutes went by.

"Henry!"

He turned and saw his partner, Bill Canazetti shrugging out of his jacket. Was it 0800 already? Canazetti laid a hand on Henry's shoulders, a heavy hand that was supposed to be reassuring. "I was so sorry to hear about Barbara," he murmured. "We all were. She was the best."

Henry took a deep breath. He had been dreading this ritual all morning. Everyone would feel obligated to say something to him. Something to remind him of what he only wanted to forget. The fact that most of them had already done so at the funeral wouldn't stop them. Perhaps it satisfied some inner need; a need to participate in another's grief. Certainly, it did nothing for Henry except pick at the psychic scab. But he could face their awful sympathy now. He really could.

"Never mind that," he told Canazetti, more gruffly than he had intended. Bill looked hurt, so he added, "It's over with. And besides, Barbry's not really gone. She's still with me. Now it's time to get on with life."

"Yes, I suppose." Canazetti looked uncomfortable. "Is there—well, anything I can get you?" He was like all the others: eager to help where no help was possible.

"A cup of decaf would be nice," Henry told him. "I do need to catch up on our project. Let me just read the notes here, and then you can fill me in on the details."

Canazetti nodded slowly. "All right." He left and Henry immersed himself in the notes on the Barnsleyformer.

He and Bill had been trying to improve SingerLabs' line of cell repair nanomachines. To achieve the elusive goal of whole body repair.

C/R nannies had changed the face of medicine over the last ten years, ever since Singer had created the first one. Repairing damage to tissues was easy now. All the doctor had to do was inject a dose of microscopic machines into the affected tissue. The nannies would visit each cell, compare it to the blueprints stored in the nucleus, disassemble any proteins not to spec, and reassemble them properly.

The problem was that, if multiple trauma was involved, only one tissue at a time could be treated. Each nanny was designed specifically for a certain tissue; and, if two nannies were introduced into the body at the same time, each would perceive the other as a foreign body and engage in a war of mutual extermination.

The information load was the limiting factor. The nannies were controlled by microscopic processors, dubbed Big NIM, that compared DNA strands in triplicate and directed the myriads of C/R machines. But even a single tissue complex involved an incredible amount of data. As Carl Sagan might have put it: "Billions and Billions of Bits." There were hundreds of different proteins:

enzymes and hormones. There were mitochondria, granules, and countless other cellular structures; each with a detailed set of "drawings" that described what it should look like. The limit seemed to be one tissue per nanny. Whole body repair seemed out of reach. There was just too much data to store and process. Big NIM always ran out of memory, no matter how much they stretched its capacity.

Bill and he had been ready to quit at one point. They had gone to see Old Lady Peeler to tell her it was impossible. There was a natural barrier, they had said, like the speed of light. Information bits must be carried on matter-energy "markers," and that set a lower limit on the scale for information processors. The machine could not be smaller than its information content. So, there was no way nano-scale processors could ever handle the data load for an entire organism, at least for an organism at the human level of complexity.

Dr. Peeler had listened to them in silence. Then she stared thoughtfully into the distance, working her lips. Finally, she had shaken her head and muttered, as if to herself, "I wonder how genes manage to do it."

And of course she was right.

Genes were natural nanomachines; yet they managed to build an entire complex organism from a single, undifferentiated cell. Morphogenesis, the biologists called it. The "unfolding" of structure from simplicity. Somehow, a zygote managed to contain all the information needed to grow a complete adult.

And that was a paradox.

Because the genes really weren't big enough to handle the information load. There just wasn't room for a complete set of elaborate blueprints in such a small space. Yet there had to be. Finally, in frustration, Henry had blurted out, "Maybe there aren't any blueprints at all!"

And that had reminded Bill of something. A dimly recalled oddity of the early 1980s. Michael Barnsley, an early chaotist, had discovered that random inputs to certain recursion formulas always generated the same precise shape. Take a simple random process, like tossing a coin, and define a positioning rule for each outcome. If the coin lands "heads," move a specified distance and direction from the current position. If "tails," a different distance and direction. Then start somewhere—anywhere!—on a grid and flip a coin. After the first fifty moves or so, start marking the positions where your random process takes you. Eventually, the recorded points will accumulate into a definite shape—the "limit shape." Iterate the process thousands of times. The limit shape is always the same, regardless of the actual sequence of coin tosses.

Somehow, the end result was encoded in the formula itself, irrespective of the input. It was like a magical machine that always produced the same product, no matter what raw material it was fed.

One set of Barnsley's recursion formulas generated a drawing of a fern leaf. The same leaf appeared every time he ran the simulation, regardless of the particular random inputs. That led him to suggest that the genes contained information, not on how the leaf was shaped, but on how to run the recursion formulas. With that information in hand, random chance took care of all the rest.

Many biologists, and even some other chaos scientists, had objected. There is no room for randomness in biology, they had argued. In biology, randomness is death.

Which was true, but they had missed the point. Randomness was built into the universe. The physicists had shown long ago that randomness underlay all phenomena. It impinged constantly upon biological growth and evolution. Yet, individuals within a species always matured into the same basic shape. Sometimes, two people, unrelated to each other, even wore the same face. And species living in similar ecological niches evolved into similar forms. There had been sabre-tooth cats in Pleistocene North America. There had been sabre-tooth marsupial "cats" in Pleistocene South America. Everywhere the same shapes asserted themselves. The stems of a flower species always branched precisely so. Every flower.

Once again, science had shown that there were always simple answers to complex questions. Barnsley's algorithm was a transformer. Like an electrical transformer, it changed one thing into another. In this case, it transformed random causes into deterministic results. Bill had dubbed the mechanism a Barnsleyformer, but Henry had his own private name.

He called it the Template of God.

Thus far, their work on that fatal Thursday, two weeks ago. Bill and he had learned how recursion formulas generated structure, but they had been stuck on the inverse process. Generating the structure from the formulas was one thing. Deducing the recursion formulas from the structure was more difficult. Now Henry saw that Canazetti had found a promising solution, and he followed the reasoning closely in the log. Bill had decided that the recursion formulas worked the way they did because certain features of the generated structures were "fractal." That is, they were invariant under changes of magnitude. He had developed a technique he called "tyling," in which the structure was tyled with smaller and smaller replicates of itself. In this way he was able to create inductively the generating equations.

"The trick," he said in Henry's ear, "was getting the number of dimensions right."

Canazetti's unexpected voice made him jerk and he looked around over his shoulder.

"Sorry," said Canazetti, handing him his coffee.

Henry frowned and sipped the brew. He grimaced and looked at the cup. It was as bad as he remembered. He set it aside. "Dimensions," he prompted.

"Right." Canazetti pulled out his desk chair and rolled it under his backside. "A coin toss gives you a Barnsleyformer with up to two dimensions, a plane. But how many do we actually need?"

"Three," Henry replied. But he suspected he was wrong. Otherwise, why would Bill have asked him?

"Wrong." Canazetti shook his head emphatically. "And, once again, the physicists have been there ahead of us. Damned mechanics. Every time a bio-scientist rolls over a new rock, he finds a physicist underneath it. No, Henry, there are actually eleven dimensions." Henry looked skeptical, and Canazetti shrugged. "Take my word for it." He held up his fingers. "Three gross spatial dimensions," he said, counting them off. "Length, height, and breadth. Seven quantum hypo-dimensions rolled up in what they call subspace. And . . ." He had run out of fingers and he looked blankly at his hands for a moment before shrugging. "And time. I've logged the references in there." He pointed at the disc drive.

Henry decided he would review the literature later. It sounded bizarre to him, but then, most of modern physics did. "Then Barnsleyformers must generate biological structure in all eleven dimensions," he murmured. "I'll be damned. The morphogenesis must be incredibly more complex that we thought. No wonder our three dimensional models— Hey, wait a minute!" His head shot up.

"What?"

"*All* the dimensions? Including time? That can't be."

"Oh? Why not?"

"Because the time dimension of an organism is its lifespan. How can the gene know ahead of time how long the organism will live?"

Canazetti shrugged again. "I don't know. It's a hunch. Did you ever read Heinlein's story, 'Lifeline'? I suspect that the time dimension of the structure only specifies endogenous death. You know, from internal causes, like old age or birth defects. Exogenous death comes from outside the organism. Accidents, like being hit with a virus or an automo—" He cut off abruptly and looked embarrassed. "Sorry."

Henry was more upset by Canazetti's circumspection than by any reference to Barbara's death; but he kept his silence. What did happen to the morphogenetic pattern when death came from the outside? Eleven dimensions. Might not some part of the pattern survive the truncation, at least for a while longer. At least until the original time span was reached? The Egyptians had believed something of the sort. That the spirit lived on—but only for a while—somewhere beyond our normal senses. There were, after all, those seven other dimensions Canazetti had mentioned. Subspace. Might the "soul" live there?

A thought began to form in the back of his head. Something nebulous and disturbing, that made his chest tremble inside. He ignored it. "Have you begun *in vivo* experimentation?" he asked.

"Just last week. I reprogrammed a scyphozoan cell-repair machine with recursion formulas tyled from its own DNA."

"A jellyfish?"

Canazetti waved his hand the way only an Italian could. "I wanted something simple enough for a first try, but complex enough to be interesting."

"And?"

Canazetti reached past Henry and pressed a few buttons on the computer terminal. A damaged molecular chain appeared on the screen. A phosphorus group was missing entirely and several carbon rings were broken. "These are the scans recorded through the digital microscope," he told him. "Watch."

Something crawled across the molecules. It looked to Henry like a slime mold, or like tarnish growing at high speed across a set of copper Tinkertoys. The colloidal agar for the cell repair nanomachines. After a few moments, it faded and the molecules underneath reappeared. Henry whistled.

"Like brand new," he said. "And fast."

Fast. What if it had been available two weeks ago?

Would it have been fast enough? Henry refused to let himself think about that.

"Yeah." Canazetti's voice was less than ecstatic and Henry looked a question at him. Canazetti waved his hand in frustrated loops. "There're still a couple of stumbling blocks," he admitted. "For one thing, if you program the nanny with the DNA of one jellyfish, it doesn't work so well on other jellyfish."

"How so?"

"Well, every jellyfish carries the basic 'I-am-a-jellyfish' information, but it also carries information that individualizes it: 'I-am-Joe-the-jellyfish.' So, if you use it on a different individual, the nanny tries to restructure it as well as repair it."

Canazetti called up another visual on the terminal. "The jellyfish on the left," he said, "was repaired with nannies grown from the DNA of the one on the right."

Henry inspected the two cell diagrams. "How close is the match?"

"Eighty-seven percent."

"Nearly complete." Henry's own voice sounded far away. He could hear the rush of his blood in his ears. He felt light-headed. Nearly complete.

"Only if the donor and recipient are the same species," said Canazetti's voice. "Otherwise it doesn't work at all. Rejection sets in. Even within a species, I suppose the greater the initial similarity, the better it would work. That's just a hunch. But it doesn't help the doctors any. We want to repair cells, not rearrange them."

Henry tapped the screen with a fingernail. "Then why not clone the nannies from the patient's own cells; tailor them individually for each patient?

"That would be fine, except for stumbling block number two. It takes time to tyle the material and to deduce the recursion equations. Remember, there are eleven dimensions to consider. And then it takes more time to grow the nannies. What's the patient doing in the meantime?" *Dying, obviously. We could have saved her, if only— If only— If only—*

Henry felt faint. He sagged in his chair and Canazetti's hairy Italian arms reached out and braced him.

"Easy there. Are you all right?"

"Yes," Henry told him after a moment. He rubbed his face with his hand. "Yes, I'm all right."

"Easy there. Are you all right?"

"Yes," Sadie told him after a moment. She rubbed her face with her hand. "Yes, I'm all right."

"You don't look all right."

It was Friday evening and he was seated at the kitchen table, eating the late supper that Sadie had prepared for him. Setting the pot back on the stove, she had staggered and slumped, almost spilling the pot. Henry wiped his lips with his napkin and pushed himself from the table. He went to Sadie and took her by the arm. He felt her forehead.

"You look flushed. Why don't you go upstairs and lie down. I'll bring you some medicine."

"No. 'M a burden, me. Too good to ol' Sadie. Time t' move on."

"Nonsense. You go upstairs. You've been working too hard these last two months. Maybe you've picked up a flu bug, or something."

He watched her leave and waited for her footsteps to die away. Then he went to his briefcase on the table in the hallway and opened it.

The zip-locked baggie lay on top of everything else. He picked it up and held it. There were three gelatin capsules inside. One was a specific against the flu bug that Sadie had. The other two— He began to open the bag but found that his hands were shaking too badly to break the seal. He set it down and leaned with both his hands on the table. He closed his eyes and breathed several long slow breaths. "*. . . the nanny tries to restructure as well as repair.*"

She's only a bag lady, after all; and an addict. It's for her own good. *"I suppose the greater the initial similarity, the better it would work . . ."*

She'll just find her way back to the streets again. I can't baby sit her forever. She'll find her connection again. An addict's need never really dies. *". . . the time variable only specifies endogenous death. . . . Exogenous death comes from outside the organism. . . . There are eleven dimensions to consider."*

And what kind of life was it, living from a shopping bag on a heating grate? She'll be much happier.

When he felt calmer, he picked the bag up and pulled it open. He poured the three capsules into his hand. He looked at them and rolled them back and forth in his palm. They felt cold and heavy, like stones; but he knew that was only his imagination.

Before he could think about it, he turned and climbed the stairs, two at a time. He stopped in the washroom and filled a glass of water and took it with him to the guestroom.

Sadie the Lady was lying in the bed. She hadn't bothered to take her clothes off. She seldom did. Henry still had to remind her to bathe about once a week. She was propped up on the pillows, but her eyes were closed and her breathing was shallow.

"Sadie?" he asked. She had to be conscious to swallow pills.

The bag lady opened her eyes and mumbled something incoherent.

"It's only an autumn cold," he told her. "Here. Take these." He thrust his hand out. The capsules seemed to have grown warmer. They were like small coals in his palm. "Take them," he said again. And his voice trembled.

Sadie reached out her arm and Henry saw the tracks of the needlemarks lining the inside. Small red circles. Craters left from years of meteoric bombardment. "Here.

Take these pills." And the words came more easily this time; the capsules had ceased to burn his skin.

She plucked them from his outstretched hand and placed them one at a time in her mouth, following each one with a swallow of water. Her throat worked and they went down. She gave him back the glass. "T'anks."

The glass rattled when he set it on the end table. He waited. The minutes dragged out. Sadie's breath came more and more slowly, until finally a light snore told Henry that she was asleep.

For a few minutes he stood there, clenching and unclenching his hands. Finally, he nerved himself and reached down and lifted her in his arms. He was surprised to discover how light she was.

He carried her to the master bedroom and laid her down on Barbara's side of the bed. He pulled off her shoes, and adjusted the sheets around her. Then he went to the stereo in the wall unit and fumbled a cassette into the tape deck. He hit "Play."

The voice that issued from the speakers was his own. He turned the volume down low, so the words were barely audible. The speakers whispered. Memories of Barbara. Her family; her history; how they had met; her life with him. Henry listened for a few minutes, but after a while he couldn't take any more, so he tip-toed out of the bedroom and eased the door shut. Behind him, memories played into sleeping ears.

The next morning, he began calling her "Barbry."

The first couple times earned him curious glances, but the bag lady seemed just to shrug it off. She seemed to accept everything he did with an odd mixture of blank fatalism and a pathetic eagerness to please. Henry dug out the old photo albums and spent all day Saturday showing the pictures to her. This is Barbry when She was six. This is the house She grew up in; and those are Her parents. Sadie nodded and grinned her gap-tooth grin. Once, passing a photograph back and forth, their hands touched and Henry was caught between a sudden desire to clasp her hand and an equally sudden desire to pull away.

She studied the pictures carefully, holding them close to her eyes, squinting, as if something had gone wrong with her vision. As if her eyes were not what they had been the previous night.

Henry peered at her face. Did it already look a little different? Were the cheekbones a little higher? The hair a little lighter? The scar a little fainter?

Or his imagination a little wilder?

A human body was more complex than a jellyfish's, and the process should take a good deal longer. But Bill Canazetti's tyling algorithm was wonderfully simple; growing a Barnsleyformer from Barbara's DNA had taken more time than brilliance. For three weeks, Henry had remained at work, after the others had gone for the day. Bill had given him some quizzical stares over the extra hours but seemed to assume that Henry was using the work as a way of dealing with his grief.

And, in a way, of course, he was right.

Henry thought he had covered his tracks pretty thoroughly. The recorded weights of the specimens in the cell library would still tally. All the reagents and other supplies were properly accounted for. There was nothing out of place that they could trace to him. Not even the flu virus. Certainly not Barbara's cell samples.

"You must have loved her very much."

He emerged, startled, from his reverie. Sadie the Lady was holding out at a snapshot. It was a picture of him and Barbara, taken during their vacation in the Rockies. There they stood, his arm around Her waist; both of them smiling foolishly, waving to the stranger who had held their camera. They were posing in front of their rented Bronco on the old railroad trestle on the Corona Pass Road. Behind them, the Devil's Slide fell a thousand feet into the forest below. Barbry was pointing back toward the Needle's Eye Tunnel that they had just negotiated. A frozen moment of happiness.

Henry remembered every detail of that day. The bite of the insects. The sawtooth sound of their chirping. How the sun had beat down on them, and how, despite that, it had been chillingly cold at the summit. Corona Pass was not a real road, but the remains of a narrow-gauge railroad bed that switchbacked up the sheer side of a mountain. It was one-lane wide, which made for interesting decisions when upslope and downslope traffic met. The Needle's Eye, a hole pierced through solid rock, had once been closed for several years by a rockslide, and the trestle over the Devil's Slide did not inspire great confidence, despite its solid timbers. The ruins of the old train depot lay astride the Continental Divide, and Barbry and he had found a secluded spot off the nature trail there, and had necked up a storm as if they had been teenagers.

"Yes. Very much," he said. "I miss her." More than anything else in the world, he wanted her back. "I love you very much, Barbry." And he looked Sadie straight in the eye when he said that.

Fear danced in her eyes, and then something else. "I lo—"

The snapshot flicked from her fingers and floated like an autumn leaf to the carpet. Sadie's left cheek twitched and she stood and trembled like a fawn. "Don't feel good," she said.

Henry caught her before she fell and carried her back to the bedroom. "You're still sick, Barbry," he told her. *(Yes, her hair was definitely lighter now.)* He laid her down on the bed. "Rest up. Everything will be all right in a little while. A couple of days, at the most."

The cheek was twitching constantly now. It tugged at the nose and the corners of the mouth and eyes. Henry could swear he saw the cheekbone beneath it *flow.* He pulled a chair up next to the bed and sat there rubbing first one hand then the other.

Sadie began to pant, short gasps, bitten off. Her eyes bulged and sweat rolled off her forehead staining the pillowcase. She arched her back and her eyes rolled up in her head. Her hands clenched into fists that twisted and wrung the sheets. A scream trickled through her tightened throat.

Henry saw a tremendous spasm run through her right thigh muscle. It jerked once, twice, three times. Then Sadie collapsed, her mouth hanging slack and her fingers curling and uncurling. Her breathing became long and shallow, as if she had just finished a long race.

Henry could not move. *The nanny will try to restructure as well as repair.* But, dear Lord, he had never imagined that it would *hurt. How long will this go on?* he wondered. He bit into his knuckles and drew blood.

Her breathing began to quicken again, rasping like a saw through pine, and Henry saw the tension build in her muscles. It was like childbirth, almost. Worse than childbirth. She began moaning and the moaning increased in pitch and tempo and would have ended in a scream except her jaw was so tightly clamped that nothing but a whine escaped. Her whole body jerked this time and she rolled halfway onto her side. *I can't take this,* Henry thought, and he pushed himself from the chair to go.

But her eyes snapped open and pinned him there, like a butterfly to a board. She spoke; and the timbre of the voice was more than Sadie, but not quite Barbara, and there was pain and hurt in it. "What are you doing to me?" she cried. And she spoke again; and again there was pain and hurt, but of a different kind. "*Why* are you doing this to me?"

The scream, when it finally came, was Henry's.

For the next three days, Henry avoided the room except to bring meals, which she did not touch; and painkiller, which she did; and to reset and play the tapes that he had made. Through the door, he would hear cries; cries that were weeping as often as they were screaming.

They were muffled and Henry knew that that was because she would thrust her face into the pillows to stifle the sound of it.

Barbara had been like that. She hated to cry and always tried to hide it.

He did not linger when he heard the crying, but fled instead to the quiet of the kitchen and, once, to the solitude of the greenbelt behind the house.

He got no sleep that weekend and when Monday came, he called in sick. Bill Canazetti took the call and Henry wanted to tell him that Barbry wasn't feeling well so he was staying home to take care of her. But he said nothing, because Bill might not have understood.

Or perhaps, he might have understood too well.

Late Monday afternoon a hammering sound brought him running up the stairs. He burst into the room and found Barbara/Sadie banging her head against the headboard of the bed. She would lean forward and then throw her head back hard against the carved wood. There were dark stains there.

His heart dropped like a stone. He bounded to her side and wrapped his arms around her to hold her back. "What are you doing?" he cried.

She grabbed her head in both her hands. "Make it stop!" she sobbed. "It hurts so much! Please make it stop!"

The brain, he thought. *The nannies have reached the brain and are restructuring it to look more like Barbara's brain.* Synapses and neurons were being rewired. Network configuration was changing. *It shouldn't hurt,* he told himself. *It wasn't supposed to hurt.* He held on to her more tightly, and she buried her face in his shoulder, making small, animal sounds.

And what will happen now? Wasn't memory stored in the arrangement of synapses? In the network? No one really knew. No one understood how the brain worked. And there were always those seven "ghost" dimensions in Barbara's DNA.

He tried giving her headache medicine, but that didn't seem to work; so he tried a sedative and that at least stopped the whimpering, although in her sleep she continued to moan and toss.

And then, after a very long while, it was Tuesday. . . .

He was in the kitchen, drinking breakfast. Bourbon, neat. An anaesthetic to dull his own pain. He had not showered nor changed his clothes since Friday and they were stained at the collar, at the armpits, at the small of the back, in the crotch; and smelled of sweat and fear. Four days of stubble had made sandpaper of his face. His eyes were rimmed with red. He had not slept since Sunday.

A footstep in the hall.

He jerked his head up. She stood there, unsteady, leaning against the doorpost from the hallway, her jeans and blouse as filthy and disarrayed as his. More so, since she had been unable to visit the bathroom during her ordeal. Her hair, dirty from sweat and oil, was ratted and tangled. It was as if she had never left the heating grate in Hell's Kitchen.

He put his shot glass down so hard that the amber liquid splashed onto his hand. He half-rose from his chair. "Barbara?"

She stared at him vacantly. After a few moments, she shook her head. "No, I— Henry?"

He stood and walked around the table to her. "You've had a bad accident," he told her. "Amnesia."

As he got closer to her he began to see more clearly that she was not quite Barbara. The facial scar was gone, but a faint line remained. The missing incisor was still missing. There were other, more subtle differences, but differences that thirteen years of marriage had made plain.

He took her hands in his but stopped short of embracing her.

"How do you feel."

"Bad as you look," she replied. "I—" A pause. A grimace. "Twinges, time to time." Her face tightened and she looked at him hard. "Y'gimme somethin', dincha? Some kinda pill."

"It was medicine. You were sick."

"I never been sick."

Henry swallowed. "Yes, you were. Five years ago. We took you to St. Barnabas. Don't you remember?"

She pulled her hands away. "Don't! Yer crazy, you." She turned, took one step, and stopped. Three heartbeats went by; then she looked back over her right shoulder. "Bright pastels," she said. "The room was painted in bright pastels. The TV set was broken and you made them replace it."

"Yes."

"No!" She put her hands to her head. "Never happened. I'se in Rochester, me. Five years 'go I'se'n Rochester!" Her hands dropped slowly. "I think I was. I—" She began to cry. " 'M confused. So confused. Henry? Help me."

He led her back upstairs to the shower and gave her Barbry's favorite baby doll pajamas. While she washed up, he stripped the bedsheets and replaced them with fresh linens. He took the soiled sheets to the laundry in the basement, but he remembered in time not to start the load while the shower was running.

While he waited for the water to stop, he gradually became aware of his own condition. He rubbed a hand over the stubble on his jaw and caught a good whiff of his own odor. *I need a shower, too,* he thought. *And a shave.*

The shower felt good, and it relaxed him to the point where his lost sleep caught up with him. He decided to take a nap, so he wrapped himself in a towel and went to the master bedroom to find a pair of pajamas.

And Sadie was in the bed, asleep.

Henry stopped short and wondered why that should

surprise him. After all, he had been putting her there himself. But, this was the first time she had gone there on her own. She had finished showering and then come to this bed, as if it were the most natural thing in the world.

His mouth twitched and he tiptoed to his dresser, where he reached around the bottom drawer for a pair of pajamas. Her breathing behind him was soft and regular. Relaxed, even; although a slight nasal blockage made a clicking sound whenever she breathed in.

He straightened and turned and looked at her. She was lying atop the sheets, her back to him. The rust-colored camisole top had ridden up to reveal her matching panties and a small, dark mole on the lower right side of her back.

He stared at the mole for a long time. He knew that mole. Even in the dark, he could have pointed to its exact location. It was not possible for two people to have that same mole.

He dropped the pajamas, and the towel, and crept gently into the bed. When he put his arms around her from the back, he felt her stiffen; but he stroked her gently, along the flank, and up and down the back—with a light touch, the way She always liked it—and, after a little while she relaxed and began making contented sounds in her throat.

Gradually, his hand widened its area of search. Up. Around. Here. There. Her breathing quickened and she twisted to face him. Her eyes were still closed, as if she were still asleep, but her mouth sought his and they embraced.

A quiet and desperate urgency followed, with quickly breathed assurances of love and pleasure. The baby dolls joined his towel.

"Barbry," he said. "Oh, Barbry."

And she stiffened again, but only for a moment. "Oh, Henry. I've missed you."

* * *

In the morning, he and Barbry lay contendedly side-by-side. The remnants of some bad dream nibbled at the edges of his mind, but he could not remember what it was. Something terrible. Something too distressing to be borne. He felt like a swimmer who had been sucked under by a sinking ship; who had kicked desperately toward the shining surface above until, lungs bursting, he had broken through into the cool, pure air.

Everything was going to be all right now.

Barbry was still asleep and Henry watched her silently for a while, admiring the smoothness of her body, the peacefulness of her face, the way her breasts rose and fell. He kept thinking that there was something he was supposed to do for her. Something important that he had forgotten. Well, it would come to him.

He eased out of bed and put his housecoat on. Then he slipped out of the room to the kitchen, where he made breakfast for the two of them. He felt like he was on his honeymoon; but that was ridiculous. Barbry and he had been married for donkey's years. He put the breakfasts on a tray and carried them back to the bedroom.

Barbry was awake when he entered, just beginning to get out of bed. She saw he was bringing her breakfast and laughed. "Breakfast in bed? Oh, Henry. No one ever done that for me." She put herself back under the covers, sitting up against the pillows.

Henry knew that the accident had given her partial amnesia, so he didn't make an issue of how often they had done this in the past. He opened the legs of the tray and set it across her, then he crawled in next to her.

She explored her breakfast with her fork. "What's this?" she asked.

"Poached eggs. Just the way you like them."

"Just the way— Course. Forgot."

While they ate, Henry noticed her giving him sidelong glances out of the corners of her eyes. She was watching him. Waiting for him, to do what? Henry took a bite of his toast and chewed. When he glanced back at her, he noticed a tear had worked its way down the side of her right cheek.

"Barbry! What's wrong? Why are you crying?"

"Nothing." She shook her head. "Nothing. Someone's died, is all."

"Died?" An unaccountable shiver ran through him. "Who?"

She looked at him and he saw there were tears in both her eyes. Tiny tears. She seemed more wistful than bereaved. She shook her head again. "No one you ever knew," she said. "No one you ever knew."

She was in the library, sitting in her chair, but with her legs pulled up under her. She had a book open and she was reading it intently. A frown creased her brows and her lips moved silently as she followed the words across the page. He came up behind her and leaned on the back of the chair.

"What are you reading?" he asked.

"The poems of Tennyson," she replied. "Tennyson was h— Tennyson is my favorite poet, but I don't remember any of his poems."

He rubbed her shoulders with his hands. "It was a bad accident," he told her. "It will take a long time to remember everything. The doctors didn't have much hope for you, you know. But we showed them, didn't we?"

She twisted and looked at him. She patted his hand. "Yes, we showed them. You'll play the tapes for me again tonight, won't you, dear?"

"Of course."

"Good. Meanwhile . . ." She turned back and reopened her book. She found her place and ran her finger down the page. "This poem. Could you explain what it means? It's called 'Tears, Idle Tears.' I'll read it to you."

She hefted the book and cleared her throat. Then she began to recite:

"Dear as remember'd kisses after death,
And sweet as those by hopeless fancy feign'd
On lips that are for others; deep as love,
Deep as first love, and wild with all regret;
O Death in Life, the days that are no more."

He felt it rise in his throat. A feeling of intense longing and loneliness. There was no question about it. The old Brit knew how to string words together. But why should those words affect him so?

He felt the tears warm his cheeks. He tried to excuse himself to Barbry, but no words came out, only uncontrollable sobbing. It was embarrassing. He was crying like a baby. He had not cried like this since . . . Since . . .

There was something that was supposed to have made him cry like this, but he had forgotten what it was. Forgotten when it was. Forgotten everything, except that he was supposed to have cried; and that now the crying may have come too late.

Bill Canazetti fidgetted nervously by the front door, waiting for . . . her to get his coat. Dinner had been uncomfortable. A mostly silent affair, broken only by the tink of glasses and silverware. Afterwards, a few awkward sallies into conversation. Then he had made his excuses to leave.

She brought his coat to him and helped him into it. "Now, be sure to button up, Bill. It chilly outside. The leaves are all off the trees. It's a lot colder here than where we used to live. It's too bad we don't get together more often."

"It's a long trip to Morristown," he agreed. He only wanted to leave. To get away from this place. To forget everything he had seen.

When he looked at his hostess, he saw Barbara Carter, smiling, waiting. He had always kissed her when leaving their house. A quick pass across the lips and a murmured quip about her husband finding out. It was a little game they had played between themselves, but there was no way this woman would know about it. Henry's theories about the seven hidden dimensions holding a person's soul and memories were just so much nonsense. Weren't they?

He put his hand on the doorknob and twisted. The chill autumn air swirled in around him. He hesitated. He had to know.

"Barbara," he said, turning around. "Tell me one thing." He searched her eyes. "*Are* you Barbara?"

Changes chased themselves across her eyes. Surprise. Curiosity. Wonder. Perhaps, wistfulness. "Most of the time," she said. "More and more nowadays."

"But—"

"But am I really her?" She laughed and shook her head. "No. I'm just an old junkie bag lady, me. He gave me something. A nano . . ."

"Nanomachine."

"Yes, thank you. A nanomachine. It rebuilt my body. It rewired my brain. I remember Sadie; but it's faint, like an old dream. And I remember some other things. Things that happened to Barbry. They're faint, too. Did they come from the tapes? Or from somewhere else? I don't know. And there are other odd memories. Things that never happened at all, either to Barbry or Sadie."

Canazetti's throat felt tight. "Sadie's memories patched onto different circuits. They're hallucinatory, those memories."

"Maybe. Still, I know who I am. Most of the time, anyway."

"Then why do you do it? Why do you stay with him and pretend? I've done some experimental work. With frogs. The nerves. When they change. It—" He didn't know how to put it. "It must have been painful," he said, not looking at her.

"Yes. Yes, it was. Very painful. But Henry saw me through it."

He turned to her. "He might have killed you," he

blurted out. "He didn't know enough to try it. We *still* don't know enough to try it. Dammit, he had no right to do what he did to you!"

"Bill, do you know what my life was like before he rescued me?"

He shook his head.

"How can I explain it? I can go to sleep and not be afraid that I'll freeze to death before morning, or that some kids will set me on fire just for the hell of it. And my new body, it's healthy. It doesn't need snow or crack like my old body did. And I can see and understand so much that I couldn't before, because my brain has been detoxed."

Canazetti looked past her shoulder, down the hallway, into the kitchen where he saw Henry carrying dinner dishes to the sink. He was humming to himself.

"Do you love him, then?"

"Yes. Both of us do."

His head jerked and he looked at her.

"When I'm Barbry," she explained, "I love him for Barbry's sake. But Sadie loved him, too. Because he had saved her life. Because he took care of her. He's given her more than she ever dared to dream about. Except for one thing."

Canazetti's voice was choked. "What's that?"

"He never told Sadie that he loved her. He never could see Sadie."

"Damn him!"

"No, don't say that."

"But, what he did to you. What he put you through. The selfishness."

"He couldn't love anyone else. He loved Her. He wasn't rational. What would you have done in his place?"

"I feel responsible, you know. It was my invention."

She put a hand on his arm. "Don't blame yourself for that, Bill. He would have tried something, even without your nano. I don't know. Brainwashing, maybe."

"I just can't help thinking that he did something wicked. A crime. And he should be punished."

She turned and watched Henry through the kitchen doorway while he rinsed the dishes and put them in the dishwasher. He noticed them watching him and grinned and waved.

"He is being punished," she said. "The cruelest punishment of all. He thinks he's happy."

Interlude

Pavel Denisovitch shut off his datalink with a clench of his jaw, and the pseudo-memories evaporated like a badly remembered dream. As always, the story of Henry Norris Carter left him profoundly troubled. There was no doubt in his mind that Carter had behaved badly; that the man's obsession had driven him quite mad, and that he had treated Sadie the Lady as no more than clay to be shaped nearer his heart's desire.

And yet, it was equally inarguable that without Carter's intervention, Sadie would have died a long, lingering, worthless death. Certainly, Sadie herself thought so. To her dying day, she had played the part of Barbara Carter to perfection. Even after Henry had predeceased her. Perhaps, in some sense, she really became Barbara Carter, as completely as poor, mad Henry had ever wished.

And does not every husband, wife, teacher, guru, reformer aspire to the same goal? Do we not—in one way or another—seek to mold others to our own ideas of who they should be?

And so, the moral knot of Henry Carter defied untangling, at least in Denisovitch's mind. Which was why he could sever the datalink and forget whenever he wished it. And why he found himself downloading the files again and again. Unwilling to remember, unable to forget.

* * *

Earthview Module was a popular spot for lovers and strangers and the pensively lonely. The huge diamond window was calculated to frame the blue planet and its white skull cap in precisely the right proportions. The Golden Ratio. For most of the spaceborn, generations removed from the home ground, the sight was nothing more than one of insufferable beauty. For a few, the sentimental, the romantic, it was the New Mecca, the great Jerusalem. For both it was a source of *yoin,* of emotional resonance; as the reverberations of a well-cast bell that continue long after it has been struck.

The carrels were attached to a structure known, for reasons lost to history, as the Jungle Gym. It reminded Denisovitch of the great gossamer bushes that grew in Hydro Town. The branching struts and tubes filled the room, blossoming at their tips into chairs and tables. Groundside rooms of this sort, Denisovitch knew, could arrange tables and chairs only in a single plane, wasting most of the volume. Denisovitch leapt and swung from branch to branch until he floated into a vacant carrel facing the viewport.

The bar server brought him his vodka without being asked. In an age when most things could be done quietly and automatically—the Jungle Gym contained all the piping needed to deliver drinks—the human touch was treasured, the more so because it was not necessary. There were those who enjoyed the personal contact, and those who enjoyed giving it. And bartenders, from saloon to saki house, filled a traditional role.

Shigehara MacDonald bowed as she attached the drinking bulb to Denisovitch's table. "Pavel, you appear troubled," she said.

Denisovitch shrugged. "Melancholy. I taught first form today. That always makes me think of . . ." With his chin, he pointed toward the great, blue globe floating below them. Below, because it used its mass to hug the fabric of space around it like a security blanket. The Cradle, some called it.

"Ah," said Shigehara. "So." Then, after a moment's proper contemplative silence, she added, "It is difficult to think of Earth without being saddened."

"Not entirely," he protested. "The *keidanren* are still in power. Tokyo and Brasilia still look toward the future. Shimizu Spaceport has never been busier." But he held his protest to him as an armor.

"So. Yet, the Russian Republic remains paralyzed in poverty, while the United States . . ."

Denisovitch grunted. "Has turned its back on greatness. We have had this conversation before, MacDonald-san."

"You and I should orbit together, d'Abreu-san. Our ancestors came from those lands—"

"To seek a better life up here. Like all emigrants."

"—and we owe it to those left groundside to give something back. To lift them up."

"We owe them nothing. You and I, we have no more ties to the Rodina or the States than these chairs built of moondust. We are a new people, the spaceborn. And that"—he gestured toward the Earth—"is the Old World." Yet even as he gestured, he saw floating into view below them the faint, sparkling lights of *Old Novy Mir*; and despite all his protests, he felt his throat close up in sorrow. *Yoin.* Ah, what his mother's folk had once accomplished! And somewhere in the same low orbit, he knew, spun the half-finished derelict that Shigehara's people had started to build.

"And yet," said Shigehara, contemplating the same sight, "your folk and mine were the pioneers; cowboys and cossacks. The first to step into the endless ocean. I have created *haiku.*"

"Please. Recite it for me." Denisovitch responded as politeness required, but he did not hear what the bartender said.

Somewhere, things had taken the wrong turn. The new

era of nanotech had bred change; and change, as Singer had so rightly noted, births uncertainty. And so, adrift in uncertainty, people turn and clutch for the old certainties with more fervor than ever. As witness: Shigehara MacDonald, longing for a land her grandparents never knew. A romanticized past. Shigehara must know, though without the *satori* that brings true understanding, that her skin color would have kept her from full participation in that lost era she longed for.

Denisovitch sighed, recognizing the old Russian sense of *grust*, as unlike Shigehara's American nostalgia as her nostalgia was unlike the Japanese emotion of *yoin*. They were joined—and separated—by the way they felt things. *Hai. A new people; but we don't yet know what we are.*

He stared at the gleaming pearl of *Novy Mir* orbiting below him. Change. Some welcomed it—embraced it, even. Others shunned it. And nanotechnology had brought greater changes than humanity had ever known. The Vingist Church was prophesying the Imminence of the Singularity, when humanity would be transformed into godlike beings of insuperable power. They were winning converts among the spaceborn, and even a few among the groundlings.

Denisovitch was less sure. He had both more faith and less in human nature. Between the Prometheans and the Luddites lay the wary majority. The surge tank of change. So while the one faction was cutting loose from the past and the other burrowing into it ever more deeply, the majority of folk continued about their daily tasks, accepting and adapting as best they could. Sometimes the new era threw new problems in their faces; and sometimes when it did, there were old solutions at hand. . . .

4. The Laughing Clone

The first suspect walked through the door into the line-up room and the lieutenant saw the little man beside him suddenly stiffen. Then, as the other suspects walked in one by one, the little man's countenance changed, first to uncertainty, then to bewilderment. The sergeant on the other side of the one-way glass told all the suspects to face front, stand straight, and take off their hats.

The lieutenant turned to the witness. "You have my assurances, Mr. Lewis, that none of the men in the line-up can see you. I want you to take your time before deciding, and be very sure. Which of these men, if any, did you see leaving the apartment of Beverly Higgins at two o'clock on the afternoon of Saturday, the seventeenth of October?"

The witness stared at the line-up, nibbling his lip like a rabbit. He turned to the lieutenant, his eyes round with dismay. "All of them!" he said in a whisper of disbelief.

The lieutenant sighed. He'd been afraid of that.

MONDAY MORNING, 19 OCT 2043

"So. How'd it go, Lieutenant?"

"Like I expected." Police Lieutenant Morris Brumbaugh threw himself into his chair and stared morosely at the accumulated paperwork. He folded his hands into a ball and looked at Sergeant Maginnis. "An eyewitness," he complained to no one in particular. "A friggin' eyewitness saw the killer clear as day leaving the apartment. Not only that, but the man's an artist; he has an eye for detail. So he gives us a top-notch description, better than the crap we usually get. And what happens? The killer turns out to be a goddam clone! Five of them, as alike as peas in a pod, right down to their friggin' DNA."

Mac knew about the case, but he hadn't read the briefing sheets yet. "Well, at least," he ventured, "we know it was one of them killed the girl. We've narrowed it down to five. That's better than five million."

Brumbaugh threw his arms up. "It might as well be five million, for all we can prove."

"Toss 'em all in jail. One of them's guilty and the other four are covering up for him."

Brumbaugh shook his head. "I think we might be on shaky grounds constitution-wise, if we tried that."

Mac shrugged and pulled a pen from his pocket. It was a cheap disposable pen, which was good because he was constantly losing them. He twirled the pen around his fingers using his left hand. Brumbaugh watched him.

"Give it up," the lieutenant told him. "You won't ever teach yourself to be ambidextrous."

Mac sighed. "I'd give my right arm to be ambidextrous." He thought silently for a moment watching his fingers juggle the pen. "I suppose we got prints and genotypes and all."

"Yeah. And so what? Forensics found a fairly decent thumbprint on the bathroom doorknob. Matches the suspect perfectly. But it matches the suspect's four clone-brothers, too. So does the DNA-print of the skin particles we vacuumed off the bedsheets and the semen the coroner found on the victim."

"Hunh. Usually it's the genotype that nails 'em. At least when we have tissue samples and a Jimmy to match them with. Hasn't been more than a handful of unsolved murders in this town for, what? The past five years? Since genotyping came into use."

Brumbaugh scowled and worried a thumbnail. "Screw genotyping. It's going to be good old-fashioned police work that solves this one."

"Do we know how it was done? The murder, I mean." Mac reached over and searched through the papers on the lieutenant's desk, looking for the briefing screen.

"Yeah. And this creep's a real scumbag." Brumbaugh's face twisted in distaste. It was an unsavory crime, even in a city noted for unsavory crimes. "According to the old couple who live downstairs, they were in bed together, screwing up a storm. The victim and the Jimmy were. Not the old couple." He smiled sourly. "The coroner confirms the fact that the victim was 'engaged in standard heterosexual copulation' at the time of her death."

Mac shook his head. "At two in the Pee-Em? Jeez." He found the briefing screen and began scrolling through it. The briefing screen was a CRT flatscreen with all current cases in memory. There was a vocoder and touchpad for the addition and editing of new information. He held the screen in his right hand, working the scroll bar with his thumb, and continued to twirl the pen in his left.

"Apparently, he strangled her at the height of passion," continued Brumbaugh. "Then, he kept going until he was finished."

Mac looked up from the sheet. "That explains the rape charge, then. A corpse sure as hell can't give consent." He thought for a moment, scratching the side of his nose. "You know, I heard some people get off on that. I mean choking off the blood to the brain right when they climax. Not screwing corpses. They say it makes it ten times better. Do you think they were just engaged in rough sex and he accidently went too far? Maybe he didn't know right off that he'd killed her."

"Manslaughter instead of Murder One?" Brumbaugh shook his head. "Not with the neck bruised the way it was." He reached over and jabbed a forefinger at the briefing screen. "See here? His thumbs didn't choke off the carotid arteries. They crushed the windpipe. Doc said it might have taken a minute or more for her to die."

Mac shivered and dropped his pen.

"Yeah," said the lieutenant. "Can you imagine what it must have been like? To lie there dying, *knowing* that you were dying, with your killer lying on top of you getting his jollies?"

Mac had picked up the pen and stuck it in his pocket. He dropped the briefing screen back onto the desk. "Christ, Lieutenant! We've got to nail this slimebucket. If he kills for kicks, ain't no one else in the City safe."

"I know. And one other thing."

"What's that?"

"It's a pretty kinky killing, right? What if he did it because of some genetic flaw? Broken chromosomes, or some defect in his hormones. Remember, he's got four identical clonebrothers."

Mac winced. "Sure, I need to hear that. I knew I was feeling too good when I woke up this morning."

"You understand," the police pathologist told Brumbaugh, "that clones are no different than, say, identical twins. Or quintuplets, in this case. Identical twins are simply a case of Mother Nature doing the cloning." The pathologist was a youngish man, long and lanky, with a wash of cynicism in the twist of his mouth. Brumbaugh had never especially liked him, but he performed his job with workman-like precision and generally gave good advice.

"How does that help me?" Brumbaugh asked him.

The doctor shrugged. "It doesn't." He was leaning back in his desk chair, his feet propped up. His white lab coat was stained with the mementos of prior cases. He pulled a piece of paper off his memo pad and rolled it into a ball. "It's just that some people have weird ideas about clones. You know. They all think alike, or they have secret powers. Shit." He threw his arms up and made a set shot toward the waste basket in the corner. The wad of paper missed, and the doctor pulled another one off his pad. "Just laboratory twinning, is all."

"I was hoping you could tell me something I might be able to use. Some way of telling them apart. We have an eyewitness, you know."

The pathologist paused in the middle of his next set shot. "Do you? Lucky you." He shot. It bounced off the rim and fell in. "I don't know," he admitted. "I'm just a pathologist. I cut up dead meat to see how it got that way. I'm no geneticist, let alone a bio'neer." He wadded up another ball. "Have you talked to their designer or their parent?"

"We're still tracking them down."

"Hunh. Well, maybe one of them can tell you something. One thing, though. Clones are like other twins. They're only identical biologically."

"Is that all?" asked Brumbaugh sourly.

"No. What I mean is, from the time they're decanted, they grow up like anybody else. Their personalities are shaped by their experiences; and even growing up in the same household, they would have different experiences."

The doctor went for another two points, but the lieutenant stabbed out his hand and blocked the shot, snagging the wad in mid-air. "Explain that."

The doctor started to reach for another sheet of paper, but seeing the look on Brumbaugh's face, he decided against it. "Think about it, Lieutenant," he said. "Alpha falls off his bike and breaks his collarbone. Beta gets stuck in a tree and develops a fear of heights. Gamma gets mugged in Central Park and has a scar on his head. Delta gets turned down for a date and grows shy and introverted." He gestured awkwardly as he answered, as if he didn't know what to do with his hands. "I'm exaggerating, but you know what I mean. Twins have remarkably similar behavior patterns. Even twins raised apart often grow up with the same habits, hobbies, and occupations. *But they can't be absolutely identical.* Nothing in nature is. If nothing else, there's always random variation in cell division."

"And what does that mean?"

The doctor solved his hand problem by shoving them into the pockets of his lab coat. He looked at him. "Have you ever seen two items that came off an assembly line? Even consecutive items? If you measure them carefully enough and closely enough, you can always find some difference. Even though they were made in the same dies on the same machine from the same material. It's the same with Mother Nature. In fact, Mother Nature invented random variation. That's why Darwin works. If you check your clones carefully, you'll find one has a slightly longer femur, say. Or one has a mole on his back that the others don't."

"All right," Brumbaugh said nodding. "I'm not sure how that might help me. The witness sure wouldn't know from a short femur or a hidden mole. But scars or behavior patterns . . . Maybe. I don't know. Like you say, there's gotta be *some* differences among them."

The pathologist eyed his memo pad longingly. "Glad to be of help, Lieutenant."

Brumbaugh opened his fist and jiggled the paper ball he had caught. "Don't mention it." He flipped the ball across his left shoulder. It hit the corner of the room, bounced off the two walls, and fell into the waste basket. The doctor looked from Brumbaugh to the basket and back to Brumbaugh.

"And watch that set shot, Doc. You're pulling to the left."

Mac and the lieutenant paused outside the interrogation rooms. The lieutenant consulted his notes. "Let's start with the first one. Barry Kavin." He shook his head. "Barry, Benny, Billy, Bobby, and Hank."

Mac looked at him. "Hank?"

Brumbaugh shrugged. "What else was left?"

"Buddy," Mac suggested. "Bubby. Bunny. Bucky."

Hank. The lieutenant wondered how anyone could give their kids such an outlandish sequence of names. But then, what would possess a man to make love to a petri dish instead of a woman? He glanced again at his notes. Rudolph Kavin, the father, lived in Milwaukee. If anyone would know how to tell the five clones apart, the father would.

"Any luck finding the father yet?" he asked Mac.

"No. No answer at his apartment. We keep getting his answering machine. We'll keep trying."

"Maybe the local fuzz can look in on him."

"The Kavins called him when we picked them up this morning. He could be flying into the City by now."

"Uh-huh. What about their designer? This . . ." He scrolled the display on his briefing screen. "Konstantin Adamides, *Dr. Gen.*? He's supposed to be at the University of San Francisco now, according to the people at CCNY."

"We left a message with the university switchboard. He's not in yet. Don't forget it's three hours earlier out there."

"Yeah." Brumbaugh twisted his shirt collar, loosened his tie some more. The older a case got, the less likely it was to be solved. This one was already close to forty-eight hours old. It had taken a full day to identify and round up the five clones. With genotyping, the round-up was usually the end of the case. At that point, positive identification was always possible. This one was the exception; the kind of case that separated cops from lab technicians.

Sherlock Holmes and Sonny Crockett notwithstanding, Brumbaugh knew that most police work was neither fancy deduction nor high speed car chases and shoot-outs. It was more like trawling. You had to hit the streets and start dragging your net around. You'd pick up a ton of junk that way. Irrelevant information; contradictory information; uncertain information. And, buried in it somewhere, a few pearls of surpassing price. Maybe. Collecting the evidence, sifting through it, fitting it together into a meaningful pattern needed patience and determination, not brilliance or quick reflexes.

Sometimes—more often than he liked to admit—no pattern ever emerged. No matter how he turned and twisted the pieces, they just wouldn't fit together. And people he *knew* were guilty as sin had walked. But there had been other times, times in the not-too-distant past, when Brumbaugh had been struck by some intuition, some flash of insight, when the pieces had suddenly fallen together of their own accord. At those times, Brumbaugh had really felt like a detective.

More than anything else, Brumbaugh wanted to crack this case. To prove that years of relying on genotypes to solve cases had not softened his wits. He cleared his briefing screen. "Okay, Mac. Let's get this over with."

Mac jerked a thumb at the interrogation rooms. "Think we'll learn anything from those creeps?"

"Hell, no. But you gotta go through the motions."

The interrogation rooms were small and dim and smelled of the sweat and body odors of a thousand nervous suspects, which the marvels of modern air conditioning had done nothing to dispel. But Barry Kavin, if looks could be relied on, was doing nothing to add to the miasma. He sat behind the table with his lawyer at his side, the picture of unconcern and nonchalance, as if he did this sort of thing every day. If he was nervous, he gave no sign of it.

Brumbaugh seated himself across the table from Barry. Mac leaned against the wall to the side. The lieutenant studied the suspect's features, looking for any telltale marks that might distinguish him from his brothers.

The clone was thin and angular, like Ichabod Crane. His face was narrow and his eyes sat too close together. It was a face you would have to work hard to trust. One that only a mother could love.

Which might be significant, because the Kavins didn't have a mother, unless you counted the agar that they grew in.

Barry Kavin wore a smile so slight that Brumbaugh had to look twice to be sure it was there. The smile irritated him. It was smug, as if the clone knew the game was already won and he was just going to dance a few waltzes with the police.

The clone nodded to the lawyer. "This here's my lawyer. Myron Kasabian." The lieutenant did not take the lawyer's hand, which didn't matter, since Kasabian did not offer it.

The lawyer was a fleshy man in an expensive three-piece suit and a tie with a below-the-knot design. A perfectly folded handkerchief peered over his breast pocket, like Kilroy in those old World War II drawings. He wore—of all things in this day and age—pince nez. Brumbaugh took an instant dislike to him.

They got the preliminaries over with quickly. Barry Kavin, aged twenty-seven, son of Rudolph Kavin, formerly of New York, now of Milwaukee; designed by Konstantin Adamides, *Dr. Gen.* Brumbaugh asked Barry what he did for a living and Barry said he was a financial consultant with an office on 52nd and Park, and he lived in a co-op in the East Eighties, and was well regarded in his circles, and why was he being grilled by the cops?

Brumbaugh didn't answer him. Could Barry account for his actions on the afternoon of the seventeenth, say between noon and 3:00 P.M.?

The clone squinted his eyes and looked at the ceiling. His tongue moved from cheek to cheek. "Gee, Lieutenant. I dunno. I was in my office making calls until a little after one. My secretary was there. Does that count?"

"Is it usual for you to work Saturdays?"

"Sure. I get a lot of tips during the week, and I like to get in position so I can hit the markets first thing Monday morning."

"When did you leave the office?"

"I toldja. About 1:15. I went to meet my brother for lunch."

"Which brother was that?"

Barry shrugged. "Search me. They all look alike." He snickered, then looked at Brumbaugh's face and shrugged. "Okay, so it was Billy."

"And where did you have lunch?"

"A Spanish restaurant at 42nd and Lex. I forget the name. We never ate there before."

"When was that?"

"I got there about quarter after one. Stayed until three, three-thirty."

"Long lunch."

"I like to savor my food."

"Yeah? What'd you have?" asked Mac.

Barry turned his head and looked at the sergeant. "*Paella Barcelona*. Billy and me, we split a pot." Barry flashed him a smile.

"Was Billy there when you arrived or did you come in together?" asked Brumbaugh.

"He came in about a quarter hour after I did and left at two."

"Yeah?" asked Mac. "Why'd you stay?"

The clone grinned again, even more broadly. "I met a coupla business aquaintances there and we shmoozed a little."

Brumbaugh probed the story. Could the restaurant's maître d' verify those times? Kavin shrugged. Maybe. He didn't know. What about the time he had spent in his office? His secretary kept a telephone log, recording who he had talked to and when. Brumbaugh asked if he could check the log and Barry said, sure, go ahead.

"Now, what about the deceased, Beverly Higgins? You were seen leaving her apartment at 2:00 on the afternoon of the seventeenth."

"Not me, Lieutenant. Musta been someone else who looked like me." He grinned again, and Brumbaugh had to suppress an urge to punch his face in. Kavin was mocking him; mocking the investigation.

"Did you know the deceased?"

"No. I never heard of her until your guys picked me up. Ask Hank, he likes that sort of thing."

"What sort of thing is that?"

Kavin's eyes flickered left, then right. "Whores," he said.

"You think Beverly Higgins was a whore?" asked Mac from the corner where he lounged.

Kavin shrugged. "How many boyfriends did she have?"

"We're asking the questions here."

"Do *you* have any girlfriends, Barry?" asked Brumbaugh.

Kavin looked back at him. "Is that any of your business?"

"It might be. Why don't you let us decide that. We're police, not morality proctors."

Kavin sucked his teeth and looked at his lawyer, who wiggled a hand in a kind of manual shrug. "No. None at present."

Brumbaugh scratched his chin and made a note on his pad. "Do you have a family doctor, Barry?"

"Sure."

Brumbaugh looked at him. The clone was smiling broadly. All his teeth showed. "Do you want to tell me his or her name?" Brumbaugh asked him.

"Why not? It's Benny."

"Benny? Your clonebrother, Benny?"

"Right. *Doctor* Benny, if you please."

"Uh-hunh." Brumbaugh stuck his pen behind his ear and stood up. "That will be all for now. We'll be checking out your alibi and get back to you. Meanwhile—"

"Yeah, yeah. I know. Don't leave town."

In the hallway, he and Mac compared notes. Kasabian, the lawyer, lingered nearby until a glance from Mac sent him scurrying for the washroom.

"I suppose that creep's the lawyer for all five of them," Mac commented.

"Wouldn't surprise me," said Brumbaugh. "Maybe they get a package deal."

Mac shrugged and glanced back at the interrogation room. "Financial consultant," he said.

"Right. Ten gets you one, Barry's clientelle is just as sleazy as he is."

"Any chance of collaring him on that?"

"Ah, why bother? Arrest one guy for financial hanky-panky and you'd have to arrest half the City. Besides this is the big M-One, we're talking about, not stock swindles or touting horse races." He tapped his screen with his forefingers. "You want to have Jersey Wilks check up on the restaurant? Have him talk to the maître d' and contact the two guys Barry met there."

"Can't. Jersey called in today. He'll be late. The PATH tubes are down—the whole friggin' loop from the airport to the Trade Center—and he has to catch the Transit train from Elizabeth."

"Wilks should move to the City," Brumbaugh complained. "What was it, temperature problem again?"

"Yeah. Fire on the tracks. The ceramics lost their superconductivity. They don't figure to have the trains floating again until the Pee-Em rush."

Brumbaugh shrugged it off. "Hell with him, then. He can work late. No, wait. Call him up. Have him work from his house. Contact Milwaukee, Frisco, anything he can handle by phone or Net. Feed him any codes he'll need."

Mac jerked a head at the interrogation room. "Y'know, if Barry *was* at the restaurant having lunch at the time of the murder, that would let him off the hook."

"Yeah, him *and* his brother."

"Too bad about the doctor, though."

"You figured that out? I was hoping their doc could clue us if there were any physical differences among the suspects. Something the witness might recall under hypnosis, maybe. No chance of getting accurate medical records, though, if *Doctor* Benny is keeping them. Ah, nuts."

"You wanna talk to Benny next?"

Brumbaugh looked at his notes. "No. Let's check out Billy. See if he remembers going to the same restaurant."

"I've got a sawbuck says he does."

Brumbaugh sighed. "No bet."

The interviews all went the same way. The brothers all had the same ferret-like habits. The same way of rubbing their chin or sucking their teeth. The same air of nonchalance.

The same secret laughter.

Billy was a sharp dresser. His suit was obviously more expensive than Barry's, and he wore a showy Yomatsu watch. His nails were buffed. He worked in an ad agency on Madison Avenue and told Brumbaugh that a dozen co-workers could vouch for his presence there between nine and one. The agency was conducting a crash campaign for a new brand of gene-tailored vegetables ("Delicious and Nutritious—on Purpose!"), and management had scheduled a Saturday morning brainstorming session. He had reached the restaurant at 1:30 and left at 2:00. Yes, they ate *paella*. He stopped back in his office around 2:20, just to clear his desk. You know how some bosses are about clean desks. Brumbaugh said he knew how some bosses were about clean desks. Two co-workers were still there, plus the cleaning woman. They could vouch for him. Brumbaugh took their names without comment. What about the deceased? Never heard of her. She wasn't his type anyway, judging by the pictures in the papers. What about his brothers? What about them?

"We know it was one of you that did it. Shut up, Kasabian. We were wondering if you had any ideas."

Billy Kavin pursed his lips. "Do you know anything about clones, Lieutenant?"

"I'm learning."

"Well, we do stick together. Even if I thought that, oh, Hank, say, was a worthless sonuvabitch, I'd never turn him over to you. I might work him over myself, but I wouldn't let you have him."

"I've heard that about clone-sibs."

"Yeah? Well, don't believe everything you hear."

"Like what?"

Billy smiled. "Like clones are so close to each other that they're telepathic. That our brains are so much alike that our minds resonate to the same frequencies and we can talk to each other whenever and wherever we want."

Brumbaugh looked at him for a long time. "No, I wouldn't believe a thing like that."

Bobby was a bartender in a 43rd Street gin mill called Hanson's, not far from Times Square, and had a bartender's personality: superficially friendly, but guarded. He told Brumbaugh that he had had a burger and beer at a nearby Blarney Stone, and he was back behind the bar before twelve-thirty. He ducked out again sometime around 1:30, to mail a letter. Things get slow right after noon. You know how it is. Brumbaugh knew how it was. There were a couple of the regulars there, passing time. Did Brumbaugh want their names? They'd tell him ol' Bobby was there. Big as life and twice as mean. Beverly Higgins? Sure, he knew her. She was one of his regulars. In the bar, he meant. Regular customer. No, not that particular day. Did she ever come there with men? Yeah, sometimes. Anyone in particular? Bobby figured she played the field, but he thought he had seen her with a couple of guys more than once. What about his brothers? Had he ever seen her with any of his brothers? Bobby grinned crookedly. "No," he said, "and I'd sure remember it if *that* happened."

"Nice ring," commented Mac.

Bobby held up his hand and looked it over. It was a heavy ring. A man's ring. A snake eating its own tail. "Yeah, I like it. I'm not much for jewelry. That's Billy's schtick. But these rings, they were a gift from Dad. He had a set made for our eighteenth birthday."

"Barry and Billy weren't wearing theirs."

Bobby shrugged. "It ain't exactly a wedding ring. Sometimes I don't wear it either. Maybe they should wear theirs more often." He turned his hand and the ring caught the light from the wire-screened window.

"Doctor" Benny was all smiles. His face seemed a trifle softer than the others. Perhaps a tad pudgier. He was well-dressed, but his clothes did not have the sharpness of Billy's. His watch was plain and utilitarian, and he wore the snake on his finger. He told Brumbaugh he had seen six patients in his office in the Chanin Building that day. Saturday hours? Sure, sometimes. That way working people could see him without taking time off from work. Mac told him he was a real Samaritan. Brumbaugh asked for the names of the patients. The lawyer humphed and reminded everyone that that was confidential information, as if anyone needed reminding. Did Dr. Kavin realize this was a murder investigation, and it was proven beyond a reasonable doubt that that one of the Kavin brothers was responsible?

The lawyer objected to that and Brumbaugh told him to shut up because they weren't in court yet and Kasabian said it would never come to court.

His nurse was there, too, Dr. Benny told them. Did that help? Mac and Brumbaugh exchanged glances. The nurse's name wasn't confidential, was it? Dr. Benny laughed. No, of course not. She was there the entire afternoon and could vouch for his every move.

Did he know the deceased, Beverly Higgins? Yes, as a matter of fact, he did. She was a patient of his. Brumbaugh reminded him that *her* medical records could be subpoenaed and the Doctor said he would be glad to cooperate in any way he could and Brumbaugh said that was nice and the Doctor said he was only doing his public duty.

* * *

Hank was different. Whether it was the psychological effect of his name or whether it was just coincidental Brumbaugh didn't know, but Hank Kavin was definitely more mellowed and laid back than his brothers. It wasn't anything in his face that showed it. It was the same, rat-sharp face that Brumbaugh had grown so tired of looking at all morning. But his voice and attitude were more pleasant. Altogether, he was more cooperative.

Which made Brumbaugh immediately suspicious.

Hank ran an art shop in the East Village. He was there from 10:00 until 2:00, when he closed up and walked home. His apartment was just a couple of blocks away. Did he leave the shop at any time during the afternoon? Well, yes. He brownbagged his lunch in Washington Square. No, no one he knew saw him there. Brumbaugh asked if anyone saw him in the shop. There were a couple of artists from Alphabet City and NoHo who stopped in a lot. He carried a special line of acrylics tailored by SingerLabs and he had an exclusive contract on some special modeling clay that could only be found in Brunei. Some of the sculptors swore by his clay and came to his shop from all over the island and even from Brooklyn. He thought he remembered a couple of them from Saturday. Brumbaugh took their names.

Did he know Beverly Higgins? Sure, he did! Such a tragedy! A great loss to the art world. She was doing some *very* interesting work in clay and chips, what the critics were archly calling IA, Intelligent Art. She'd been exhibited at Greenfeld's and The Parting Shot. In fact, she was one of those who came in for the Brunei clay. He always called her and a few other friends whenever a shipment arrived.

Was she in his shop on the seventeenth? Yes, about 10:30. She bought some clay. She was going to make a life mask, she said. Brumbaugh asked him whose face and Hank said he didn't know. How did she seem to Hank that day? Worried? No. Excited, maybe. Like she was on the verge of a big breakthrough. Artists are like that, you know. Excitable. Brumbaugh said he didn't know and asked him his personal opinion about Higgins.

Hank sagged back in his chair. "I liked her," he admitted. "I know my brothers wouldn't. Especially Barry and Billy. At best, they might tolerate her. But you know how that type is."

Mac asked if Hank had ever dated the victim and Hank said he had.

"We did a few shows together. Had some fun. Nothing serious, you know. I'm not into that scene. But, shit, she was good folks. I hope you catch whoever choked her, Lieutenant. I really do."

Brumbaugh blinked in surprise. "You realize that the genotyping shows the killer was one of you. You or one of your brothers."

The lawyer began to sputter but Hank waved him silent. "Sure, Lieutenant, I know it looks that way, but I just can't figure it myself. I mean, I *know* those guys. You know what I'm saying? I know those guys as well as I know myself. And I can't see any of them as a killer. I don't mean that Barry wouldn't bilk an old lady out of her last dime; or that Benny wouldn't find the right pills for you; or that Bobby doesn't rake off the till at Hanson's; but Jesus, Lieutenant, those aren't in the same league as murder."

The lawyer looked about to have apoplexy and Hank laughed. "Ah, don't worry, Myron. I never said my brothers *did* any of those things. I only said I could imagine that they *could*. But not murder. No way. There's gotta be a mistake somewhere."

At the water cooler afterward, Brumbaugh asked Mac what he thought of Hank.

"The most cooperative one of the bunch. Certainly more likeable. More . . . normal."

Brumbaugh scratched the back of his head and stretched his muscles. "I know what you mean. The others are whaddaya call 'em? They don't like women. Not gay, but they just got no use or interest in the ladies."

"Misogynists."

"Misogynists, right. That's what they are. But not Hank. He likes 'em."

"Or he acts like he does."

"Yeah. This whole City's full of friggin' actors. What do you think? A man needs a woman every now and then, unless he's gene-gay and hasn't been re-tailored. That's a physical fact. What happens inside a guy's head if he needs women but despises them?"

Mac tossed off his drink and crumpled the paper cup and threw it in the basket. "He holds it in for a while. Until he has to explode. Then he does what he has to do, and afterwards he's disgusted."

"At who? The woman, or himself?"

Mac wiggled his hand. "Could go either way. If he's an introvert, he might crawl off and slit his own throat in loathing because he's so despicable. If he's an extrovert . . . well, 'the woman tempted me,' so it's her fault."

Brumbaugh smiled grimly. "That's an old excuse."

Mac laughed. "The oldest one in the Book. Genesis, Chapter 3, verse 12."

"Uh-hunh. What do you make of Hank? He's the only one admits he had a relationship with the Higgins woman."

"Yeah, could be. And Barry and Billy both mentioned Hank, too. But don't forget Dr. Benny. He gets to see her naked all the time; or whenever she comes in. Maybe after a while, he wants to do more than look."

Brumbaugh sighed in frustration. "A lot of maybes. What about Hank? He's the odd one out, and he says he liked Higgins. Maybe we can work on him; get him to rat on his brothers."

Mac fingered his ear. "I dunno, Lieutenant. Clones have pretty strong sibling bonds. Even stronger than most twins. It's the look-alike thing. My brother is myself. Or my sister is. And they bond to the parent, too—at least when they're the same sex. The parent is just an older version of themselves. Sure, they go their own ways as adults. Everyone does. But they keep in closer touch than most sibs, and they support one another when they're in trouble. I don't think you'll break their fraternity, Lieutenant."

Brumbaugh grunted and pulled on his ear. "What did you make of Billy's remark? About clones being telepathic."

Mac made a face. "You hear stories, you know what I mean? Some people say they do and some say they don't. Me, I think when guys are as alike as that, they can't help thinking the same things now and then."

"Yeah, I know what you mean. Sometimes Tillie does that to me. Answers my questions before I ask them."

"You been married too long, Lieutenant. That's your problem."

"Maybe. You did notice one thing about their alibis, didn't you, Mac?"

Mac pulled up his briefing screen and thumbed the scroll. "Sure. I even made myself a little Gantt chart. Take a look. They all got alibis for the afternoon. Not for the whole afternoon; but for enough of it that, if the alibis hold up, they're all off the hook."

Brumbaugh studied the little timelines as they crawled across the screen. There was one for each clone. The intervals were annotated with references to location and witnesses. Each clone could account for enough of the afternoon to make it impossible for him to be the killer. Brumbaugh smiled a little smile of satisfaction. "People with alibis," he said, "have something to hide."

MONDAY AFTERNOON, 19 OCT 2043

The maître d' looked down his nose at the holograph. He turned it, first one way, then another, checking it from all angles. Then he handed it back to the Lieutenant.

"Yes," he said. "That is the man. There were two of them."

"You are positive about the identification?"

"Absolutely. I have seen him in here many times before." He blinked rapidly. "That is, I have seen one of him in here before." He seemed to be confused regarding the proper syntax.

Brumbaugh was about to correct him. Both Barry and Billy had said it was their first visit to this restaurant. Then he remembered that Dr. Benny's office was only a short distance away, in the Chanin Building. He probably ate here occasionally. "Could you tell me what time they arrived?"

The maître d' consulted his reservation book. "We normally do not take reservations for lunch, but I remember that this one called ahead and insisted. Ah, yes. Here it is: Barry Kavin, party of two, for 1:30. He arrived quite early, about 12:30, I should think, and waited in the bar for his . . ."

"Brother."

"Of course. His brother. One of them left after lunch, sometime around 2:00, I think; but the other encountered some aquaintances and spent the remainder of the afternoon in our bar."

"Your memory is pretty good."

The maître d' shrugged. "One does not normally see twins of such exacting likeness. It was a sight to remain in one's memory."

Mac rang the buzzer and waited. After a few moments, a voice answered from the grill over the buzzer. "Yes?" It was a harsh voice, made more harsh by the ancient wiring and speaker.

"Sergeant Maginnis of the NYPD. Are you Karen Jo Lincoln, Benjamin Kavin's nurse?"

"Yes," the voice admitted cautiously. "Why?"

"I'd like to ask you a few questions."

There was a long silence. Then the door lock buzzed and Mac, taken by surprise, missed grabbing the latch. Irritated, he pressed the buzzer again.

It was a four-story walk-up and Lincoln had the rear apartment on the third floor. When he reached it, the door was partway open on its chain. An eye looked at him from the crack. Mac pulled out his wallet and held the shield up. The door closed, then it opened again, this time unlatched.

Karen Jo Lincoln was middle-aged and brown-skinned. She wore a pair of 'round-the-house coveralls; the baggy kind that covered her from wrists to ankles and hid whatever sort of shape she might have had. It was the style rage for the last several years, since the Reverend won the election; but Mac had never cared for it, nor for the sort of woman who wore it. Lincoln cut her hair in mannish fashion, parted and combed over, and wore no make-up of any sort. In fact, except for the curves of her face and neck, she might almost be taken for a fine-featured man.

All in all, she was exactly the sort of woman that a Kavin might hire.

Mac learned that "Dr. Benny" did indeed schedule Saturday appointments twice a month. The appointments on the seventeenth were routine, no emergency work. Two of the appointments had failed to show up. And Nurse Lincoln could vouch for Dr. Kavin for virtually the entire afternoon.

Mac asked her if she had left the office at any time during the afternoon. She admitted she had, but only between 12:15 and 12:45, when she ate lunch at a deli across from Grand Central Terminal, and again around 1:30, when the doctor had sent her on an errand to the pharmacy on the ground floor of the office building. During the remainder of the afternoon in question, the doctor had been with her or with a patient.

As far as the victim went, Nurse Lincoln had very little use for that sort of woman. Constantly flaunting and exposing herself to men, in direct contradiction to God's commandments. Lead us not into temptation. Whenever Higgins had come in for an examination, Lincoln had been present in the examining room. Otherwise, there would have been a potential for scandal. Yes, she did that for all of the doctor's female patients.

Was she herself a patient of Dr. Kavin? Well, certainly! Dr. Kavin was a gentleman. She would never trust her virtue to some stranger. Mac didn't ask her if she insisted on another nurse being present during her own examination.

After leaving the restaurant, Brumbaugh walked to the Grand Central Station and took the Number 7 to Woodside. The ride over was slow and rattling, since the Queensboro line had not been converted to magnetic floaters. Which was just as well, he thought, since the PATH tubes, which *were* converted, were frequently down due to temperature problems with the superconducting ceramics.

The neighborhood he found himself in was shabby and run-down. At one time, it had been Irish and Italian, and not too safe. Now it was largely Haitian and Filipino, and not too safe. Some things were constant, at least; although he supposed that a policeman's view was likely to be cynical, at best. The row houses had probably been decent when new, but time, neglect, and the weather had taken their toll. Children played in the wreckage of one of the buildings. Their laughter seemed out of tune with their surroundings. The autumn wind was colder than it had been in Manhattan, and Brumbaugh turned his jacket collar up.

The house he sought was neither better nor worse than the other buildings in the block. Keeping up a house needed money, and the residents didn't have it and the landlords wouldn't spend it. He walked up the porch and rang the bell.

An old woman answered.

"Mrs. Genata? I'm police Lieutenant Brumbaugh from Manhattan Midtown. I'd like to ask you some questions about some former neighbors of yours." He showed her his badge and she studied it. Then she studied him and thought about letting him in. Maybe it was his craggy good looks or maybe she was just resigned to fate, but she finally decided in his favor and opened the door.

Mrs. Genata was ninety-two years old and looked it. Singer's Flu might have extended the human lifespan, because a lot of what was called aging was the cumulative effects of background radiation damage, but most people had themselves Carterized to keep their appearance reasonably youthful. She was dressed in a "granny" dress and "earth" shoes. Psychedelic posters adorned the walls; pictures of the Beatles and Joplin and the Stones and others that Brumbaugh didn't recognize. Faint odors of pot and sandlewood clung to the curtains and carpet. She sat him down in a chair that was every bit as uncomfortable as it looked and offered him a cup of herbal tea.

Brumbaugh didn't care for tea, herbal or otherwise, and he wasn't sure what Granny Genata might have put in it; but he accepted politely. He set the steaming, earthenware cup down without tasting it and got down to business.

"You were once a neighbor of Rudolph Kavin and his children," he suggested.

Mrs. Genata screwed up her face. "That fascist? That male chauvinist pig? Sure, he used to live in the house next door, on the right. But I wouldn't call those clones his children."

"Oh? Why not?"

"Because they were *artificial, unnatural.* Humans shouldn't interfere with nature like that." She shook her head slowly from side to side.

"I understand your feelings, Mrs. Genata, but what I want to know is how well you knew the children. Could you tell them apart?"

The old lady cocked her head, giving his question serious thought. "Police, hunh? I suppose you got the goods on one of them but you don't know which one. That's a real bitch, all right. Those brats were as alike as peas in a pod. They used to play tricks on me. Not just on me. On everyone in the old neighborhood. They'd pretend to be each other. Trade places, you know. I'd say, 'Now, Benny, you stop that.' And he'd say, 'I'm not Benny, I'm Billy.' And it was really Bobby all along." She shook her head, remembering. "It was enough to drive everyone crazy."

"Surely there must be something. No two people are exactly alike. Perhaps their behavior, or some personality trait. I realize it was a long time ago, but it would be a great help to us if you could recall something. We have an eyewitness we could autoregress, *if* we knew what questions to ask his subconscious."

She shushed him impatiently. "Now it seems to me," she said, "that one of them—was it Hank?—was friendlier toward me than the others. The others were real pests. That son-of-a-bitch Kavin was a real chauvanist piggy. Hated women. Opposed the ERA. And he taught his kids to be the same way."

"Perhaps it was a genetic tendency they inherited from him," Brumbaugh suggested.

"Bullshit. That's fascist hereditary bullshit. It's environment and upbringing that makes people behave the way they do. You young folks should listen to your elders more often. Besides, if it were genetic the way you say, why was Hank friendlier than the others? He used to come to the house and do chores for me, and I'd give him granola or wheat germ snacks." She sighed, remembering small kindnesses. "He didn't do it often, and *never* when his brothers or his father were around."

"What about the others? Do you remember any other habits or traits? Broken bones?"

She thought about it for a long time. Then she shook her head. "I heard something about one of them breaking an arm in a bicycle accident." She looked at him shrewdly and added: "That's just hearsay. I didn't see it myself. Let's see, though." She looked into the distance. "Was it Benny or Barry? One of those two, I'm sure."

She shook her heads. "What names! It was hard enough telling them apart without giving them sound-alike names, too."

Mac stepped into Hansen's and looked around. It was a typical neighborhood bar in the West Forties. Old, splintered wood and plastic lamination. The smell of stale beer and liquor. The mirror behind the bar was fogged and a crack ran diagonally across it. Business was slow. Monday afternoons, it was always slow. There were five customers, one of them semi-comatose, huddled over their drinks. Mac wondered what drove some people to spend their lives in places like this. The bartender was cleaning a glass with a bar towel and watching Mac suspiciously. He could smell fuzz a mile away.

Mac stood up to the bar and flashed his shield. The bartender looked at it and shrugged. He'd seen them before.

"Bobby Kavin work here?"

The bartender put the glass away. "Yeah, but he ain't here now. Monday and Tuesday are his days off. Come back Wednesday evening." He turned away.

"Nice place you got here," Mac said, watching a cockroach run along the moulding at the bottom of the bar rail. "Board o' Health been here lately?"

"Yeah. An' they gave me a clean bill."

"Yeah? And how many bills did you give them? You know . . ." He looked around the room. "You know, this looks like a bad place. A hangout, you know what I mean? Maybe you could use some extra police surveillance. To keep it safe, like."

The bartender sighed. "You made your point. Waddaya wanna know?"

Mac asked him about Bobby Kavin's Saturday stint.

"Yeah, we was both here Saturday. Saturday's a busy time, you know. People going out, they stop here for a quick one. People coming home, from wherever they were Friday night, stop here, too. Right after noon is the only slow time. You know how it is. Bobby was on from 8:00 till 3:00. I came on at one. So I know he was in here from one to three."

"He says he went out at 1:30."

"Did he? I don't remember. Yeah, I guess he did. More like 1:15. Had a letter to mail or something. He was out about half an hour."

Mac nibbled his lip. If the bartender placed Bobby here between one and three, he could not have committed the murder, no matter where he went between 1:15 and 1:45. Well, that eliminated another brother. At least they were narrowing the list down. He showed the bartender the names of the regulars Bobby had claimed to be present on Saturday.

The bartender told him that one of them was in the bar now and Mac asked him who, afraid it would be the comatose one, and the bartender pointed to a man in the corner scowling into a shot and beer.

The man was surly, but grudgingly cooperative. Sure, he was here Saturday. He was here *every* Saturday. He was here every single goddamned day. Like, sitting here was his only job since he got laid off, see? Bobby Kavin? Sure, the geek was here. He was a sonuvabitch. He always watered the drinks when he thought you couldn't see what he did behind the bar.

Mac thanked him insincerely. Bobby's story had checked out; but he would be sure to chase down the other witnesses, too. Like the lieutenant always said, you had to touch all the bases. Check out all the stories five ways from Sunday. Find the loose thread that would unravel the whole thing.

He snapped his notescreen shut and stepped out onto Eighth Avenue and took a deep breath of air that, while not precisely fresh, at least did not smell of beer. A huge billboard atop the building across the street reminded everyone that God saw everything. In the poster, God looked suspiciously like the Reverend President Sawyer.

Mac wondered if God would come forward as a witness. He hoped the lieutenant was having better luck.

MONDAY EVENING, 19 OCT 2043

By coincidence, they met on the steps to the precinct house. Brumbaugh waited at the door for Mac to catch up with him. "How'd it go?" he asked the sergeant.

"Depends."

"On what?"

"Well, both stories I checked out are holding up. That's bad news, because we can't pin it on Bobby or on *Dr.* Benny. But it's good news, because that narrows it down to three."

"One," said Brumbaugh. "Barry and Billy were definitely at lunch together during the time Higgins was being murdered. We'll check out the rest of their stories in the morning, at their offices; but hell, we know the killer went into Higgins' apartment about 12:30 and left at 2:00. So if they've got alibis for any part of the afternoon . . ." He finished with a shrug.

"So that leaves Hank. The one who doesn't mind girls."

"Yeah. Odd man out. The different brother with the different name. That's so damned pat it stinks."

"Yeah. And you know what I think?"

"What?"

"*His* alibi is gonna check out, too."

When Brumbaugh entered the bullpen to clear his desk for the day, he experienced a shiver of *deja vu.* Seated in the wooden chair beside his desk was one of the Kavins. For a split second, he wondered if the clone had come to confess, or to rat on one of his brothers. Then he realized that it was a different person entirely, because this particular individual had grey hair, cut short in what they used to call a "buzz."

He walked to his desk and stuck out his hand. "You must be Rudolph Kavin, from Milwaukee. I'm Lieutenant Brumbaugh, in charge of the case. I'm glad you're here, because you can help us clear up—"

"Why are you holding my boys?" the visitor demanded. "You've got no right to do that. I talked to them and that lawyer of theirs while I was waiting for you. They were all somewhere else when that tramp was getting what she got. You know that and I know that."

Instinctively, Brumbaugh shifted his mental gears. The acorns had not fallen too far from this particular tree. This man had not come to help, but to get his sons off. While behaving as offensively as possible.

He studied Kavin closely. Aside from the buzz cut and the grey coloring, the man looked surprisingly youthful. Brumbaugh noticed the tell-tale face-lift scars behind the ears. The natural diamond stickpin. The Yomatsu watch. The carefully manicured nails. *Vain,* thought Brumbaugh. Here was a fellow who thought highly of himself; and felt everyone else should, too.

"We have probable cause," he said without amplification. "We can hold them for another forty-eight hours." *After which, they walk,* he thought disgustedly. He had never been in a situation where he had such positive identification, yet no grounds to hold a particular individual.

"Nonsense. You're picking on them because they're clones. Naturalistic chauvinism. You think you can pander to the prejudice of the public. Of the Men Born of Women."

The scornful way Kavin uttered that last remark made Brumbaugh wonder. Chauvinism could run both ways. The Men Born of Women. And who were The Men *Not* Born of Women? he wondered. The new *Übermenschen?*

"Things may be different out in Milwaukee, Mr. Kavin," he told him, "but here in the City, no one cares about clones. Here, *everyone's* a minority. We've got people in every conceivable size, shape, color, and birth. Homo and hetero. Black and white. Natural and gene-tailored. Hell, we've got a detective on the force who . . . well, never mind. Just rest assured that, if your sons are under arrest, it's because of reliable evidence and not birthism."

Kavin grunted and looked unconvinced.

"In the meantime," Brumbaugh persisted, "you can help us find grounds to release those of your sons who *are* innocent. Is there any way at all of telling them apart?"

Kavin looked at him and something new came into his eyes. Brumbaugh wasn't sure what it was. He couldn't place the look. He only knew he didn't like it.

"Is that all? Some way of telling them apart? Lieutenant, they are clone-children. Do you know what that means? It means that they are exactly alike."

"Didn't one of them break an arm one time, in a bicycle accident?"

"Who told you that? No, never mind. It was a leg, not an arm. The damnfool driver ran right into my boy. Smashed the bike."

"Which boy was that?" Brumbaugh asked. *Maybe one of them still walks with a slight limp. Some way of carrying himself that the witness's subconscious might have noticed.*

Kavin looked at him for a moment, as if making up his mind whether to cooperate or not. "That was Bobby," he said at last. "He was eight at the time."

"Are there any other distinguishing behaviors? Any nervous tics, or habits?"

"Nervous tics or habits. Not that I . . . No, wait. Benny. He always drops his eyes when he talks to you. I wanted my boys to look me straight in the eye when they answered, but he always dropped his eyes first. And Billy, whenever he's nervous, he runs his left hand through his hair. Like this." Kavin demonstrated, running his fingers front to back. He chuckled. "Of course, it's different when you wear long hair, like my boys."

"Anything else?"

Kavin paused and seemed to think. "No, nothing that I can think of off hand."

"Could you think about it some more? We'll talk again tomorrow."

"I'll do my best, Lieutenant. I'm staying at the Holiday Inn Midtown. Room 104."

He stood to leave, hesitated, then stuck out his hand. "Sorry to be so hostile at first, but you know how it is when your own flesh and blood is at stake. It's even more so when they're clone-children. We have a very special feeling and relationship for each other. I'm sure this is all some gruesome mistake."

Brumbaugh shook his hand and watched him leave. He became away of Mac standing behind him. He turned and saw Mac twirling a pen between his fingers and lounging up against Jersey Wilks' desk.

"How did you like that performance?" he asked him.

Mac grinned. "I liked the Jekyll and Hyde act."

"Yeah. Turned real cooperative all of a sudden. Something I said made him happy."

Mac made a long face. "A happy Kavin is not a good thing."

TUESDAY MORNING, 20 OCT 2043

The next day, Brumbaugh sent his team out to comb the City. He told them to check everything they could think of, then to check everything they couldn't think of, then to check it all again.

Jersey Wilks was in and gave his report. The PATH tubes were up at last and he had floated in early, to make up for yesterday. Jersey was a black man, dark black, and built like an angry defensive linesman. Crowds parted instinctively when he walked down the street. Only Brumbaugh knew Wilks' dark secret: he was a bird-watcher and butterfly collector.

He was also the best records man Brumbaugh had.

"So, what'll it be, Lieutenant?" he asked. "Public school records? Bank accounts? Credit cards? Police records?"

"We already know they got no priors," growled Brumbaugh.

"Did you know Benny was rich?"

"I figured it. He's a doctor, isn't he?"

"Sure. He rakes in the credits like leaves on a fall day. But it all goes in and hardly any of it goes out."

"What do you mean?"

Wilks shrugged one shoulder. "He don't spend it. And when he does, he doesn't buy top of the line, even though he can well afford it."

"Why do you suppose that is?"

"How should I know? Maybe he found out Hell is expensive and he's planning to take it with him."

"Uh-hunh. What about the others?"

"Barry and Billy are both well off, but Billy's the real spender. Lives on the edge. Barry, he's like any other wheeler-dealer. He could be dirt poor or filthy rich. No one can tell. The other two? Hank's shop keeps him comfortable, but Bobby is pretty much hand-to-mouth. Barry's loaned him money from time to time. Never paid back."

"What else you got?"

"Well, Bobby was in the hospital once, when he was a kid. Traffic accident. They all five came down with neo-mumps. In school— How much of this do you want?"

"Wilks, if I knew what was going to be important in this case, I'da told you to get it."

"Have it your way. They were all B+ students in high school. They all went to the same college—CCNY. They all joined the same frat. They're all registered Independents. Oh. Police record." He grinned at Brumbaugh's surprise. "No, none of 'em were ever arrested. But the father was a complainant on a case back in 2024. Claimed his sons were being harrassed because they were clones. Seems Barry was beat up pretty bad by some neighborhood kids. Sawyerite families." He shook his head. "I guess they ran out of blacks and Hindus." He scrolled some more pages. "Let's see. I wasn't able to locate their father, Rudolph," he told Brumbaugh. "Local cops cruised by his house, but no one was home."

"He flew into the City. Showed up on my desk late yesterday."

"Yeah? Still want my report?"

"Just give me the highpoints. I'll read the rest later."

"Okay. He works at Matusiak and Kobesky. Genetic counselors. They told me he called in around 0900 Monday morning. Said he wasn't coming to work because Billy had called him from New York. Said 'his boys' were in trouble and he was going there to straighten things out." Wilks scrolled his notescreen. "Matusiak wasn't too thrilled because Kavin had taken an early start on his weekend, but he gave him three days off with pay. Says Kavin's a good worker. High productivity. Not many client complaints."

Brumbaugh grunted. "How do you measure productivity in genetic counseling? Never mind, I don't want to know. What about Adamides? Did you locate him?"

"Uh-hunh. He said there was nothing out of the ordinary about the Kavin cloning. No special designs or modifications. Strict specs, though. Straight carbon copies, was the way he put it. I could tell he didn't want to open up to me. You know how you can sense when someone is holding back? Well, I got that from this Adamides guy. So I leaned on him a little. He didn't want to admit anything at first, but I finally got out of him that there were originally *eight* Kavin clones."

Brumbaugh straightened up. "Eight, did you say? Where are the other three?"

Wilks shrugged expressively. "Well, he was a little evasive about that. He says that one of the clones didn't 'take' and that the other two failed in morphogenesis."

"Morphogenesis?"

Wilks grinned. "Look it up."

"So what did he do with the three rejects?"

"He says he aborted them."

"You don't believe him?"

"I don't know. Something I sensed. I think maybe one of them wasn't."

"Wasn't aborted."

"At least, not the way Adamides said."

"So there may be a sixth Kavin running around town. One that Daddy and the Carbon Copies don't even know about." A sixth clone. That would explain how the five Kavins could have such good alibis and still leave a tissue sample at the scene. If it were true. He wondered who could have raised it. Adamides? What must it be like to be part of a brotherhood, but outside it? He tried to imagine the outcast clone, lurking in the background. Resentful. Wistful. Jealous. Watching. Copying. It might work. If it were true.

"That's about the size of it," admitted Wilks. "Of course, maybe this Adamides character is speaking sooth; but I just get a feeling, is all."

"All right. Someone has to go down to CCNY and check their cloning records. Especially the Tissue Sample Traceability Records and the Lab Reports."

"From twenty-seven years ago? Sounds like a bitchin' job."

"It sure does—and it's yours."

Wilks made a face of great joy. "Gee whiz, thanks, Lieutenant. You're a pal."

Hank's alibi checked out, of course.

Brumbaugh took the Lex to Bleecker and walked to Great Jones Street. Hank Kavin's art supply store was open. The stressed glass sign projected in the window gave the Saturday hours as 10:00 to 2:00, in glowing letters. Brumbaugh studied the sign, trying to see how it was done. Intelligent windows, they called them. Window glass and computer chips were both silicon.

Inside were two clerks (one male, one female, both young) and a handful of customers (in assorted shapes and sizes). The place smelled of clay and paint. Brumbaugh browsed for a few minutes while the clerks dealt with some purchases. He studied the rack of acrylic paints, wondering how anyone could distinguish among so many subtly different shades. Blue-green and green-blue. What the hell was the difference? And all the different browns. Burnt Umber. Sienna. Some of the colors had fantastic names. Martian Rust. L5 Ebon. He wondered what would happen if he switched some of them around. Would any of the artists really notice, or was it some sort of game they played among themselves?

Thinking about artists reminded him of Lewis, the witness who had seen one of the Kavins leaving Higgins' apartment. Did they have enough new data to make auto-regression worthwhile? Speakeasy caused total recall. Under the *smertechka* the witness could recall details the conscious mind overlooked. But you had to know what questions to ask.

And Speakeasy was a rough drug, too. It opened *all* the doors in the subject's mind. Shook loose every forgotten sorrow, every buried secret. All the petty and shabby acts of a person's life bubbled to the top of the conscious mind, like the froth on a wastewater settling pond. It was a harrowing experience and, by law, could not be performed without the subject's consent, nor repeated for at least six months.

At last the clerks were free and Brumbaugh presented himself. The announcement that Hank Kavin was a suspect in a murder investigation disturbed them. They didn't think it was possible. Brumbaugh assured them that anything was possible and asked if either of them had worked the previous Saturday.

The young man had. He told Brumbaugh his name was Kyle Karson—with a K—and he had worked all day Saturday until they closed up. They were in the shop until maybe 2:10, locking up. Brumbaugh questioned him closely about Hank's story, and he confirmed all the particulars. He asked him if he knew where Hank had gone for lunch and Karson with a K told him he wasn't sure but he thought that he had bagged it to the Square.

Brumbaugh thanked him and left the shop. He walked down Great Jones until it changed into West Third. Then he turned north and walked to the park. There was the usual potpourri of hangers out. Painters painting the arch. Dicties scoring dope. Young lovers sitting demurely on blankets afraid to do what they wanted to do because who knew when a morals proctor might come along?

The dicties and their pushers were playing it so cool they were superconducting. The little packets and the big wads changed hands quickly, surreptitiously. Fooling the proctors was how the game was played. A handshake. A pat on the back. An *abraço.* It was easier to disguise that sort of transaction than it was to disguise an illicit kiss, but Brumbaugh's practiced eye was not fooled.

Neither were the pushers. They saw him, made him, and dismissed him. They were almost defiant. They knew with a glance that he was not there for them.

There was no chance that he could confirm Hank Kavin's presence in the park. Some of these people had undoubtedly been here that day, but the probability that anyone would nark to a policeman was as close to negative as you could get.

He continued through the park and caught an uptown Eighth Avenue train at Fourth Street and rode it to Columbus Circle, coming up in the Hearst Building. He walked the two blocks to the hotel.

At first, the desk clerk did not want to cooperate, but a look at Brumbaugh's credentials effected a marvelous transformation in attitude. Actually, the clerk was perfectly correct, Brumbaugh reflected. Information on guests could not be given out to every Jimmy that trucked in from the street. He studied the register screen.

R. Kavin. Room 104. Address 1227 N. 23rd St., Milwaukee. Checked in at 12:08 on the afternoon of the nineteenth. Brumbaugh copied the credit card number.

R. Kavin bowed him into the room with the same false heartiness that he had shown the day before in the police station. "Ah, Lieutenant . . . Brumbaugh, right? What can I do for you? Have you released my sons yet?"

Brumbaugh shook his head and looked around the room. "Not yet. We started the paperwork this morning, but it'll take a while to get it processed." Brumbaugh thought that "lost paperwork" was the greatest invention of the criminal justice system. For some reason, the NYPD computers had more timely disc crashes, keystroke errors, and accidental erasures than any computer system in the world.

"Just a few questions we're doublechecking. Which of your sons called you Monday morning to tell you of the murder?"

Kavin sat on the edge of the bed. Brumbaugh remained standing, but he leaned his backside against the dresser to take some of the weight off his feet. There were a brush and comb, a razor—the old fashioned kind—and some toiletry articles. Idly, he moved them around with his left hand, playing a kind of chess game with them. Kavin scowled at him, resenting the familiarity, but unwilling to make an issue of it.

"It was Billy who called," Kavin answered.

Brumbaugh looked up, abandoning a checkmate on the deoderant. "Are you sure?"

"He told me it was Billy. My sons don't lie."

"To you, maybe. But one of them's lying to us."

Kavin shook his head. "I don't believe that."

"What time did Billy call you?"

Kavin frowned. "I'm not sure. I don't remember. Early. Maybe eight or so. I packed a bag immediately, called work and told them I wasn't coming in, and grabbed the next flight to New York."

"Yeah? How was it? The flight."

"Bumpy coming over the Appalachians, but the landing in Newark was smooth."

"Yeah, I know what you mean. It's the take-offs and landings that get me. That's when the most things can go wrong. Once you're up, you're up." He scrolled across his notescreen, glanced at it. "Have you given any more thought to what I asked you yesterday?"

"About differences among my sons? Yes, I have. I'm sorry I can't help you much. I mean, *I* can tell them apart, but I'll be damned if I know how."

Brumbaugh thought that R. Kavin knew exactly how he could tell his sons apart, but he wasn't going to cooperate. The family bonds were too strong.

"Bobby has a scar on the back of his scalp from that bike accident," Kavin continued. "I don't know of any other physical differences, though I'm sure they must have picked up random scratches over the years."

Sure, thought Brumbaugh sourly. *But none of them on the face.*

"What about non-physical differences?" he asked.

"Psychological? Not much there, either. They're as alike as peas in a pod."

Brumbaugh was tired of hearing that. "Have you ever seen peas in a pod?" he asked.

"Hmmm? Oh. They aren't very much alike, are they?" He laughed shortly. "Silly metaphor, isn't it."

Brumbaugh crossed his arms. "Suppose you tell me a little about each of your sons. Just give me an impression of each."

Kavin sucked his teeth. "I don't suppose you mean about how gentle they are and how they wouldn't hurt a fly? No, I didn't think so." He tilted his head back and pursed his lips. "Well, let's start with Barry. He's the best of the lot. Serious. No nonsense. Billy's the most like him, I guess, except maybe he lives a little faster. Barry's more a nose to the grindstone type. Billy will wear the Yomatsu watches; Barry prefers a cheap, reliable Brazilian one. Chances are, where you might find Billy in an after-hours joint, you'll find Barry working late in his office." He looked at Brumbaugh steadily. "I don't want to exaggerate the difference, understand. This ant and the grasshopper thing. To anyone else, their behavior might seem pretty much the same. I'm their father, so I notice little things."

"Uh-hunh. What about the others? How would you characterize them?"

Kavin pursed his lips and looked past Brumbaugh's shoulder. "Well, there's not much to say about Bobby. He doesn't have his brothers' drive and ambition. The others are all professionals or own their own business. Bobby's satisfied with being a bartender in a crummy beer joint. If I had to sum up his personality, I'd say he'd rather watch life than live it."

"And Benny?"

"Benny." Brumbaugh thought he saw a faint twist of disapproval in Kavin's mouth. "Benny's all right, I suppose."

"You don't like him."

Kavin looked surprised. "What? Don't be absurd. He's my son. More than my son. I love him as much as I love all of them."

Brumbaugh wondered how much that was. He didn't think Rudolph Kavin loved any of them half so well as he loved Rudolph Kavin. In a sense, he had had children by making love to himself. There was more than a little narcissism in such an act. "So, tell me about Benny."

"It's not so much Benny," Kavin admitted. "It's that . . . employee of his."

"The nurse? Karen Jo Lincoln?"

"Yes. The woman."

"What about her? Too dark for you?"

"Too . . . female, if you must know."

Brumbaugh thought that, from what Mac had said, "too female" would be the last description he would apply to Lincoln. Though, come to think of it, the repressed sexuality of both the doctor and his nurse implied a rather considerable psychological tension. Who knew how that might express itself after hours?

"You do know that if Benny is seeing female patients,

then he must have a female nurse to chaperone the examinations?"

Kavin sighed. "Yes, I know that. I told Benny he should see only male patients; but he said that would give a wrong impression in some quarters, and he would be in violation of some absurd civil rights rule. Besides, women being the weaker sex, they are more prone to ailments and psychosomatic ills, so there was a lot of money involved, too."

"And the money is important," Brumbaugh stated flatly.

"It is to Benny. Now Billy, he's a spender. He likes what he can buy with the money. And for Barry, the money is just the scorecard and the fun comes from playing the financial game. Benny just likes the money. He went into medicine because he thought he could rake it in faster. He didn't love it the way Barry loves finance."

"Scrooge, hunh?" Brumbaugh made a mental note never to see *Dr.* Benny professionally.

Kavin shook his head. "Scrooge? No, not the way most people would understand it." He shifted his place on the bed, looked at Brumbaugh, then looked away again.

"Which brings us to Hank," Brumbaugh suggested.

"Yes. Hank is the loner. He's different from his brothers. Even when he was young I could tell."

"Did that bother you?"

Kavin opened his mouth, closed it, and opened it again. "A little. What parent is there that doesn't fear his child may be defective?"

"Different isn't defective."

"Isn't it? It all depends on your standards, doesn't it? If you have standards. Or are you one of those egalitarians, who think that there is no one best way?"

"My beliefs aren't the issue here. One of your sons is a murderer. My job is to find out which. Or doesn't murder violate your standards?"

Interestingly, that seemed to strike something in

Kavin. His face grew sad and a little wistful. "No, Lieutenant, I never raised my sons to be killers."

"But one of them is. That makes him 'defective,' doesn't it? Help me stop him before he does it again."

Kavin gathered himself together. "No, again, Lieutenant. You see, I don't accept your contention. There's been a tragic mistake here, that's all."

Brumbaugh shrugged. "All right, then. Tell me how Hank is different from his brothers."

Kavin paused in thought for a while. "Hank has been a disappointment to me, even more so than Bobby. He hasn't measured up to my expectations."

"Meaning he likes girls."

Kavin looked at him sharply. "He associates with them. More than he should. But I'm positive he hasn't done anything filthy."

"You don't like women yourself, do you?"

"They are no longer necessary. With human cloning legally available once more, men can reproduce themselves without the sloppy and painful need of forming a . . . a 'relationship,' I believe they used to say."

"Relationships can be painful," Brumbaugh admitted. "Only the dead feel nothing."

Kavin laughed. "Very facile, Lieutenant. I'll not convince you that my way is right. And you'll not convince me that the random mixing of genes with chance aquaintances is the best way to produce offspring."

Brumbaugh grunted but said nothing. There was more to the business than producing offspring. Tillie was sterile, had always been sterile, but he couldn't imagine the last thirty years without her.

"And what about Number Six?" he asked gruffly.

Kavin looked blank. "Number Six?"

"There were six clones, weren't there? We've spoken with Dr. Adamides."

Kavin snorted. "Then you know that there were originally eight embryos. Three were defective and were aborted."

"Were they? We have information that suggests that one was not." He didn't really have such information. It was a shot in the dark. He wanted to see how Kavin would react.

The reaction was interesting. Kavin's face grew red, and his eyes took on a wary look. "That's a lie!" he said. "Whoever told you that was lying! There are only five surviving Kavin clones."

Brumbaugh saw that the other was concealing something. Clone Number Six struck very close to some sort of nerve. "Maybe so. We'll check into it anyway."

Kavin stood up and walked toward the door. "If you are finished now, Lieutenant? I was planning to visit with my sons today." Brumbaugh pushed himself away from the dresser and followed him.

"Thank you for your help, Mr. Kavin," he said at the door. He stuck out his hand and Kavin shook it perfunctorily.

"You should be out on the streets looking for the killer, not persecuting my sons."

"We'll catch the killer," Brumbaugh promised him.

In the hallway, he looked at what he held in his left hand. A hair. He had pulled it from the brush on the dresser. It was long and brown. Kavin's hair was short and grey. *Well, well, Mr. Misogynist. Have we had a visitor? Maybe a woman?* Or maybe a man. No telling Kavin's tastes.

He stopped at the desk on the way out. He asked the clerk if Kavin had taken anyone to his room. Male or female. Did he pick up anyone in the bar or on the street?

The clerk tossed her head back. The hotel did not monitor the behavior of its guests. That was for morals proctors. She looked around quickly as she said that, in case a proctor was nearby. Brumbaugh thanked her and left. What Kavin had told him pretty much bore out his own impressions of the five clones. But he had the nagging feeling that he was missing something important. Something about the sixth clone.

TUESDAY AFTERNOON, 20 OCT 2043

Mac was on the phone when Brumbaugh returned to the station. He waved at Brumbaugh and pointed to the phone. "A tip," he said, covering the mouthpiece. "Wait just a minute while I get this down."

While he waited, Brumbaugh sent the hair to the lab for an analysis. Detective Pizzuli came over and handed him a large manila envelope. Brumbaugh raised his eyebrows questioningly.

Pizzuli was short and chunky, with a swimmer's build. She opened the envelope onto Brumbaugh's desk. Sketches in charcoal and pencil spilled out. Kavins. A coven of Kavins. Kavins scowling. Kavins laughing. Kavins looking thoughtful. "What is this?" he asked.

"We found them in Higgins' apartment. The police artist tells me they're 'studies' or preliminary sketches."

"She was going to make a life-mask, too," Brumbaugh said absently. "Hank told us that." He looked through the sketches. Identical faces. They all seemed to be laughing. He paused over one. There were six faces scattered across the page. Were they six studies of the same man? Or had Higgins learned about the sixth clone?

Pizzuli reported that Barry Kavin's secretary could corroborate Barry's presence in their office until 12:50, when Barry had left to meet his brother for lunch. Brumbaugh asked when the secretary had eaten lunch and Pizzuli told him that he had gone out between 11:45 and 12:15. Also, she said, nobody at the Blarney Stone remembered Bobby stopping there for lunch. Which didn't necessarily prove anything.

Brumbaugh handed her a photograph of Rudolph that he had taken with his tie clasp camera and told her to go to Kavin's hotel and see if she could get him to pick her up. He told her to talk with the bartender and other guests, unofficially, and ask about his activities the previous evening.

"Why the interest in Rudolph?" Mac asked when Pizzuli had gone.

Brumbaugh turned. His partner was off the phone. "Nothing, really. I'm just trying to get a handle on this crazy family. Some feel for what makes 'em tick. The father made them what they are."

"Tell me on the way, Lieutenant. We just got a tip. Manager at some East Side fleabag called and said one of the Kavins checked into his hotel late Friday night. He recognized the picture in the paper."

They took a staff car and drove up Third Avenue. Mac listened while Brumbaugh recounted his findings at the art shop and at the Holiday Inn. He told Mac about the hair.

"Hunh," the sergeant said. "Know what I think? I think this whole female thing is a facade. I think they like women, but they won't admit it even to themselves. Like they got an image to keep up."

"Is that so?"

"Yeah. Like *Dr.* Benny and his nurse. Methinks they do protest too much. I bet they're getting it on after hours. Don't you? And I bet *both* of them get a big kick out of examining women patients."

Brumbaugh looked at him. "You got a dirty mind. You gonna turn them over to the proctors?"

Mac made a face. "Don't ever mention a proctor to a cop. You know what the word means? Proctor? It's from the Greek. *Proktos,* meaning 'the asshole.' And the suffix is Latin, *-or,* meaning 'one who is or does.' So proctor means 'one who is an asshole.' " He laughed.

"That's not what the word means," Brumbaugh told him.

"Shit, I know that. But that's what it *should* mean. Bluenoses playing at being cops. Who needs 'em?"

* * *

The Hotel Calypso was for transients. Brumbaugh wondered if the manager appreciated the irony in the name, then decided that he did. The manager was short and skinny and wore glasses thicker than a boot heel. The table behind the check-in desk was littered with dog-eared paperbacks. Dostoyevsky. Sartre. Joyce. And, of course, Homer. The manager's name was Boris Quint. There was a sign over the desk giving monthly, daily, and hourly room rates.

Brumbaugh showed him a photograph of the Kavins and Quint said, yes, that was the man. At least, one of them was. No, he couldn't say which one. He showed them the terminal and pointed to the entry, Jason Medwick, and said that was the name the man had used. Brumbaugh noted that "Medwick" had checked in at 9:00 P.M. on the sixteenth, paying cash. There was no home address given, which didn't matter since it would have been as phony as the name.

Quint told them that Medwick had met a woman in the bar. Mac looked at Brumbaugh and Brumbaugh looked at Mac. They showed him a holograph of the murdered woman. It was a morgue holo. Head and shoulders. Eyes closed. No complexion, except the purple markings on the throat. Quint stared at it, holding it close to his eyes, and licked his lips.

"Was that the woman?" Mac asked.

"Maybe. I can't be sure, but I think it was. The bar's dark and I don't see so well." He blinked at them and the effect, with the eyes magnified by the lenses, was like twin signal lamps on a battle cruiser.

"What about the bartender?"

"That's my brother-in-law. He never sees anything, if you know what I mean."

Mac laughed. "I've got a memory improvement course." He took the photo and headed for the bar. Quint watched him go.

"When did he check out?" Brumbaugh asked.

"What?" Quint turned.

"This 'Medwick.' When did he check out?"

"He didn't. That's why I called you guys."

"You mean he's up there now?"

"Oh, no. I haven't seen him since Sunday. But he didn't check out. Didn't pay his tab, either," he added, aggrieved.

"Rent the room yet?"

"No. Say, Lieutenant?"

"What?"

"The story in the paper. About what he did to the girl. Do you think . . ."

"Think what?"

"Do you think she knew he was a clone? Was she doing it with all five of them? Maybe all of them together at once?" Quint's eyes were big; his mouth was slightly parted. He was hoping for the worst, eager to believe anything if it was bad enough.

"I wouldn't know," said Brumbaugh. He thought: *She had to know. She knew Hank, and she went to Bobby's bar, and Benny was her doctor.* Group sex was illegal, of course; but if the group was a set of clones, you could argue that it was really only one individual. He wondered if Higgins had been playing on a kind of sexual merry-go-round, and if so, whether she had found a way tell the brothers apart. Maybe she had wanted to try it with each one of them. People should have goals in life.

"It must have been kind of kinky," Quint insisted. "The five of them, like that."

"They don't like girls."

"What?"

"The clones. They don't like girls. Women."

"Y'mean they're queer?"

"No. They don't like sex at all. Too unsanitary." That should give Quint enough material to elaborate on with his patrons. *The investigating lieutenant, he tol' me. . . .* Maybe it would make somebody think of something. Bread upon the waters.

"Couldn't prove it by me. Not the way they were muzzling in the bar."

"How's that?"

"They were in each other's faces. You know . . ." He blushed. "Kissing and all. In public."

Brumbaugh thought Quint was overacting. If he didn't want that sort of thing going on in the bar, why did he keep it dark? So passing proctors couldn't see anything.

Mac returned from the bar with a positive ID. The brother-in-law had fingered the Higgins woman as the one who had been with "Medwick."

The most obvious thing about "Medwick's" room, when Quint had let them in with a pass key, was that there was nothing in it. No clothes. No personal effects. The room was bare.

"Mac, go call forensics. Tell 'em we want a search for tissue samples and fingerprints and all." Mac left and Brumbaugh wandered around the room. He was careful not to touch anything. Quint watched from the doorway, storing up material to tell his buddies. "Has the maid cleaned in here?"

Quint laughed. "Maid?"

Brumbaugh hadn't thought so, but it was nice to check. He took a stylus from his pocket and lifted the sheet where it hung to the floor and peered under the bed. Dust bunnies. No bodies or anything.

He stood up and brushed his knees off. There was a clock on the side table by the bed. It read 13:13. Brumbaugh scowled and checked his watch. "Your clock's slow. It's 13:56."

Quint shrugged. "No one who stays here wants to know the time anyway. I tell them when their time's up."

"Yeah." For most of the transients who stayed here, time had stopped anyway. He looked around the room again. Nothing to do but wait for forensics. He wondered if Higgins and Kavin had come up here. And, if they were meeting here, why did he go to her apartment the next day? And which one was "Medwick"? Barry, the most woman-hating of the lot? Hank, who actually had dated her? Benny, whose secret lust, Mac believed, boiled just below the surface? Or maybe . . .

Or maybe Clone Number Six? A sixth clone would explain an awful lot.

"Ever see either of them in here before?" Brumbaugh asked. "Medwick or the woman?" Quint shook his head.

Mac trudged back up the stairs and stood with Brumbaugh for a moment, surveying the room. He pulled a pen from his shirt and began twirling it. "I had a new thought."

"That's good. Don't let me stop you."

"Who says it was the same Kavin that was here on Friday as was at Higgins' place on Saturday?"

Brumbaugh looked at him. "You thinking about what Quint here said?" Then he remembered that Mac had been in the bar when Quint had said it. "That Higgins was playing with all five of them," he added.

"More than one, at least. She knew three of them." He fumbled the pen, caught it in his right hand. "I got a theory."

That was bad. When Mac started getting theories. "What is it?" Brumbaugh asked.

"One of the clones was fooling around with Higgins. Let's say it was Hank."

"Why Hank?"

"Why not? It's just a theory. Maybe I should say 'Alpha.' "

"No, Hank is fine."

"OK. Hank and Higgins are getting it on. Or getting it off," he laughed. "Dancing around the maypole. Barry finds out about it and goes into a rage. The worst thing a Kavin can do. He can't kill Hank. That would be like killing himself. So, he finds out where Higgins lives—maybe from Benny's records—and goes there. She thinks it's Hank and lets him in. Gets undressed before he can say boo. He's *never* seen a naked woman before; and

Higgins wasn't exactly Tugboat Annie, if you know what I mean. Can you imagine the effect it must have had on him? He does what comes naturally. He can't help it, despite all the conditioning from his father. Afterwards, he's disgusted, but it can't be *his* fault, because he's pure of heart. So he removes the source of temptation."

Brumbaugh nodded. "It's a good theory."

"Yeah. Maybe it wasn't Hank and Barry, but they fit best."

"Uh-hunh. There's just two problems with your theory."

"What's that?" Mac sounded hurt.

"Number one. There's no evidence to support it. Number two. Barry was eating lunch in a public restaurant during most of the time that the killer was at Higgins' apartment."

"Not in front of blabbermouth here." Mac jerked a thumb at Quint, who looked more disappointed than insulted.

Brumbaugh smiled at the manager. "Don't worry. Boris isn't going to say anything. You know why?" Mac asked why. "Because the Kavins have themselves a fancy lawyer whose suits cost more than this whole friggin' hotel; and if Boris here so much as breathes a word of your theory, Kasabian'll be all over him like a garbage slick on the Jersey shore." He swiveled his head and looked at Mac. "Not that I would compare Myron Kasabian to a garbage slick."

"Naw," Mac agreed. "He ain't that slick."

TUESDAY EVENING, 20 OCT 2043

When Morris was stuck on a case, Tillie thought, *he was impossible to talk to.* She watched him pace back and forth across their Staten Island living room, scowling like thunderclouds. Morris always kept everything inside him. Police troubles, anyway. He liked to lick his problems on his own. He would share it with her in his own good time.

She knew which case was troubling him. The papers were playing it up, more because of the clone aspect than the sex, which was, after all, routine for New York. The *Times* had editorialized that cases like this were justification for reinstating the anti-cloning ban. The *News-Post* wanted to know why Brumbaugh hadn't solved it yet, and had invented an entire new type size for its headlines. They had interviewed three well-known advice columnists, four psychics, and a Hollywood starlet to get their ideas on the case.

The holovision stage was mute. Morris didn't care for most of the shows on HV; although, with 125 channels to choose from, it was hard to decide which ones he disliked the most. Every week, they studied the published schedules and Tillie programmed the unit to record the ones they were interested in and play them back on their days off. Instead, Morris paced to the background of Alpine music. Franzl Lang yodeled his way through *Freunde der Bergen.* Absurdly cheerful, given Morris' disposition.

Tillie sighed and resumed her study of the chain diagrams. When Morris wanted to share his burden, he would. Meanwhile, there must be a reason why her protein assembler wasn't folding the way it was designed to.

Finally Morris sighed and stalked into the kitchen. She heard the potato chip bag rustle. "Morris!" she called. "You know what the doctor told you about greasy foods." He always began stuffing his face when he was unhappy.

"Screw the doctor," her husband replied. "I'm changing doctors. Gonna go to Dr. Benny from now on." She recognized the sarcasm, just as she recognized Dr. Benny from the news stories.

She laid the chaingrams down. The clones bothered her, too, but for a reason having nothing to do with Morris' case. She had been born sterile. Yet, she had always wanted to have children with Morris. Not adopted, and certainly not surrogate. Old fashioned, maybe, but it had been a real need within her. Cloning had seemed like the answer. Clones didn't have to be single-parented. They could be grown by combining DNA from both parents. (Or, for that matter, from three or more; but that was still illegal.) They could even be designed with the best gene combinations from both parents. Medically, there was no need for any couple to be infertile.

But Morris had drawn a line there and would not cross it. No cloning. He was seldom stubborn about anything, but on this issue, he would not budge. It made no sense to Tillie, but she couldn't force it on him. Children had to be made willingly or not at all. Now, she was too old for it to matter.

Morris returned from the kitchen. He stood in the doorway, the potato chip bag in his left hand, his right hand scrounging inside it. "Damn Kavin," he said. "Damn the five Kavin clones. Damn anyone who won't damn Kavin and his clones."

He went to the sofa and planted himself in it. Franzl Lang was singing about mountain climbing. *Um die Wände zu bezwingen, braucht man Kraft und braucht man Mut.*

Um den Gipfel zu erringen braucht man Schneid und ruhig Blut.

"I really thought we were on to something with that Number Six clone," he announced.

"Yes, dear."

"But Wilks checked the CCNY records, and it looks like everything matches. He says there was a date altered on one of the Tissue Disposal Forms. Wilks thinks that was why Adamides and Kavin were so nervous. It looks like one clone was aborted *after* quickening."

Tillie blinked at him. "Oh, dear. That is serious."

"Damn right. We could get them both on manslaughter, if the statute of limitations hadn't run out." After quickening, the fetus was legally a person, with class five rights. Just as Higgins had been an adult with class one rights. "We're not after a twenty-seven year old murder; we're after a twenty-seven year old murderer," Morris finished.

Tillie grimaced. The penalty for murder was alteration by Carterization, which she had never liked. It was better, in her mind, to execute the killer outright than to tamper with his personality.

Morris told her about the investigation. Tillie listened attentively; not because she thought she could help him, but because he needed to throw his own thoughts around and hear them out loud.

"We're going to regress our witness in the morning," he told her. "It's a longshot and we really had to argue to get him to agree. You know what Speakeasy is like. And even if he remembers noticing something, like Bobby's limp or scar, or Billy's running his hand through his hair, it won't mean diddly squat because we can't prove opportunity. Every single one of those bastards was somewhere else when the crime was going down."

"All of them?" she asked.

"Wilks and Pizzuli and Mac," he added, "have tracked down every witness we could identify. The businessmen Barry met at the restaurant. The patrons who were in Bobby's bar. The cleaning woman in Billy's office building. And they all corroborate the stories. We can't find a single hole in any of them!"

"That's too bad."

"It's more than too bad. It's impossible. We've got DNA prints. We *know* it was one of them! That's why I was counting on the Sixth Clone Theory. It would have explained all the facts."

"Could the geno-assay have been mistaken?"

He shook a handful of chips at her. "Not a chance. We had the lab run two more replicates. All three agreed."

"Well, you'll think of something." She smiled, patted his arm, and took the chips away from him. "It can't be easy with them being clones. It's like telling peas in a pod."

Morris laughed and Tillie smiled tentatively, not sure of the reason. He began to tell her how Rudolph had said the same thing, and how he used to shell peas as a boy and how peas in a pod weren't really alike, but a funny look came into his eyes. "Shelling peas," he muttered. "Well, I'll be damned. They *are* like peas in a pod!"

WEDNESDAY AM, 21 OCT 2043

Mac arrived at the station house early, but he found Brumbaugh already there, hard at work, when he walked in. "Hi, Lieutenant," he called. "What's up?" He inspected the clutter on the desk. Street and subway maps of Manhattan. Matrices with times and places filled in. Mac recognized them as Time-and-Position diagrams. He looked them over. "Laying out the afternoon of the crime?"

"It came to me last night," explained Brumbaugh without explaining. "Take a look at this map. I've marked the locations of Billy's ad agency, Hanson's bar, the Spanish restaurant, and the other locales. Notice anything?"

Mac studied the layout for a minute. Then he shook his head. "No. Should I?"

"None of them are more than a block away from a subway stop."

Mac shrugged. "No one in Manhattan is more than a block from a subway stop."

"That's an exaggeration. Here, look. Four of them are practically on top of the Lexington Avenue subway. Benny doesn't even have to leave his building to catch it. Fifty-first Street station is right outside Barry's office building. Billy is a block west of 33rd Street station, and Hank is close to the Bleeker Street station."

"Yeah, and Bobby is one block west of the 42nd Street station on the Eighth Avenue line. So what?"

"So none of them are ever more than fifteen minutes away from each other."

Mac frowned and looked at the map. "What about

Bobby? He can reach Barry or Hank easy enough on the E train, but what if he wants to see Billy or Benny?"

Brumbaugh pointed. "He walks the two blocks to Times Square. From there, the shuttle goes directly to Dr. Benny's building, and the Broadway trains to 34th Street, which is two blocks from Billy's ad agency. That last one is pushing the fifteen minutes, but it doesn't matter, since Billy spent a good part of the afternoon at a restaurant across the street from Benny's office."

Mac looked up from the map. "Okay. They're clone-brothers. They like to stay close to each other. I must be stupid this morning. Why is it so important?"

Brumbaugh handed him the the T/P diagram. "Look this over and then you tell me."

Mac sat down in the chair and pulled a pen from his pocket. He whistled while he read. The old Hitchcock theme music. Abruptly, the whistle turned into a single, high-pitched note. The pen fell to the floor and rolled under the desk. "I will be dipped in shit! How come we never noticed this before?"

Brumbaugh smiled. "Because the mind is the first thing to go when you get old—"

"The second thing," Mac answered him. "Son of a bitch. And we thought they all had alibis."

"Tillie and I were talking last night, and she used the old 'peas in a pod' cliché. I started to explain about peas not really being alike and remembered back when I used to shell peas for my mom, and that made me think about the old shell game. So, I thought, if four of the brothers kept changing places, they could make it look like there were five of them."

"Yeah," Mac said, running his finger down the chart. "None of the alibis account for all five of them at the same time. There was always one or two of them out to lunch, or on break, or just plain unobserved." He tapped the sheet. "Like when Barry's secretary was at lunch from 11:30 to 12:15."

"Right," Brumbaugh nodded happily. If it made sense

to Mac, it probably made sense. "*He* says he stayed in the office. *She* says he was there when she left and there when she got back. *But there was no observer in the meantime.* And an unobserved fact isn't a fact."

"Like Schrödinger's cat?"

"Who's Schrödinger, another detective?"

"In a way," Mac grunted. "So, you're thinking that when she got back from lunch, it wasn't really Barry there at all."

"Hell, maybe it wasn't even Barry to begin with. Mrs. Genata, their old neighbor, told me how they used to play the switcheroo game when they were kids. They got a kick out of it. It didn't really click with me at the time."

"Since they were all close to the subway, they could trade places whenever they wanted. And, if four of the five brothers can account for all the alibis . . ."

"That leaves one of them free to commit murder."

"Fine, but which one?"

"Easy. The one who suggested playing the game that afternoon."

"And that means they all know who really did it."

"Which makes them all accessories after."

"So now, what do we do?"

"Now we start asking different kinds of questions. 'Barry' was supposed to be shmoozing with some business aquaintances at the restaurant. Did he seem unsure of the details of finance or of past deals? Did anybody order a drink from 'Bobby' that he didn't know how to mix? That sort of thing."

"Uh-hunh. You know, if they do this sort of thing often, they'll have briefed each other pretty thoroughly."

"Sure, but they couldn't know *everything* about each other's lives. The meeting in the restaurant, for example, must have been a chance thing. Suppose it was Hank instead of Barry. He might have made some minor slip."

"Unless . . ."

"Unless what?"

"Unless clones really are telepathic."

Brumbaugh stared at him for a moment. "You sure are one cock-eyed optimist, aren't you?"

Mac shrugged. "When a pessimist is wrong, he's happier."

"You know what I think? I think Billy brought up telepathy just to make us wonder."

"Maybe. It'd be hard to test for it, too."

"Yeah. How can you tell the difference between someone who's not telepathic and someone who's *pretending* to be not telepathic?"

Mac refused to worry about it. "You can't. What about Lewis? We all set up?"

Brumbaugh checked his watch. "The tech has everything set up in Interogation One. Lewis hasn't shown yet."

"Think he will?"

Brumbaugh considered the question. Then he nodded. "Yeah, I think so."

The door opened and they both looked; but it was the lawyer, Kasabian, who entered, followed by a morals proctor. Kasabian nodded curtly then planted himself in a cracked plastic chair against the wall. He picked up a magazine and leafed through it. The proctor continued past him toward the desk.

"Hey, Myron," Mac called, jerking a thumb at the proctor, "they finally catch you?"

Kasabian gave him a sour look, settled his pince nez, and shook the magazine to a new page.

The proctor looked at Mac, then at Brumbaugh. "Police Lieutenant Brumbaugh?" she asked. Brumbaugh grunted, "That's me," and the proctor offered her hand.

"Assistant Warden Rebecca Morton. I'm your Official Witness. Is the subject here, yet?"

"Not yet, Warden Morton." He shook her hand briefly. "Have you read the case?"

"No, I haven't." Mac snorted, and Morton turned and looked at him. "The case isn't within my jurisdiction," she told him. "I'm not interested in it, per se. My only roles are to certify the transcripts and to assure that you do not abuse the truth drug."

"We don't mess around with Speakeasy," Mac growled.

"I'm sure you don't," the Warden replied in a voice that implied she wasn't sure at all. "Neither do ninety-nine percent of the secular police forces. But you must remember the scandals of 2037 when some departments used it to obtain illegal evidence and—in one instance—to destroy a suspect psychologically."

"Thompkins was scum," Mac told her. "He was guilty as sin."

The proctor shrugged. "Sin is for my department to judge, according to our Laws. The police, however, are bound by secular laws. Who shall guard the guardians?"

Mac's reply was forestalled—fortunately, in Brumbaugh's view—by the arrival of Lewis and his lawyer. Lewis' lawyer introduced herself as Jayne van Hook and Mac introduced the others. The proctor asked everyone to call her Becky. No one did.

"And the scuz over by the wall," added Mac, "is Myron Kasabian, the Kavins' lawyer." Kasabian smiled and waved. Insults were wasted on him.

Brumbaugh passed out sheets of paper. "These are the questions we plan to ask you, Mr. Lewis. By law, we may ask only these questions, or questions intended to follow up or clarify your answers to these. Hey, Kasabian!" He waved another copy of the list. "Don't you want to review the questions?" Kasabian looked up from his magazine and shook his head.

"Pretty damned confident," growled Mac.

"Yeah. He doesn't think we're going to get anything out of this, does he?"

"Screw him," said Mac. Then he looked at the proctor. "I was speaking metaphorically. That wasn't an actual request." Brumbaugh kicked Mac in the ankle.

"Of course," she replied through thin lips.

Lewis handed Brumbaugh the copy of the list. "These look . . . These look fine."

"Nervous?"

"I've heard stories."

"Well, I won't say don't worry. We'll all do our best to make this as easy as possible. You're a witness, not a suspect. You will be given a tranquilizer along with the drug. Your lawyer is here to see we stick to the list. She has the right to terminate the questioning on your behalf if the resurrected memories seem to be causing you great emotional distress. If you do blurt out some embarrassing memory not relevant to the investigation, it will be erased from the record."

"Sure." Lewis licked his lips, glanced at the proctor, then away.

"Do you want to take the Oath, now, Warden Morton? Everyone's here."

Morton agreed and Brumbaugh opened his lower right-hand desk drawer. There were a number of small, bound books. "Which one?" he asked. "Douay? Upanishads? Quran? Torah?"

"King James, of course."

Brumbaugh selected one of the books and pulled a small printed card from it. He handed the miniature to Morton, who held it in her left hand, palm up. It looked ludicrously small. Mac set the video camera on his shoulder and nodded.

"Do you swear or affirm," Brumbaugh read from the card, "on your Faith in God and your Hope of Salvation that your Witness to these procedings will be true and complete; and that, further, you will take no account of, nor otherwise notice, any extraneous information divulged by the subject while under the influence of the drug; nor will you turn any such information over to the Proctor General's office."

"I do so affirm. God be praised!"

They trooped toward the interrogation room. Mac whispered to Brumbaugh, "How much protection is that Oath if she really gets it in for someone?"

Van Hook heard him. "It depends on whether you

really Believe," she said. "I wouldn't worry about the Sincere so much. It's the opportunists and cynics you need to look out for."

The technician looked up when they entered. "Just finished, Lieutenant."

There was a padded chair, with restraining straps set in the middle of the room. Two drip bottles hung on their racks, one on either side of the chair. The table had been pushed to one side and was now filled with monitoring equipment. The leads hung loose.

The witness looked at the setup and wet his lips again. "Let's get this over with," he said.

He sat in the chair and the technician administered the sedative. Then he began attaching leads. When Lewis was under, the technician inserted the intravenous needles. He turned on the Speakeasy drip. "I'll turn on the tranquilizer drip," he told them, "if I need to counteract any agitation."

He watched the α-monitor for a few minutes, while Mac set up the videotape. Finally, the tech nodded. "Go ahead, Lieutenant. He's in the *smertechka.*"

Brumbaugh nodded. He leaned toward the witness. "Can you hear me, Mr. Lewis?"

"Yes."

"I want you to go back. To 17 October 2043, four days ago. It is 12:30 in the afternoon. Are you there?"

A hesitation. "Yes. It's Saturday." The voice was heavy, zombie-like. *Smertechka* was Russian for the "little death." It had been used originally to create "zombies" during the purge of the *glasnostniki.*

"What do you see, Mr. Lewis?"

"My room. It's dim. Overcast outside. The light's no good for painting."

"What do you hear?"

"Nothing. Traffic sounds from Third Avenue. The buzzer in the hallway. Someone wants into the building and one of the residents has triggered the door lock. I open the door and peek out."

"Why?" That was Kasabian. Brumbaugh gave him a venomous look.

Lewis continued. "Mugs do that sometimes. They press buttons until someone lets them in."

"What do you see in the hall?"

"A man. Thin. Long, brown hair. Five-nine. He's wearing a light blue windbreaker. He climbs the stairs. I hear knocking from the third floor. Bev Higgins' apartment. Bev is an artist, too. Works in clay, like Cyndy. Cyndy was my wife. She left me. We didn't—"

Brumbaugh interrupted the stray thought. "Can you hear anything from the third floor, Mr. Lewis?"

There was a silence while the man in the chair squirmed. He cocked his head in a listening attitude. "No. I hear a car horn from the street." Abruptly, Lewis' face twisted in terror. "No! Hit the brakes! Hit the brakes!"

The technician jumped and turned on the tranquilizer drip. He glanced at Brumbaugh. "Memory association," he apologized. "The automobile horn reminded him of something."

"Don't let him get off the track," warned van Hook. "The accident was very traumatic for him."

Brumbaugh looked at the lawyer as if to say he was more interested in staying on track than she was. But he said nothing and turned his attention back to the witness.

"Mr. Lewis. It is now . . ." He consulted his time sheet. ". . . It is now 1:57 P.M. Tell me what is happening."

"A door slams. Upstairs. Heavy steps on the stairway. Someone in a hurry. I open the door a crack. I peek out. I must be quiet. Mommy and Daddy will be angry. I can see them through the bedroom door. They are—"

"Stop, Mr. Lewis."

"I'm sorry. I'm so sorry." Tears forced themselves through Lewis' closed eyelids.

"Mr. Lewis. It is the year 2043. You are not a child.

You are in your apartment on Third Avenue, not your parents' house. You are looking out through your apartment door at the hallway."

"You should have let me drive, you stupid bitch!"

"Mr. Lewis. It is the year 2043. You are in your apartment. You are looking out through your door at the hallway."

"There is a man on the stairs," the witness said, suddenly calm. Brumbaugh relaxed.

"Go on. Is it the same man you saw earlier?"

"Yes. He is coming down the stairs. He looks worried. He glances back over his shoulder. He rubs his hands together and shoves them in the pockets of his windbreaker. I know him."

"What is his name?"

"Hank Kavin. He runs the art store where I buy my paints. I've seen him and Bev together sometimes."

"Does he see you?"

"No. Yes, I think he does. He glances at my door and sees it is open a crack. I see his pupils dilate. He takes a step toward my door. He stops and runs for the street door. He's running, the sonuvabitch. That'll teach him we don't want his kind on our turf. Damned wops."

Brumbaugh realized that the image of a running man had triggered another association. "Mr. Lewis, I want you to make time reverse until the man is on the stairs. Then I want time to stop. Do you understand me?"

"The dagos think they can come in here anytime they want. We'll show them, won't we? This is white boys' turf."

Brumbaugh repeated himself patiently. "Mr. Lewis, I want you to back up until the man is on the stairs. Before he puts his hands in his pockets. Then I want time to stop. Do you understand me?"

"He is on the stairs."

"Do you see him in profile or full-face?"

"I see a three-quarters figure, from the front and the left. Lighting is soft white, from the left."

"Good. Time is now frozen. I want you to zoom in on

the man. Let your eyes get closer. I want you to focus on his . . ." He consulted the checksheet that he and Mac had put together. It was a list of distinguishing features, based on what Rudolph had told them, and on their own and others' observations. "Focus on his feet, Mr. Lewis. Can you describe his shoes?"

"They are black shoes. Six-hole laces. Brazilian styling, but not Brazilian made."

"Are there any scuff marks? Or soil?"

"No. They are worn-looking. They are probably comfortable."

Brumbaugh gradually worked his way up the suspect. When Lewis described the prominent bulge in the pants, Morton blushed. When they reached the hands, Brumbaugh asked him if the suspect was wearing any jewelry.

"He has a ring on his fourth finger."

"Describe the ring."

"It is the worm Ourobouros. The snake that swallows its own tail. A powerful symbol. Primordial. Jungian. The *ur*-snake. The snake is striking her. She is gasping. She is laughing. She is laughing at me. She is laughing at the snake. I am so ashamed." Lewis turned in the chair and tried to curl up, but the straps held him in place. The technician adjusted the tranquilizer flow.

"Mr. Lewis. What else do you see on the man's hand? Is he wearing a watch?"

Lewis quieted. "Yes. He is wearing a watch. It is expensive. Japanese. I can read the logo. Yomatsu. It reads 13:18."

"Now look at the man's scalp. There may be a scar there, above his ear on the left side. Look carefully. Let your eyes go into the hair."

"His hair is not combed."

"Can you see a scar beneath the hair?"

"So fine," Lewis murmured. "Her hair is so fine. I run my hands through her hair. She turns her face toward me. We . . ."

"Please, Mr. Lewis. Do not digress. Stay in the hallway of your apartment building."

"I'll never see her again." A sob escaped from his throat. Van Hook sat up and laid a hand on Brumbaugh's arm.

"Just a little while longer," Brumbaugh pleaded. Van Hook frowned, looked at Lewis, and nodded slightly.

"Mr. Lewis, are you back in your apartment? You were inspecting Kavin's scalp for a scar. Can you see a scar?"

"Yes. A small scar, just behind the ear. I see it when he runs his hand through his hair."

"Is it Kavin you are seeing? Are you back in the hallway?"

"Yes. I wonder why he looks so worried. Worry. Worry. Do you think the show will go off all right? What if the critics don't like my work?"

"The critics will love your paintings," Brumbaugh told him. "Now let Kavin walk toward the door. Let time resume. There may be a slight limp. Tell me if he limps."

"He is coming down the stairs. He looks worried. He glances back over his shoulder. He rubs his hands together and shoves them in the pockets of his windbreaker. He stumbles on the third step."

"Which foot?" asked Brumbaugh sharply. Lewis told him it was the right and Brumbaugh made a note. "Go on."

"He looks at my door and sees it is open a crack. I see his pupils dilate. He drops his eyes. He takes a step toward my door. His hair is not straight. He stops and runs his hand through his hair. His lips move . . ."

"Stop! Can you hear his words?"

"He is whispering to himself. He says, 'Sonuvabitch. I didn't want to. I'm a sonuvabitch.' Then he turns and bolts for the street door. I see no limp."

"Thank you, Mr. Lewis. We will go through it once more."

Van Hook stopped him. "Is that really necessary? Look at him." Brumbaugh watched the witness twist and squirm in the chair. Lewis moaned and tears stained his cheeks. A thin drool of saliva stained his collar. "The longer he stays under," van Hook reminded him, "the more buried memories will bob to the surface of his mind. Every mean and petty act. Every embarrassment and disappointment. Every mistake and slip of the lip."

"Yes, and every joy and fondness."

"On the balance, Lieutenant, of which is any life more full?"

Brumbaugh bit his lip, then he shook his head. "You can stop me at any time, counselor. But I need a second run-through, so I can sort out the stray remarks. Remember, he volunteered. Beverly Higgins was a neighbor and a friend. He *wants* to help us."

Van Hook gave in and they went through the questioning again. Five times, Lewis lost his train of thought, as his subconscious segued through associated images into other memories. Four times, the recollections were painful. Once he screamed, "The baby! The baby!" And Brumbaugh wondered what private torment he was reliving.

Brumbaugh felt that Hell must be very much like this. Total and complete recollection, without any illusions or excuses.

Afterward, they left Lewis alone so he could compose himself. Mac and Brumbaugh went to their desks. Kasabian laughed and waved to them as he left.

"Sonuvabitch," muttered Mac. "He doesn't think we learned anything useful."

"Did we?"

"Hell, no; but I can't stand it that he knows it."

"Lewis didn't see a limp."

"So what? Negative evidence doesn't prove anything. You know that."

"What about the lowering of the eyes?"

"You mean, was it Benny? Anybody can lower their

eyes. Or run their hand through their hair. Or wear a fancy watch."

"Like Billy."

"Yeah, like Billy. I still like Barry for the Jimmy, you know what I mean? But we didn't get any proof from Lewis. Hell, it's like the Jimmy was deliberately mimicking his brothers' habits. We've got to dig deeper."

Warden Morton took her leave. "I've sealed the video with my official seal," she told them. "Sorry you didn't learn anything, but don't worry. Our Father, Who sees all in secrecy, will act justly. The killer, whichever he is, will be punished."

Mac watched her go. "What an attitude for a cop! Don't worry if you don't catch the Jimmy, because God'll get him. That must be comforting if you're a crook."

Brumbaugh rubbed his nose. "Actually, I think she was trying to comfort us."

"Us?" Mac seemed surprised that anyone would think he needed comfort. "Hell." He lapsed into silence. "You know what bothers me most of all?"

"What's that?"

"That we put Lewis through hell, and it didn't help our case any. I mean, it'd be one thing if his subconscious remembered something important. Then, at least, we could all tell each other that it was worth it."

"Yeah." Brumbaugh felt depressed. It seemed as if they had made no progress at all on the killing, despite everything that they had learned. None of it seemed to hang together. None of it pointed at any particular individual. Even if the clones *had* played musical chairs that afternoon, it didn't tell them which one was odd-man-out.

Mac told him he was going to the corner deli for lunch and asked did Brumbaugh want to come with him. Brumbaugh told him no thanks. They were releasing the Kavins that afternoon and he wanted to make sure the paperwork was straightened out. Mac said that was a hell of a note and Brumbaugh agreed. It was a hell of a note.

* * *

He fiddled with the papers on his desk. Printouts. Interviews with Nurse Lincoln; with the bartender at Hanson's. The lab report on the hair. Time and position notes. Maps of subway stops. Quint's fleabag hotel. Forensic reports on the DNA found on the scene. The transcript of Lewis' testimony. His own scribbled thoughts on scratch paper. He picked up the map showing the hypothetical movements of the clonebrothers during the afternoon of the crime. He studied it silently for a while. Then he threw it down in disgust. The "musical chairs" gambit just wouldn't work. *Benny.* Brumbaugh watched his carefully erected theory collapse like a house of straw. Benny was the key and he just wouldn't fit in the lock. *Dr.* Benny loved money. He would never risk a malpractice suit by letting one of his brothers take his place in the office. It didn't matter that all the appointments that afternoon were "routine." When even the slightest chance of a slip-up could have multi-million dollar repercusions, Benny just wouldn't take the risk. The "old switcheroo" was a fine theory, in the abstract. But it couldn't stand up in the face of practical human realities.

And if Benny was out of it, the other three couldn't pull it off. There was no way they could have traded places without Benny's cooperation. The timing wasn't right. Only the clone manning Benny's office could make it to Hanson's Bar by noon.

So, where did that leave him?

Nowhere, dammit. He propped his elbows on the desk and cupped his chin in his hands. He found himself staring at the litter on his desk.

And that was when it all fell into place.

There was a tiny click in the back of his head and the pieces all came together and fit. There was no rhyme or reason for it. He had stared at the same reports countless times already. He picked one up and studied it. It just might be possible. He sniffed at the idea from different angles. By God, it smelled right!

He picked up the phone and dialed a number and talked to someone on the other end for fifteen minutes. Then he transmitted a photograph using the DataNet. He made more phone calls and confirmed some times that he had noted.

Lewis and van Horn were just leaving. He called them over and showed them a statement in the transcript. He asked Lewis whether he could now recall that moment consciously. Lewis looked at him with haunted eyes and agreed that he could recall a great many things that he had long forgotten. Brumbaugh made a suggestion. Could that be what Lewis had noticed?

Lewis started and looked thoughtful. Yes, he agreed. Now that he thought of it. That might have been what struck him. An artist notices such things. Brumbaugh thanked him and returned his attention to the Net terminal.

After a half hour his terminal screen blinked and began scrolling. Brumbaugh read the material as it downloaded. He smiled in satisfaction. Yes, indeed. A very pretty picture.

Mac came back from lunch in the middle of it. Brumbaugh told him what he was thinking and Mac thought about it, too, and agreed that maybe—just maybe—it was possible. Brumbaugh told him he was a cock-eyed optimist.

When he had everything he needed, he gathered the evidence into a file and printed out a hardcopy file as well. Then he checked his watch and sat back to wait.

Rudolph Kavin and Myron Kasabian arrived right on time. The baliff had just brought the five Kavin clones from the holding cells and returned their possessions to them. The elder Kavin looked at Brumbaugh.

"I see you've given up."

"I never give up," Brumbaugh told him.

"I meant you've given up trying to blame my sons for it."

Brumbaugh shrugged. "Time will tell."

Rudolph looked to the lawyer. "Can we leave now, or is there more bureaucratic red tape to go through?"

"Oh, why not wait a moment," Brumbaugh said. "I'd like to bounce some ideas off of you. All of you."

The Kavins looked at him suspiciously. It was an identical look, timed identically. With all of them standing together like that, the resemblance was more than startling. It was eerie.

Mac pulled up a couple of chairs and they spent a few moments sorting themselves out. When they were finally seated, one of them—Brumbaugh thought it was Barry—said, "All right, Lieutenant, what's up?"

"I am trying to solve a murder."

They looked at each other. They knew that. Brumbaugh couldn't tell if one pair of eyes was warier than any of the others. Kasabian slouched in his seat and inspected his fingernails.

"The first thing to note," Brumbaugh began, "is that we have a positive make, through genotyping, that the Jimmy was one of you."

They scowled at him. And three of them simultaneously crossed their arms.

"What made it difficult," Brumbaugh continued, "was that you all had airtight alibis." (And *that* got him seven satisfied smiles.) "So we figured there must be something we were overlooking. There were three possibilities. Possibility number one was maybe the alibis were not as airtight as they looked. That happens. Sometimes people lie or they don't remember right. That's why we always look for corroboration. For example, we couldn't find anyone to corroborate Bobby's lunch at the Blarney Stone, or Hank's in Washington Square."

Two clones started and sat up straight. "Hey," said one. But Kasabian put a hand on his shoulder. "It doesn't matter," he told him.

"That's right," Brumbaugh agreed. "Given a long enough time and even Myron will be right. You see, even if we couldn't acount for a half hour here or there, we could still place each of you for some portion of the time that the killer was at Higgins' apartment."

They all relaxed at that and Rudolph gave him an I-told-you-so glare.

"So, no matter how deep we dug, everything seemed to check. Then we tried possibility number two." He waited, wanting one of them to ask.

One of them did. "What was number two?" Brumbaugh thought it was Hank.

"Or maybe I should say number six, instead."

Rudolph Kavin's head jerked and his eyes flicked from side to side. He opened his mouth, as if he wanted to say something. Then he closed it tight.

"You see, originally, there were eight of you."

That did surprise them. Their arms unfolded. They looked at each other, at Brumbaugh, at their father.

"Two of the other clones failed to develop. They died as embryos. But there was something funny about the paperwork on the other. Let's call him Number Six. It looked to us like the termination dates had been altered. So we began to wonder if maybe there weren't another one of you running around the City." Brumbaugh noted the odd look in the clonebrothers' eyes. As if the idea of a sixth brother were both unnerving and exciting. "You see, a sixth clone would explain everything. The tissue samples. The airtight alibis. Imagine how your brother would feel, knowing he was a part of you, but excluded from the group, We pictured his resentment building into hate, and eventually into a kind of vengence by implicating all of you in a murder."

"Very nice, Lieutenant," said Rudolph. "Except that Number Six is dead."

The brothers all turned and looked at him.

"Yes. Your father's right," Brumbaugh said. "Number Six was aborted two months after quickening. That's why the dates were altered. Not to feign a termination, but to conceal the late termination."

"But . . ." Brumbaugh didn't know which of the clones it was who interrupted. "But, that was a crime back then."

"It still is. Manslaughter. But let me tell everyone—especially you Kasabian, because I see you're itching to say it. Fetuses, from quickening up to one year post-partum, are class five persons. They are neither infants, children, adolescents, nor adults. The statute of limitations on this particular crime has run out."

"Then what's the point of bringing it up?" demanded Rudolph.

"Oh, nothing, really," Brumbaugh answered casually. "Just the *reason* for the illegal termination. Your geneticist didn't want to talk, but we finally got it out of him. It seems Number Six was flushed because he was not developing *exactly* like the rest of you. A few minor deviations. Nothing major. Not even anything overt. Poor Number Six was just not a precise copy."

Identical frowns creased five brows. They looked at each other and saw the frowns were identical, and the implications of that began to sink into them and the frowns deepened. Identically. One of them turned to the father and said, "You killed our brother just for that? That he wasn't exactly like the rest of us? Damn you!" Brumbaugh was almost certain it was Hank that spoke, so he was surprised when Rudolph said, "Be quiet, Barry."

"What about me?" asked another. "How close did I come to your friggin' spec limits?" The clone on the far right had risen from his chair and was glaring at his parent. The others looked troubled and one nibbled his lip.

"Boys," said Rudolph Kavin. "Boys."

Brumbaugh smiled to himself. He had driven a wedge into the Kavin solidarity. Now to exploit the crack. He played with his folder for a moment. He was being childish, he knew, drawing it out like this. But they had been playing games with him up till now, so turnabout was fair play.

"Then we went on to possibility number three. Musical chairs." He saw their looks of puzzlement and explained how it was possible for them to switch places often enough that they could mask the fact that one of them had actually been somewhere else. "After all," he said, "your alibi witnesses could swear only that they were with one of you. But not with which one!"

The Kavins looked at each other. Bobby bit his lip. Barry laughed and glanced at his father. Benny looked frightened. That's when Brumbaugh realized that they really had done it! *I'll be damned,* he thought. He wondered how they had talked Benny into risking a malpractice suit. Then he remembered that some of the patients that day had canceled. So it didn't matter if the right Kavin was in the doctor's office or not. Brumbaugh kicked himself mentally. Could he be wrong? No, he was sure of it. The fancy footwork was only a red herring.

"You can't prove that they did it," said Kasabian. "You can't prove a negative from the lack of evidence." He smiled smugly.

Brumbaugh agreed. "Not only that," he said, "but even if it were true, it put us no closer to the killer; since there was no way of telling which of the five of you was odd man out. Still," he added wistfully, "whoever the killer was, he seemed go out of his way to throw suspicion on all the brothers."

That remark got him a stone-faced look from all of them except Kasabian, who looked bored.

The elder Kavin smiled grimly. "So. That takes care of possibilities one, two, and three," he said. "What's left? Nothin'. You got no case against any of my sons."

Brumbaugh smiled at him. He was going to enjoy this. "What's left is I went back to possibility number two."

"Number t—" The father shook his head. "I don't get it. What are you trying to pull? You already eliminated that one. There is no sixth clone."

"Yes, there is. Tell me, Hank, what makes the five of you clones?"

The Kavin on the far right looked at him and shrugged. "We're all exact genetic duplicates."

"Duplicates," Brumbaugh repeated. "Duplicates of whom?"

Hank paused and his mouth parted. Bobby's head jerked up and he turned and looked at Rudolph. "*You?*"

"That's right," Brumbaugh said. "The Sixth Clone Theory was too good to abandon. Then I realized that there was a sixth clone all along."

The elder Kavin grew red-faced. "That's impossible! I wasn't even in the City the day of the murder!"

"Yes, you were. You were checked into a flea-bag hotel up on Third Avenue. You flew in Friday night and met Higgins in the bar there. It was a casual pick-up. You had your fun and she left. How often do you do that sort of thing, once a month? Never mind. We'll find out. What you didn't know at the time was that she recognized you. That she knew three of your sons. She asked you to come to her place the next day so she could do a life-mask. You didn't know why until you went to her apartment."

"Impossible!"

"Well, it doesn't matter. You were already disgusted with her because of what she 'made you do.' Now there was the certainty that she would tell your sons about your weakness. You couldn't accept that. So, you choked her. What you didn't count on was Lewis seeing you as you left. If he hadn't identified you as a Kavin, we might never have matched the genotypes."

"Lewis saw a man with long brown hair." Rudolph rubbed his greying brush cut for emphasis. "I read Kasabian's copy of the transcript."

Brumbaugh shrugged. "Anyone can wear a wig."

"I don't have a wig," Kavin protested.

Brumbaugh shook his head. "Sorry. I found a hair in your hairbrush. Long and brown; not like your own hair at all. The lab report came back and said it was artificial fiber, not natural hair. And one of the things that Lewis noticed about the man he saw coming down the stairs was that 'his hair was not straight.' He thinks now that his eye might have caught a wig slightly askew. Not only that, but he noticed the scar from your facelift. We've asked him to come back and compare yours and Bobby's to see which one he remembers."

There was silence in the office. None of the Kavins said anything. They didn't even look at each other. Kasabian, the lawyer, looked unconcerned. The father, after all, wasn't his client.

Finally, Kavin heaved a breath. "I was in Milwaukee until Monday morning," he said steadily. "When Billy called me and told me what happened, I called Matusiak and asked for some time off to come here. You can call them and check."

"We did. You told me you called your office around 0815."

"That's right."

"But *they* said you called in a little after 0900. Ten o'clock, our time."

"I . . ." Kavin looked confused. "Maybe it was nine. I don't remember. So what?"

Brumbaugh shook his head. "You know why? Because when you came from Milwaukee, you changed time zones. You had to reset your watch. You probably didn't bother to do it until after you had checked into the hotel, *ipso facto.* The clock in your room was slow by about three quarters of an hour. You didn't think to check it. Even by Monday morning you were still off."

"Bullshit! Just because I misremembered the time—"

"Billy," said Brumbaugh. "What time did you call your father?"

The second clone from the left answered. "Sometime around eight, eight-fifteen. It was just after you brought us in."

"And what did you say to your father?"

Billy sucked on his teeth. He looked at Barry, then at Bobby. "I didn't talk to him," he admitted. "I got his answering machine. Left a message. He called back later through Kasabian and said he was flying out right away."

"How much later was that?"

Billy answered slowly. "About an hour."

"Uh-hunh. Sometime around nine." Brumbaugh looked at Kavin, Sr. "We checked with the long distance companies. Matusiak and Kobesky received a call from a New York public phone booth at 0851 Central Time on Monday morning. Now, if Billy called you around 0800 Eastern Time, you would have known about the arrests at 0700 Central Time, if you were in Milwaukee. So why wait two hours to call your boss?"

"I didn't call right away. I waited an hour. Matusiak isn't in until—"

"Patience," said Brumbaugh. "To make it look right, you wanted to wait until 0800 Central Time to call in. There you are in the hotel room. You've just checked your answering machine, long distance, so you know Billy's tried to notify you. So you call Kasabian, here, pretending you are calling from Milwaukee. You tell him you're flying out. Now to call Matusiak. Your clock says it's 0815. That's 0715 in Milwaukee, you think. Matusiak ain't there. So you wait an hour. That's reasonable. It might take you an hour to pack a bag, right? At 0951, your clock says 0908 or thereabouts. So you think its a little after 0800 at your office. Actually, it's 0851, their time, about when Matusiak remembers you called; and 0951 our time, when the phone company says a long distance call was placed."

"I told you, maybe it was nine o'clock! I don't remember clearly. I was upset. That long distance call was just a coincidence."

"Yeah? Matusiak doesn't remember talking to anybody from New York that morning. No matter how you cut it, it was two hours between Billy's call to you and your call to your office. So, I checked the airline schedule, too.

You told me you landed in Newark. The first flight leaving Milwaukee, after your phone call to the office, doesn't arrive in Newark until 11:28. Now how could you do that and check into a Midtown hotel at 12:08?"

Kavin laughed. "That's easy. Since they extended the PATH lines to the airport in the 1990s, the trip has been a piece of cake."

"Except, the PATH tubes were down the day you said you came in."

Kavin's mouth set. "I think I better see a lawyer. You're desperate to solve this case and you obviously feel a need to pin it on one of us."

Brumbaugh shrugged. "You couldn't possibly have flown in on Monday. The way we reconstruct it is this way: You knock off work early on Friday and fly into New York. A gate agent in Milwaukee thinks she recognizes your holo from Friday afternoon. You arrive late, check into the hotel, call—it's, oh . . . early evening—call into your answering machine to see if there are any messages you need to return. Then, on Monday, you check into the Holiday Inn, pretending you just arrived." Brumbaugh settled back in his chair and let a satisfied look creep across his face. "We have people out now with your holograph, checking places where you might have gone. And we're still checking with the airline people in Milwaukee and Newark to see if any of them can give us a positive make. Someone will. Maybe your buddy, Boris."

"Boris do—" Kavin gave him a thin smile. "Boris who?"

"Boris Quint. He runs the hotel you stayed in up on Third Avenue. By the way, he wants to know when you're checking out."

"I've never been to the Hotel Calypso in my life!"

"Did I say the name was Calypso?" Brumbaugh made a surprised face. He looked at Mac. "Did I say Calypso, Mac?"

Mac shook his head. "I never heard it."

Kavin's face grew red again. "Yes, you did! A few

minutes ago. I heard you. You said the Hotel Calypso." He turned to his sons. "You heard him, didn't you?"

Hank shook his head. "He said, '. . . the hotel, *ipso facto*.' Later, he said, '. . . the hotel call—it's, oh . . .' "

Brumbaugh raised his eyebrows. "Did I say that? Gee, you must have *thought* I said 'Hotel Calypso' instead." He smiled and showed his teeth. "It's a natural mistake. Sometimes you hear what you expect to hear. Especially when you're under a lot of stress."

"I want a lawyer." He twisted in his chair. "Kasabian! You want the job?"

Kasabian looked up from his fingernails. "I thought you'd never ask."

"Good, I—"

"And my first piece of legal advice is to shut your goddamn mouth! You already got more feet in it than the Rockettes." Kasabian smiled and looked at Brumbaugh. "Sorry to spoil your fun, Lieutenant. I was enjoying it myself."

"I bet you were," Brumbaugh said.

"That's why you called me Friday night," said Barry, staring at his father. "I wondered why you wanted us to play the switch game."

"It was *his* idea?" asked Bobby. "I thought it was yours!"

"Yeah. Which means you been thinking I set it all up, so I must be guilty, right?"

"Well . . ."

"Yeah, I'd'a thought the same thing if it was you. But *I* knew it was Dad's idea; and by Monday morning I had a good notion why."

"Barry!" Rudolph Kavin reached out toward his son. "Don't."

Barry brushed the hand away. "So, I went along with it. Given the choice between my clone-father and some woman I didn't even know . . . Well, it's like Billy sometimes says: Me against my brother, but my brother and me against the world. We don't break ranks." He turned and looked at Hank and Bobby and Benny. "I didn't know then that you guys knew her."

"Then why are you breaking ranks now?" asked Mac.

Barry twisted in his seat and looked at him. "Look. The woman was dead. Nothing I could do to change that. All right? It bothered me a little when I realized that he had put suspicion on all of us, deliberately. But, that's why we all worked up our alibis. I knew that in the end you could never pin it on any of us. And by playing our games we could make it *seem* like it coulda been one of us. Distract you from Dad."

"But . . ." Brumbaugh threw the word out and let it hand in the air.

"But, he killed our brother. For nothing. I know we're all identical twins. We like it. You can't imagine what it's like to have someone who understands you, totally and completely. Part of that's genetic and part of it's the way we were raised. But I know we're also a little different, *and that's all right, too.* It'd be incredibly boring if we were all exactly the same. I didn't know your obsession ran that deep, Dad. I didn't know how ruthless you were about it." He turned from his father and looked at Brumbaugh. "That's why you told us that, wasn't it? About the sixth brother, I mean. So we would know that Dad had broken faith with us a long time ago." Brumbaugh wasn't sure, but he thought he saw tears in the clone's eyes.

Hank Kavin was glaring at his father. His hands were tight balls pressed against his knees. "Why, Dad? Bev was good people! She was a good customer and a good friend. Why'd you do it?" He took a ragged breath between stiff lips. "You know what you are? You're a son of a bitch! You're a God damned son of a bitch!"

Brumbaugh laughed and they all looked at him. "That's what made me think of Rudolph in the first place. Lewis remembered that when the killer came down the stairs he muttered, 'I'm a son of a bitch.' And really . . ." He showed his teeth again. "When you come to think of it, there's only one of you that fits that description."

Interlude

The pseudo-memories vanished and Pavel Denisovitch finished his vodka in silence. Shigehara had left to attend to others perched about the room. Denisovitch watched as *Old Novy Mir* curved around to the planet's night side and flashed diamond-white in the false sunset. For a while he contemplated the memory of it. Then, applying his mind, he computed the orbit of the old habitat, relative to *Evening Mists'* frame of reference. He sucked in his breath. If he left now . . .

Decision kicked him loose from his perch. With a flex of his legs he shot through the tangle of the Jungle Gym, caroming off the tubes and struts with practiced hands. As he did, he downlinked to the taxi stand and had a broomstick reserved for him.

The shower sprayed over him and Denisovitch turned and twisted until he was thoroughly wetted down. The colloid streamed and pooled across his face and body, crosslinking and spreading until it covered him completely. When the film closed up over his mouth and nostrils, Denisovitch remembered to hold his breath for a few moments until the membranes were activated and the nanoskin allowed the air to pass through.

The vacuums sucked out the last of the residual colloid

and Denisovitch stepped before the scanners, standing arms and legs akimbo. It did not happen often, but occaisionally the nanoskin formed with pinholes or voids, which could cause severe discomfort or even injury once Outside. In the mirror, the skin suit sparkled like sequins over his red-and-yellow bodystocking. Sausages, the spacefaring called themselves, and Denisovitch grinned at the image. The robust frontier humor of the Brazilian *bandierantes* more than balanced the formal mannerisms of their Japanese partners. At what other time of history, he wondered, had the frontier spirit evoked by wide open spaces coexisted with the rigid codes of politeness and circumlocution imposed by living cheek-by-jowl in the habitats? There were nine words in Japanese for "yes," and none of them meant "yes." Perhaps that was why the spaceborn habitually used Japanese on the Inside and Brazilian Portugese on the Outside.

He buckled on his air tanks, regenerator and equipment belt, and straddled the broomstick. Then, afixing his face plate, he tested the breathing system. He sucked cool, sweet oxygen out of the tank and through the membrane. Breathing out, the nanomachines in the membrane disassembled the CO_2, replenishing the oxygen tanks and saving the residual carbon for the food tanks. He gave the portmaster the thumbs-up sign. The broomstick kicked off and Denisovitch jerked back in his harness while he sailed through the iris. The burn lasted a precise twenty-seven seconds, slotting him into a spiral down to *Novy Mir*'s orbit.

He floated in an endless hole where down was every direction. And he found himself with time for thought. Newton was flying the broomstick now; and Newton was an unrelenting pilot. So, Denisovitch settled himself for the trip.

The American detective, Brumbaugh, had lived virtually untouched by the sea of change around him. Nanotechnology had thrown challenges in his face: the clonebrothers, the body-snatcher, the gossamer thief. And always Brumbaugh had seen beyond the technology to the eternal human truths at the heart of things. He had seen more clearly than most that tools were only tools, whether wielded by hero or villain. They did not change what people did, only how they did it.

But what happened when human truths were no longer eternal?

5. Werehouse

Me and Pinky and the Wag was sitting around bored one day when we decides to pay a visit to the carter. We was just hanging out on the corner and there was nothing going down, so Pinky ups and says he'd like to get himself informed.

Well, it sounded okay. We never went in for that stuff before; but you know how it is. You keep your ears open and you hear things, and it was supposed to be a real kick. Besides, it was a slow day and we was itching for something new, and we wasn't too particular what. You know how it is: different day, same shit.

It was Pinky who brought it up. Pinky was an albino. His hair was as white as a Connecticutt suburb and his eyes was red, which was spooky. He was skinny and liked to dress in black. He wore vinyl bomber jackets and pants tucked into his boots. The Wag always told him how it made him look like a prock.

We was flush and we figured to blow it on something, because what the hell good was a wad if it just sits in your pants? So we knowed we was gonna buy some kicks, the only questions being what kind and how many. Gambling? That was for suckers. Besides, the crap games had floated downtown and the numbers was run by the State and was crooked as a snake. Drugs? Most drugs didn't kick no more. Not since that guy Singer doped the water supply with Anydote; and that was a long time ago.

Sex? Like I said, what good is it if it just sits in your pants? There was plenty of janes in the neighborhood, and they didn't charge much; but then they wasn't worth much, neither. We figured with what we had on us we could get parked about two million times each; which, no matter how you look at it, is a tough row; and, whatever enthusiasm we might start with would wilt a whole lot sooner than our wad., And there was always the chance of catching something—State Cleanliness Certificates not being worth the paper they was forged on.

Besides, we had all them janes so many times already there wasn't no more kick to it. I mean, how many different ways can you do it? It was a long time since we seen anything new along those lines.

And what was there worth doing, besides gambling, drugs, and sex?

So Pinky, who was maybe thinking about parking Red Martha for the millionth time and not thinking too highly of it, gives a shudder and says, "I don't want to dribble this wad away. How bout we try something really new?"

The Wag looks at me and shrugs. "What?"

"How bout we go look up a carter? I hear there's one up by 72nd Street."

"A carter?" The Wag touches his lips with his tongue and rubs his face with his hand to show how he's thinking it over. "That's a stiff tick." He says that to show how cost conscious he is. As if it was our money to start with.

"Hey," I said. "You only live once." (And yeah, I know it shows religious prejudice, but the Dots live mostly over in Jersey, so who gives a shit?)

Pinky looks at me. "You wanna do it?"

What I heard is that informing hurts like hell. They dope you up with Thal, which helps; but which also makes you a dick, which is how they get a lot of repeat business. "I dunno. You gonna?"

We kick it around and what it come down to is that

each of us would do it if the other two would; so it ain't like nobody made a decision or nothing. Shit happens. You know. So we started walking north. We wasn't exactly going to the carter, but if we found ourselves near there, we might look in just to see what it was like.

Werehouses was never easy to find. Seeing as how they was illegal, they tried to stay quiet. Make too much noise and a prock was sure to come nosing around. Carters didn't exactly hang out no signs, so if you wanted to get informed you had to listen to the Street. The Street knew, like it always did.

We was passing 69th when a crop of janes come a-cruisin' the other way. They was dressed in twin glitterbelts. One on top and one below and neither one much wider than a promise. The Wag, he smiles at them and unzips so richard can wave at them. That's how he got his name. "Hi, jane," he says. "Show me your smile."

The janes, they look at him and one kinda raises her eyebrow the way a proctor might, but they don't stop walking and one glance is all they make. So the Wag, he points and says, "Hey, don't you know who this is?"

And the chocolate one, with the eyebrow, she answers and says, "It looks like richard, only smaller."

The janes laugh. And Pinky and me, we kinda laugh, too; cause it was funny, you know. But the Wag, he gets red in the face.

"Oh, he be blushing. Ain't it cute?"

The Wag growls deep in his throat and makes a snatch at them, but Pinky and me grab him instead and hang on. He stretched his arms out like claws and tugged and twisted himself, trying to break our grip. He called them janes some pretty bad names, but they didn't pay him no mind. Hell, they was called those things near every day of the year and some of it was no more than the truth anyway, so who cared? That made him madder and he screamed some more. I admired his vocabulary and studied some of it for future use.

The Wag is like that. Most times he's as sweet as your mama's milk. Other times, he's as sour as the smile. There was no telling what would yank him off.

"Hey, Wag," I says. "Calm down. Get hold of yourself."

He looks at me and cusses. There's spit at the corners of his mouth. He tells me what he's gonna do to them janes—and I had to admit it was real creative—but they're gone around the corner, and out of sight out of mind. The Wag laughs high and funny like he does sometimes. Then he does get hold of himself, and after a while he smiles.

"Let's go find the carter," he says when he's done.

I kinda scuff my sneaks a little. "You sure you wanna?"

He looks where the janes went. "Yeah. I'm sure."

The werehouse was in an old Chink restaurant uptown on Serpent turf. When we passed 70th and saw the local colors policing, we knowed we was close. Carters bring a lot of cash onto a turf; so the colors, they don't let nobody bother 'em. An op gets ripped off too much, he shifts the scene and the colors lose the Tax. And werehouses was about the biggest op around, legal or illegal. Some of the colors even put the word around through the Street sayin' they would cut breaks to any op what staked out on their turf.

Pinky asked a jimmy on 71st if he knowed where we could get informed, and the Serpent, he looked us up and down like we was procks. He spit a gob into the street and allowed as how he might know something or he might not. So the Wag goes how much was the Tax and the Serpent goes how much you got and they haggled a little. No big thing and we all knew it. The little shit wanted some grease on top of the Tax. Pinky and me kinda waited around, pretending to be scenery. The Serps were a Chink gang and were supposed to be straight as any colors north of 48th, but who ever knew for sure? I hadn't hearda no wars on the East Side lately, but we seen plenty of old burned out buildings when we crossed the line.

I studied the jimmy's jacket a while, trying to read his badges and pins. Some of the colors go in for a lot of deco, showing how long the jimmy been stooled or how much weight he threw. But the gangs all used different systems and some didn't use any at all, so who cared?

Besides, the lookout who was lounging in the fifth-floor window across the street got my attention. Not that I ever thought the Serps would leave their man uncovered, but that jimmy with the smear gun made me a little nervous, you know what I mean? If he was a dick he might not care if we was legit or not and blow us away just for fun. He didn't have no expression on his face, and he wore flatshades so I couldn't make out his eyes. He was dressed all in black, and nothing reflected any sunlight. Not his shades; not his leather; not his gun barrel. Nothing to make him stand out against his background; except that he was so damn flat that he did stand out.

Pinky sees him, too, and leans over and whispers, "To keep their man here from getting too much grease on his fingers. He's probably got a mike so's he can hear what goes down."

"So shut up, stupid. We ain't supposed to notice him."

Pinky shrugs. "Why pretend?" And the sonuvabitch *waves* at the lookout.

I don't want to see the lookout's reaction, but I can't help myself; so I kinda glance sideways. And the jimmy hasn't moved so much as a muscle since I first seen him. His flatshades look like two more gun barrels, and he stared at us like we was meat.

The Wag punched us on the shoulder. "C'mon," he said. "I got the skinny."

I don't know how long the restaurant was abandoned. I could still smell the chop suey and mustard sauce and the Wag makes a joke about sweet and sour park which we didn't think was too funny. The tables and counters was layered in dust and grease. There was newspapers and broken glass all over, and the heavy smell of urine.

There was a zombie crouched by the kitchen doors, watching us, and I kinda stop for a second or two, you know. Not that I'm scared or nothing. I know that they don't have no more brains than a dog, but he gimme the creeps. You look in a zombie's eyes and there ain't nobody home, you know what I mean? Even when they juice a stiff with his own DNA, there's always something missing. What they call free will and innerlect. So all a zombie's good for is fetchin' and guardin' and stuff like that.

The Churches wasn't too happy about zombies when they first come out, but even the legit ops all said they was good, cheap labor that couldn't be organized. So everyone looked in the Book and found out that, sure enuf, old Jesus H. had pulled the same stunt with Lazarus and a little dead girl, and maybe even with Himself. It was a great thing, that Book. You could find whatever you were looking for, if you only looked hard enough.

(Golems was tougher to find. That's where they juice the stiff with someone else's DNA. And sometimes the stiff wasn't really a body, but just buy-o-mass or whatever. They hadda go all the way back to Genesis to make golems legit. You know. The part where God breathes on a lump of clay. Golems had to be registered with a synagogue and have a special mark their forehead; but zombies could be marked and registered by anyone, even a mosque.)

The Wag walked up to the zombie and said something which I suppose was the password, because it pushed the swinging door open and let us go in with no more than a hungry look in our direction.

The carter was a skinny man who looked like a ferret. He must have been fat once, but went on a diet and forgot to tell his skin, cause it hung on him kind of loose.

His green doctor gown was all stained and tore and his chin was a mess of stubble, like his whiskers couldn't decide whether to grow or not. He paid us no mind at first, but sat behind a battered old metal desk marking a tablet with a stylus. Every time he made a mark the computer screen beside him would wink at us.

After he made us wait long enough to show us he was important and we wasn't, he looked up and blinked his red, watery eyes. "Well?" he said. "What do you want?" His voice said he didn't particularly approve of us or what we wanted, which was funny because what we wanted was him.

Pinky looks at us, then at the carter. "We wanna be informed." Me, I wasn't so sure, but I didn't want to make Pinky look stupid.

The carter scans us, like he was checking the janes at a smile auction. "Have you ever patronized a werehouse before? No?" He steepled his fingers. "I thought as much. Go home to your mamas, boys. This is not for you." He bends over his stylus and pad.

Have you ever seen how a little kid acts when you try to take a toy away, even if he wasn't too sure he wanted to play with it in the first place? The carter talked like an educated man, maybe even high school—there was ragged and stained papers thumbtacked to the wall that looked official—so he ought of knowed that. And maybe he did. Maybe he was playing games, teasing us. Maybe he liked to see people beg for it.

The Wag pulls our wad from his purse and waves it at the carter. "We got the cash. You selling or what?"

The carter looks at the stash and wets his lips. "Is that government money?" he asks and the Wag nods. "It might be enough for one treatment," he allows.

"Nuts. It's all three of us or none of us."

The carter nods his head at the wad. "That is insufficient to cover three fees."

"You ain't counted it."

"That isn't necessary. I can gauge its thickness."

The Wag looks uncertain and I'm keeping my mouth shut; but Pinky, he ups and says, "So, what's better: three cheapies, or nothing?"

Well, I can see how that makes him think some. "You're too young," he says again, but his heart ain't really in it. Nobody makes money turning customers away.

"We're old enough to park janes," says the Wag, which makes me wonder if he's still thinking about them smilers that shot him down on 69th Street. "I probably got a dozen kids around the City."

"An accomplishment requiring great skill and study, I'm sure." The carter makes a steeple of his fingers again. "Very well," he says through the fingertips. "You understand that the treatment will be quite painful. I will give you drugs to deaden the pain; but nevertheless, the nanomachines restructuring your cells will twist your bones and organs into new shapes. That there will be some pain involved is regretable, but unavoidable."

Me, I could feel my organs twisting already, but the Wag says, "Yeah. We can take it."

The carter looks doubtful, but shrugs. "Very well. The original procedure was developed by Henry Carter over a generation ago when he adapted some of the earliest cell repair nanomachines to change the body's shape. Of course, it was far more painful and took much longer than it does now. Great strides have been made since then. I have an extensive library of DNA samples"—and he points to a refrigerator humming in the corner—"that I can use to program the cell machines for the original alteration; and I will, of course, retain your own DNA samples in my cell library and culture nanomachines from them, so that I may restore your bodies to their original configuration when you return."

He pulls open a drawer and lays some papers on his desk. "These are the usual release forms stating that I have explained the procedure and the risks to you. Read them and sign where I've indicated."

Read? He's gotta be kidding. I couldn't understand none of his explanation, and I didn't care. What difference did it make how old informing was, or who done it first? I see Pinky and the Wag look at each other. Then they take pens from the desk and scratch their X's. They show the carter their City passes so he can copy their vitals onto the form.

I try to read my form like he says. I wasn't from the City original, so I can read some. I can recognize some of the words on the form, which makes me happy; but too many are long or unfamiliar, so I give up. I stick my tongue out the corner of my mouth and draw my name. I'm proud I can do that, but the carter, when he sees what I done, looks kinda sad and says, "Are you sure you want to go through with this, son?"

No, I'm not. For just a second the carter sounded like my old man and I wanted to tell him everything and let him tell me what was right. But what can I say with my friends sitting right next to me? The next second I remember the carter is a smelly old man who doesn't shave and that reminds me what my old man was really like so it doesn't bother me anymore.

"Yeah, I'm sure."

He sighs. "Very well, then." He gives all three of us a look. "My cell library includes several of the more famous pornstars and athletes. You understand, by the way, that the transformation will not be total. Your brain cells, in particular, will be affected only to the extent necessary to, ah, 'run' your new bodies. That was the law when this procedure was legal, and I still abide by it."

That explained why he made us sign release forms. I didn't think he would file them with the proctors, though.

"After you have been informed by the nanomachine, your bodies will become a reasonable compromise between your present form and that of your chosen model. You will not look precisely like Big Pete Hardy does on his videos, if he should be your choice; but you will have his craggy good looks and his, shall we say, virility?" He waved us to a row of cracked plastic chairs salvaged from the restaurant and asked us what form we wanted.

Pinky looks at us and says. "I'll tell you when we go in there." And he nods toward the curtained off area that I been trying not to look at.

The carter doesn't say anything to that. "And you gentlemen?"

"I ain't decided yet," says the Wag. "Me, too," I agree.

The carter looks disgusted but it ain't his problem. So he takes Pinky behind the curtains. I hear all kinds of sounds, like metal and glass and stuff. As soon as they're gone the Wag was out of his chair and at the refrigerator. He opened it and began pawing through the vials racked inside.

"Hey, Wag. What you doing?"

"Shut up. I wanna see if he got what I want."

"What's that?"

"Wolf."

Before I can say anything, the curtain parts and the carter comes out. He sees what the Wag is doing and shouts. "Get your ass away from there!" And aims a kick at him. The Wag rolls away from it and bares his teeth in a snarl. For a second I thought he would flip out again like he did with those janes, but he calmed down right away and grinned. "Just wanta see what you got."

"Don't mess with things you don't understand." The carter reaches into the fridge and pulls out a vial. When he closes the door, he puts a deadlock through the handle. Before he retreats behind the curtains again, he turns and looks at us.

"Your friend is under anesthetic now. Do you wish to watch the transformation? It is quite remarkable to see the bones and muscles changing shape before your very eyes. There are some who find the sight enjoyable."

"Nah," says the Wag, who's thinking about more important things. I just shake my head.

After that it was quiet and I wondered what form Pinky picked for himself. It was his idea to get informed, so he musta had something in mind before we ever come uptown.

I look at the Wag. "Wolf?"

When he grins back, I see all his teeth.

Screams I think I could have took, but what we heard was moans. Long, low, and drawn out, like someone having a bad dream. The Wag and me look at the curtain, then at each other; and the Wag's tongue darts out and wets his lips. A jimmy moans, you know the pain goes on and on and he can't do nothing about it, like he gives up the struggle. I began to wish for one, pure, defiant scream.

After a while, it began to get to me, so I stood up and walked around. The carter had some old yellowed newspaper clippings tacked to the wall and I spent the time trying to sound out the headlines. Some had pictures and, if the words weren't too long, I could mostly figure them out, which made me feel good. *Clones Not Legit, Sez Council. Sawyer Rules on Zombie Law. Kops Katch Killer Klone.* Before my time, all of it. Some of the clippings was so old they was falling apart, but I did figure out from one old photo that the carter's name was Benny.

Then the carter pulls the curtain aside and Pinky walked out dressed in a tattered, white robe. He was wet and shiny, like he just took a bath. The carter stood to one side, watching us. Pinky was walking unsteady and looked a little dopey from the drug. I looked and the Wag looked and neither of us said anything for a while.

Cause Pinky was a jane.

I knowed it was still Pinky. If anything, his skin and his hair was whiter than ever, so his eyes looked like spots of blood. He looked about the same mass, but it was all set up different, you know what I mean? His face looked like a Chink ivory carving I seen once in a picture book. I remembered a phrase I heard one time: alabaster body. Pinky sure enough had that.

"Well?" he says after a minute of us gawking.

"Shit, Pink. You're parking beautiful." And he was, too. Richard tried to sit up and look for himself. It embarrassed me and I hoped nobody noticed.

Pinky looks kinda pleased—and, who knows, maybe he did notice—and turns to get his clothes. But the Wag jumps up and grabs his wrist.

"Hey, hold on there," he says. "We ain't seen everything." And he pulls Pinky's robe open. "Show us your smile."

I was kinda curious myself to see how complete the informing was. Pinky lets us look for a moment, then he pulls it shut again. "It's your turn now," he says. "I'm gonna get dressed."

"Wait up a sec," the Wag says to the carter. "Me and my friends got some talking to do."

The carter shrugs and points. "Use that room over there."

It was a small room, that used to be a storeroom or office or something, and there wasn't no furniture. The Wag kicked the door shut and it got dark, with just a little light coming in a small, dirty window high on the wall.

"Hey, Wag," says Pinky. "Leggo my arm."

"What's up?" I ask. Then I hear the Wag unzip and I know what's up.

"C'mon, jane," he says. "Smile for richard."

"Hey—!" And Pinky sounds scared. "Quit foolin."

"No foolin." And the Wag pulls the robe so hard it tears at the sleeve. Pinky is whiter than the robe and he glows in the light from the window. He always was built light and he makes a fine looking jane; so I can't help it if richard wants to look, too.

The Wag hooks a foot behind Pinky's ankle and trips him down. I can hear Wag's boots scraping on the dirt. Then he kneels hard on Pinky's belly to make him smile. "Quit yer bitchin," he says, and his voice was hard and angry. "We was looking for something different, weren't we?"

"Yeah, but—"

"C'mon. Don't you even wanna know what it's like from the other side? Whydja change if you didn't want to do it?"

Pinky yells a couple times and says it hurt, but the Wag goes shut up and enjoy it; and it wasn't like Pinky never said the same thing to janes himself. The Wag says over and over how good it feels, but I look close at his face and he ain't smiling no more than Pinky is.

After a while I can't look no more. I ain't squeemish or nothing. We'd all watched each other plenty of times. But this was different, somehow.

Wag doesn't take long. He never does. When he's done, he tells me it's my turn. "I gotta see the Man about a dog." And he laughs that laugh of his again and leaves us in that little dark room.

Pinky watched him go. "Bastard," he said, hugging himself.

"Hey, Pink. You come dancing out with nothing but a robe on, what do you expect? It ain't his fault. Shit happens."

"Yeah." He didn't sound like he believed me.

"And it ain't like you never done it to janes yourself."

He looked at me and his eyes were twin pools of blood. "It's different being done to."

I didn't say nothing. I didn't want to be in the room with Pinky. I didn't want to be in the werehouse at all. I don't know where I wanted to be.

I looked at Pinky out of the corner of my eye. He was sitting there, naked, picking little pieces of wood or plastic off the floor and tossing them into the dark. I had to admit he made a good-looking jane. Better looking than he ever was as a jimmy.

He sees me staring. "Well?" he says, and his voice has a defiance to it. "You gonna take your turn or what?"

I look away. "I dunno. I'm not real interested."

He pointed. "I got eyes. You wanna do it. So why don't you?"

"Christ, Pinky. You're a jimmy."

"Hey! Look at me. Look at me," he demanded. I looked and he showed me the smile. "Does this look jimmy to you?" I had to admit that it didn't and he leaned back on his elbows. "So go do it. It ain't like I'm a virgin or nothin."

I put my hand out and touched him/her. He looked like a jane; and he felt like a jane; and he smelt like a jane. And the eyes and the skin and the nose are a lot smarter than the brain any day. Besides, it was getting hot in that little room. So, what the hell? Shit happens. You know what I mean?

Afterward me and Pinky was back in the waiting room and the Pink was all dressed up and ready to go. He was wearing the same clothes he come in with, but they fit different. Snug in some places, you know. His hair hadn't grown any longer, but s/he had combed it different. S/he didn't look butch or nothing. Pinky was a real cruising jane. If I seen him on the street, not knowing who s/he was, I don't know what I'da thought.

Pink shouldered his bag and paused kinda awkward. "Well," he said. "So long."

"See you later," I said.

Pinky shook her head. "I ain't coming back."

I wasn't surprised. Somehow I knowed that already. "Cause of the Wag?"

His face hardened. "I'll fix that bastard good," she said, looking toward the ratty curtains. "And that carter. He knowed what the Wag wanted. I'll fix him, too. But they ain't the real reason. I always wanted to be a jane. I don't know why, but I always did. Now I am, and I ain't changing back. It was too boring, doing the same stuff every day."

"Yeah, I know." Life's a bore. Different day, same shit.

But I wondered how long it would take Pinky to get bored of smiling, too.

That was a scary thought. Anything new is a thrill the first time you try it, but the thrill wears off. So what do you do when there ain't no more new thrills to try? The Ultimate Thrill? The one that no one ever does twice, because you only can do it once? The one you could never get bored of? A lotta jimmies and janes I knew tried it. No one ever came back to say how it felt.

A long moan came from behind the curtain and me and Pinky look that way. Pinky spits on the floor. "I hope that sonuvabitch hurts for a week. What did he pick? Pornstar?"

"Wolf," I say, and Pink looks at me funny.

"Wolf?"

"Yeah. He's gonna be a 'laskan grey wolf."

Pinky shook her head. "Wolf ain't possible. The size . . ."

"Nah. He tol' me how a wolf is 150 pounds or less, which is about all any of us mass. So there shouldn't be too much stretching or squashing."

"Too bad," says Pink. "He should hurt more. But then, he always was part animal." She looks at me. "What about you? You gonna do it?"

I shook my head. "It ain't sounded like too much fun so far."

She grins and claps me on the shoulder. "And why change what's perfect, right?"

"Yeah. Something like that." I grin back at her, knowing I prob'ly won't never see him again. "I'll miss you, Pink."

She looks at the curtain once more. "Yeah. Look me up. I better be going. Good luck."

"Yeah. Good luck." And I waited a while longer in that dank, empty room, listening to the moans from behind the curtain, smelling the medicines and the zombie outside the door, and Pinky, even tho she was gone. Well, we wanted something different, didn't we?

* * *

The Wag looked like a wolf, but you could tell he really wasn't. His head was bigger than a real wolf's and was shaped different. The muzzle was shorter and blunter. The carter goes how that's because the human and lupine (that's what he said, human and lupine) their DNA juices had to blend together. The brain stayed mostly human; which meant the skull had to be bigger, which took away from the jaws. The carter told me all about it. He called it Morfo Jenny, or something like that. I almost understood what he was saying.

"Can he talk?" I asked the carter.

"Somewhat. He has vocal cords, but the lips and palate and teeth are shaped differently. That was part of the humano-lupine compromise. So—"

"Of course I can talk," says the Wag/Wolf. Except I have to ask him to repeat a couple times before I get it, which pisses him off.

"What's it like, being a wolf?" I ask. I see his tail whisking back and forth and thought: *He's still the Wag.* I thought it was kinda funny but I didn't say nothing to him. The Wag had a bad temper and a lot of teeth.

"I'll tell you later. Better yet, why don't you join me? It'll be more fun the two of us together." He barked. "Tonight's my night to howl."

Yeah. A load of laughs. "Well . . . I tol' Pinky I wasn't gonna do it."

His hairs stood up and he growled at me. "You wimping out on me, shithead? You hop in the vat like I did, or I'll tell the janes tomorrow how you couldn't do it."

"Well . . ." I didn't want to do it, not really. But I didn't want to back down, either. I mean, you don't let your friends down, right? And I didn't want Wag to think I was scared or nothing.

"Come on," he goes. "Ain't you never wondered what it was like to park a dog? This way you can do it without being no prevert or nothing." He made a whuffing sound, which I thought might have been laughter. "Everything looks different. Everything smells different. I can tell how many people been in here just by the number of smells. Shit. You wanted something different? This is as different as you can get."

Just before I climb into the vat, the carter leans over and whispers in my ear. "Last chance to back out, boy."

I don't look at him. "I ain't scared. Why should I back out?"

"Because you don't really want to do this. Because you aren't like your two friends. Because—" He hesitates and rattles a couple of needle valves in his hand. "Because you can read," he says.

I tell him I can't read nohow, and he better not let on. People find out you can read, even a little, and they call you a nerd. A 'worm. "Besides," I tell him, "reading ruins your eyes. They proved it."

"Who's 'they'?" The carter looks angry for a moment. Then he sags and shrugs. "To hell with it, then. Climb into the vat." And he turns on a faucet and a thick, greenish liquid oozes into the tank. I climb in and it's like swimming into gelatin.

I won't bother telling you what it was like. If you been through it, you already know; and if you ain't, nothing I can say will mean shit. I hoped I would die and was afraid I wouldn't. I felt like I was made of tiny twisted threads and every thread was on fire. It was a nightmare even with the dope.

Afterwards, I scampered out of the vat and stood on the floor. I shook the excess water off and it come to me that I was standing on all fours and I was covered with fur. My eyes was three foot off the floor, about level with the Wag. I felt like I was on hands and knees, with my legs cut off at the knees. I twisted my head to try and get a good look at me and saw long, hairy, grey flanks. Things looked a little blurred. Out of focus like.

Shit. I was a wolf.

"Hey," I said. "I can't see so well." Were wolves near-sighted? Or just my wolf?

"Take a deep breath," says the Wag. He's grinning with his teeth.

I do and all of a sudden I can "see" real well. Not colors and shapes, but smells. The far corner of the room smells pungent, like stale yourn, but it fades off toward the ceiling into something more like mildew. There are fireflies dancing in the air. Molly Cools, the carter tells me. Chemicals and medicines he's used. I know it's my nose, not my eyes, but my brain is telling me it's my eyes. So, I "see" sparks. The floor has a million smells from a million feet, and each footprint glows with its own individual color. I snuffed one or two like I was tracking, and it was like blowing on a hot coal. The smells seemed to brighten.

Wag and me stagger around the waiting room a while until we get our coordination back. The carter tell us our physio-jimmy has all the wolf's nerves. What he called the auto-something nervous system. That way it didn't take long to learn our new bodies.

"Hey," I says, "this is all right."

The Wag shook himself. "Then let's howl." He looks back at the carter. "We'll be back in the morning. You have our juice ready by then."

The carter was already planting himself behind his desk. He looked at us with those empty eyes of his and shrugs. "Certainly. Mind the zombie as you leave."

We bounded out from the old restaurant and onto the streets. The zombie howled and shook its chains as we passed, which made me feel good; a zombie being afraid of me and all.

It was night when we come out and I was surprised 'cause I didn't think we'd been in there so long. *Evening Mists* was shining bright high overhead in its orbit and me and the Wag howled at the gooks up there.

I always thought the City smelled; but shit, I never smelled it like I did that night. The smokey grey of old, burnt out buildings, and the fresher yellow of a new fire somewhere off downtown. The garbage along the curb and in the alleyways. The greasy trails of cars, their exhaust plumes twisting like brown streamers in the air long after the cars was gone. The black smell of rubber on the road.

And the people! I didn't know they could stink so many different ways. They stank in stripes. The carter smelled one way, the footprints on the sidewalk smelled another. I could smell Serpents: Chinks smelled different from regular people. I knowed some of the smells were me and Pinky and the Wag, but I couldn't tell which was which.

And there were dogs and cats and pigeons and rats. Each one unique. Each one different.

Somehow, that rat smell made me hungry.

I could smell the Wag Wolf, too, and that made me nervous. I don't know why; but every time we got a little too close, he would growl or I would growl, and we'd back away from each other. In-stink, the Wag called it.

"Hey," he said. "Let's go find those janes we saw before and give 'em a scare."

I knew he was wanting to get back at them for what they done to him earlier; but hell, it sounded okay to me, so we bounded off downtown. It was a wonderful feeling, the way I could run and leap. I was strong. I was fast. The air was a wind on my face, sparkling with odors.

A jimmy and jane was walking toward us, up Fourth. She was leaning on him and rubbing her hand over his chest. He had his hand on her ass, squeezing. I could hear them whispering to each other from half a block away. They wasn't saying nothing too original.

We streak past them like an express train, leaping into the air and snapping our teeth in their faces. She shrieks and he cries out and tries to pull her in front of him and the Wag and I disappear around the corner on 71st. I find out what fear smells like. It is a heavy, pale smell.

It rolls off them in waves and makes me want to chase them.

I can hear the slap she lays on his face as clear as a bell. The Wag and me look at each other and we both rear back our heads and howl at the moon.

We zig-zagged our way down the avenue, snapping and growling at pedestrians. Mostly, they yelled and ran. Some of them yelled and froze stiff. One man pulled out a cross and aimed it at us, but it didn't hurt none. The fear smell made me jumpy. I don't remember ever feeling so high before. I wanted to jitterbug.

I remembered the Serp lookout at 70th just in time. The Wag was all set to have a go at the turf guard, but I gave him a bump and he went ass over teakettle.

Man, he whipped up and was on me in a flash. He bit me on the left hind leg, but I shook loose. "The lookout!" I shouted. Except it was more like "The woof-au!" and he was so excited that I had to say it over and over before he got the idea. When he did, he quieted down.

"Don't screw with the Serps," I said. "Or any of the other colors when we're on their turf. They don't mind a little hell-raising; but you can't touch one of their own."

He growled at me a little, but he had to admit that I was right. "Don't never bump me again," he said. "I couldn't help myself. Biting you. It was those in-stinks again."

He wasn't gonna get no closer to an apology. I didn't know if it was wolf in-stinks or Wag in-stinks, though, that made him do it. I twisted my neck backward and sniffed at the wound. There was a metallic smell I recognized as blood. I sniffed again and licked at it. It was stopped already, clotting up.

We cut down an alleyway, bumping over all the trash cans. One of them fell and a couple of big, grey rats cut out in front of us. *I struck like lightning!*

That rat was in my jaws before I even thought about it. I bit down hard and felt the bones crack. Bright, hot copper-smelling blood gushed around my teeth, down my thoat. The rat squealed once and tried to bite back, but he never had no chance. I dropped the body to the ground and snuffed it. It sure did smell good.

Then I realized I was thinking about eating a dead rat, raw, and I wanted to puke. Except that it didn't really make me feel sick. Just in my head I wanted to feel sick. I backed away a step or two.

The Wag had lunged at one of the other rats but had missed. He come over and looked at mine. "Lucky bite," he says.

Lucky, hell. I think I was just quicker to learn the body, is all. He sniffs at the rat and I feel the hairs on my back go up. So I growl at him and he backs away.

"You gonna eat it or what?" he asks.

I didn't want to, but the thought of the Wag eating what I killed don't feel right. "Just leave it," I say. "You wanna eat, we can get steak from the market."

"Yeah? With what?"

"Our smile." I show him my teeth and he catches on.

When we reached 69th, the Wag snuffed around some looking for the trail the janes had left. But the trail was cold. We'd met them early in the afternoon and now it was late night—about one A.M. About a million feet had walked around that block and the smells was all the color of mud.

We tried around the corner on Sixth, where we seen them go, and all of a sudden Wag pulled up sharp. He took in a sharp sniff and let it out. "Park," he says.

I sniff, too; and suddenly I know what got him. A scarlet smell mixed with pink shimmering in the air. A bitch in heat.

My wolf's body responded. I sat on my haunches and yipped at the moon. Wag did, too. Then we set off following the scent. We could tell we was going the right direction cause the smell got brighter as we loped along.

She was inside an alleyway taking a leak by a trash

dumpster. She was a regular dog; a collie mix, I think. She looks up and sees us, and her head darts left, then right, but we got her cornered. Between the brick wall of the building and the dumpster there wasn't no way out except past the Wag or me.

Understand. She wasn't pretty or nothing. Hell, she was a dog. But I guess the lupo- part of my "lupo-human" body didn't go by looks. It was the smell that hooked us, and it was automatic. Pure in-stink. I could no more *not* want to do it than I could play the saxaphone with my paws.

We was sliding up real slow and easy. The Wag, he was sweet-talking her as if she could understand a word he was saying. I was starting to realize that I didn't know *how* to do it and figured to rely on those in-stinks again, when she howled and the decision was taken away from us.

He came bounding toward us from the dark end of the alley, snarling and snapping. The Wag and me, we cut out of there real fast without even looking. He sounded a whole lot meaner and tougher than we was. We didn't turn around till we passed a lamppost that had his marker scent on it. Then we looked back to see what it was that had chased us.

I don't suppose we was the first jimmies ever to get ourselves informed with wolf juice. Still, it was kind of a surprise to meet another one. He was standing by the entrance to the alleyway, pacing back and forth and growling at us. Three, four other dogs, all bitches, crowded up behind him, and one other wolf-man guarded the—harem?—and kept a watch in the other direction.

We tucked our tails. I could tell the Wag wanted to fight, but he wasn't any dumber than I was. Two against two and both of them was bigger than us. We slunk off. I wondered if them wolf-men we seen made the changeover regular-like; or even if they'd given up being men at all. A short-timer can always tell a lifer, and them two had acted like they knowed what they was doing.

Wouldn't you know it. The bitch had took our minds off them janes we was trying to track, and as soon as we stopped looking for them, there they was.

We saw 'em when we turned crosstown on 67th. There was only three of them by now. The others had probably found customers to stay with, or maybe these three was working overtime. Anyhow, I recognized the tall chocolate one that put the Wag down earlier and figured the other two orbited with her.

The Wag sees them, too. He pushes me back around the corner before they can spot us and takes a strong whiff of the air so he'll know their scent. He put his muzzle next to my ear and whispered, "Let's run at 'em barking and knock 'em down. Snarl right in their faces; show 'em some teeth. Maybe tear their glitterbelts off. Make 'em pee their pants, if they was wearing any." He looked once at the corner. "The nigger bitch is mine. I'll teach her a thing or two." I think he was wondering if a wolf could do it to a human.

"We're just gonna like scare 'em, right?"

He sniffed the air again. "Get ready. They're almost here . . . Now!"

We cut around the corner and spring into the air. The janes see us and scream. I hit the skinny white one and knock her down. She tries to squirm away and she hits me with her fists, but it's like being hit with feathers. I put my face close to hers and growl and she freezes with her mouth wide open and not a sound coming out. "Don't move," I say. I don't think she understands me, but she understands I spoke.

"Werewolf!" She tries to scream it, but it only comes out a whisper.

I smile with my wolf-mouth to show she's right. She's afraid of me, all right. I can feel her shivering underneath me. It makes me feel funny. Nobody was ever afraid of me before. The fear smell is starting to get to me, so I take a snap at her torso-belt, to pull it loose. It's vinyl or something like that, so it doesn't tear, but I stretch it enough so that she pops out of it like twin seeds from a melon. I start licking and she squeezes her eyes shut and gets real stiff.

"Son of a bitch!"

That was the Wag.

I turn and look and see that his jane is loose. Maybe he missed his jump and didn't hit her square on. I don't know. All I know is I see she's loose, but she ain't running. She's backed up against a lamppost and has a gravity knife in her hand. Her lips are pulled back from her teeth and she looks for the moment every bit as dangerous as we do.

A swipe with the knife and a line of red opens up along the Wag's side. He howls with rage and leaps at her. She tries to put her arm in front of her throat. And that's all I see, because the jane underneath me decides to fight back, too. She swings and connects to my nose.

None of her other punches so much as bothered me, but that left to the nose was another story. It was like I was poked in the eyes. All the smells around me shattered into a kaleidoscope. I howl and snap and my teeth sink into something tender.

There is a scream in my ear and the fear smell is overpowering. I snap again and the scream turns into a gurgle. My mouth is full of warm, salty water. I pull and tear and swallow. It tastes good. Almost like pork. I hadn't realized how hungry I am.

There are more screams, too, from somewheres else; and that warm liquid squirts at me like from a hose. I keep biting and tearing until the pain in my nose goes away. I bite and I chew and . . .

And I realize what I done.

I jerk away from the body like I was burned. I see it twitch two, three times as the last of the blood spurts out. Then it gets real still. Part of the rib cage is sticking out. The smell—a blend of fear and blood and yourn—starts to cool, and I commence to shaking, but I can't tear my nose away from it.

"Wag?" I call, and I can hear the strain in my own voice. He doesn't answer and I turn and look. "Wag!"

And he's still at it.

The chocolate jane is lying stiff and her eyes is like glass. One arm still has a tight hold on the knife, which stands there sharp and upright; but the rest of her is limp. She flops all loose every time he takes a bite. Her throat is all tore up and there's blood sprayed all over everything. The jane is covered with it and the street is covered with it and the Wag is covered with it.

"Wag!" I call again.

This time he hears me because I can see him come into focus. He looks at me and at the janes and he snuffs the body. Then we both cut out for the alleyway.

When we was back in the alleyway, we turned and looked. It was all blurred at that distance, but I could smell what it looked like. The two janes laid there not moving. Not that I expected them to. If they had, I might have lost my mind. But there was a tiny shred of thought that maybe it was just a bad dream.

"Wag," I said again and reared back my head and howled. "What did we do?"

"We didn't do nothing," the Wag said. "It was all them in-stinks. When the bitch cut me I couldn't think. I went crazy. Like you. It ain't our fault. Shit happens. They shouldn't have fought."

I sniffed a little at the Wag's idea. It sounded right and I wanted to believe it. That wolf juice gave us wolf in-stinks along with our bodies. It was like we was just along for the ride. You know what I mean? It all happened without me wanting it, and it was over before I knowed it.

I remembered how good it felt, though. Like catching prey was what I was built to do. I don't remember ever feeling that good about something, and I didn't ever want to feel that good again. I began shaking again.

"Where'd the third jane go?"

"What?" I look at him.

"The third jane." he snarled. "She'll nark to the proctors. We've got to find her!" And he was off like lightning. I didn't know what else to do, so I followed him.

We picked up the scent real easy. It was so heavy with fear that it glowed like neon. We trailed it down the street and across into the alley opposite. We ran like the wind, knocking over trashcans and newspaper stands. There wasn't no one around at that hour.

Then we seen her, about a crosstown block ahead of us. Wag howls as he runs and the jane turns and sees us coming and shrieks. She's running, too; but she's tired and clumsy and she stumbles and the Wag is on top of her.

"Wag, wait! What are you doing?" I jump around a little, feeling skittish from the scents around me.

He was getting better at it. Practice, I suppose. He knew to go for the neck right off and I suppose that was the fastest and kindest way to do it. But the jane kept right on trying to scream, even with no throat to make the sound; with the blood spraying the walls instead of going up into her head. Then her brain finally got the message and shut down for good. It couldn't have taken more than a minute, but it seemed to last forever.

When he was done, the Wag was breathing heavy. He took a bite from the thigh muscle. "You want any?" he asked me.

I just shook my head. "No! Wag, what's got into you?"

"It ain't me, chickenshit. It's the wolf. I ain't the one doing it. I'm just inside watching. This is great, man. When we go back to the carter and get reinformed, it'll be like we never done it ourselves."

And he took off again, howling. Somewhere off downtown I heard an answering howl and I thought about those other wolves we seen.

I chased after the Wag. I didn't know what I'd do if I caught him. I wanted to be back at the werehouse. I wanted to be myself again. I hated Pinky for ever suggesting we try it, and I hated the Wag for making me climb in the vat.

Something had gone terribly wrong with the Wag. He never was any too right to start with, but he was never a stone killer. I didn't know too much about wolves, but I didn't think they acted this way, either. Even wolves have rules.

I caught up with him in another dark alley. He was crouched at one end, watching and sniffing. There was two figures at the far end of it. I sniffed a jimmy and a jane parking it and I could hear them telling each other lies. They was doing it standing up, with him pushing her up against the wall. But it was too far to smell any more than that through the garbage.

"Watch this," says the Wag. "Two at once." And he runs and leaps.

The two screw-balls hear him. The jimmy turns and starts to shout an obscenity, but then he sees what's coming, and he pulls out and she falls on her ass. He tries to run, but his pants are down around his ankles and he trips and sprawls into the trash along the building wall. Then the Wag is on him; but he just makes a snap in passing. The jimmy, he shrieks and grabs himself with both hands between the legs. He twists and curls along the pavement, splashing in the rancid puddles that dripped down from the gutters overhead. He was dressed downtown slick, and I wondered what he would tell his wife when he went home to the suburbs.

The Wag bounced over him and snapped the jane. I thought he would make short work of her like he did the other one. But he bites and tears; then he freezes, and backs off.

By that time I catch up with him. The jimmy is moaning and cursing. His legs and hands is all bloody, but I got no eyes for him. I sniff the jane and know who she is.

It's Pinky.

She ain't dead, but that's just a formality. She's all messed up, blood everywhere; the red sharp against her milky skin. Her jaws is clenched tight so no scream'll come out. She don't look decent. I want to pull her glitterbelts back in place—sometime during the night she musta got herself regular cruising clothes—but I don't got the hands for it. Folks should look decent when they die. I look into those blood red eyes and she's looking right back.

"You, too?" The words trickled from her ruined throat. "You did it anyway?"

I sat on my haunches. "Yeah. I was bored. Didn't know what else to do."

"Pinky," says the Wag. "I didn't mean it. I was just—"

"Doing what . . . always . . . wanted." The words came fast, in bunches. Short gasps of sound. "Fuck . . . both. Fixed . . . good, Wag . . . Narked . . . carter." She sucked in her breath and held it. "No screams. Finish job . . . bastard."

The Wag looks at me and I look at him.

"Finish it!" she screamed.

The Wag howled and lunged and it was over.

Then he laid down and put his head on his forelegs and whimpered. "It ain't my fault," he kept saying. "It was the in-stinks."

I just kept looking at Pinky, not thinking anything. Until I thought: *Narked on the carter?*

I stood bolt upright. We had to get back there fast! That carter had our juice.

We ran back uptown as fast as we could. The Wag was winded already from what he done, but he found his second breath when I told him what was coming down. While we ran he kept trying to tell me that it wasn't his fault about Pinky. I wanted to tell him to shut up but I wanted to save my breath.

The Wag was tired from all his running and leaping, and maybe he had too full a belly, you know what I mean? So I pulled ahead and it wasn't in me to wait up for him. I wished I'd never see him again.

Then I turned the corner on 72nd and seen I was too late.

I stop short by a brownstone on the corner and scramble behind some ashcans under the stairway. The grating is hard and cold on my flanks. I listen and sniff.

The proctors is all over the Chink restaurant like a fungus. They got the zombie on a leash and it's just sitting there snuffling in confusion. The carter is standing nearby with his hands clasped over his head. They got dart guns aimed at him from all over but I don't smell no fear. I'm not sure what his smell was. It was dull colored with sparks. He's just watching everything and not saying nothing. I think maybe he's relieved.

I smell some Serpents nearby watching. I know they don't like losing the Tax on the werehouse, but they ain't about to mess with no proctors. And for that matter the procks ain't gonna mess with the Serpents. Officially, this was City turf and the Serps didn't have no legal standing. I see one proctor, though, in his flat black leathers, watching the window at the far corner. He's standing easy with a smear gun over his shoulder. I think he's admiring the view the Chink lookout has. Hell, maybe they was saluting each other. One colors to another.

It gradually came through to me that I wasn't going to get reinformed. The carter had my juice, and the procks had the carter. I began to shake, but I didn't dare move. I couldn't let the proctors see me. By their code I committed not just a crime, but a sin. Just being a wolf was a sin; and since changing me back would be a sin, too, there was only one thing they could do.

The Wag comes panting around the corner just as the procks start smashing the vials with the juices in them. They got the fridge hauled out, and they got the rack of glass jars, and they're picking them up one by one and throwing them against the wall of the building. I flinch with each smash. They crash and splash and stain the bricks. The broken glass sparkles in the light from the streetlamps. They sparkle with the odors of men and beasts.

The Wag sees what they's doing and he lets out a howl. It sends a shiver down my spine. It is a howl filled with such anger and hopelessness that I hope never to hear it again.

The proctors spot him right away and a squad takes off in his direction. That brings them close to where I'm hiding, so I hunker down close in the shadows. My heart is doing a rock beat.

The Wag knows he done a stupid thing. I could hear him in my mind blaming his in-stinks. He turns and runs, but he's all run out. The procks get him in range and one of them brings him down with a dart. He flops down in the middle of the street right where I can see him. He's stunned and looks around with glazed eyes. The fear stench is so strong it makes me want to run myself, but I keep ahold of myself, fighting the in-stink, and don't so much as twitch.

The procks reach where the Wag is lying and one of them pulls a shiny spike and a mallet from his kit. The Wag sees what they're doing and starts to whimper and tries to lick the hand of the nearest prock, but the prock yanks his hand away as if there was acid on the tongue.

Four of them get down and grab the Wag's legs, and a fifth his head, and they pull and the Wag is all spread out. The fur on his underbelly is pale and bright in the streetlight. Then the prock with the mallet positions his silver spike and drives it home with two well-aimed blows.

There is a pause like a freeze frame in an old movie. The Wag staring at the spike in his chest. The procks crouching around him on one knee, almost like they was genuflecting. The carter, still under guard of the other procks, watching with no expression on his face.

Then the blood spurts out around the spike, and the proctors let go, and the Wag starts to twist and jerk in the street, and the carter closes his eyes and his head sags down on his chest.

And I cross my forelegs over my muzzle so I can't see or smell anything.

It was a long time before the procks cleaned out the werehouse. They were coming and going all night and I began to get worried that it would get light enough that they would see me where I was hiding. But there was still only a hope of grey in the east, when the last of those black cars with the star-cross-and-crescent pulled away and roared down the street and I was alone.

I lay there shaking for a long time, not daring to move. Not even knowing where to go. I couldn't go back. I was a wolf now, for good. I didn't even know where another carter might be. And no one else had my juice, anyway; and he couldn't get it from me anymore because I was a "lupo-human compromise." Funny how I remembered that phrase of the carter's. I was alone. No family; no friends. There'd be no more janes; no more numbers or dice. No more pizza and hoagies and soda. No more . . .

It come to me that I wasn't losing a lot. That there never was much to lose. Yet, I felt sad, like I had lost everything in the world.

I looked at myself and I couldn't see what to do. Sure, when the three of us went hunting kicks yesterday, this was never what we intended.

I remembered the other wolves we seen on 69th and thought maybe they could use a new jimmy. Maybe there was a whole gang of us hiding in the alleys and sewers of the City. It wasn't much, maybe; but it looked to be all the future I had.

I left my hiding place and darted from stairwell to stairwell until I reached the corner. When I looked back, I saw *Morning Star* rising. It shined bright and steady and I snarled at it. There was men up there, and women, too; looking down on us from orbit. But hardly any of them spoke English and they never paid a mind to what happened in the City. And then it come to me that I had lost a lot, but that I had lost it a long, long time ago, and there wasn't no going back.

I sat on my haunches and bayed at *Morning Star.* A mournful cry that echoed between the old decaying buildings. Then I tucked my tail between my legs and slunk off to find the wolf-pack.

Interlude

The answer to his question, Denisovitch knew, was that human values were whatever you held most closely to yourself. The thief, the grifter, and the psychopath were as human as the saint. What they did with the tools handed them depended on their own natures, not on the tools themselves. A crowbar could be used to break into a store, to smash a human skull, or to pry a child from the wreckage of an earthquake. And the tools of nanotech could create a heaven or a hell.

Americans had wanted someone to tell them they were *safe.* To tell them that they could be comfortable and secure in a universe full of danger. And they had found no shortage of prophets willing to tell them so. They had found danger in their appliances, in their apples, in their insulated basements; and the prophets had told them to ban and regulate and control.

Americans never did anything by halves. To avoid the chance of hell, they had foregone heaven. In the end, they had banned, regulated, and controlled themselves into slavery. Because the only way to assure the security they craved was to surrender some of the freedom they treasured. You had to *make* your neighbor stop doing things you knew were wrong. So one coercive law had followed another. Save us, save us. From acid rain, from filthy song lyrics, from crime in the streets, from ozone holes, from the breakdown of family values. Only later did some thoughtful people note how often the dangers were exaggerated to justify the powers sought to fight them . . . and by then it was too late. As the sage, Franklin, had noted, those who surrender freedom for the sake of security will find neither freedom nor security.

The would-be coercers of left and right had groped their way to a wary alliance, united by their common fear of change and their common hatred of science. Pornography was not just dirty, it degraded women. Evolution was not just contrary to God's Law, it was modeled on capitalism. Pollution was not just harmful, it violated the precepts of stewardship set forth in the Bible. "Cleanliness is next to Godliness!"

Abram Sawyer had been elected on the God-&-Green ticket. It was a peculiarly American theocracy: both ecumenical and secular. Four years later, Sawyer was re-elected in a landslide. The Constitution might have stopped him then, but the travesty of the Election of 2060 changed everything. And nanotechnology had bored a loophole through the 23rd Amendment.

So they elected Sawyer again. And again. And again.

Finally, someone asked why they bothered holding elections anyway?

* * *

The air inside *Old Novy Mir* smelled musty and stale from disuse. Few of the spaceborn bothered to visit. It was *hari kuyo*—a shrine to the past. Every few years there was talk of boosting it into a higher orbit, but nothing ever came of it. Denisovitch marveled that people had ever lived in it. Compared to *Evening Mists* or *Morning Star* or *Alto Rio* it was like living inside a closet.

He found the shrine. One of the old cosmonauts—perhaps in the last crew, before the Union in its death throes had recalled them forever—had written the Names in small, precice cyrillics upon the bulkhead. *Gargarin. Titov. Glenn. Tereshkova. Schirra* . . . Some names, like

Grissom, Komarov, Resnick, were marked with black Orthodox crosses. They were all there. Soviets, Americans, Canadians, French . . . Denisovitch smiled. Even a Mongolian and a Saudi. Comrades now, because it mattered less whence they had come than that they had come at all.

He could feel the *grust'* well up within him. A tear started in his eye and the pseudoskin absorbed it and fed it into his canteen, reserving the salt for savor.

When he left *Old Novy Mir* at last and remounted his broomstick, he let his gaze linger on the looming backdrop of the earth. The cloud-scudded Brazilian coast was coming toward him and he studied the waters off Recife wondering if he might see the flash of a heavy lift launch. There was no point in watching Florida.

Denisovitch sighed. It seemed wrong to have a future without the pioneers who had begun it. He set his feet in the stirrups and kicked the boost pedal. He wondered what was happening groundside. Was there any hope, at all?

6. The Blood Upon the Rose

They showed her into the grey stone prison and led the way to his cell, treating her with cold politeness. Politeness, because she was after all the daughter of Elder Praisegod Johnson, entitled to a few privileges; and because, in all fairness, she had been convicted of nothing herself. Equally important, she had been accused of nothing. At any rate, of nothing worse than poor judgement in love. And love, as they say, is blind to the faults of the beloved.

But the beloved in this case was the notorious rebel and heretic, Sebastian Jack, caught at last after lo these many years of fruitless search. Caught, accused, condemned. Someday, in a more reflective mood, the State might even find time for the trial. Just for the record. There was no doubt the man was who he was; no doubt that he had done what he had done. Nay, he even bragged of his deeds. He had printed leaflets of the old secular humanist Constitution. He had planned and executed the notorious raid on the Jericho arsenal. He had killed five proctors with a car bomb in Bethlehem. Given that the truth was already known, of what purpose, then, a trial?

And so, the coldness behind the polite smiles and bows. Even a woman should show better sense in friends.

* * *

Stone walls do not a prison make; nor iron bars, a cage.

Ah, but they surely do help.

Sebastian Jack's cell sat high in the northeast tower of the prison they called God's Scales, a gloomy, dark stone keep that brooded over the pale Potomac ruins. This was only prudence where so important a prisoner was concerned. At ground level, a man might jump and run; in the dungeon, he might burrow. But from the pinnacle there was no escape save that a man grew wings and flew with the birds.

He was standing by the barred window, watching those selfsame birds, when she entered. The solid steel door closed behind her with a metallic crash, and she flinched a little from the sound, noticing the odd little detail that he did not.

The cell stank, as the whole prison did. She saw the thin mattress laid upon the cold, stone floor. The rude, wooden stool. The honey pot in the corner—the source of the stench—unemptied in who knew how long. She fumbled in the purse they had searched and let her keep, and pulled out the deodorizing spray. Even the guards, insensitive as they were, carried spray cans to ward off the ever-present miasma of the prison. As for the prisoners, few survived long enough for the stench to matter; and for those who did, it was no worse than they deserved.

"Sebastian?" She sprayed the mist into the air around her. She sprayed it at the walls and ceiling and, from a discreet distance, at the honey pot itself. The odor of pine and woodland flowers suffused the cell, incongruous in the barren, stone room. "Sebastian?"

He did not turn around, but reached out and grasped the window bars. "Mary, why did you come?"

"I wanted to, Sebastian. It was my right."

A short pause. "Yes, they are very careful about rights. Those they have left us."

"Why won't you turn around and look at me?"

When, after a heartbeat, he did turn, she sucked in her breath. His face was a massive bruise. Purple welts closed the left eye. His cheeks and lips were swollen. When he smiled, she saw that two teeth were missing in the front. "Not so handsome anymore, am I?"

She went to him and put her arms around him. "My love is not so thin as that. I don't care what your face looks like."

He pulled from her embrace. "Thanks," he said wryly.

"I didn't mean it that way." Mary knew she sounded petulant and that that would irritate him. She reminded herself that he was going to die and why. "I mean I will always love you, regardless."

"For another twenty-four hours at least."

"Forever. I know who you are and I love you. I don't care what they say you did."

He twisted his lips together. "No, you truly don't care what I've done, do you? You are the daughter of the junior senator from Kentucky. You think that God's in His Heaven and all's right with the world." He turned and grasped the bars of his window and gazed outward at the freedom of the birds once more. "Well, I don't. Those people out there. Once upon a time, they were Americans. They knew what freedom meant. They could say what they pleased and not worry that a proctor might hear them. They could chase a president from office if they took a mind to."

"The Old Days, Sebastian. It's all stories. No one alive remembers those things. It's all different now."

He turned from the window and faced her with his arms crossed over his chest. He shook his head slowly, from side to side. "Oh, yes. It's all different now. Thanks to the Reverend Sawyer." He raised his voice, ignoring the hands she held up to stop him. "The Reverend Phony-Clone Sawyer," he shouted at the walls. "It isn't even him, anymore, you fools. It's his clone. He isn't a God-damned immortal!"

"Hush, dearest. That's blasphemy."

He laughed. "What can they do? Execute me twice?"

"Oh, Sebastian." She let her hands hang by her side and dropped her head. "I did not come here to talk politics."

"No." His voice was heavy with regret and relief. "You never would talk politics." Unspoken, the phrase echoed: *Because, if you had . . .*

"I just wanted us to spend this last time together." She held her arms out to him again and he stepped into them.

"And I, too."

"I only wish it were more than tonight."

She felt the earthquake of his laugh. "And I, too."

"Let's not talk of the morning."

"No, let's not. If there is to be no future, of what use then to discuss it?"

The thought of his coming death distressed her more than she had thought possible. She reached up a hand. And let it drop. "Please, Sebastian."

He pushed her away slowly, but firmly. "Why did they let you see me? Did they hope you would turn me around? What did they ask you to do?"

"Sebastian, it isn't necessary for you to die. You could . . ."

He laughed again. His laugh had always caused shivers in her back. "I could what? Recant? Go on 3V and tell the world I was wrong?"

"Yes! Live a while longer. I don't want you to die."

He took her by the arms and held her away from him. "I don't want to die, either. God Above knows I want to live. But what does it matter? Even if I did what you want me to do—even if I recanted everything, I would only live long enough to make the videotape. I can't trade my principles for a few more weeks of life."

"Don't scorn another week of life. It can be precious beyond all counting."

"What is life without honor?"

"What is honor without life?"

Sebastian Jack heaved a sigh and sank down upon his mattress. He sat on his haunches with his hands folded into a ball before him. "Oh, Mary, you don't understand."

"I know I am only a woman, a Frail Vessel . . ."

"No, it's not that at all. No one understands any more. They've forgotten. That's why we formed the Sons and Daughters of the Revolution. To place the stars back in the flag, where they've pasted their star-cross-and-crescent. To remind them of everything that once was."

She made two fists of her hands. "How can you know what once was? It was too long ago."

"I've read the books. Old books. Forbidden books."

"Forbidden because they contain errors."

He shook his head once, violently. "No! Because they contain the Truth. Freedom. Individual choice. The right to be secure in one's property. To speak and publish as we please. The right to bear arms. The right to privacy and our own bodies. The right to peaceably assemble and petition for redress of grievances. Those are not errors!" Then, louder, toward the thick, barred door: "We hold these truths to be self-evident: That all men are created equal. That they are endowed by their Creator with certain unalienable rights. That among these are life, liberty and the pursuit of happiness!"

She went to him and hunkered down beside him. The paving flags were hard and sharp on her knees. She saw the tears inching down his scarred cheeks and took one of his hands in hers. "But we do have freedom of thought in this country," she reminded him. "We can think anything we want."

"We just can't say it aloud," he said sadly. "That was how it started, even before Sawyer. When the courts decided that Mormons must not practice polygamy; or

Indians, the peyote ceremony. They could believe in it, but they would not do it." He shook his head. "Your regime only built on a foundation of rot that was already lying there."

"It is not *my* regime."

"Your father's, then. You never questioned it."

"Should I have? It has given us so much."

He gave her a look of disgust that froze her heart. "They have given us nothing and taken it all. Once, we had the planets within our grasp. Once, we had it in us to produce such a wealth of plenty that no one need starve or go in want. Nanotechnology—"

She gasped. "Was a blasphemy in the eyes of God!" She stood and stepped away from him. "Sawyer and Rifkin and the other prophets saw that. The Old Regime that you worship . . . They were Secular Humanists. They believed in Evolution and Capitalism. They blasphemed God and His Church. They polluted the fragile Earth with their demon technology. Your nanotech is well forgotten. It was a Pandora's Box. Horrible things were done. To people; to animals." She shuddered. "They say some people *became* animals. It would have destroyed the world. That was blasphemy, wasn't it? Blasphemy against the environment, just like Reverend Sawyer preached. In the Book, it says that God made us stewards over the Earth; and what steward lays waste to his charge?"

He rose from his mattress pad and turned his back on her. "Why do I love you?" she heard him ask. "We always argue. Nanotechnology isn't completely forgotten, even today. Otherwise, how could Sawyer have cloned himself? We had the power to assemble and disassemble any material, molecule by molecule. . . ."

She went to him again and put her arms around him from the back. She felt how his bruised flesh cringed from her touch. "Let's not talk of that. There is no point to such talk."

He released a long slow breath, like a balloon deflating. "Ah, no. There is not. But my death . . ."

"Hush, dearest! I want you to speak of nothing but our love."

"Why?"

"Because you are going to die." The words were hot, almost angry. She saw how they hurt him and regretted it immediately. "I don't understand why you have to die. You could have kept quiet. You could have lived your life . . ."

"As a slave."

"With me. Is that so terrible?"

"No, for I do love you, too. You don't understand me, Mary. I serve a cause larger than either of us." She saw how his hands shook and marveled at the bravery that graced him in the face of such fear. "Some things are more important than life itself," he finished.

"Yes. Love."

"Love of country."

"Your country doesn't love you. They curse you for a terrorist."

He smiled bitterly. "Unrequited love, then. The purest sort."

"Do I mean so little to you?"

"Never. But I am a patriot, and my country needed me."

"To die. But I need you, too. I needed you to live for me. And now I can never have you."

He nodded. "Yes. It is too late for that."

She bowed her face against his chest. "I know. Too late."

"I only regret that I have but one life to give for my country."

"A fatuous expression from a forgotten book. Patriotic posturing. What is worth dying for?"

"Freedom." His words were defiant. "To be able to say what I wish. To go where I wish. To worship God—

or not!—as I please. That is worth the greatest sacrifice."

"Your life. That is not the greatest sacrifice."

"No? What is?"

She would not answer him. "And so useless. So useless."

"Not if it awakens the masses. To sacrifice one's own life is the hardest thing of all; but if my death becomes a symbol . . ."

She buried her face against him. "But it will not. Most will never know of it. And those who do will say you received no more than your desserts. For the masses to rise, they would need a grander symbol than that."

He took her by the chin and tilted her face toward his. "Oh?" He smiled in self-mockery. "And what would that be?"

She smiled sourly. "If God's Scales itself were to collapse into rubble . . . If these stones were to tumble like jackstraws, and this fortress vanish . . . Then might they rise up."

He laughed. "I shall beat my fists against its walls until it does."

She turned her mouth up to his. "Kiss me. It is all I will ever have of you."

He gave her the rakish half-smile that always made her heart flutter. "The proctors are watching."

"Let them," she said. "I can take my flogging and wear the stripes with pride."

He held her close and for a moment she let herself float in his arms. Across his shoulders she could see the window and the birds beyond. Ah, if only he could fly with them!

"I love you Mary Rose Johnson," she heard him say.

"And I love you, Sebastian Jack."

By early the next day, when the sun's first rays had stained God's Scales a dusty rose, the nanomachines that she and the other women had sprayed upon the walls had done their work; and the building collapsed in a cloud of rubble, taking all: proctors, guards, and prisoners alike into ruin beneath it, and Sebastian Jack, for a few brief moments flew at last among the birds. She wept then an ocean of tears. When all the sorrows had fled Pandora's Box, left behind was Hope; but even Hope could be a sorrow. She could not tell him now what she had always kept close in her heart. That patriotism need not speak its name aloud; that silence was ofttimes the bravest act. And that sacrificing one's own life was not at all the hardest thing to do.

MICHAEL FLYNN

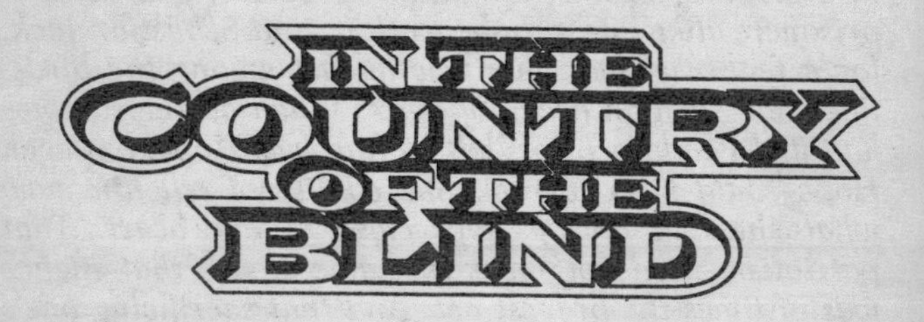

What if it were all a plot?
What if there really *were* a secret conspiracy running things behind the scenes . . . and they were incompetent?

It is a little-known fact that over a hundred years ago an English scientist-mathematician named Charles Babbage invented a mechanical computer that was nearly as powerful as the "electronic brains" of the 1950s. The history books would have it that it was unworkable, an interesting dead-end.

The history books lie. In reality, the Babbage Machine was a success whose existence was hidden from view by a society dedicated to the development of a "secret science" that could guide the human race away from war and toward a better destiny.

But as the decades passed their goals were perverted—and now they apply their knowledge to install themselves as the secret rulers of the world. Can they do it? Even though their methods are imperfect, unless they are stopped their success is assured. *In the Country of the Blind*, the one-eyed man is King. . . .